Other Tales

by

Kathleen Murphey

Published by Kathleen Murphey LLC

Printed by CreateSpace 4900 LaCross Road
North Charleston, South Carolina 29406

Cover Illustrations:
Front Cover, "Thou little child." William Heath Robinson. 1915.
New York Public Library. Public Domain Collection.
Back Cover, author photograph, Tony Skorupski.
Cover Design, Tony Skorupski.

For interior illustrations, see "Illustrations."

Library of Congress Control Number 2018906456

ISBNs

978-0-9992471-3-6 PCN/loc paperback
978-0-9992471-4-3 Kindle (Mobi)
978-0-9992471-5-0 iBooks (ePub)

Fiction publication, short stories, alternative fairy tales, sex-positive fairy tales. English.

Adrienne Rich called for new visions of female sexuality nearly forty years ago in *Of Woman Born* (1976), and though feminists from Riane Eisler to Naomi Wolf to the contributors of *Yes Means Yes! Visions of Female Sexual Power and a World without Rape* (2008) have added to this call for new visions, truly empowered images of female sexuality, particularly adolescent female sexuality, are rare in popular culture. For too long, girls and women have thought it was necessary to choose to be either asexual to be given respect and to be taken seriously or to be sexual within the narrow confines of male constructed notions of female sexuality (wives and mothers who produced legitimate children or sluts and prostitutes who they used and condemned). It is time to reject both choices (asexual and sexual) and redefine female sexuality as just as natural and desirable and powerful as male sexuality is seen and to see alternative sexualities as just as valid as heterosexuality.

Each of the stories included in this volume challenges at least one aspect of the traditional fairy tale scripts in the hope of helping create new visions of what girls and boys and women and men can be: full human beings who are ambitious and affectionate, analytical and compassionate, assertive and sympathetic, intellectual and sexual, competitive and gentle, independent and understanding, outspoken and soft-spoken, physical and emotional—in whatever mutually consensual, respectful, and pleasuring relationship they choose.

To Natasha, Katarina, and Tatianna Skorupski, my three princesses, who are ever my inspiration and fascination, in the hope that your world will be a better place because of bold new stories that re-envision the world and the relationships between the people and the creatures in it.

For above all, this gylanic world [a world where women and men are truly equal] will be a world where the minds of children—both girls and boys—will no longer be fettered. It will be a world where limitation and fear will no longer be systematically taught us through the myths about how inevitably evil and perverse we humans are. In this world, children will not be taught the epics about men who are honored for being violent or fairy tales about children who are lost in frightful woods where women are malevolent witches. They will be taught new myths, epics, and stories in which human beings are good; men are peaceful; and the power of creativity and love—symbolized by the sacred Chalice, the holy vessel of life—is the governing principle. For in this gylanic world, our drive for justice, equality, and freedom, our thirst for knowledge and spiritual illumination, and yearning for love and beauty will at least be freed.

Riane Eisler, *The Chalice & the Blade* (1987)

We are laying the foundations of a way of life that may become so world-wide that it will have no rivals, and [human beings'] imaginations will be both sheltered and imprisoned within the limits of the way we build. For in order to think creatively, [human beings] need the stimulus of contrast. We know by sad experience how difficult it is for those who have been reared within one civilization ever to get outside its categories, to imagine, for instance, what a language could be like that had thirteen genders. Oh, yes, one says, masculine, feminine, and neuter—and what in the world are the other ten? For those who have grown up to believe that blue and green are different colours it is hard even to think how any one would look at the two colours if they were not differentiated, or how it would be to think of colours only in terms of intensity and not of hue.... We stand at the moment in history when we still have choice, when we are just beginning to explore the properties of human relationships.

Margaret Mead, *Male and Female* (1949)

Real sex education is not the same as porn education. Instead, it's about teaching that pleasure is an important part of any sexual relationship. It's about teaching that there is nothing wrong with wanting to feel sexual pleasure and seeking it out, so long as it is done safely and responsibly. It's about teaching comfort with one's body and a lack of shame over desires, and that there is more to sex for all people than sticking penises inside vaginas. Real sex education teaches how to go about making intelligent, safe choices, rather than just stating the choices available. I believe there is a big difference. And I believe that teaching teens to make smart choices about sex must involve teaching them that having sex, partnered or alone, can be a smart choice.

Cara Kulwicki, "Real Sex Education," in *Yes Means Yes! Visions of Female Sexual Power & a World Without Rape* (2008)

Acknowledgements:

Several of these stories have been published previously. "Ruby and Romulus" was published in *The Fairy Tale Whisperer* edited by Evelyn Zimmer by Zimmbell House Publishing in 2015. "The Twelfth Princess" was published in *Pagan* edited by Evelyn Zimmer by Zimmbell House Publishing in 2015. "The Frog and the Transgender Prince" was published by *Writing in a Woman's Voice* in 2017.

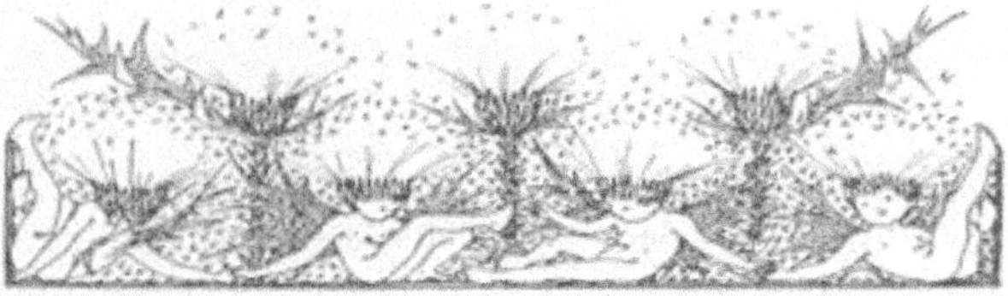

Contents

Illustrations

Cover, "Thou little child." William Heath Robinson. 1915. New York Public Library, Public Domain Collection.

Three fairies image. *When Life is Young: A Collection of Verse for Boys and Girls* by Mary Elizabeth Dodge. 1894. British Library, Public Domain Collection, Children's Book Illustration Album.

"End-paper design." Walter Crane. 1909. New York Public Library, Public Domain Collection.

Fairy border image. Helen Stratton. *Songs for Little People* by Norman Rowland Gale. 1896. British Library, Public Domain Collection, Children's Book Illustration Album.

"Entrée de Monseigneur Henry de Lorraine, Marquis de Moy soubs le nom de Pirandre." Jacques Callot. 1627. New York Public Library, Public Domain Collection.

"Canis Lupus, var. Nubilus." Thomas Landseer. 1829-1837. New York Public Library, Public Domain Collection.

Dancing couple image. Sarah Selina Hamer. c. 1890. *An Old Chronicle of Leighton*. British Library, Public Domain Collection.

"A floral fantasy in an old English garden." Walter Crane. 1899. New York Public Library, Public Domain Collection.

Castle image. A. Jourdain. *Notice Historique sur le Chateau de Chenonceaux*. 1845. British Library, Public Domain Collection, Castles Album.

"The Dragon Flies Off With The Empress." Henry Justice Ford. 1901. New York Public Library, Public Domain Collection.

"She had stepped down into the cool clear water." William Heath

Robinson. 1915. New York Public Library, Public Domain Collection.

Two girls' heads in a circle of flowers image. L. Housman. *Goblin Market* by Christina Georgina Rossetti. 1893. British Library, Public Domain Collection, Children's Book Illustration Album.

Mermaid rectangular image. Helen Stratton. *Songs for Little People* by Norman Rowland Gale. 1896. British Library, Children's Book Illustration Album.

"Ringel Tanz." Walter Crane. c. 1900. New York Public Library, Public Domain Collection.

"Thou little child." William Heath Robinson. 1915. New York Public Library, Public Domain Collection.

Two boys looking up border image. Helen Stratton. *Songs for Little People* by Norman Rowland Gale. 1896. British Library, Public Domain Collection, Children's Book Illustration Album.

"The prince knocks at the door of the poor, mean, little house and not the great, rich one." Howard Pyle. 1915. New York Public Library, Public Domain Collection.

"Vereenigde Provincien der Nederlanden." 1910. New York Public Library, Public Domain Collection.

"To die will be an awfully big adventure." Francis Donkin. 1911. *Peter and Wendy* by J.M. Barrie.

"Looking glass in silver and bronze, designed and executed by Elkington & Co." 1880-1883. New York Public Library, Public Domain Collection.

Steadfast Soldier image. Anne Anderson. 1924. *Hans Andersen's Fairy Tales*.

"The End." 1894. *Jack's Partner and Other Stories* by Stephen Fiske. British Library, Decorations & Designs Album.

Andersen's "The Little Mermaid": The Wicked Woman Version

The king of the sea lived in a grand palace at the bottom of the sea with his people and his six daughters and mother. Since he was a widower, his mother kept house for him. Being a proud merwoman, she wore twelve oyster shells on her tail (when most only wore six). The youngest daughter was the most fair. She was also strangely fascinated with the human world, and in her garden, she had a statue of a handsome boy that she had found on a wrecked ship. The youngest daughter never tired of hearing her grandmother's stories about the human world. It was tradition that when each of the children reached the age of fifteen, she would be able to surface and look at the ships that sail by and the forests and the cities of humans.

(The human patriarchal divisions of power and labor are the repeated in the merpeople world. The ruler is male, and his mother takes care of domestic affairs—keeping house and minding and educating his children. The old woman wears twelve oyster shells on her tail when most people/women? wear six. This information seems innocent enough, but later it is clear that wearing oyster shells is painful. So the old woman wearing twelve oyster shells is the first association that women should endure pain for the sake of beauty or adornment.)

The eldest princess turned fifteen, and she journeyed to the surface, and she came back and told them all about the wonders she had seen of the human cities. Next the second oldest sister went to surface and returned with her tales. When the third sister went, she swam up the rivers and journeyed farther into human territory than the older two but retreated when a dog scared her. The forth sister went, and then the fifth sister. The little mermaid listened to all their tales with rapt attention. The sisters found their initial encounters with the human world and the natural world above the water fascinating, but with time, they preferred the merrealm to the human spheres.

At last the little mermaid turned fifteen, and it was her turn to journey to the surface. Her grandmother helped her get ready, putting flowers in her hair and eight oyster shells on her tail. When the princess complained about the pain of the oysters, the old woman said, "You must suffer a bit to look pretty!" On the surface, the little mermaid could see a big ship. Through the windows of the ship, the little mermaid could see a young prince having his own birthday celebrated with music and festivities. Though the ship grew quiet, the little mermaid couldn't make herself leave. She was very taken with the young prince; he reminded her of the statue in her garden. A storm came and broke apart the ship. The little mermaid found the prince and held his unconscious head above water. In the morning, the storm had cleared, but the prince did not wake, and the little mermaid kissed him. Down the coast, there was a convent, and the little mermaid swam the prince to it. The little mermaid watched as a girl from the convent found the prince and went to get others to help her. The prince revived and smiled at the women around him, and the little mermaid felt sad because the prince did not smile at her (hidden as she was) or know that she had saved him.

(Girls and women should endure pain to be pretty is clearly expressed here and gives meaning to the grandmother's wearing of twelve oysters. That the little mermaid is different from her sisters has already been noted. She was always curious about the human world. Her saving and kissing the prince show affection, but she does not reveal herself to him. Why? Because humans don't believe in merpeople? Because as a merperson, she is not worthy of his affection? The answer is not given. But if we project the standard tropes of gender behavior (male active/male sexual initiator and female passive/female not sexual initiator), the little mermaid can't save the prince, kiss him, and reveal herself if she is a good girl. Only a "slut" would act so boldly. Additionally, girls and women are supposed to subject themselves to pain for beauty and also for love or affection.)

In the merrealm, the little mermaid withdrew herself. She told no one of her encounter with the prince, not even her sisters. In her garden, she would hug the statue of the young man who reminded her of her prince. Finally, she told one of her sisters, and she told all the rest and some very close friends who wouldn't tell anyone. Someone had seen the ship and the prince and knew where the prince's kingdom was. So the little mermaid's sisters took her one night to palace of the prince. Knowing where he lived, she would visit him and yet did not reveal herself to him. She would swim up the canal and watch him when he thought he was alone. She listened to the fisherman talk about how good the prince was. She longed to be among the humans. She asked her grandmother questions about the humans. If they didn't drown, did they live forever? No, they lived quite short lives compared the merpeople's three hundred years. But humans had immortal souls, so there was a life after life for them whereas after merpeople's three hundred years, they turned into the foam on the water. The idea of having an immortal soul captivated the little mermaid, and she asked if there was any way she could get such a thing. Her grandmother told her that only if a human loved her so much that he would marry her, only then could she share his immortal soul. But the grandmother said it was impossible because the little mermaid was a mermaid, and humans didn't like merpeople and tried to distract her by ushering her to the great ball the merking was giving.

However, the little mermaid couldn't stop thinking about her prince and an immortal soul, and she left the ball and went to the sea witch to see if the woman could help her. As she grew close to the house of the sea witch the seascape became barren, and then a strange forest appeared full of polyps (half plants and half animals) that looked like worms and that grabbed at her. She was frightened and nearly turned back. She came to an opening in the forest where the sea witch house stood made from skeletons of wrecked human ships. The sea witch sat at the entrance with a toad eating from her mouth and sea snakes circling her breasts.

(The sea witch is a being of contradictory natures. That the seascape near her house becoming barren suggests death and petulance. The forest of polyps suggests un-natural beings—living beings but not of species that should ever mix. They threaten the little mermaid as an extension of their un-natural mother. That her house is made of human wreckage points to her low opinion of human beings. Yet for all her associations with death and the un-natural, she is associated with life—with a toad and snakes—both species which are associated with rebirth and transformation (toads shifting from tadpoles to toads and snakes through their changing skins). Both toads and snakes (reptiles) are also associated with witches; snakes being further associated with Satan and Adam and Eve's expulsion of the Garden of Eden—which adds a link to the half-plant/half-animal/worm-like/snake-like forest/garden outside the sea witch's house. The sea witch is old power—female power;

she has the power of life and death and everything in between. She is outside patriarchal power and, therefore, someone to be feared.)

The sea witch knew why the little mermaid had come. She agrees to do what the little mermaid desires because it will cause the little mermaid sadness. The time is right. The sea witch can make a potion for the little mermaid that will give the little mermaid legs and transform her into a human-like being. But the sea witch warns the little mermaid that it will hurt. It will be like being stabbed by a sword—the splitting of her tail into legs. She will retain the grace with which she moved through the sea, but every step she takes will feel like she is walking on knives with blood flowing from her feet. The sea witch also warns the little mermaid that she can never be a true mermaid again and that if she fails to make the prince love her and he does not marry her, the morning after he marries another she will turn to foam on the water. The little mermaid agrees.

(The sea witch's powers extend beyond life and death to merging life-forms into the un-natural and to mind-reading or being able to divine the little mermaid's desires. She can make the potion to transform the little mermaid, but it will hurt. Getting legs is a symbolically violent rape—it is like being stabbed with a sword with the connotation of blood and trauma. Beauty is pain, after all. Her mermaid fluidity in the water she retains, but actually using her legs and by extension her feet causes more stabbing pain which is coupled with the image of blood flowing. The odd implication is that as a mermaid she is immune from full female sexuality—having nothing between her legs like a vagina or clitoris—only a fish tail. Once she has legs, there are things between them, a vagina, a clitoris, and more. A human girl's vagina bleeds, so acquiring legs and all that is between them again causes pain and blood—these are further violent images—stepping on knives—self-mutilation. The deal cuts her off from her family and species, and if it fails (the misfortune the sea witch desires), it will cause the little mermaid's death.)

The sea witch warns the little mermaid that she will have to pay dearly for the potion. The little mermaid has a beautiful voice, and the sea witch demands that as payment for her potion—the best of the little mermaid for the potion the sea witch will make that contains some of the sea witch's own blood to make it "sharp as a two-edged sword." When the little mermaid protests, the sea witch says that the little mermaid will have her shapely figure, her elegance of her movement, and her beautiful eyes. With these powerful assets, the little mermaid should be able to "enchant" the human prince's heart. The little mermaid agrees, and the sea witch makes the potion, putting many things into it including blood from her breast that is black and drips into the potion. When it is done, it is clear. The sea witch then cuts out the little mermaid's tongue, leaving her unable to sing or speak. The sea witch sends her on her way telling her that she can use drops of the potion to ward off any polyps that bother her, but the little mermaid doesn't need to—the polyps all shrink away from the shining potion in the little mermaid's hand.

(Though the little mermaid mutilates herself to appear acceptable (human-like) or even attractive to the human male gaze, it is a woman who commits the mutilation. One of the powerful achievements of patriarchy is setting women against women so that men do not always need to "discipline" rebellious or troublesome women—women do it to other women. The sea witch moving from desiring the little mermaid's unhappiness to mutilating and silencing her are such acts. The added dimension to the sea witch's actions is that it takes away the little mermaid's voice. She cannot speak about what has been done to her, and she cannot speak for herself. Further, since the mouth and tongue are used sexually and since the orifice of the mouth and tongue mirror to a certain extent the orifice of the vagina and clitoris which will be bestowed on the little mermaid upon drinking the potion, the amputation of the little mermaid's tongue can be seen as a symbolic clitorectomy—a taking away of one aspect of her ability to be sexual. That the blood from the sea witch's breast is black is a reversal of a mother's white breast milk. Whereas a mother's white breast milk is symbolic of life and bonding, the sea witch's black breast blood is un-natural and symbolic of death and, even perhaps, the devil (she is a witch after all). The black un-natural blood will make the potion "sharp as a two-edged sword," again associating getting legs with violent penetration by an unyielding weapon that is not just pointed but two-edged—causing the maximum amount of damage. Lastly, the idea that women "enchant" or "ensnare" men through their voices (and words), their looks, and the way they move is demeaning. The implication is men are helpless against "womanly wiles" and that it is only through such entrapment that men attach themselves to women.)

Going past her father's palace, the little mermaid enters the gardens and takes a flower from each of her sisters' gardens—her heart full of sadness because she was separating herself from them forever. The little mermaid goes to the prince's palace. On the marble stairway, the little mermaid drinks the potion. It burns, and then she feels as though "a two-edge sword" has pierced her body. The pain is so intense that she passes out "as though dead." When she wakes, she again feels shocking pain, but the prince is there in front of her. She realizes that she has legs and that she is naked. She robes herself in her long hair, and the prince asks her who she is and how she came to be there, but she cannot answer him. When she moves, it is just like the sea witch said: each step is like stepping on "pointed awls and sharp knives." But she accepts the pain and walks with him where everyone marvels at her grace (unaware that her ability to glide and float across any surface is a legacy of her mermaid ability to glide fluidly through the sea).

(In patriarchy, girls and women are separated from their families at marriage to live with their husbands' families where they are at the mercy of their husbands and his family members. The little mermaid's alienation from her family is made more absolute by her changing species or appearing to become human, but she accepts this as necessary. The potion burns and then feels like it is cutting her, penetrating her. In a sense, the fish tale is split, cut in two, to form the human-like legs, but the continuing violent assaults (when she walks and with every step she takes) are disturbing. The stabbing pain of swords, awls, and knives imply the flow of blood though it is not mentioned in this description. In gaining legs, the little mermaid has also gained a vagina, a clitoris, and a womb; she has moved from asexual mermaid with single fish tail that cannot be penetrated to a human-like girl/woman whose menstrual blood does flow and can be sexual and sexually penetrated. That such a transformation is worthy of so much painful punishment speaks to the deep fear and distrust of patriarchy for female sexuality. Additionally, that women should endure such awful pain to be physically appealing to men is also a toxic message.)

The little mermaid is given beautiful clothes to wear, and she is with the prince and his parents when they are entertained by a slave girl who sings well to the delight of the prince. The little mermaid is sad at this, because she knows that her voice was so much prettier and that the prince will never know that she gave up her voice for him. The slave girls danced for the royal party, but when the little mermaid dances, all are amazed by the way she moves, and though every movement hurts her, she dances for the prince. The prince calls her "his little foundling" and says that she will stay with him always, but he treats her like a pet instead of a person and lets her sleep on a cushion outside his door. At times, she rides with the prince, and despite her feet bleeding, she pretends it doesn't hurt and follows wherever he chooses to go.

(Without a voice, the little mermaid cannot sing for the prince nor can she correct his misconceptions about her nor insist that he treat her differently. Of course, the little mermaid can figure out no other way to communicate to the prince. She doesn't know how to write or to draw pictures, so she becomes his companion and plaything. Though others see the little mermaid's bleeding feet, the prince does not appear to or does not find it troublesome enough to stop leading her through the countryside. Her pain and blood are not enough to stop him from doing what he wants when he wants to do it.)

At night, after everyone is asleep, the little mermaid goes down the marble stairway to the sea and tries to cool her aching feet. One night her sisters find her. They tell her how much they miss her, and after that, they visit her each night. Even her grandmother and sea king make appearances to wave at her from a distance. The prince loves the little mermaid but in a platonic way. He explains to the little mermaid that she reminds him of the young woman who found him after his ship wreck and who he loves. He believes the young woman, a novice of the convent and therefore pledged to the convent, is the person who saved him. The little mermaid is sad, because the prince doesn't know that she saved him and what she has sacrificed for him.

(The little mermaid's family only visit her in secret—their statuses as merpeople and the little mermaid's family both forcing them not to seek her openly in front of the prince and his parents. They are taboo both as alien species and as a support system in the domain of patriarchal authority (the prince and his kingdom). Again without her voice, she cannot tell the prince that she saved him or what she has done to be with him.)

The king has arranged for the prince to marry a neighboring princess, and the prince gets ready a grand ship to travel to the kingdom and see it and the daughter. The prince knows his parents will not force him to marry, and he is convinced that he will never find the young woman from the convent. While they were travelling, the little mermaid saw her sisters and her grandmother. The sisters wanted to help the little mermaid but all they could do was look at her sadly and wring their hands.

(Are the little mermaid's sisters powerless because they are merpeople and cannot meddle in the human realm or because they are female?)

The prince's ship entered the neighboring king's harbor, and there was much festivity. Parties and balls were held. The princess was not there but was travelling to the kingdom from the place she had been educated. When at last the princess arrived, she was the young woman from the convent, and the prince was overjoyed. The little mermaid was devastated. She would die the morning after the prince married the princess and become foam upon the sea. The little mermaid held the bride's train during the ceremony. That night she danced more spectacularly than ever before though every step caused her stabbing pain. But the pain of her feet was nothing compared to the pain in heart for losing the prince and his immortal soul. That night alone as she looked over the ship's railing, she saw her sisters rise out of the water. She noticed immediately that their hair had been cut off.

(Without her voice or the capacity to find another form of communication other than her voice, the little mermaid is powerless to correct the prince's misconceptions of his rescue. As an obedient woman, she mutely participates in the prince's wedding, carrying her "rival's" wedding gown train and keeping up appearances despite her looming death. She dances spectacularly in an effort to gain the attention of the prince despite the pain in her feet and heart. Women are expected to feel pain and still move gracefully and look pretty.)

The little mermaid's sisters explained that they had cut off their hair for the sea witch, and the sea witch had given them a knife to give to the little mermaid. Before sunrise, if the little mermaid stabbed the prince in the heart, his blood on her legs would cause her fish tail to return, and she could come back to the merrealm and live her three hundred years with her family and then become sea foam. They urged her to hurry and return to them.

(The little mermaid's sisters and the sea witch have come together to offer the little mermaid an alternative to death—an unusual image in patriarchy of women working together to help another woman in distress (the little mermaid).)

The little mermaid took the knife and went into the chamber of the prince and his bride. She kissed him, but he murmured the name of his bride. She couldn't kill him, so she threw the knife into the sea where it looked like blood. She threw herself into the waves and felt her body come apart. She thought she was becoming foam, but then she could hear voices. They floated around her, and she realized that she floated too. The voices explained that they were daughters of the air and that by doing good deeds for three hundred years they could earn immortal souls. Because of all the little mermaid has suffered, she had been transformed into a daughter of the air, so that she too could earn an immortal soul.

(The little mermaid cannot bring herself to do violence to the prince and chooses to sacrifice herself instead. In the patriarchal world, women are raised to sacrifice themselves for those they love, their husbands and their children. She casts the knife into the water where her sisters' sacrifices are acknowledged by the blood red color it casts. Transformed into a daughter of the air, the little mermaid has shed herself of her physical body; she has become asexual again. Through good deeds, the little mermaid as an asexual being can achieve an immortal soul on her own instead of sharing the prince's immortal soul (through marriage) or end as sea foam at the end of her mermaid life. Being asexual also stops her pain, the pain in her feet and the pain of her heart. Thus, two disturbing messages seem to be that only an asexual woman can find grace with God and that sexual women must endure pain. Finally, did the little mermaid ever truly love the prince? Or was her fixation on him just a strategy to get an immortal soul? If the immortal soul is the prime motivator then the little mermaid is every bit as manipulative and deceitful as patriarchal society labels women. She was using him to get part of his soul instead of truly loving him for himself.)

The Little Mermaid: The Sacred Version

Once upon a time at the bottom of the sea, there was a great city of merpeople. The old queen of the merpeople shared her rule with the sea witch and her eldest granddaughter, and they guided their people with compassion and authority. Merchildren were schooled in many subjects. They read and wrote literature and music, they studied history. They learned the languages of dolphins and whales. They helped with the cultivation of kelp and sea weed fields, with the harvesting of crustaceans, and with fishing. They learned different crafts; they sang songs and performed plays and dramatic productions. Merchildren were vital to the city and its inhabitants: gifts from the gods and the merpeople's legacy to the future. The young queen and king had been blessed with six daughters, Adrianna, Marina, Salacia, Galene, Catalina, and Sirena, but their girls were nearly all grown now.

The merpeople lived in proximity to the human world, but they were careful to avoid it, and human beings were too unimaginative to suspect the beautiful city of the merpeople hidden below the waves. When merchildren were seventeen, they could venture to the surface under cover of night, but they had to be careful and not seen by the humans. This restriction was perfectly sensible to the merpeople who had witnessed the wars between humans—both the fighting on the land and the battles by sea where mutilated human bodies polluted their seas and choked the rivers. They had seen too the brutal slaughter and butchering of whales by the humans. Humans were dangerous and violent. The old queen and the sea witch were convinced that if the humans knew of the merpeople's city, the merpeople would be hunted, and they had no weapons of war like the humans did, nor did they want them.

All kinds of merpeople lived in the city. There were merpeople with dark brown and ebony skin with dark hair and brown/black eyes with brownish-gold fish tails that sparkled in the light with every imaginable shade of brown and gold. There were merpeople of what might be considered yellowish skin with straight dark hair, slightly slanted eyes of dark brown—their fish tails sparkled in myriad shades of gold and yellow. There were merpeople with slightly reddish skin with straight dark hair and dark brown eyes with reddish/purple fish tails that flashed with a profusion of shades of red and magenta. There were merpeople with fair skin and light colored hair and eyes whose fish tails sparkled in a pale mix of white, silver, light blue, and light pink. And there were merpeople of mixed ancestry who could have the most startling combination of features: a merwoman with fair hair and crystal blue eyes but red skin and a brown-gold tail or a merboy with fair skin and red hair but with brown-black eyes and red/purple tail.

Sirena was the youngest mermaid princess, and she was very beautiful. She had light brown skin and dark wavy hair, but her eyes were a light golden-brown and her tail was a dark brownish-gold. She had a beautiful singing voice and enjoyed helping the sea witch, Circe, with healing and tending to the infirmed or sick at the hospital. On her seventeenth birthday night, she rose to the surface of the sea and found one lone ship sailing toward the coast. There were music and voices coming from the ship. Curiosity made her approach the ship and peak through the widows. A beautiful young man sat at the head of a large table and was being toasted many good wishes for his birthday. Sirena found that a startling coincidence that they should both have the same birthday. It caused her to look at him more carefully. He had fair skin and light brown hair and brilliant green eyes. He was quite handsome for a human. Though he tried to hide it, Sirena could tell he was bored. Suddenly, he turned his gaze toward her—as if he felt her eyes watching him. She ducked away from the window and swam away from the ship—not far away—but enough so that she was hidden from view.

Slowly activity on the ship decreased, and lights started to go out all over the ship. Sirena swam closer again. She looked in the window again, but all was dark. She swam around to other windows, but they were all dark too. She felt disappointed, and annoyed at her own foolishness, she accidently slapped the end of her tail against the surface. A shaft of light pierced through the darkness lighting her up. Startled and blinded, she tried to shield herself against the light with her hands.

"Who are you?" said a stunned male voice.

Sirena froze. She had been seen by a human. The queen, the sea witch, her parents, her sisters—they would be so disappointed. She was about to dive when he must have seen the fear and panic on her face and guessed that she was about to flee.

"Please, don't go!" he said urgently. "Please! I only want to talk to you." The light was suddenly extinguished.

She knew she should have left, but he had begged her. Her eyes began to re-adjust to the darkness, and she could see him hanging over the railing perhaps ten feet above her searching for her as his eyes too adjusted to the darkness. He was the birthday boy—the one she had seen through the window. She must not have ducked fast enough. He had seen her and waited to try to see her again. But most humans didn't have imagination to see her kind. That made him either very interesting or very dangerous. She thought of leaving again.

"What's your name? At least tell me that," and there was again an imploring quality to his tone that made her hesitate. She could see his fair skin even in the moonlight, but his eyes and hair were black in the dark—though his eyes seemed to burn with curiosity and sincerity.

"Sirena," she answered quietly. "Why should it matter to you?" she asked.

"Because I've never met a mermaid before, and it is nice to be able to call you by name, Sirena," he said honestly. "My name is Brendan," he added.

"Happy birthday, Brendan," she said.

He smiled at her, "I thought I saw you at the window. I hoped I had seen someone. It is the best birthday present ever, seeing you, meeting you," he amended.

He really was quite handsome, Sirena thought, but it didn't matter. This was foolish, talking to a human, and yet she didn't feel ready to go.

"Do you only come at night?" he asked.

"This is my first time. It is my birthday, too. I am old enough to come to the surface, now," she tried to explain.

He smiled again. "Happy birthday, Sirena. Will you come again tomorrow night?" he asked with so much longing in his voice that she found it difficult to say no.

"Perhaps," she said evasively, "for a short time, maybe."

"Please," he implored her. "Come later, like now, when the others have gone to sleep. Please."

She smiled by way of answer and then dove beneath the waves and made her way to the merpeople's city. She told no one of her encounter with Brendan, but she found herself thinking about him—trying to picture how he looked through the window with what she had seen leaning over the railing of the ship.

The next evening, when she surfaced, she was alarmed to see the little dingy tethered to the side of the big boat, but only Brendan sat in the little boat waiting for her. He smiled radiantly at her as soon as he saw her, and she swam slowly toward him. In the little boat, they would be very close to each other. They could even touch, and Sirena wasn't sure how she felt about that.

He sat staring at her intensely. "You are very beautiful, Sirena," he said quietly. "Even more beautiful than what I saw in the lantern light last night," he added blushing with embarrassment.

"You are very handsome yourself, Brendan," she said. They fell into an easy conversation talking about themselves and their likes and dislikes. Brendan told her about his kingdom; he was a prince, but he was careful not to press her about where she was from or her people. He seemed to sense that she had reason to fear him or at least fear his people, and he seemed to desperately want to convince her that she did not need to fear him. He had brought her some walnuts which he cracked open for her; he put the cleaned nuts in her hand. They were different than anything she had ever eaten, but they were good. Next, he peeled an orange and split it with her. The fruit burst in her mouth and was delightful.

They continued to meet in secret for a few hours every night for some weeks, growing more intimate with each other. He often took off his clothes and joined her in the water. They kissed and explored each other's body as much as they could. It was more difficult for Brendan because he had to keep his head above the water. Slowly, Sirena told him about how the merpeople lived, not where they lived, but how they lived. Brendan was fascinated by their peaceful ways, their generosity, their adoration of all the merchildren, the responsibility that all members of the merpeople felt for each other, their arts, their desire to live in harmony with the sea and its creatures and plants, and their desire to be the best individuals that they could be. He longed for such a world. His father and older brother had been killed in the last war. He had been young, but he remembered the destruction, the bodies, the suffering, the sicknesses, and the grief.

It surprised her when Brendan told her that he loved her and asked her to marry him. She knew from their conversations that human marriage was like merpeople bonding. Bonding—the whole situation was impossible. He was a human—and even if he liked her—loved her even—his people would never let him be with her—and even if he left them—turned away from his people forever—he couldn't survive under the sea. And she—she was betraying a strict rule of her people by having contact with a human. She would never leave her people—and yet, she realized painfully that she did love Brendan. She longed for him all the time they were apart. Was there any way to reconcile their absurd situation? Sirena realized that she needed to tell, to tell someone about Brendan, someone in authority. She was closest to her sister, Princess Adrianna, but Circe, as the sea witch, had the power to not only approve but to help perform the magic necessary. She told

Brendan that she would appeal to the sea witch and ask for her help.

"Could she make me like you?" he asked plaintively.

"Would you want that?" she asked uncertainly.

"I … I love you. I would do anything to be with you, for forever or for as long as we can have," he said earnestly.

She looked at him. His eyes pleaded with her. He meant it. Was this possible? They kissed tenderly for a while, and then she left him. She needed to talk to Circe and throw herself at the sea witch's mercy.

The next day, Sirena worked with Circe at the hospital, and then asked the older woman to lunch with her.

When they were alone, Circe looked at Sirena thoughtfully and asked, "What is it, child?"

"I need help, Circe. I … I have fallen in love," Sirena blurted out.

The sea witch looked at her carefully, a rueful smile playing at the corners of her mouth. Sirena felt uncomfortable under the sea witch's scrutiny. She blushed and looked down at her uneaten food.

"You have been preoccupied and distracted enough to be in love, but I have been watching you, and you don't spend your time with anyone out of the ordinary—your sisters, me, a few friends. Who is this mystery lover?" the older woman asked teasingly.

It scared Sirena slightly to think that the sea witch had been watching her behavior. In the time she spent away from

Brendan, she had been so preoccupied in missing him that she had not really thought about how she appeared to others. She hesitated, but she had to tell. "I have been sneaking out," she whispered.

Circe's expression changed from amusement to a vague wariness. "Sneaking out? Why?" she asked puzzled.

Sirena understood Circe's confusion. Sirena was free to have a relationship with nearly anyone she chose—except a person bonded to another. Guilt and embarrassment must have shown on her face, because Circe gasped and her eyes went wide.

"Sirena," Circe said cautiously. "You wouldn't," the sea witch shook her head as if the motion would banish the thoughts she didn't want to entertain.

Sirena forced the words from her mouth, "I … have … been … going … to … the surface."

"The surface?" Circe echoed, but her eyes flashed dangerously. Growing anger hardened the features of her face. "Tell me, all of it," she said in an icy voice.

Sirena sighed. She was in so much trouble; though Circe was very fond of her, this was beyond Sirena; this was about the merpeople and their safety, but Brendan wasn't like that. She had to explain; she had to make Circe understand. She began very slowly. "On my birthday, I went to the surface." Circe looked alarmed and even angrier. Her birthday was a month past. Circe was about it explode, but Sirena pressed on, the words tumbling out. She told the sea witch about the ship, about Brendan, about how he had seen her through the window and then over the railing. She told Circe about how gentle he was, how different he was from everything she had ever heard about humans. She told Circe about their growing affection, their intimacy. Finally, she told the sea witch that they loved each other, and that Brendan wanted to be bonded to her and live with the merpeople. Circe's face as she listened flashed so many emotions it was hard to keep track: disbelief, outrage, fear, uncertainty, speculation, wonder, more disbelief, a grudging sympathy, determination, and resignation. When Sirena was finished, she sat silently, waiting to hear what Circe would say. It was such a relief to tell someone that she felt a sudden calmness that steadied her for what would come next.

Circe sighed, "You know you have put the merpeople in danger. In fact, you have had them in danger for a month. You could be banished for such a crime," she said gravely.

Sirena nodded mutely, tears pooling in her eyes. She had known that she was endangering the merpeople, and she had known that her actions were probably punishable, but she had not explicitly thought about what that punishment might be.

"We will have to see your grandmother and your sister. The queen and princess will not be pleased." Circe paused and looked at Sirena searchingly. "You are sure of this human, Sirena?" she asked.

Her tears were now mingling with the sea water around them, but they sparkled as they left her cheeks. "Yes," Sirena answered in a sob.

The sea witch stood and took Sirena's hand, "I hope you are right for all of our sakes. Come, let's find Morgan and Adrianna," and the sea witch led Sirena to the public room where the queen, the sea witch, and the princess heard petitions from the merpeople. There were only a few merpeople left to be heard. Queen Morgan motioned Circe to join her and the princess on the dais, but Circe declined, and the queen's eyes flashed from the sea witch to Sirena and back, taking in that there was something important to be discussed when the queen and the princess were done with the others.

When the last of the petitioners took his leave, Circe ushered Sirena forward; Lord John, the queen's current consort, sat next to Queen Morgan, and Lord Peter, the princess' bonded partner, sat next to Princess Adrianna. All of them nodded to Circe, who did not take her chair but stood with Sirena. Prompted and encouraged by the sea witch, Sirena told them. The look of betrayal on her grandmother's face when she realized the full extent of the potential danger Sirena had put the merpeople in made her heart sick. She cast her eyes down after that and talked determinedly to the floor. She heard gasps of indignation and surprise at various points, but she couldn't bear to look up, not yet. When she was finished telling them, it was utterly silent in the public room. It was so silent, Sirena was sure they could hear her heart hammering away with anxiety.

"My Lady," Circe said quietly, interrupting the silence. "Sirena is very young. She has done a rash thing. A punishable thing, but if this human truly wants to join us, perhaps the breech in security would take care of itself."

Sirena looked up. The queen's face was pale, but her eyes rested on Circe, considering her words. Lord John's face was rigid with disapproval. He whispered something into the queen's ear, and she shook her head ever so slightly in response. The princess's face was less severe, and her eyes looked at Sirena with an exasperated fondness, and Lord Peter just looked stunned. The queen looked at Sirena; her eyes were cold and clear. "You know this is beyond just you and me, Sirena?" she asked.

"Yes, my Queen," Sirena answered quietly, and she bowed before her grandmother to show how sorry she was and to show her willingness to do whatever the queen deemed necessary.

"Get up, my child. We don't prostate ourselves before others here, and though you have done something wrong, you should not be bowing before anyone." The queen paused, glancing at the princess. "What do you think, Adrianna?"

Lord Peter whispered to Adrianna, and she nodded and squeezed his hand. "This is a public matter. It needs to go before the people. There seem to be two matters. Can Sirena be forgiven for her actions? If she can be forgiven, are we willing to adopt this human—assuming that he can be transformed in a manner that will allow him to live at the bottom of the sea?" she added, looking at Circe for confirmation on this later matter.

Circe smiled, "Yes, I could transform him. There is a special potion which we would need to make contributions to and some magic to make, but it could be done."

Sirena had thought that Circe could do it, but she had not known for certain. Hearing the words made her face shine in relief and joy. If it could not be done, she knew that eventually the relationship between her and Brendan would fail, and that loss had seemed unbearable to her and now that dreadful fate did not threaten them. The queen gasped, and Sirena looked up to find the queen gazing at her wide-eyed.

"You care for this human that much?" she asked, incredulity clear in her voice.

"Yes," Sirena answered immediately.

The queen looked at Sirena probingly, her eyes softening. "We will need to talk to his human. Someone will need to go."

"I will go, my Lady," Circe said. "I can interview him and read his soul. Sirena and I can report to you and the princess in the morning. If you approve, it can then be put before the people. They will need to time to consider the matter."

The queen and princess nodded their approval, and Circe and Sirena agreed on a time to go to the surface to see Brendan. Sirena spent the rest of the afternoon and evening reading and trying to distract herself. As merpeople made their way to their beds, Circe and Sirena made their way to the surface. Brendan was there in the little dingy waiting for Sirena; he gasped when he saw Circe and fell back onto bench seat of the dingy. He was not just startled, he was frightened.

Sirena had never given much thought to the different appearance of the sea witch. She was not a mermaid. She was a seal-soul. She had volunteered herself many, many years ago to live with the merpeople to give them guidance and the use of her magic in accord with dictates of the Great Goddess (to live in harmony with the seascapes and oceanscapes of the world and be stewards and benefactors of all their plants and creatures). As a soul—she was a shifting ethereal form of whites, silvers, and the palest grays. She could take the form of her seal-self, but among the humanoid merpeople, she took her seal-woman form. Circe had been co-ruler and part-manifestation of the Great Goddess for the merpeople's city for so long, no one alive could remember the city without her, and yet, how would she appear to a human? How did she appear to Brendan?

"Brendan?" Sirena said in a soothing voice. "Brendan, it is okay. This is Circe, the sea witch, I told you about. Remember?"

The sound of Sirena's voice seemed to calm Brendan. He turned his face toward her, and his fear faded some to be replaced by his relief and happiness in seeing her.

"Brendan," said Circe gently. "Can I come sit with you? I have some questions to ask," she said, explaining. Circe looked at Sirena and said quietly, "Go comfort him."

Brendan glanced back at Circe, his fear returning. "It's okay, Brendan," Sirena said reassuringly, and she dipped under the waves and rose right next to the dingy. She took his right hand in hers and squeezed it. Circe waited until he seemed comforted and then rose past the water line and floated onto the bench beside Brendan.

"Are you a ghost?" he asked in a terrified whisper.

"Perhaps, to your way of thinking," Circe answered quietly. "I am a seal-soul, but also a sea witch, and one of the rulers of the merpeople's city. We need to decide if we can trust you, Brendan. Do you understand how important that is?" she asked.

Brendan did understand. His reactions now would determine what would happen—whether he could be with Sirena and whether he could join the merpeople. He mastered his fear and squeezed Sirena's hand gently. "Yes, my Lady," he answered, his voice strong and determined.

And so they talked. Circe probed him about himself, about why he wanted to leave his people, about why he thought it would be better with the merpeople, about his love for Sirena. Sirena kept mostly silent, but chimed in at some points with added information. Circe then explained about the potion and the magic. There was a risk to Brendan in making the transformation; he was willing to take that risk. There would be no going back. Circe could think of no way to undo the transformation. When Circe was completely satisfied, she told them that she approved. The next steps would be to get the approval of the queen and princess and then the people. Circe took her leave of the young couple and made her way back to the city of the merpeople, leaving the two lovers alone.

The next day Circe and Sirena reported all that had happened with Brendan to the queen and princess and their consorts in the queen's private apartments. It was agreed that the matter should be put to the people that evening at dinner. They would give the people three days to consider the matter. The situation was described to the merpeople—and the reactions ran the gamut: shock, outrage, anger, fear, amusement, annoyance, disapproval, and curiosity among others. The hissed conversations that followed un-nerved Sirena, and she found that she couldn't eat. She retreated to her bedroom to wait for evening and her visit with Brendan.

The days dragged by. Everyone looked at her strangely. Some with open hostility, but some with sympathetic smiles and winks. Everyone was talking about her. She hid when she could, but she also spent time at the hospital with Circe. Finally, the three days had passed, Circe stood with Sirena as the queen announced that the merpeople had forgiven her and that Brendan could join them. Sirena was so relieved that she swooned on the spot, causing an outbreak of tittering sympathy.

After dinner, Circe had the queen, the princess, their consorts, and Sirena meet her in her chambers. In her workroom, she had a special container laid out and her wand (which she rarely used in her day-to-day activities in the city). She would need a drop of blood and a scale from each of them. She would need tears of joy and sorrow from both Sirena and Brendan (they would get his later). She needed mother's milk and a crushed pearl. Adrianna agreed to provide the mother's milk since she was still nursing little Meredith. The queen provided the pearl, and each allowed Circe to prick his/her finger and take the blood and pull off a scale. The scales and the pearl were crushed in a mortar and pestle, and then mixed with the blood, Sirena's tears, the mother's milk, and a little sea water—all in the special container. Circe then picked up her wand and placed the tip on her forehead and extracted a fine silvery thread and added it carefully to the container.

"What is that?" Sirena asked in an awed whisper.

"Each manifestation of the Great Goddess must give some of her essence for the potion; the queen and the princess have given blood and scale; I have no corporal form anymore, so I have given a strand of my soul," she answered quietly.

Sirena could only mumble a lame thank you, but the sea witch smiled and dismissed them all for the night.

The next day, Sirena spent in an anxious torment. She was both terrified that it would all go wrong and somehow equally terrified that it would go well. Sirena and Circe were to find Brendan after dark, make the transformation, and return to the city. When darkness finally fell, Brendan was waiting for them on the beach as had been previously agreed. Sirena waited in the shallow water while Circe floated her way out of the surf and stood with Brendan. Circe collected his tears. It was easy for him to cry in sorrow at thinking of leaving his home forever, but it was also easy for him to cry for joy at spending the rest of his life with Sirena. His tears were added to the potion. Circe prodded the potion with her wand and handed it to Brendan. As he drank it, Circe murmured an incantation that Sirena didn't understand. A mist of sea water rose and swirled itself around Brendan. The mist thickened, and Sirena felt a wave of panic when she couldn't see him. He cried out—not in pain, she thought. Frantically, she called his name. The mist cleared, and Brendan lay on the beach flapping his tail and looking slightly stunned. Even in the moonlight, his tail was spectacular—the scales were the full rainbow of their species' scales because they had been mixed from more than two races. Every possible color shone in a dazzling glory. Circe urged Sirena to grab Brendan's hands and help pull him into the water. Circe's ethereal form didn't allow her to help very much, but finally between Brendan's struggles to get to the water and her pulling him toward it, they managed, and they dove into the water together, splashing their tails against the waves and delighting in his ease of movement in the sea.

Circe led them back to the city indulging their giddiness and turning a blind eye when they stopped to kiss or embrace. To Sirena's surprise, Circe led them to the great ballroom, where the queen, the princess, their consorts, and most of the inhabitants of city were there to have Brendan presented to them. Brendan, slightly staggered at this reception, did his best to look appropriately humble and appreciative. After much swimming, dancing, and eating, Sirena and Brendan fell into bed together and were content to know that they never had to be parted again.

Ruby and Romulus

Once upon a time, there was a little girl named Ruby Red. She had flaming red hair and golden green eyes and was a joy to her family. Ruby grew up surrounded by women. Her grandmother and her great aunt, the grands, lived on the other side of the great forest, and her mother, her Aunt Lauren, and her cousin, Cathy, lived in the small village by the river. The grands were healers and mid-wives, and they kept to themselves except when they were summoned to tend to someone who was ill or a woman in labor.

As Ruby grew up, she was sent to spend more and more time with the grands, so she could learn the ways of healing. They would show her pictures and samples of herbs, plants, flowers, barks, or mushrooms, and send her into the great forest to collect samples. They taught her how to treat the different items, which to mix together, which to make into various teas, salves, poultices, and remedies, and so on.

At night in the cottage, the grands had Ruby read old myths and folk tales. They taught her to spin, knit, and sew. They had presented her with a basket and a sack with which to collect samples, an athame (a special dagger that healers used), and a bow and arrows to help her protect herself in the great forest. The athame also helped her collect samples. They regularly had her practice with the dagger and the bow. She got so good that she could supplement their goats' milk cheese, chicken eggs, cultivated and foraged fruits and vegetables, and occasional chicken dinners with hares, ducks, geese, fish, and other small game she hunted or snared in the great forest.

Most of the great forest was safe for Ruby to explore. Within the great forest, however, was a dense black woods that the grands warned Ruby never to enter. The black woods was a realm where the magical and the real world mixed, and strange things could happen there.

The grands explained that being a healer and mid-wife in their country in that time was a great honor, a great responsibility, and a great risk. "Men fear us, particularly church men, for we are women of power, and they don't like women to have power," they warned.

When Ruby's blood began to flow regularly, the grands also explained another unspoken fear that men had of women. They gave her a beautiful red velvet cloak that was lined with brown velvet, so the cloak was reversible. She could wear it with the red side underneath, hidden, like her sexuality, or she could wear it brazenly and with risk.

"Red is the color of life, of blood, and of passion. Men are hypocrites. They preach asexuality because what they fear most is female sexuality and passion, but what they really do is indulge or tolerate male sexuality and repress female sexuality. Look at the godly figures they hold up to the world: the Father, Son, and Holy Ghost, and the Virgin Mary. None of these is sexual, unlike the ancient gods of the Greeks or the Romans or the Great Goddess religions. Do not fear your sexuality but be very careful with it.

Some men would curse you for being sexual and perhaps even kill you, but you should know yourself as a sexual being even if that means only by self-exploration. Your blood flows now, child, and you will soon be capable of bearing children yourself. Men fear menstrual blood too because it is a part of women's ability to bear children that men do not possess. Red is the carnal color—of life, of passion, of blood, and of the flesh. Be carnal, but be careful with whom you share your carnal self."

Ruby loved her cloak and pondered the words of the grands. Their words frightened her, and she knew they were supposed to. She wondered, not for the first time, why it seemed so much more complicated and dangerous to be a girl and young woman. She had, of course, touched herself. She had heard the grands pleasing themselves in their beds in the small cottage, and she had heard her mother and her aunt do the same when she lived with them. It felt good. She didn't understand how something that felt so good could be considered so bad, but she had also seen how badly a young woman was treated if she was unfortunate enough to get pregnant out of wedlock. The same consequences never applied to a young man. Mostly, she wore the cloak with the red side as lining. It was easier to move through the forest among the animals with the brown side showing. Some part of her also knew that she wore the red inside trying to grow comfortable with herself as a sexual being, not quite ready to wear it outwardly for all the world to see.

Time passed, and she blossomed into a young woman, sexually aware, but as yet, only sexually known to herself.

Ruby enjoyed the great forest. It felt like a sanctuary to her, a holy place full of stillness and quiet and yet teaming with life and noise—a place of life and death—like all the great mysteries of life—or at least that is what the grands said.

"Blood is a symbol of both life and death, and we find life and death in the great forest and in the river and in all places of great power. Respect the great forest for its bounty as well as for its dangers," they warned.

Sometimes the grands let Ruby take the pony into the great forest, and while she loved Gray Lady, she also liked how quietly she could walk through the great forest alone. One day Ruby was following a stream and collecting different mosses for the grands. She ventured further than usual into the great forest. She was humming contentedly to herself when she felt the small hairs on the back of neck stand up and goose bumps course over her skin. She whipped around scanning the great forest, but she could see nothing. Though she could see no animal or person, she felt eyes watching her. She drew her athame and backed away, retracing her steps until she felt comfortable enough to turn face-forward and hurry home.

She tried to explain that she felt like she was being watched to the grands, and they exchanged a worried look and admonished her to stick closer to the cottage for the next few days. Though she meant to stay close to the cottage the next day, she felt herself drawn deeper into the great forest until again she felt eyes watching her. But this time their presence did not alarm her so much. She felt them upon her, but the hairs did not stand up and the goose bumps didn't come. Slowly she turned, searching for the source of the gaze upon her, but she couldn't find it. She didn't run away this time, but lingered, more curious than afraid. The eyes did not reveal themselves, and eventually, Ruby knew she had to get back, so she left, almost reluctantly.

When she next entered the great forest, she again felt drawn into its depths until she felt the presence of the eyes upon her. Again she couldn't locate their source, and frustrated now, she moved forward looking for them. And then they were gone; she felt their absence. They weren't looking at her. She froze in confusion. Had she scared their source? Why would they stop looking? What or who did they belong to? Then, as she stood there thinking, she felt them settle on her again but from further away. She realized that she liked the feel of the eyes upon her. She wanted to move forward again, but she didn't want to frighten them away again.

"Who are you? What are you?" she called softly, but there was no answer. Again she lingered, but nothing changed, so she moved forward again. As she passed a great oak tree she saw a small clearing and then the black woods came into view. She sensed that the gaze now came from the black woods, and she stopped, knowing that she shouldn't enter. "Come out," she said. "Show yourself to me, please," but her request was met with silence.

The next time Ruby went into the great forest she brought with her a lunch that could feed two with four apples and some goat cheese and a little bread. She sought out the black woods, and it didn't take long for her to feel the mysterious gaze settle on her. She walked toward it as far as she dared, and then she took off her cloak and spread in on the great forest floor with the brown side down and settled herself on the red cloth, taking off her weapons, laying them down next to her, and taking out an apple. She bit into the apple and ate it slowly and quietly, straining her ears to see if she could hear anything moving toward her and combing the great forest for eyes or movement.

After a while, she suddenly caught sight of a pair of big, glowing, golden/yellow eyes looking at her through the trees. She couldn't see a face, but she saw the strange eyes, bigger than animal eyes with a color that she didn't associate with human eyes. They stared at each other for a moment, and then the eyes closed and disappeared, reappearing in another spot. Again and again, they would appear, disappear, and reappear in a different spot, slowly getting closer.

"Who are you?" Ruby whispered.

And suddenly, a young man stepped out from behind a tree. Ruby sucked in her breath, startled by the sudden revelation. Somehow the young man heard her change in breathing, and he froze, anxiety clouding his face. She realized he was thinking of running away.

"Stay," she said softly. "You surprised me." She looked at him. His face relaxed slightly as he took in her words. He was a little older and taller than she was. He was muscular and darker skinned than she was. He had shoulder-length, brown, wavy hair, eyes that stared at her with such intensity; she felt like they could almost burn her. He wore leather pants and a home spun shirt that was loosely laced across his chest. He was bare foot, and scattered stubble marked his cheeks. He was beautiful in a different, almost animalistic way.

"Who are you?" he asked back, in a voice that was deep and rough. "Why do you come here?"

"I come to get things for my grandmother and great aunt, herbs and mushrooms and things," she said trying to answer him.

"Young women don't usually enter the great forest alone," he said.

"Maybe I am not your typical young woman. You've been watching me, why?" she replied.

He moved toward her cautiously. "I like the way you smell, and you're beautiful," he said softly, his face flushing with color. He squatted down just at the edge of her cloak, just feet from her.

"What is your name?" she asked, taking the opportunity to look at his eyes and his face more closely. His eyes were almost cat-like, glowing yellow-gold, but his pupils were normal, human. His eye lashes were unusually long and thick for a young man's. He had full reddish/pink lips, and his nose was straight and short.

"I am Romulus," he answered hesitantly. He was still looking at her hungrily and warily at the same time, as if some part of him desperately wanted to be with her while another part told him he should run away and hide from her. "What is your name?"

Romulus, suckling of the She-wolf, Ruby thought to herself. "I am Ruby, Ruby Red. I brought some food," she said gesturing toward the sack in which she had the apples, cheese, and bread. "Would you like some?" she asked, patting a spot beside her on her cloak.

He looked at her with mingled horror and fascination. "You shouldn't be here," he said harshly, but he moved slightly closer to her.

She pulled out an apple and offered it to him, holding it in her hand. He moved closer, sitting himself on the very edge of her cloak. He started to move his hand toward her, but he seemed afraid to take the apple for some reason she didn't understand. She reached out and put the apple in his hand. As she did so, their hands touched, her finger tips brushing against his palm, and it was like an electric charge passed between them. He jerked his hand back, but she didn't move hers. It hadn't felt bad, just intense and different and full of something she couldn't describe. She stared at her hand and then at his hand.

"What was that?" she asked softly.

"I don't know," he said, blushing again. The apple was still in his hand, and after he recovered himself a little, he ate it—more like devoured it, in what seemed like three bites. "It is good. What is it?"

"It's an apple," she answered incredulously. "Haven't you ever had an apple before?"

"No," he hesitated. He was holding something back yet wanting to reveal it too. "There aren't any where I am from."

Here she sensed was the source of his unease, the conflict that made him want to be there and yet told him to run. "And where are you from that there are no apples?" she asked.

"I live in the black woods," he whispered so quietly that it was hard to hear him, and she almost wasn't sure she had heard him correctly.

"The black woods?" she repeated in a whisper to match his own. She looked up to find him scrutinizing her face with brutal intensity, searching for signs of recognition or revulsion or fear, but she returned his gaze evenly and calmly. She knew what he had to be. He was a werewolf in his human form, a werewolf young man who was attracted to a human young woman, and he was beautiful and here with her, risking himself to be with her. She knew how the villagers would react to meeting one of his kind.

"How long have you been following me?" she asked.

Again his eyes searched her face demandingly as he tried to read her reactions to his answers. "I didn't mean to at first. I began to recognize your scent when you were in the great forest, even from the black woods, and I was drawn to it. But I would stay out of range and just watch you from afar or listen to you. I like your singing and humming. You have a pretty voice. Maybe a few weeks like that. You're not like other human young women, and then I wondered just how different you were."

Nothing he said alarmed her, so she continued to look at him calmly. She had been drawn to him as well. She was drawn to him now. She wanted to see what would happen if they touched again. She moved a little closer to him, but she stopped as she felt his body go rigid in alarm. "What do you mean 'just how different I was'?" she asked him.

"You're so beautiful, Ruby," and she was shocked at how pleased she was to hear him say her name. "So bold wandering the great forest. I ... I ... wondered ... if you would be ... bold enough ... to talk to me," and his voice was quiet again, barely audible. His face flushed as he said the words. She reached her hand toward his, and he tensed but didn't move away. Slowly, he moved his hand back toward hers, and then very gently, he placed his hand over hers. Her skin burned and tingled where he touched her. Her breath caught, but so did his. They stared at each other, watching and waiting and feeling. Sensation seemed to move across their skin surprising them with the intensity. He moved closer.

"Is that why you came closer four days ago?" she asked breathlessly.

"Yes," he breathed. "I shouldn't have crossed out of the black woods, and you shouldn't want to see me, but I want you to want to see me, and impossibly, you are here." They were very close now, and they both knew they were about to kiss. His face bent toward hers, and she inclined her face up to his. Their lips brushed against each other teasingly, full of anticipatory longing, and the burning sensation was there too, tingling with a rush of desire. Then the kiss started for real, his lips parting hers, his tongue probing hers, his hands knotting into her hair, and she was kissing him back and winding her arms around his neck. The intensity of the kiss grew. Everywhere they touched burned with sensation, and perhaps it was so much that they forgot to breath because they had to pull away from each other panting.

He was laughing, and she realized she was too, with relief and happiness. She had found a young man who she liked, and though he was a werewolf that didn't seem to be a barrier that had to separate them. He had found a young woman who he liked, and though she was a human that didn't seem to be a barrier to separate them either. They talked softly, asking each other about everything and eating the food that she had brought. He had never had cheese or bread before either. Mostly he ate meat, fish, grasses, berries, herbs, and some wild varieties of vegetables. She told him about the grands and what she was learning from them. His pack was small, nine or so werewolves, mostly bonded pairs, but two were only cubs and then himself. He didn't know how much trouble he would be in when he returned. He could try to bathe in a stream before going back, but they would still smell her on him. She knew she would need to tell the grands, and she had absolutely no idea how they would take the news. They weren't like the villagers with their irrational prejudices, but they had warned her not to enter the black woods and she knew that would also mean not cavorting with beings who lived there.

She realized it was getting late and that she needed to go so that she would return home safely before nightfall. He realized it too, and he pulled her into his lap for another kiss. They were touching in more places than ever before, their bodies pressed together, and everywhere burned and tingled. The blood surged through their veins, and she could feel their hunger for each other. She wanted him to touch her more, in the places that she had only explored by herself, and she could tell that he wanted her to touch him in his private places too. They contented themselves with the kiss, letting it flame with intensity until she was wrapped around him and he was pressing her closer to his body. Finally, she pulled away panting and disengaged herself from his body. He let her go reluctantly, and they stood up and moved off her cloak. He bent to retrieve it for her, shaking off the great forest floor debris and placing it around her shoulders. She retrieved the sack and her weapons, and they said good-bye with a fleeting kiss and a promise to see each other the next day.

The grands could tell Ruby was agitated, and they wanted to know what was going on. She told them she had met a young man in the woods and that she liked him. When she told them his name, they knew immediately that he was the one who had been watching her and that he was a werewolf. They were filled with a mix of emotions.

"You have managed to engage yourself with one of the few beings that the village men and especially the church fathers would find more offensive than a sexually active young woman. You *do* realize that?" they demanded. They huffed and puffed. They didn't like it, but they wouldn't forbid her from seeing him. A condition they mandated was meeting him, which she thought was only fair. She would have to talk to Romulus about it. She wondered what he would think of that. She wondered how he was faring in the black woods.

Romulus bathed in the stream, rolling over and over and scrubbing his skin uncomfortably against the rocks, but he knew it would not be enough. He entered the black woods and made his way cautiously to the pack. As he neared, he heard the growling as they picked up Ruby's scent on him.

"Have you killed a human?" demanded the angry voice of the alpha male.

"No," Romulus started to answer.

"No," cut in the elder male. "He has touched one and been touched by one."

"Are you insane?" asked the alpha male. "It is too dangerous. It is not done!"

Romulus cowered before the alpha male. "She is the grand-daughter of the healers. She is not of the village," he said in his defense. "She is different."

"Grand-daughter of the healers? The Red women?" the elder male said questioningly. "Clan leader, there could be advantages in this to us."

"Perhaps," conceded the alpha male, "but there is risk too."

"There is always risk," the elder male answered calmly.

The alpha male beckoned to Romulus, "Explain yourself."

"I like her. I like her a lot.... I ... I love her," he choked out.

The alpha male stared at him, caught off guard by the depth of the young man's feelings. "And she is not afraid of you—repulsed by you?" he asked skeptically.

"Apparently not," Romulus answered blushing furiously.

"She reciprocates your feelings, your desire?" he asked incredulously.

Romulus hesitated. "I kissed her, and she kissed me," he said very quietly, and he heard the collective gasps as the whole pack digested this information.

"We will consider this matter," said the alpha male.

Romulus retreated and watched warily as the alpha and his mate consulted with the elders.

The next day, Ruby entered the great forest eagerly. Romulus found her easily, catching her in his arms and holding her closely. The shock of their touch rocked them both, and they kissed and pulled apart before they could be overcome.

"The grands want to meet you," she said breathlessly.

"The alpha, his mate, and elders want to meet you and them too," he answered.

"Really?" she asked.

"Really," he answered. "Perhaps tomorrow. Could the grands make it to the northern stream where it forks at noon?"

Ruby considered this. They could ride and tether the horse and pony a safe distance away and walk to the fork. "Yes. They would ride most of the way. We could tether the horse and pony far enough away, so the animals wouldn't be spooked by your scents, and we could walk the rest of the distance to the meeting point."

Ruby set down her basket and took off her weapons, and Romulus pulled Ruby back into his arms. She looked up at him with shining eyes; they stood there a moment, memorizing the features of their faces until Romulus reached up to pull back the hood of her cloak and free her hair, running his fingers through it and letting it spill down her shoulders and back. "I missed you," he said softly.

"As I missed you," she answered back. He pressed his lips to hers, gently, and they could feel the intensity of their touching, even through their clothes. His hands reached to undo her cloak, and when they fumbled, her hands met his and pulled the tie free. Gently he pulled the cloak from her shoulders and spread it on the great forest floor as she had done the day before to make a circular blanket for them.

Self-consciously they moved to the center of the cloak and seated themselves next to each other. He reached up to cup her face in his hands, and then he was scooting closer to her and inclining her face towards his and bending his to hers. Her lips trembled against his, spiking a wave of desire in him, and he greedily parted her lips and kissed her. Her arms wound around his neck, and the feel of her fingers running through his hair made him growl softly in the back of his throat. The sound and soft vibration made her crazy with desire, and she found herself climbing onto his lap, straddling him with her legs, her skirts settling around them. She kissed him fiercely, and their bodies felt like they could burst into flame.

Finally, the kissing and the touching through clothes was not enough, and Ruby reached for his shirt, and he helped her pull it over his shoulders and head in a smooth motion, casting it aside. Her hands combed over his chest, and everywhere she touched burned. Her fingers traced over the muscles of his chest, and she played with the hair there at the same time as her mouth moved to his neck. The kisses changed to sucking and gentle biting. He groaned with pleasure, feeling like he could completely dissolve in her arms. Then he wanted to touch her too, to feel her naked skin against him, but her clothing was so much more complicated than his. He reached for her bodice, and she pulled away slightly so that she could help him unlace it and show him how. With it unlaced, they pulled it and her blouse off and cast them aside. He stared at the soft, pale flesh of her naked chest for a moment, and marveled at the fullness of her small, rounded breasts, so different from his own flat, muscled chest.

She was so beautiful, even more beautiful than he could have imagined. Her shapely breasts aroused him painfully, and the hungry way he looked at her made her blush. He pulled her against him, so that their bare chests pressed against each other and their skin burned and their blood raced. He moved his mouth down her neck, mauling her throat as his hands caressed her breasts until she moaned in pleasure, and he pulled away from her because if they didn't stop, they would continue until they were naked and mated. They stared at each other, panting and trying to calm and steady themselves.

"I never knew I could feel like this," he whispered.

She nodded in agreement. "So totally overcome," she added.

"Yes." He reached for her blouse and helped her dress, enjoying lacing her into her bodice. He put on his shirt reluctantly. They got up, and he retrieved her cloak for her, shaking it off and draping it around her shoulders. She armed herself and took up the basket. He asked her to show him some of the things she collected for the grands, so they walked through the great forest, pausing as

Ruby took samples of this or that. She paused at one point. She was so curious, but she wasn't sure how to ask. He looked at her searchingly.

"What is it, Ruby?" he asked.

"I just wondered … what … you," she began but blushed before she could finish.

But he guessed easily, "What I look like as a wolf?"

"Yes," she breathed.

"Are you sure you want to see me like that?" he asked and his voice was conflicted, afraid that he would scare her, and yet also hopeful, that his beastly form wouldn't.

Understanding his hesitation and desperate to show him her devotion, she answered him firmly, "Yes, I want to see you, every way that you are."

Carefully, he stepped away from her, and he fell to his knees and then rose up, four legged and furry with a tail, and his face elongated, his nose and mouth becoming a muzzle and his teeth transforming into canine teeth. His eyes remained the same, glowing golden-yellow, and his hair was the same brown, with the hair around his chest and neck thicker and longer than the rest. He was magnificent, strong and lean. Her breath caught as she looked at him, and she could see the anxiety in his eyes, but she moved close to him and ran her fingers through his hair, bending only slightly to kiss his forehead. He growled that same low growl of pleasure in the back of his throat that he had done earlier, but it sounded different, louder and lusher, in his wolf form. He stepped back from her and barked, a happy bark of relief, and then he changed back into himself or at least the human young man she knew.

He moved toward her catching her in his arms. "You're really okay?" he asked, unsure but hopeful.

"You're just as beautiful and impressive as a wolf as you are as a young man," she said, looking deeply into his eyes, and she saw him fight back the sudden tears that welled in them. She touched his cheek and brushed her lips across his.

"You are everything to me," he whispered, and then he kissed her until they had to break apart for air. Then it was time for Ruby to return home, and they parted.

The grands agreed to the meeting, explaining that a relationship between Ruby and Romulus would be a special kind of alliance, filled with both risk and opportunity. They grilled her on her feelings toward Romulus. She explained about their powerful physical attraction to each other, not without blushing furiously. They nodded and told her that they thought, though Ruby would be associating herself with werewolves, that she could be fully sexual with him without danger, unlike with a young man from the village. They talked to her about the ways that women and men could be intimate. They explained that it could hurt her a little the first time. They warned her that wolves mate for life and asked if she was willing to take on that responsibility and commitment. They warned her that she might have to become a werewolf herself, and they told her about her great-great grandmother, Little Red Riding Hood, who had married a werewolf and had been found out by the villagers and eventually had to change into a werewolf to escape them. The villagers had changed the story, of course, but the real story was that Little Red had been happy with her wolf and he with her. They didn't press her for answers, but asked her to think on things during the night and to try to have some answers in the morning.

Ruby thought fitfully over the all the grands had brought to her attention. What did she feel for Romulus? Was she the one for him? Was he the one for her? What would the black woods be like? What magical things would she be able to see and find? What would it be like living with a pack of werewolves? What if she became a werewolf herself? It was overwhelming. She didn't know what to think. She tried to calm herself.

Did she love him? Could she love him? She felt for him powerfully. She knew in her heart that he was a better match for her than any young man in the village. Yes, she decided, she could commit to him. The black woods? What scared her the most was how she would be received by Romulus' pack, but perhaps she would feel better after meeting with the alphas and elders.

In the morning, Ruby told the grands how she felt. She did her chores around the cottage and farm: feeding the chickens, gathering eggs, milking the goats, setting the milk for cheese, and tending their kitchen garden. Soon it was time for them to travel, and she saddled Blaze for the grands, who rode together, and Gray Lady for herself. They rode as close to the meeting place as they felt was safe and tethered the horse and pony, and then walked the distance to the fork in the stream.

The alpha male was a powerfully built man with flowing golden-brown hair and dark blue eyes. His mate was blonder and slighter, feminine, but imposing. She had yellow-gold eyes similar to Romulus'. The elder male had salt and pepper gray hair with glowing green eyes; his body was muscular and imposing but obviously diminished from his former glory. His mate was brown haired with streaks of gray and wide gray eyes. They wore simple clothing. The men in leather pants and home-spun shirts and the women home-spun frocks belted at the waists. Romulus stood with them, his face baring the emotions that he felt: anxiety, happiness, relief, and longing—all at the same time.

Little Red and her wolf were the precedent for the relationship between Ruby and Romulus, both sides acknowledged that. That Ruby was not a village young woman, but a healer/mid-wife in training and the grand-daughter and grand-niece of two very capable healer/mid-wives were all to her favor. Ruby would not draw as much attention to herself since she wasn't of the village. Further, she could use her training on the pack members, and in cases that were beyond her care, she could get the assistance of the grands. To Romulus' favor was his devotion to Ruby and his and the pack's ability to protect her in the black woods. (What was also in his favor but left unsaid was his werewolf appreciation of Ruby's sexuality instead of the typical human male fear of it and hostility toward it.) Ruby would be able to spend time there in the black woods with the pack and with Romulus, but she would also be able to gather things, magical things that were unavailable elsewhere, and bring them to the grands. It was acknowledged that in the course of their relationship it might be necessary to turn Ruby into a werewolf for her own protection. Both sides understood the risks, and yet both sides could see and feel the obvious delight that Ruby and Romulus took from each other's company. Consent was given. Ruby walked the grands back to Blaze and Gray Lady, and the two older women rode Blaze home with Gray Lady trailing behind them. The alpha and his mate and the elders disappeared into the great forest, and Ruby and Romulus were left alone.

They walked for a while until they found a spot they liked and then they spread out Ruby's cloak on the great forest floor. Soon they were kissing and touching with a frenzied excitement. His shirt came off and then her bodice and blouse, and then that wasn't enough and more clothing was shed. He touched her all over and then between her legs until she cried out in pleasure. She touched him too, but when she reached for him, he stopped her.

"If I come too, they will think we have mated. They will be able to smell you on me in this new way as well as just the scent of your skin and hair. If I come too, they will smell that and assume," he explained.

She looked at him, and she could tell that it was painful for him to stop, not just physically but emotionally too. He wanted to go further so badly, but he was trying to protect her, and she realized that she didn't care what they thought. She wanted to go farther too. If they thought they were mated if he came, then why not mate? "Then, let's mate," she whispered, color flooding her face.

"Ruby?" he said, his golden eyes searching her face.

"Don't stop touching me, Romulus," she implored him.

He growled softly, and the rest of their clothes were off, and he entered her gently at first and then more forcefully. He came quickly, and she had brought some spare rags for the fluid that the grands told her would be the result of the sexual union of a woman and a man. They lay together in each other's arms, a little stunned at what they had done.

After a while, he propped himself up to look down at her, and she laughed thinking of the village story.

"My, what big eyes you have," she teased.

His eyes danced with amusement. "The better to leer lustfully at you, Ruby Red," he answered playfully.

"My, what big ears you have," she continued.

"The better to hear you moan with pleasure, my love."

She flushed and added, "My, what big hands you have."

"The better to touch every inch of your body with, my darling," and he traced his hand over her breast and down to her hip.

"My, what a big mouth you have."

"The better to kiss you with and lick you with and suck you with, my sweet," his lips turning up in a grin.

"My, what big teeth you have," she said, finishing her parody of the village tale.

"The better to bite you with," and he put his mouth to her throat and mauled her neck until she was panting and running her fingers through his hair.

"You know that wolves mate for life," he said cautiously, his heart racing in his chest, his lips just below her ear.

"Yes," she answered softly.

"Marry me?" he whispered, afraid to look at her, afraid she would say no.

"Yes," she said. She had already decided it would be him, both last night after talking with the grands and in the decision to mate with him. "I love you," she added, saying the words out loud for the first time and knowing that they were true for her, and she pulled away a little so that she could see his face.

He laughed with relief, "Really?"

"Yes, really, Romulus. Will it make it easier for you, us getting married?" she asked.

"I am not sure," he answered slowly. "They know I love you, but that we have mated … so quickly … well … I think that will surprise them. It sort of surprises me," color flushing his face. "Will the grands know? Will they be surprised?"

She reached out to touch his face, "I don't know if they will know, but they have made it clear to me that my sexuality is mine to explore and do what I want with. Their main concern is that my partner loves me."

"I do love you, Ruby," and he took one of her hands in his and brought it to his lips so that he could kiss it. "I have loved you since the first time I really saw you with your green-gold eyes and flaming red hair and the way you smelled of lavender soap and human female." He paused, "You know it won't be an official human marriage, don't you?"

"What, no village riot at the reception lead by the church fathers themselves?" she teased.

He smiled slightly, "It is funny, but it's not, and the not funny part is that it could all be too true—we could become the hunted. Ruby, are you sure this is what you want—a life with me?" And there was pain in his voice and in the look in his eyes.

She looked at him, her hand tracing down his cheek, around his jaw, under his chin, and up the other jaw and cheek. His eyes closed to savor the sensation of her touch. "I know it hasn't been very long, but we are past the point of going back. We're mated and engaged. How soon do you think we can be married?" she asked.

"Whenever the grands agree to it," he answered, relief clear in his voice, and he leaned over her, bending down to kiss her gently, tenderly. They dressed quietly, each lost in thoughts about how their lives had so completely changed in the last few days and how much more they would change again once they were married.

Romulus again tried to wash the scents of Ruby from his body in the stream. His return to the pack wasn't met with growling but with blatant stares of disbelief. The alpha male glanced in the direction of the deeper black woods, and Romulus jogged to his side and followed him through the trees.

When they were some distance away, the alpha slowed his pace, "You've mated with her?" he asked. "Already?" the shock and disapproval clear in his voice.

"Yes," Romulus answered quietly. "I told you that I loved her. She loves me too. We couldn't stop. She said that she would marry me."

"Couldn't or wouldn't stop," the alpha said harshly. "You could offend the Red women. They could go to the villagers," he paused. "Marry? She understands about our bonding?"

"Ruby doesn't think her grandmother or great aunt will be offended. Yes, she understands about our bonding."

They heard the approach of the elder male and waited for him to join them. "You rash pup, what were you thinking?" chided the elder, but a smile played at the edges of his mouth.

"He wasn't thinking. That's exactly the problem. It's too impossibly sudden, too reckless, too intense," said the alpha.

"I can't explain it. She's all I can think about." Romulus struggled to explain, "I noticed her weeks ago. I could smell her from the black woods. I had to be around her, and then she was willing to see me a few days ago. When we touch, it's like fire," he said blushing furiously. "Sometimes I feel like we could burst into flame. I know it is too intense, but I don't know how to make it less so. She drives me wild."

"That is how the attraction between Lucian and Little Red has always been described when I have heard about it," answered the elder, "as a love almost like madness. That's why I came, Alpha. I thought you might want to know that before judging the young man too harshly." He turned then, returning to the pack and leaving them alone.

"Romulus, we will wait to see what the Red women say of this new development. I hope it will be received as you say, for all our sakes," and they returned to the pack.

Ruby returned to the cottage. She was subdued but happy, not sure exactly how to present Romulus' proposal to the grands and equally unsure about how they would react. They watched her carefully at dinner as she toyed with her food and was unusually quiet, but they didn't press her about it until after dinner when the dishes were cleared, washed, and put away.

"Out with it, child. What happened today with you and Romulus? What is it that you need to tell us?"

She paused and looked at them cautiously. "He asked me … to … marry him," she said very quietly.

"Marry him?" they stammered, exchanging alarmed glances and looking back at her. "It's been three days, child," and they watched the color flood Ruby's cheeks. She heard them gasp in unison, and though she couldn't imagine her face getting even redder, she felt like it had. "You've mated, haven't you?" And though there was accusation in their tones, there was also an amusement and even a little admiration for her boldness. They clucked at her and at each other. "You'll need to tell your mother. You'll need to visit the village. Hopefully, it goes without saying that you will tell her and only her. A wedding. A great forest wedding at sunset and then under the stars," they gushed. "A great grandbaby in less than a year! There are herbs and teas you must start taking, my dear."

Early the next day, the grands helped Ruby saddle Gray Lady, and after they loaded her up with herbs and salves and gifts for her mother, aunt, and cousin, they waved her off. She was highly uncomfortable leaving with Romulus unaware of where she was and what she was doing. She wondered if he would find her in the great forest before she got very close to the village. If he didn't find her, she thought she might cry. However, she also knew she had to see her mother and the sooner the better.

Just as she was afraid that she had gone beyond where he would dare to go, she heard Romulus call her name from a distance, giving her a chance to tether the pony and walk to him.

Anxiety lined his face, and it pained her that she was the source of his discomfort.

"Where are you going?" he asked.

"The grands told me that I needed to tell my mother, about us, about the wedding," she said, and she saw to her horror that this explanation did not relieve him but drove up his level of distress. She realized he was drawing the most negative conclusion possible. "No, not like *that*. She is my *mother*. She *needs* to know; no one in the village will know."

He didn't seem particularly assured, but he pulled her into his arms, pulling the hood of her cloak down and nuzzling his face in her hair, and then they were greedily kissing and touching each other. When they broke apart, he led her to a small stand of trees, and they spread out the cloak, so they could be together once more, kissing, licking, touching, sucking and gently biting, moaning in pleasure, making her come, and then mating. They had been too frantic to do much more than murmur each other names and profess their love, but as they cleaned up and dressed, they told each other what had happened when they faced their families. She was interested in what the elder male had said about the love between Little Red and Lucian, and he was intensely relieved to hear how the grands had taken the wedding news. He didn't like the idea of her being in the village at all. She would spend the night in her mother's house and leave again in the morning. She promised to see him the next afternoon, and he reluctantly let her go, kissing her in parting.

She rode again, and as she neared the village, she noticed some people in the great forest. Several wood cutters labored, and a few young men were hunting, with no particular success. A group of children gathered sticks under the supervision of one of the wood cutter's wives, but Romulus appeared to be right. Girls and young women didn't enter the great forest alone, and almost no one traveled so far alone in the great forest as did she and the grands, but she wondered if the grands counted the same way because they normally traveled together.

Her mother was pleased to see her and pulled her into a tight embrace. They put Gray Lady in the barn and got her oats and water and took off her saddle and tack. They caught up on household news, and though her mother knew Ruby had come for a specific purpose, she waited for Ruby to tell her in own time and in her own way. Aunt Lauren and Cathy seemed almost as pleased to see her as her mother. After Ruby had had some tea and cheese and fruit, Ruby asked to see her mother alone, and they retreated to her mother's bedroom. Ruby told her mother everything—about feeling watched in the great woods, about meeting Romulus, about how intensely they seemed feel for each other, and about their mating and his asking to marry her. Ruby's mother listened to her daughter intensely, studying the features of her daughter's face as she spoke.

"And you want this, Ruby? You want to marry this werewolf young man when you are so young? When it will put you both at risk? Put even your families at risk?" she asked her voice full of concern and wariness.

"I do, Mother. He is all that I think about. I mean I can think about other things, but he is always also on my mind. I feel like I need him, being so far away from him now is painful, and this morning when I thought I wouldn't see him for two days, I was utterly miserable."

"When?"

"The grands were thinking next Saturday night."

Her mother looked at her for a long moment. "All right," she said at last. "But I want to make you a gift. Come with me." Her mother led Ruby out of the house and down the street to her uncle's smithy. He was wrapping up his work at the forge, but he looked up as they entered, and he smiled warmly at his sister and Ruby. Ruby's mother explained that she wanted a set of copper rings, one for Ruby and one for a young man. Uncle William seemed to take note of the vagueness of her mother's references to a young man, but he said nothing.

He took Ruby's hand and wrapped a piece of string around one finger, cutting the string so that the ends just met. Then Uncle William held out his own hand and asked Ruby to estimate which of his fingers was closest to the index finger of the young man in question. Uncle William was a full-grown man and a smith. His fingers were thick and calloused. If Ruby had to guess, she thought his pinky was the closest. Her uncle saw her hesitation and called for his oldest son, Will, who was nineteen. Will presented his hands to Ruby. She blushed as she did it, but she took one of Will's hands in one of her own and interlaced their fingers together. Yes, she thought Will's hands were of a similar size to Romulus', so her uncle cut another piece of string to fit around one of Will's fingers.

Her mother pulled her brother to the side and spoke to him softly, and then she left with Ruby. She said nothing until they were back at the house. Wedding rings were normally made of silver or gold, she explained. Gold was too expensive for her to afford, and silver wouldn't do for a werewolf. Copper would work, but William would suspect the reason, which would be confirmed when Ruby didn't get married in the village. She had told her brother. Seeing the alarm run over Ruby's face, her mother assured her that William wouldn't tell a soul. The Red family knew its history even if the rest of the village had fabricated its own version of that history, her mother explained.

They ate a pleasant meal with Aunt Lauren and Cathy. Ruby brought out the various supplies and gifts that the grands had sent to her mother, aunt, and cousin. They swapped more news and stories, and then Ruby went up to bed with Cathy. Ruby fell asleep thinking about her reunion with Romulus.

Romulus had bathed on his way back to the black woods. His return was not remarked on, but as the day wore on, his anxiety and agitation were noticeable. The elder male approached him, "What is it, my boy? Walk with me and tell me," he requested. When they were out of ear shot of the rest of the pack, Romulus told him that Ruby was going to the village to tell her mother of the wedding. At first, the elder was as alarmed as Romulus had been, but then Romulus had explained all that Ruby had told him including the grands' suggestion of the following Saturday night for the wedding.

"So this agitation, this restless energy, is from being separated from her?" the elder asked wonderingly.

"Yes, I guess—that and her being in the village—even for a good reason," Romulus answered, perhaps a little too sharply.

The elder raised his eyebrows. "You have it bad, Romulus."

"I know," he admitted. "What will happen once we are married? Where will we live? How can we be together without the whole pack listening?" he asked miserably. Though the pack members lived in small cottages grouped together, pairs did their mating in the black woods in places where they knew they could be alone. Romulus wasn't sure he could take Ruby that far into the black woods, which was why he had risked the places in the great forest that were closest to the black woods—places that were far away from both humans and werewolves.

"There is Little Red and Lucian's cottage not all that far from here. It hasn't been used since then, and the disuse has made it largely hidden, but it could be cleaned up for you," the elder said pensively.

"Could we go there? Would you show it to me?" he asked pleadingly.

"Not tonight. But I will take you tomorrow. It will give you something to do while you wait her return," and the elder smiled at Romulus.

"What about during the full moon?" Romulus asked hesitantly.

"It was my understanding that the cottage was enchanted somehow—that Little Red could not be harmed there even during the full moon, but Ruby has an additional option. She has her grandmother and great aunt. It might be nice for her to spend those nights with them, so she does not completely lose her human family," the elder said thoughtfully.

With Romulus comforted, they returned to the pack.

In the morning, Ruby was surprised that her mother and her aunt had combed through their belongings looking for fine clothing. They had come up with a beautiful linen blouse that was trimmed in lace, a midnight blue velvet bodice and a matching long-fitted shirt. There were several other plainer linen shirts and a brown leather bodice and a burgundy brocade bodice. They presented these items to her in the morning and packed them in her bags. Her mother would make the trip for the wedding, and they all said a teary good-bye. Despite the sorrow she felt at leaving her family, Ruby also felt a sense of relief at being able to leave and return to the grands, the great forest, and Romulus, so the ride was pleasant.

Romulus was up early, but he forced himself to stay calm and contain his energy. The elder male would take him, so he couldn't afford to annoy the elder before he was ready to go. The elder seemed to sense Romulus distress and hurried. They ran part way to burn off some of Romulus' energy, and then they came to a densely wooded area. In fact, it seemed almost impassible between the denseness of the trees and the debris that littered the spaces in between. By squeezing through the trees and pushing debris out of the way, they got through about ten feet. Suddenly, the density ended, and a clearing rose before them in the center of which was a little cottage. It had only two rooms: a kitchen area with a hearth and stove and work surfaces and a small bedroom. It was dirty and dusty. The roof was in disarray, and the shutters weren't hanging straight. But it was miraculous to Romulus. He could clean it and fix things before Saturday, and he and Ruby could be in the black woods alone, not with the pack all the time.

Romulus looked at the elder, and he flushed to see that the elder had been looking at him for some time with a bemused look on his face. "*Thank you*," Romulus choked out, and the older man smiled and said, "I'll leave you to it then," and left Romulus alone with his project. Romulus found a bucket and went outside; there was a small stream not far from the house, so he filled the bucket and went back to the cottage, wiping down surfaces until the water needed to be changed, and he spent the morning cleaning and passing the time.

At mid-afternoon, when it seemed possible for Ruby to be home, Romulus left the cottage and headed toward the great forest. Ruby had gotten home, and having attended to Gray Lady in the stable and relating the most pressing news to the grands, she went looking for Romulus. He heard her and smelled her before she knew he was there. The relief he felt, in seeing that she was all right and had returned to him from the village, was as if a physical weight had been lifted from his shoulders. He ran to her, catching her in his arms and spinning her around. She laughed at the enthusiasm of his embrace, but she was pleased too. It had filled her with anxiety when he hadn't met her in the great forest during her return.

He pulled down her hood and pulled her hair free running his fingers through it as he did so. He bent to kiss her, and though he tried to tame it, he couldn't stop the urgency of the kiss, of his physical need for her, and she wound her arms around him in response, kissing him back with a kindred passion. Finally, they pulled apart gasping, and he undid her cloak and spread it hastily on the great forest floor. He pulled her down on the cloak where he unabashedly started liberating her from her clothing. Soon they were both naked and kissing, touching, licking sucking, biting, and pleasuring each other, moaning and murmuring as they went. After he made her come, he came quickly, and they lay together in each other's arms for a few moments before pulling apart and cleaning themselves.

Sated physically, they began to catch up with each other. She took his hand and looked at it closely, confirming that his fingers were much like those of Will's. She explained that her mother wanted them to have rings for the wedding, and he was charmed by the idea of a copper wedding ring. She told him that her mother intended to come to the wedding, and he told her about the cottage that had belonged to Little Red and Lucian. They parted reluctantly, agreeing when and where to meet the following day.

And so it went for the days up until Saturday with Romulus spending time at the cottage cleaning it, fixing things (the roof and the shutters), finding fresh pine needles for the mattress and restuffing it, finding sweet smelling herbs to hang in the kitchen and the bedroom. He still found time to spend with Ruby, mating with her and talking to her. Ruby enjoyed her time with Romulus but was commandeered into all sorts of wedding preparations, which largely meant food preparation. Extra cheeses were made; fruit was collected from their trees and gardens but also from the great forest. In the two days before the wedding lots of bread was made. Ruby's mother arrived the Friday afternoon before the wedding, bringing her own stores of butter and jams and throwing herself into the food preparation.

That Saturday at late afternoon, the grands had attached a flatbed cart full of food to Blaze's saddle and had ridden close to the fork in the northern stream. They unhitched the cart at the closest point they thought Blaze could stand and then moved him safely away. The alpha's mate and the elder female met the grands. They were supervising spits of venison and wild pig, and the four women moved the food from the cart to tables that had been constructed and lined the area where the wedding would take place.

The four women realized they respected each other—both sides had made an effort to make this a special event. The werewolves realized the care the human women had taken to provide them food they couldn't get in the black woods. They asked about each other carefully, gleaning information. Both sides found that they shared much, including the love of their young people and the child they suspected was growing or would be growing in Ruby's womb.

Ruby's mother had helped Ruby dress in the fine white linen shirt with the lace trim and the midnight blue velvet bodice and skirt. She had brushed Ruby's hair, then woven an array of pretty white flowers in a cascade of braids and curls that framed Ruby's face elegantly. As they were leaving the cottage, Ruby moved to put on her cloak in her usual manner, but her mother took it from her and reversed the linings so that the red side showed and the brown was hidden. Her mother's gesture made Ruby blush. It was time for Ruby to acknowledge herself as a fully sexual female with the carnal color wrapped around her like a mantle instead of hidden. With the sun flashing its fading golden light, Ruby, in her cloak, glowed like fire, moving through the great forest—or at least that is how she looked to Romulus, as he watched her approach—a flaming light to give meaning to his life. He could only hope that he could provide her with as much inspiration and comfort.

Rough logs had been placed on either side of a narrow path so that the werewolves and their few human guests could sit while Ruby and Romulus said their vows publicly. Most of the pack members had been milling around, but they began to take their seats when they saw that Ruby had arrived. Ruby and her mother were met by the grands and the alpha and elder couples and Romulus. Over the past two days, this group had met several times to meet and get to know each other better. The elder couple and the grands seemed to find the situation inevitable and even romantic, but perhaps that was because they had heard the genesis of the current story from people who actually seen and witnessed the love between Little Red and Lucian. Ruby's mother and the alpha couple were less enthusiastic but accepting. After speaking briefly, they dispersed to take their seats leaving Ruby with Romulus.

Romulus pulled Ruby toward him and kissed her forehead. "I like the red," he whispered huskily. Then he untied the cloak and pulled it from her head and shoulders, setting it aside so that he could look at her. "You look so beautiful," he said softly. His normal attire had been replaced by a slightly finer set of leather pants, shirt, and leather jacket. He took her hand, and they walked together to stand before their families. The ceremony was simple, but cast against a magnificent blazing sunset, it made the scene almost magical. Ruby and Romulus said their vows and exchanged the rings that Ruby's mother had given them. After the words were said, they kissed, and then there were embraces and introductions. Ruby was introduced to the pack members she had not yet met, as were her mother and the grands. Torches were set, and the food and the company were pleasant.

When everyone had eaten his or her full, the company broke up. Ruby's mother and the grands were given torches to light their way back to Blaze and then to the cottage, and the werewolves disappeared into the night. Romulus wrapped Ruby in her cloak, and her hand in his, he led her through the forest and into the black woods to the cottage that had been Little Red's and Lucian's and would now be theirs.

Someone had lit a merry little fire in the hearth. Romulus suspected the elder male, so there was soft light in the cottage when Romulus carried his bride over the threshold. He set her down so she could look around. She was charmed by the little cottage, and almost forgot herself in thinking about their shared future life there until she felt his hands at the tie of her cloak, undoing it and pulling it from her head and shoulders. He cast it aside and pulled her up into his arms again, carrying her into their bedroom. Somehow he managed to rip the top sheet and blanket down and place her gently on the bed.

They scrambled out of their clothes, and though they had never minded mating in the great forest, there was something wonderful about being alone in a proper bed in a bedroom, and even more wonderful still was the knowledge that they didn't need to be parted. They didn't need to separate to go home because they were home. Basking in that sweet knowledge, their kisses and caresses began slowly, tenderly. Her hands explored his body, and his hands explored hers. The kissing, touching, licking, sucking, biting, and pleasuring each other continued until they had both come, and after they had wiped themselves off, they snuggled into each other's arms, savoring the contact between their naked skin and whispering to each other until they fell asleep—not as innocent characters in a fairy tale but as fully aware sexual partners.

The Prince Rejected

Once upon a time, in a tiny kingdom long ago, there was a farmer, Henry Tinge, and his wife, Lenore. He was a strapping man, and Lenore was petite but strikingly beautiful with thick long blond hair and crystal blue eyes. At first, they didn't think they could have a child, but after ten years of marriage, Cindy was born to them. Cindy's parents adored her. They read to her, sang to her, danced with her, and taught her everything they could think of so that she could have a productive and rewarding life. That meant that she learned the kinds of things people associated with women's work: cooking, cleaning, sewing, spinning, knitting, caring for the smaller animals on the farm, herb and garden cultivation, milking, etc. But it also meant that she learned many of the skills of her father: riding, using a bow and arrows, plowing and harvesting a crop, slaughtering and butchering animals, mending fences, etc.

One horrible winter, Lenore fell ill, and she did not get better despite repeated visits from the mid-wife and various infusions and salves. She died before the last the snows melted and was buried on the farm. Time passed, but it was hard on the farm with just Cindy and Henry. When their neighbors, Eva and Tom Fenn and their three children, had a visit from Eva's widowed sister and her daughters, Henry seemed glad of the extra company in the village. Lucinda Miller seemed like a cold woman to Cindy, but warmer than her two haughty daughters, Tara and Sara. There was a village dance, and Cindy watched in dismay as her father paid a lot of attention to the Widow Miller. Soon enough Lucinda and Henry were married, and Lucinda became Cindy's step-mother and Tara and Sara, her step-sisters.

At first everyone was careful to treat everyone else well, but after about three months, the true natures of the Miller women became apparent. They were lazy, proud, unkind, and demanding women. Henry considered divorcing Lucinda, but before he was able to go see the mayor, he was struck by a terrible stomach illness from which he never recovered, and a year after her mother's death, Cindy was orphaned and at the mercy of her awful step-mother and step-sisters. If it was hard before with Cindy and Henry running the farm by themselves, it was even worse now because though Lucinda, Tara, and Sara were able bodied, they did very little to help Cindy with the farm and housework. Cindy worked like a slave doing the work that she could manage, but she could not plow all the fields nor take care of all the animals and do the house work. She rotated the single field she could manage to plow, and some of the animals were either sold or slaughtered. Lucinda and her daughters did some of the housework, but the heavier tasks of cleaning and laundry were left to Cindy.

With little legal recourse, Cindy tried to put up with her appalling treatment as best she could. When she was alone or with the animals, she sang, and she had a beautiful voice. The hard work made her body lean and supple, and though she did a lot of manual man's work, her years of being read to and danced with left her quite knowledgeable and graceful. She still recalled her parents' favorite books for comfort and company rather than endure the hazing and teasing of her step-sisters and their loathsome mother. Though Cindy dressed largely in her father's old overalls and other raggedy clothing, she bloomed into a beautiful young woman. When she was clean after a bath or a swim in the nearby river, she was stunning. She was taller than her mother, but she had Lenore's beautiful blond hair and sparkling blue eyes. She was shapely and strong. However, she, normally, appeared quite plain with her hair covered, her face and hands dirty, her clothes in rags, and shod in wooden clogs.

The Fenn's oldest son, Jeremy, was nineteen; as he grew, he had taken on the responsibilities of the fields that bordered the Tinge's (or at this point the Miller's), and he had increasingly taken notice of Cindy and her transformation into a young woman. He found excuses to ask her about what crop she was planting where, how her animals were breeding, what chores she enjoyed and didn't. They even talked of books, which disconcerted Jeremy because he realized that he was less well-read than Cindy and strove privately to remedy that situation. Jeremy quite clearly saw through the dirt and the ragged clothes to the beautiful woman beneath, but he also saw a smart and kind-hearted woman who refused to let appalling circumstances make her bitter and hateful. He watched her handle her animals with skill and care. He loved to listen to her sing, stealing up on her to listen because she stopped when she saw other people around, even him. He longed to hold her in his arms. Cindy, for her part, found Jeremy's attentions sweet and flattering. He was handsome and gentle. He was a good farmer and good man, but she felt that she had nothing to offer him since Lucinda and her awful daughters would get her parents' farm.

Now it happened that the tiny kingdom was ruled by a king who had a son of marriageable age, a fine lad of twenty. The surrounding kingdoms had princesses, but all seemed to be too old for him or too young for him, so the king had suggested a series of grand balls to be held where all the free born girls between the ages of seventeen and twenty-two were invited to attend. The kingdom buzzed with gossip and anticipation of the event. People swarmed to the capitol, and almost every inn and tavern room were filled. Some of the fallow fields surrounding the capitol had been turned into camp grounds to accommodate those who couldn't find city accommodations.

The Widow Miller had once lived in the capitol, and she imposed herself and her daughters on her brother who still lived there. She had sold anything she could find of value in Cindy's parents' house for suitable clothes for herself and her daughters to wear to the balls, but they only had three sets of gowns, and the balls would be held for seven nights. Cindy was expected to stay home and mind the farm since she had no gown to wear to the balls. She wasn't even sure she minded not going since it meant she would be alone on the farm and perhaps she could spend some time alone with Jeremy. But when she found out that Jeremy was accompanying his sister, Lilly, to the balls, she had a desperate desire to attend. She sought out her god-mother, the old mid-wife, and asked her for her advice. The old woman told her to pray to the woodland fairies because they had old magic and had been friends with her mother who had prayed to them for a child and had been granted that wish.

Cindy searched for suitable tokens to give the fairies. At the river, she collected a range of the smoothest and most colorful stones she could find. At the farm, she collected swatches of aromatic herbs. Over the years, she had collected some of the feathers that birds had lost either in the fields or on the farm, and she looked through those now, selecting the most colorful and unusual. As she traveled to the small wood near the farm, she collected wild flowers. She wasn't sure where the best place would be to make her offering and her prayers, but she felt compelled to enter the wood more deeply. Finally, she found herself inside a ring of twelve tall pine trees, and she knew this was the place. In the center of the stand of trees, there was a small stone table and she laid the stones, the herbs, the feathers, the flowers, and her mother's wedding ring (the only precious thing she owned) on this and knelt beside it to pray.

"Oh, woodland fairies, help me, please. There is a series of balls where the prince searches for a bride, and though I have worked so hard for so many years, I have nothing appropriate to wear. You were friends to my mother, won't you befriend me too?"

Nothing happened though Cindy stayed there for some time. Discouraged but still not bitter, Cindy rose to leave, and when she turned, she found she was facing an unnaturally beautiful female child clothed in new spring leaves. Looking closer, Cindy realized she wasn't a child. She was a fairy. Her ears were pointed, her hair like the silk from maze, her eyes unnaturally green, like dark bright emeralds. Around her head was a thin golden circlet. Cindy took a step backwards in surprise.

"Do not be afraid, child. I am Maeve, queen of the woodland fairies, and your mother, Lenore, was a friend to us as we will be friends to you. But beware what you wish for and remember that your parents hoped that you would have a rewarding and productive life."

Cindy bowed. "I will try, My Queen. Thank you."

"Close your eyes, child, and listen to me. When you open your eyes, there will be two horses, one as black as night and the other as white as snow. One carries two chests and a guide for you; the other which you will ride carries a tent for you and supplies. You should pitch your tent close to the woods on the northside of the capitol. The afternoon before each ball, one of my fairies will come to help you bathe, dress, and adorn. You will be the fairest woman at the ball, but you must consider who is the fairest man. When you have made your decision, do not tarry, but make it known. Someone will look after the farm in your absence. Our blessings are upon you. There is also one gift you should understand: your step-mother and step-sisters will not recognize you at the balls."

Cindy listened with her eyes shut. She murmured her thanks again and felt the queen kiss her forehead, but she remained with her eyes closed until she felt the breath of a horse in her face. When she looked up, she saw that they were magnificent horses, tall and powerfully built, with beautifully groomed manes and tails. Her guide inclined his head to her in greeting. He was a tall fairy knight, beautiful and slender. He rode the ebony horse. He jumped down gracefully to help her onto the white horse, and then he led the way out of the forest to the main road. He played the pipes off and on to pass the time. Many of the songs she didn't recognize, but some of them she did. In two days, they reached the capitol, and the fairy knight led her to the north side close to a wood where he set up camp for her and disappeared into the woods. The next day the first ball was to begin. As promised, in the afternoon, a fairy woman appeared in the tent, and she bathed Cindy, washed her hair, and anointed her with sweet smelling oils.

She did her hair in a beautiful elaborate series of braids, put her in a shimmering dress of white, and adorned her with pearls.

"Of everything you see before you, what is the one thing that pleases you most, child?" the fairy asked in a sing-song voice.

Cindy looked at herself in the mirror that the fairy woman held before her and pointed to the delicate pearl necklace at her throat.

"So be it. When the magic is spent, the necklace will remain with you as our gift."

Cindy gasped. "No, my lady, it is too generous. You have offered me so much all ready."

"Shh, shh, child, what mortals think of as wealth is fleeting and unstable. You must decide what makes yourself truly wealthy in the fullest sense of the word. Now go, the first ball awaits."

Cindy went, and the palace was beautiful and enormous. It seemed that thousands of people were in the great ballroom. Jackets and dresses of every imaginable color floated about the room. With a flourish of trumpets, Prince Daniel was announced with his royal parents, King James and Queen Isabelle. Royal scouts mingled through the crowd looking for young women to bring to the prince's attention. One had seen her and dashed off immediately to tell the prince. She felt giddy from the compliment.

She heard someone call her name, and she turned surprised to find herself standing in front of Jeremy Fenn and his sister, Lilly. They both gaped at her—at her hair, her clothes, and her jewels. She didn't know how to explain. They were both dressed well for farm children with a little extra money, but Cindy realized she was dressed like a princess. "My god-mother helped me," she stammered.

"I wish she was mine," Lilly said appreciatively.

Jeremy tried to recover himself. He didn't even remember ever seeing Cindy wearing a dress. "You look *so* beautiful. Would you … would you like to dance?" he asked. "Lill, you don't mind do you?" he added quickly.

Cindy looked at Lilly, who said quickly, "No, I am fine. You two go ahead."

Jeremy held out his hand; as he had wanted to do a hundred times, he pulled Cindy into his arms and spun away from his sister. At first, he just savored the feel of her in his arms, her pressed against his chest. He could smell the sweet oils that scented her skin like flowers, and he could feel her body through the soft delicate fabric of her dress. But then it wasn't enough, he wanted to look at her some more. He moved her to the edge of the dance floor and separated himself from her, looking down at her as she looked up slightly into his eyes.

Cindy was flattered by Jeremy's attentions. She found it pleasant to be in his arms, dancing. She liked him, and if the fairies were really giving her one gift for each night of the balls, she might have something to offer Jeremy other than her destitution. He was handsome with curly brown hair and dark blue eyes. He was tall and strong from farm work, and even through his jacket, she could feel his muscled arms and shoulders. When she looked into his eyes, she was surprised with their blazing intensity.

"I have never seen you so clean," he said. Hurt and annoyance flashed over her face. Though it was true, it was obviously the wrong thing to say, but before he could explain or make it right, a royal scout interrupted them.

"Excuse me, Miss, Prince Daniel would like the next dance. Would you follow me?" he said extending his hand to take Cindy's.

She hesitated, and then said yes, and was led away. Jeremy watched her go, feeling crushed. He'd insulted her, and he had nothing to offer that could compete with a prince. He looked around the room trying to find his sister, but also trying to see if there was any young woman there who was nearly as breathtakingly beautiful as Cindy. There were lots of pretty young women in pretty dresses, but none of them looked as stunning as Cindy. Lilly found Jeremy before he found her. She read the distress on his face and demanded to know what was wrong.

"I told her I had never seen her so clean," he said.

Lilly clapped her hands over her mouth, and squeaked between her fingers, "You didn't?"

"I did, and now she is dancing with the prince," he added despondently.

Prince Daniel was tall and elegantly handsome with fair skin and coppery auburn hair and dancing green eyes. He was muscular and soft-spoken, a perfect gentleman. He thanked the scout and Cindy, and then he held out his hand to take her into his arms. Cindy fit against him differently than against Jeremy; she was smaller in his arms. His clothes were much finer than Jeremy's, and he danced superbly, twirling them through the crowd so that they seemed to float across the floor rather than move their feet.

After the dance, he pulled her aside to talk to her. He was surprised that she was essentially a farmer, but he was pleased about the books she seemed to know, and he told her he thought she was very beautiful. She blushed under his flattery and attentions, but his life in the palace seemed so remote from life and the earth and her animals and plants. It made her uneasy.

Though he danced with other young women, the prince danced with Cindy two more times that night, taking the opportunity after each to talk with her again.

Lilly convinced Cindy to dance with Jeremy again, and though his clothes were new, he smelled vaguely like hay which Cindy found comforting. Cindy danced with other partners that night but none of them held her attention as much as the prince or Jeremy. And so the evening passed with dancing and music and food.

The next afternoon, a different fairy woman came to bathe, anoint, dress, and adorn Cindy. The dress this time was a soft yellow, her blond hair was pulled on top of her head where it cascaded down her neck and shoulders in pretty curls. Flashing crystals set in gold adorned her ears, neck, and wrists. When asked what she wanted to keep, she picked the dangling, flashing earrings.

She was again the most beautiful young woman at the ball. She found her step-mother and step-sisters and watched them for a while. As the fairy queen had promised, they did not recognize her and stared at her with envy and malice. Neither Tara nor Sara had danced with the prince.

The prince danced with Cindy though. Again three dances followed by short conversations after each. He was handsome indeed, and Cindy felt her attraction to him, but she also found herself looking for Jeremy and his sister. She liked their company, and she dance that night three times with Jeremy as well. Again other partners asked her to dance. Some had danced with her the night before, but others were new. Some danced well and some awkwardly, but none compared to either the prince or Jeremy.

And so it went. The third night she was dressed by yet another fairy woman in a dusky rose gown, her hair pulled up in a tight twist with small corkscrew curls strategically framing her face, dark burgundy stones ringed her neck and wrists and shone from her ears. When asked what she wanted to keep, she chose the dress. The prince danced with her four times and took her briefly to the various palace gardens to show them to her. They were magnificent and dazzling. There was a whole garden of roses. The herb garden off the kitchens was as big as one of her father's fields. The fountains seemed magical to Cindy who had never seen anything more complicated than the village well. She had other partners too, and she danced again with Jeremy, though he seemed sad and conflicted when they were together.

The afternoon of the fourth night, another fairy woman appeared to help Cindy get ready for the ball. The dress was a bright bold blue, and light aquamarines lit up her throat, wrists, ears, and a finger. The combination of blues, the dress slightly darker than her eyes and the stones slightly lighter, made her eyes glow and seem unnaturally blue. Dazzled by the effect to her eyes, Cindy chose this dress as well for her fourth gift. The prince danced with her three times, and after each dance, he showed her a part of the palace, the library and then some of the royal suites. Everything was opulent and spectacular—leather-bound books from floor to ceiling, velvet curtains, marble floors and gilded woodwork, beautiful tapestries, paintings by masters, sumptuous furniture, stained glass windows, and spectacular views of the gardens and grounds. She asked to see the kitchens, and he took her to see them. To her amazement, they were a series of large rooms with many different types of ovens and cooking surfaces, work surfaces and basins, cabinets upon cabinets of pots and pans, foodstuffs, and china and cutlery. Countless servants bustled with activity trying to prepare the evenings delicacies and get them to the guests.

To Cindy's surprise, the king danced with her, and then the queen requested an audience with her. Queen Isabelle talked to Cindy about life at the palace. It became apparent to Cindy that the current king and queen had many years still to rule the kingdom before the responsibilities would fall to the prince and his princess. Though the idea of raising children in such luxury was immensely appealing, the idea of years of being entertained by palace life left her feeling like a doll or play thing of some kind. She left the audience with the queen with much to consider.

Cindy found herself relieved to find Lilly and Jeremy and went willingly into Jeremy's arms for a dance. She smiled at the hay scent that clung to him, but as he held her in his arms, Cindy realized that he was miserable.

"What is it, Jeremy?" she asked.

He looked down at her, his eyes somber, "The gossip is rife, Cindy. The prince is smitten with you. You'll be the princess, and the only way I'll see you again is here as my princess and then as my queen." He paused, and when her face crinkled in confusion, he added hastily, "Don't get me wrong, I am happy for you, but I've loved you for so long."

They had talked often over the past year and flirted even, but he had never said the words before, and she looked up at him in surprise. "You love me?"

"Of course," he said simply.

"But I have nothing—no dowry, no inheritance," she protested.

"I don't care about any of that. Nor do my parents. That beastly Widow Miller, my aunt, murdered your father and stole your farm. We all know that. We want to take you away from them—to make it right between our families again."

"Jeremy … I don't know," she began, struggling to take in the significance of his words.

"I know you'll choose him. How can you not? You're so beautiful and kind and smart. You're also obviously touched by fairy magic of some kind. You deserve better. It's just hard to say good-bye. I'll miss you."

Her heart ached. The prince was sweet and tempting, but she knew Jeremy was a farmer like she was. Life with Jeremy would help her find a rewarding and productive life she realized. "Jeremy …" she began, but he interrupted her.

"No, it's too painful. I can't," and he disengaged himself from her and walked away.

She came to a stop and watched him make his way through the crowd. He didn't believe she could choose him, but there was one way she could show him. She could return home. The fairy queen had told her not to dawdle when she knew her own mind. Though the ball was not over it was late, and Cindy retreated to her tent for the night.

The fifth afternoon, Cindy waited anxiously for the fairy woman to arrive. When she did, Cindy bowed to her and said, "My lady, I don't need your help tonight. I want to return home."

"You know your heart's desire, child?" she asked.

"I know that I won't find it as a princess, my lady. Please thank your queen for all your help and her guidance. I think my parents would be happy with my choices."

"You have three nights of gifts left, my child."

"I just want to go home, please," Cindy said.

"Very well, I will send the fairy knight to lead you home." She took her leave, and the fairy knight appeared, saddled the horses, took down the tent, and packed the baggage. Cindy was surprised that the knight's midnight horse carried a chest but said nothing.

Again it took them two days to reach her parents' farm, the fairy knight playing his pipes off and on to entertain them. When they reached the farm, he tethered the horses in the stable, and took the tent and a supply chest in his arms and walked until he disappeared into the woods.

The fifth night of the ball began with anticipation heavy in the air, except that the beautiful, blond, young woman who everyone was talking about was not there. Royal scouts combed the crowd. The prince was agitated. Lilly and Jeremy walked through the ballroom searching for Cindy. Jeremy was afraid that she was ill or hurt. Perhaps she was just late, but she didn't appear all that night. The prince distracted himself by dancing, but his eyes combed through the crowd searching for her.

The sixth night was the same. Cindy didn't come. The prince was melancholy but resigned. He danced—trying desperately to find a new partner, a new princess. Jeremy was distracted trying to figure out what Cindy's absence could possibly mean. He longed to leave and go home, but he knew his parents and Lilly would be disappointed. Only another couple of days he told himself.

The seventh night was the same. The prince danced and talked privately with a few young women. Jeremy was beside himself. He didn't know what to think. The gossip said that Cindy had left the afternoon of the fifth ball. She wasn't ill or hurt. It appeared that she had gone home to the farm and the village. She appeared to be rejecting the prince and being a princess. Did that mean she would accept him? But he hadn't even formally asked her, he realized. His thoughts made him dizzy and giddy with the sheer impossibility of her picking him. He danced a few frantic dances with his sister.

"Jeremy, calm yourself," she admonished. "We'll only know when we get home."

"Could she really choose me?" he asked, struggling to hide the desperate desire in his voice.

"Why not?" answered Lilly. "I mean you can be an annoying brother, but to a non-sibling, you could have some appeal," she teased.

He elbowed her. "Thanks. Can we leave? I want to leave first thing in the morning."

She smiled at him, and they quit the last ball and returned to their tent.

Cindy found it a relief to be home. The smells and the noises and the quiet—all this was familiar to her and beloved. The palace was stunning and overwhelming, but she doubted that she could ever feel at home there. Now safely back at the farm, she had the feeling of a disaster averted. If she had married the prince, she would have felt like an outsider for her entire life there. She wandered through the house and yard to the stable and into the fields. The animals had been fed, watered, and stalls, where necessary, cleaned. The gardens had been watered, but the place was in disarray, only the minimum had been done.

She had been surprised that the magnificent horses had been left with her as was a chest that she was too intimidated to open. She struggled with what to do with these things. She didn't want them to fall in the hands of her step-mother or step-sisters. Finally, she decided she would ask the Fenns to keep them for her. She set off for the Fenn farm. Eva Fenn received her kindly. She was such a different woman than her sister, Lucinda; it was hard for Cindy to believe they were sisters at all. Tom Fenn was more disabled than Cindy had remembered, and he sat by the hearth with his feet up listening as the women talked. The youngest son was out tending to the farm. Cindy explained vaguely that she had come by two horses and gone to the ball and had been given the chest and that she didn't want her step-mother to have these things. Mrs. Fenn agreed, that with all Cindy had suffered, these things should be kept away from her sister, and she hinted that they might help a young couple set up a household by themselves. That the Fenns seemed to know about their son's affections for Cindy both surprised and pleased her. They bade her to fetch the horses and bring them to their stable.

When she brought the horses to the Fenn's stable, she found them both waiting for her, Tom Fenn leaning heavily on a cane. They both gaped at the horses. They were magnificent creatures. Eva Fenn looked at the box strapped to the black horse, looking at it curiously.

"This is marked with fairy marks, Cindy." And her wonderment at the box changed focus and landed on Cindy herself.

"Yes, Mrs. Fenn ... I have had fairy help," she said quietly.

Recovering herself slightly, Mrs. Fenn continued, "Well, Lucinda shouldn't have access to any of it." Then her face grew thoughtful, and she said almost to herself, "In fact, I wonder if she even could... perhaps she wouldn't be able to see them .... It doesn't matter." Eva paused in her musings, and her focus sharpened and returned to Cindy. "The horses can stay with us, until you and Jeremy figure out what to do. The box was given to you by the fairies, and I think that only you should touch it. If you take it off the horse, you can place it in this cabinet by their stalls," to which she gestured.

Cindy did as she was told. She thanked the Fenns and returned home. She set about weeding and tending the animals more closely. She worked hard over the next three days to groom the farm into looking as if she had never left to fit the ruse that her step-mother and step-sisters believed. The hard work distracted her from thinking about just exactly what would happen when she saw Jeremy again.

Jeremy woke Lilly early the morning of the eighth day, and they rode hard on the journey home, making it in only a day and half. As they neared home, they could also see Cindy's parents' farm with smoke drifting out of the chimney. Jeremy let Lilly talk him into going home and bathing before rushing to see Cindy and confirm his dreams.

Entering their stable, they were amazed to see the two beautiful horses there. Their mother was soon there helping them take the baggage and tack off their horses and explaining that the beautiful beasts were Cindy's. Lilly and Jeremy explained to their mother about the balls and about the enchantment that seemed to surround Cindy with her stunning clothes and adornment. Then, Jeremy explained that he had confessed his feeling for Cindy when it seemed clear that he had no hope at all and Cindy would marry the prince, and Lilly told her mother that Cindy had left the very next day and had apparently returned home. Eva Fenn's eyes sparkled with joy for her son.

"I want to marry her, Mother," and his voice was tinged with anxiety and excitement.

"Yes, my son, you should marry Cindy Tinge. Go get yourself cleaned up and go see her. If she is willing, we need to get you two before a minister before Lucinda gets home and tries to ruin more of that poor girl's life."

Cleaned and freshly dressed, Jeremy rushed off to find Cindy. She was in the kitchen in a pair of her father's overalls cooking a small dinner for one or two people. He burst into the kitchen.

"You left," he said, but it was more of a question, asking her to explain. She took the food off the heat and moved toward him.

She answered calmly, "I didn't see the point of staying. I figured out who I wanted even if he couldn't see it himself."

"And you want me?" he asked bemused and baffled at the same time.

"Yes, Jeremy. I know you. We have so much in common, and you said that you loved me."

"I do love you," he said. "But I am just a farmer, Cindy."

"And so am I."

"No, you are something more," he said with conviction.

"As you've guessed, the fairies have given me things, Jeremy. I thought that perhaps we could sell the things for money for our own farm or to buy back my parents' farm, but I had a dream, and the fairies told me to keep the things as my gifts and told me there was gold in the remaining chest that we should use instead."

"I had a fairy dream too, Cindy," and he dropped to his knees and held out his hands to her.

She took his hands in hers and looked at him curiously, "Jeremy?"

"In the dream, the most beautiful creature looked at me and said, 'She has chosen you with her heart and her mind, and you are worthy. My people have given her gifts because of an old debt to her family, but you should have a gift for her that expresses your love, and we are willing to provide that for you. It is now in your pocket, a ring that will ever remind you of the crystal blue of her eyes. Cherish and worship her, Jeremy, or you were the wrong choice.' I knew every word was true, and this is the ring she gave me. Will you marry me, Cindy?"

Cindy looked at the ring. It was the aquamarine ring she had worn from the fourth night of the balls. It was a beautiful thing. She held her left hand out, and he slipped the ring onto her finger, "Yes, I'll marry you," she said softly, and he stood up and pulled her into his arms, hugging her at first and then bending down to kiss her. His lips meet hers, and it was a gentle kiss at first, and then it flared in intensity, leaving them both surprised and gasping when they pulled apart. Though they were giddy with happiness, Cindy's step-family was a threat.

"My mother thinks we should marry today, before your step-mother gets home," he said gently.

"Today is almost over, Jeremy."

"Almost, but not quite. Come, my love," taking her hand and leading her to the Fenn farm.

They could tell that something had happened to the house, it seemed to glow in an oddly pleasing and enchanting way. Flowers garlanded the doorways, and candles flickered everywhere, casting magical light. The kitchen tables and chairs had been pushed to the walls. Minister Brown stood in his church robes with his prayer book, a Bible, and a record book at hand. Eva and Tom Fenn were neatly dressed and both wearing beaming smiles. Tommy and Lilly were also neatly dressed, and Lilly moved to take Cindy's hand and led her upstairs to her bedroom, shooing her inside and leaving her alone. The fairy woman from the first ball was there as was the queen. The fairy woman used the wash basin and bowl to clean Cindy up. Then she anointed her in the sweet-smelling oils and did her hair. The beautiful white dress of the first ball appeared and was put on Cindy, and she was again adorned with pearls, the necklace she had chosen as a gift magically appearing around her neck. When she was dressed, the queen gave her back her mother's ring and kissed her forehead once again. "Your mother's ring is too precious to you for you to ever give it up. I give it back to you, my child."

Then the queen herself led Cindy out of the room and down the stairs. Soft music filled the house, and the minister began the ceremony. Cindy Tinge became Cindy Fenn, Jeremy's wife, and Jeremy Fenn became her husband. When the minister had the wedding party enter their names in the book, Cindy was slightly surprised to see the queen enter her name as Lucinda Miller, but that was for the benefit of the minister she realized, who didn't have the imagination or courage to believe in things beyond church teaching, but the Fenns all seemed pleased and blessed by the miracle taking place on their farm. When the ceremony and recording details had been taken care of, the minister left, and the queen took her leave pointing out to Cindy and Jeremy that Cindy's tent from the balls had been set in the fallow field, so that they could enjoy their first night of wedded bliss alone beneath the stars.

Though Lucinda Miller denied that she had been present for her step-daughter's wedding and denied that she had given her consent, the minister and the Fenns all bore witness to her being in attendance. Without Cindy as their slave, the Miller women were forced to sell the farm, and they moved back to the capitol. Cindy and Jeremy bought the farm and lived contentedly, returning the farm to its former glory, having a swarm of children, and visiting, every so often, the stand of pines in the woods to leave little tokens of gratitude to the fairies.

And to the amazement of their children, at village dances, Cindy would pull out one of her fairy ball gowns and adorn herself with her fairy jewels, and she and Jeremy would dance the night away, not like farmers, but like a princess and a prince from a fairy tale.

Jill and the Beanstalk

Once upon a time, in a little village, there lived a woman and her daughter, Jill. They lived on a little farm which they worked quite well. They had an herb and vegetable garden full of things like parsley, rosemary, thyme, peas, beans, spinach, potatoes, and carrots. They had a small orchard with apple trees, pear trees, and walnut trees. They kept chickens and a pair of goats. They had Milky White, the cow, and Faithful Hans, their horse. With Faithful Hans' help, Jill or her mother plowed one of their four fields with winter wheat, oats, and hay each season while the other three fields lay fallow in the rotation cycle.

Most years they made a decent profit with which they did repairs to the farm house and the barn, bought feed for the animals, bought new books and new material for clothes, helped to fund the village school, and gave to the church's fund for orphans and widows. Though the field crops were largely how they made their profits, Jill often sold cheeses, eggs, vegetables, and fruits at the village market on market day. They were kind and generous neighbors, and they were well liked in the village. Jill also often helped at the village school, and Jill and her mother donated the books they had read and were finished with to the school mistress, Miss Blue Stocking.

Jill and her mother had read stories about magic and magical creatures like mermaids and fairies and giants and trolls, but neither one actually thought such magic or magical creatures actually existed. Though Jill and her mother choose to ignore the magical world, the magical world did not choose to ignore them. The fairy queen, Tatiana, watched these industrious women and admired them. Their charity and generosity in particular made Tatiana watch them and wonder. It was legend among the fairies that a human girl of the downworld might have the generosity of heart to transform the upperworld and restore it to the peace and harmony of before the dark magic.

The upperworld was a land of magic, and centuries before, all the creatures lived in peace and harmony there: the unicorns and the dragons, the fairies and the giants, the humans and the centaurs, the elves and the dwarves, and so forth. Then a dark magic fell upon the land, and the magical crops died and a madness settled on the giants. At first, they fought themselves until only a few survived. These remaining few carved up the upperworld into territories and slaughtered the people and creatures, driving the few survivors deep into the mountains and far away places, and life in the upperworld had been a living hell ever since. Some of the fairies escaped to the downworld where they waited and watched for the human child of the prophecy.

The question was, was Jill that child? Tatiana was unsure, and the responsibility of sending a human girl against even one murderous giant let alone the six most murderous surviving giants weighed on her heavily. Tatiana was sure that love was the power that would arm this unlikely champion, but she wasn't sure how to test Jill for this quality. Then it occurred to her to ask Jill to tell her three stories about love.

One cold and stormy night, Tatiana transformed herself into an old beggar woman, and banged on Jill and her mother's kitchen door begging for mercy and shelter from the storm. Knowing their generosity, she was not surprised to be taken in immediately and brought to the fire, given a blanket, hot soup, and hot tea with which to warm herself. Jill and her mother let the old woman eat in peace, but when she was done, they sat beside her and asked her to tell them about herself. Tatiana explained that she was a widow who had been driven out of her village and was seeking their village because of the aid they gave to people like her but that she had lost her way in the dark and come across their farm. They said they would happily take her to the church shelter in the morning after the old woman had spent the night with them.

As they talked, Tatiana looked carefully at Jill. She was a young maiden, perhaps sixteen. She was pretty for a human child with long wavy brown hair and sparkling blue eyes. She was shapely and of medium height. She was strong from her work on the farm but carried herself with grace and assuredness. Tatiana asked if Jill had a beau or a great love, and Jill blushed and said that all she knew of love were love stories. Smiling and pouncing on the opportunity, Tatiana asked Jill to tell her three love stories she thought were important.

Jill thought for a few moments then named "East of the Wind and West of the Moon" as the first story, and she told the story. "Once the youngest daughter of a very poor man went to live with a great white bear in a magic palace. She was alone in the magic palace during the day, but during the nights, when all the lights were out, a man joined her in her bed, and after months of talking together and touching each other, she knew that she loved him and that he loved her. Though she saw her mysterious lover every night, she was lonely during the days and begged to be able to visit her family. Her lover gave his assent but warned her not to listen to her family members. When she was home, her mother was horrified to hear how an unknown man slept with her daughter. Her mother told her that she should wait until he was asleep and light a candle so she could see whether he was a monster or a man. The youngest daughter knew that this was exactly what the man had warned her against doing, and yet she could not seem to help herself. One night after her return, she lit a candle and looked at him, and he was so beautiful that she did not extinguish the candle immediately but leaned over to look at him more closely and, as she did so, dropped hot wax on his shirt burning and waking him. If she had been able to wait a year without looking at him, the enchantment making him a bear by day and a man by night would have been broken, but she had not lasted that long. He explained that now he had to return to the Troll Queen, who had cast the enchantment, and marry the Troll Princess in the castle that was east of the sun and west of the moon. The wind rose up, and he disappeared as did the magical palace, and the youngest daughter was left all alone. She cried, but she also vowed to find him and redeem her love. She searched everywhere, asking everyone where the castle east of the sun and west of the moon was. Finally, she came across an old woman with a golden apple and a horse, and the old woman told her she did not know but that perhaps her sister did, and she gave her the golden apple and the loan of her horse. The second old woman did not know either but gave her golden carding combs and the loan of her horse and sent her to her other sister. The third old woman didn't know either but she gave her a golden spinning wheel and the loan of her horse and sent her to ask the East Wind. The East Wind didn't know but took her to the West Wind who blew farther than he did. The West Wind did not know but took her to the South Wind who blew yet further than he. The South Wind did not know but took her to the North Wind who blew the furthest of them all. The North Wind had been to the castle east of sun and west of the moon only once, but he agreed to take her. It took all his strength to get her to the shore by the castle. The next day, after her arrival, the youngest daughter sat outside the castle wall playing with her golden apple. The Troll Princess saw her and agreed to trade a night with the prince for the golden apple, but the princess drugged the prince, so no matter how hard the youngest daughter tried to wake her lover, he slept. The next day the youngest daughter sat outside the castle playing with the golden carding combs. Again the Troll Princess wanted them, again they were traded for a night with the prince, and again the prince was drugged, so that he did not wake despite the youngest daughter's efforts to wake him. The next day the youngest daughter sat outside the castle playing with the golden spinning wheel, and again the Troll Princess wanted it, again traded a night with the prince for it, but this time, the prince had been warned that a young woman had been in his room at night trying to wake him and crying because she could not. So that night he only pretended to drink the drink that the Troll Princess brought him. Thus, the youngest daughter was reunited with her lover, the prince, and they devised a plan where he would insist that his future wife be able to wash his wax-spotted shirt clean (which he knew no troll could do). In fact, the shirt turned black under the Troll Princess' efforts, but when the youngest daughter touched the shirt, it turned as white as freshly fallen snow. The trolls flew into a fit of rage, which blew them apart. The prince and the youngest daughter then freed the people imprisoned there and took as much gold as they could carry and set off to make a new life for themselves as husband and wife."

"Why do you like that story?" asked the old woman.

Jill hesitated. She had never had to articulate why she liked this story—she just liked it. "I like it for many reasons," she began slowly. Then her thoughts focused and the words poured out. "She makes a mistake, but she is able to fix her mistake—not all by herself (she gets the aid of the old women and the winds) but through her initiative. I like that she saves him instead of the usual boy saves girl. I like that three old women help her instead of pitting woman against woman. I like that the youngest daughter gets to know him by talking with him at night before she realizes that she loves him."

Tatiana smiled warmly at Jill. Jill's answer pleased her. A girl heroine would need to be active and resourceful such as the youngest daughter had been. "And the second love story?" she asked.

Jill knew the story she had in mind was not a romantic love story, but it was such a beautiful story. "The Selfish Giant" by Oscar Wilde," she answered quietly.

The old woman raised her eyebrows in surprise. She did not know this story. It was not a true fairy tale; it was written by a mortal. Further, the title had a giant in it.

Seeing that the old woman seemed confused, Jill launched into the story. "Once in a little town there was Giant who lived in a house that had a beautiful garden. He had been gone for seven years visiting an ogre friend, and during that time the Giant's garden became the town's children's favorite place to play. Because the children were so happy in the garden, strange things happened there. The birds loved to linger in the garden singing sweetly to the delight of the children. In the spring, the flowers in the Giant's garden bloomed longer and more beautifully. In the fall, the fruit trees bore more and sweeter fruit. Then the Giant returned, and he was angry to find the children in his garden, and he chased them away. To keep them out, he built a high wall around the garden and put up a no trespassing sign because he was a selfish giant. The children missed their garden, and the seasons passed. Spring came all over the country, but spring would not enter the garden of the Selfish Giant because there were no children there, so it stayed winter. The Selfish Giant thought it strange that it remained winter in his garden. In the rest of the country, spring became summer and summer became fall, and still it was winter in the Selfish Giant's garden. One morning, the Selfish Giant heard the most beautiful music he had heard in a long time, but it turned out to be just a bird singing in one his trees. Apparently, a hole had formed in the wall around the Selfish Giant's garden, and the children had climbed through, and in every tree that a child climbed in, spring had transformed it into a blooming, budding, living thing with singing birds in it. Underneath one tree at the far side of the garden was a small boy who couldn't reach the lowest branches, so that tree remained locked in winter's frost. The Selfish Giant saw the children and the transformation of his garden from his window and realized he had been very selfish. He decided to help the little boy into the tree. When the children saw the Selfish Giant, they ran from the garden. Only the little boy, crying because he could not reach the branches, did not see the Selfish Giant, so he did not run. The Giant gently picked up the boy and put him in the tree, and the tree burst into blossom and the birds sang from the tree's branches. The little boy was so delighted that he hugged the Giant and kissed him, and when the other children saw this, they came back to the garden, and the Giant gave the children the garden. He knocked down the wall and played with the children. The little boy who the Giant had placed in the tree was his favorite, but he disappeared before the day was over, and no one knew where he was. The children came every day to the Giant's garden, and he played with them willingly, but he longed for the little boy who he loved the most. One winter morning, when the Giant looked out his window, he found the tree at the far side of the garden covered in blossoms and underneath stood the little boy he had missed so much. He ran to the little boy and was enraged that the child had been hurt: there were cuts on the boy's hands and feet where nails had been driven through. He demanded to know who had done this so that the Giant could punish that person, but the Christ child said that his wounds were the 'wounds of Love.' The Giant knelt before the little boy," Jill paused. When she read the story silently to herself, she was fine, but whenever she read or told the story out loud, the beauty of the story choked her with emotion. The tears were coming now, and her voice trembled as she said the last part. "The little boy told him that as the Giant had let him in his garden so he would take the Giant to his heavenly garden, and that afternoon, the other children found the Giant dead under the tree covered in white blossoms."

Tatiana stared at Jill, watching this girl struggle with telling the last part of the story. "Why do you cry, child?" she asked.

"It ... it's just ... so beautiful and sad," she said trying to recover herself.

Tatiana realized that this was a Christian story, but it was, as the girl had said, sweet and beautiful. "And what do you like about this love story?" the old woman asked.

More in control, Jill answered, "I like the emphasis on the magic of children—that they make the garden bloom sweeter and longer—that they transform the Giant. I like the fact the Giant learns that in giving he finds happiness, not in hoarding. I like the fact that the Giant is rewarded with a spot in heaven, especially since some people only think humans can go to heaven."

Tatiana's heart leaped in her chest. She could be the one! Tatiana struggled to maintain an impassive or neutral expression on her face. "And the third love story?" she asked.

"I wanted to tell stories of the three different loves, romantic, altruistic, and familial. So ideally, this would be a story of the love between a parent and a child instead of romantic love or altruistic love, but 'The Happy Prince' also by Oscar Wilde comes to mind, and it is also beautiful and sad. Would you like to hear it?" Jill asked.

"Yes," the old woman answered.

"I will probably cry with this one too, just to warn you," and she started the story. "In the city, there was a tall, tall statue of the Happy Prince. His armor was gilded, his eyes were sapphires, and there was a ruby in the hilt of his sword. In life, he had spent most of his time in the palace, and because his life was so carefree and sheltered, he was known as the Happy Prince. It also happened that there was a little swallow which was late in flying south for the winter because he had fallen in love with a reed. When he realized the relationship was hopeless, the swallow flew south and arrived at the city and found shelter in the feet of the Happy Prince's statute. Just as the swallow was getting ready for sleep, a drop of water landed on him and then another, and he realized that the statute was crying. The Happy Prince explained his sheltered life and explained that now high above the city he can see all the 'misery' and 'ugliness' of his city, and it made his leaden heart ache and him cry. The prince got the swallow to take the ruby from his sword to a poor seamstress who was desperate to comfort her sick son. Because she had nothing, she was working feverishly to embroider a dress for one of the queen's maids-in-honor for the next ball. It was the only way she could get money to buy something for her son. The swallow resisted at first and then consented. The next day the swallow intended to fly further south, but the prince convinced him to stay and to deliver one of his sapphire eyes to a young playwright, so he would have the time to finish his play. The swallow didn't wish to take the prince's eye, but he did so and delivered it to the playwright. The next day the swallow again intended to leave, but the prince convinced him to take his other eye and give it to a little match-girl who had ruined her matches and was in danger of getting beaten by her father for returning without any money. The swallow did so and committed himself to staying with the prince since he was now blind. The little bird became his eyes and told the prince about what was happening in his city. Hearing about starving street children, the prince had the swallow take off his leaves of gold and give them to the children. With winter fully upon the city, the swallow died from the cold, and the heart of the prince broke with the death of his little friend. The town officials, dismayed at the barren appearance of the Happy Prince, had the statute taken down and smelted, but the broken leaden heart would not melt. It was cast on a garbage heap where there also happened to be the dead body of the swallow. The Lord God asked one of his angels to go through the city and find its two most precious things, and the angel brought the Lord God the broken heart and the dead bird, and …" she paused again, struggling to fight back her tears and to quell the tremor in her voice, "the Lord God … said … he had … chosen well."

"And you cry again because it is a sad and beautiful story?" asked the old woman.

"Yes," Jill answered simply.

"What do you like about this love story?"

"The selflessness of the Happy Prince when he truly understands the suffering of his people, and the selflessness of the swallow—the idea that it is in giving that we find true reward and accomplishment—not in isolation or through self-indulgence," Jill said.

Tatiana was satisfied. Mistakes could be redeemed, a girl was an active and resourceful heroine, giving was its own reward, sacrifice was sometimes necessary—these were the messages of the love stories that Jill loved most. They were the qualities that she herself would need. Tatiana transformed back into herself, the small radiant queen of the fairies, and Jill and her mother gaped at the fairy queen. Recovering themselves, they curtsied.

"My Lady," Jill stammered. "To what do we owe this honor?"

"It is both a great honor and a great burden, my child. There is a prophesy among my people, and I think you may be the child of that prophesy," she said.

"Me?" Jill choked. "Surely, you must be mistaken."

"Perhaps, but I do not think so. Let me tell you about it, and then we can judge together," and fairy queen told them about the upperworld, how it had been many years before, how the dark magic had come and changed the giants so that they slaughtered the inhabitants, and how the few survivors had been forced to flee and hide themselves in the mountains and far away places She told them of the prophesy of the human girl of heart who might mend the upperworld. When she was finished, no one spoke. Jill's mother looked shocked and scared. She shook her head gently. She wanted no part of this adventure for her daughter.

Finally, Jill spoke, "What could I possibly do against murderous giants?"

"The point is not to fight them, Jill. You must understand that. Violence only begets more violence, and there has already been too much of that. The human girl must be generous of heart—she must love, and you do. You love your mother, you love the animals on your farm, you love the children at the school, you and your mother provide for the poor and vulnerable. The love stories you chose were powerful stories of love and sacrifice. You believe those characteristics are noble. Noble acts move you to tears. You would not go alone. Two of my best fairies would accompany you. They will provide you what aid they can. You would receive my blessing—something that would stay with you until the end of your days. Upperworlders would be in your debt. Can you honestly think of any other human girl you know who is better matched for this quest than yourself?" the fairy queen asked.

Jill stared at her. The queen was making her sound exceptional, and she didn't think of herself that way. "But I am just a regular girl," Jill protested.

But her mother shook her head again, "No, dear, you are not. Very few people in the village and surrounding areas are as generous as we are. The minister has often remarked on our exceptional generosity—not only to the orphans and widows' fund but to the school and to our neighbors. Also we are independent and self-sufficient and resourceful women. You are well read and exceptionally kind and sweet. I do not want you to make this quest because I fear for you, but I cannot deny that what the queen says is true—you are as suited to this task as if you were born for it, and though I didn't believe in magic until a few minutes ago, looking at and talking to the undeniable manifestation of a magical being, I am also afraid to earn her wrath."

Tatiana smiled, "Thank you. I am glad we understand each other."

"So that's it. I have no choice. I have to do this?" Jill cried in alarm.

"No, you do not have to do anything, but I can be quite persuasive, and I have time to make you see the advantages of choosing this task," Tatiana said innocently, but the threat was there.

Jill considered the implications of these words. The farm was thriving now, but if the fairy queen was denied, what would she do to compel Jill to the quest? The terms were favorable now—fairy aid, the blessing, the gratitude of the upperworlders—but would they be later? Jill reached out and took her mother's hand. Her mother looked at her with tears in her eyes but with a resigned and a trying-desperately-to-put-a-hopeful-look-on-her-face look. "Fine, my Queen," Jill said, realizing that by accepting, she was one of the queen's subjects, "I am willing to try, but I can't promise any results."

"All I can ask of you is that you try," the queen said. She reached into her pocket and pulled out three beans. "Plant these in one of the fallow fields tomorrow. I will return in the evening with my fairies and some more instructions. You honor us, and we will honor you," and with that she took her leave. She left out of the kitchen door before Jill or her mother realized she intended to go out into the storm. They rushed to the door, but when they opened it, they could see no trace of her. Realizing that the fairy queen could use magic to go home in the blink of an eye, they shut the door and went back to the fire to talk over the extraordinary events of the evening.

The following morning Jill took a trowel and a full watering can and walked to the closer of the fallow fields. In the center of the field, she dug three small holes in a triangular arrangement and dropped one bean into each. She covered them with soil and watered them, and then she went home. She busied herself around the farm, trying to get as much work done as possible so that her mother would not be overwhelmed with the tasks while Jill was gone. The work helped to distract her. She didn't like to think about how dangerous this quest would be or the real possibility that she might not survive it. As the sun began to set, the fairy queen arrived with a small group of fairies. They were small—like children in a way—and their faces were impossibly youthful and ancient at the same time. They were clothed, it seemed, in leaves and flowers, and they were shockingly graceful and delicate in their movements.

Jill and her mother curtsied in front of the fairies who inclined their heads in acknowledgement. The queen presented Jill to her companions, and then she had two fairies step forward. One was a male fairy called Juniper. He was slender and graceful, and though his hair was golden blond, his eyes were a shocking color of green and his clothing, a long jacket over close fitting leggings, was of a similar bright, strong green. The second was a female fairy called Dusty Rose. She was also slender and graceful; her hair was wavy, long, and brown while her eyes were a deep and almost disturbing mauve color like the flower she was named after and matched her clothes, also a long jacket and leggings. Both were armed with small swords, and each had a bow and a set of arrows.

The queen presented Jill with a set of clothes similar those of her fairies but bigger to fit her considerably larger form, in shades of deep blue that matched her eyes. Jill hastened into the house to change. Better outfitted, the queen gave her a small back-pack in which there were several knives, a length of silvery rope, and three shining stones. The queen explained that the rope could change sizes as the need arose and that each of the three stones could become something she needed most when and if she needed to use them. Juniper and Dusty Rose had powers that they would explain to her on their journey.

They would leave the following dawn. The beans would overnight create a giant beanstalk that would take them to the upperworld. With sky flaring into deep red and gold tones behind her, the queen kissed all of three of them, Juniper, Jill, and Dusty Rose, on the foreheads and spoke words of blessing as she did so. What Jill did not realize was that the kiss of fairy queen left a mark that would be recognizable to all magical creatures and beings. To them there was a brilliant, glittering star on Jill's forehead—almost like a jewel. It was a promise of protection to Jill and a threat of retribution to any who dared harm her. When this was done, the fairy party took its leave, leaving Juniper and Dusty Rose behind. They declined human food, but delighted Jill and her mother by singing some fairy ballads before turning in for the night.

Early the next morning, Jill was not surprised to find Juniper and Dusty Rose waiting for her in the kitchen. Jill's mother struggled not to cry in front of her daughter, and she hugged her tightly before they left. In the middle of the fallow field was indeed a massive beanstalk. The three vines curled around each other like a great swirling cord. It reached so high that they couldn't see the top of it. Despite its great size, it was relatively easy to climb. There were handy gaps in which to place feet and hands, and they climbed and climbed and climbed.

When Jill thought they would never reach the top and wasn't sure she could drag herself any further, they suddenly burst through the clouds and arrived at the upperworld. Jill looked around, and what she saw, scared her—the earth was scorched and the land barren. It hurt to look at it. Jill walked as she had been instructed and came upon a massive deteriorating castle. The fairies left her and told her how she could call them when she needed them. Alone and feeling very small, Jill walked closer to the back of the castle. She found a kind of kitchen yard with a scraggly herb garden, a large compost heap, a large wood pile, a large shed, and a large chicken coop with hens the size of fairies. The giant's wife came out a door holding a large pail which she proceeded to dump onto the compost heap. Turning, she saw Jill standing by the herb garden. The giantess was at least ten feet tall, and though she was inhumanly big, she was not ill proportioned. Her face was pretty in a way, but there was strain or pain or both that lined the skin around her eyes and mouth. The giantess eyed Jill with amusement and surprise and a certain amount of what seemed to be caution.

"Ho, ho," she cried. "A girl. We don't get girls very often. In fact, I don't remember having had a girl here in very long time. I doubt you'll last longer than the boys. My husband is good at smelling human flesh. I dare say if you won't be the tidbit to start off his breakfasts some morning soon unless you take yourself away from here as fast as you can."

"Oh, please, Madame. I'm very hungry. If you give me something to eat, I'll work for it." They had climbed all day, and Jill had nothing to eat since her hurried breakfast.

"What can you do?" the giantess asked.

"I can cook and clean and garden," Jill said looking at the herbs. "I can sew and mend things," she added.

The giantess considered Jill and shrugged her shoulders. "Don't say I didn't warn you."

She led Jill into the kitchen which was a vast room with a twenty-foot ceiling. The giantess fumbled in a closet and pulled out a curious stool. On the one side, it was just a stool with a high bench seat (about four feet off the ground), but, on the other side, there was a series of small steps which Jill could easily climb to reach the top of the stool. The giantess placed this stool by the sink, and Jill climbed up it to the sink ledge, where she could see the sink filled with enormous dirty dishes and pots. Jill set about scrubbing them clean. She hummed or whistled while she worked, and the giantess seemed to like the sound. She hovered near Jill whenever she was making music. Jill took the opportunity to learn as much as she could.

"How is your husband?" she was bold to ask.

The giantess looked at her startled, as if people rarely asked her opinions or thoughts. She considered for a moment. "He's become a beast of a giant—cruel and violent when he wasn't always so. They made themselves that way—fighting and plundering instead of farming and raising families. We have no surviving child," she said bitterly. "He was slaughtered."

"I'm sorry," Jill said. She washed and scrubbed; she hummed or sang folk songs as she worked—again the giantess hovered near Jill to listen to her, and when Jill was finished, the giantess set out some cheese and bread for her, but her manner was softer and gentler somehow.

The ground shook, and Jill looked at the giantess whose face had become stony and tense. "He comes, child. You should go and run away," and Jill heard the regret in the giantess' voice.

Inspired by some force, Jill said boldly, "I have been sent to restore love to the upperworld. Help me! Hide me! I will figure out a way to make your husband see."

The giantess looked at her wildly, "Are you mad? Haven't you understood what I have told you? He is a beast now. You will die if you stay here, and I am beginning to like you. I don't want to see you hurt. GO!"

Jill looked at the giantess with all the resolve she had. "This is my task, and I have made a pledge to try to complete it. I wish you and your people to have love, children, and happiness again."

Tears swelled in the giantess' eyes. She struggled to say something but couldn't. "Who are you?" she squeaked.

"My name is Jill," Jill said quietly.

"I am Theresa, and my husband is Killroy (killing king) —at least now. His name used to be Gabriel. Hide in the closet. He will smell you, but stay quiet, and I will try to distract him."

Jill buried herself at the bottom of the closet and tried to calm her thrumming heart. The ground shook more and more violently. Just when she thought the ground would break and she would be swallowed up by the earth, it stopped, and a terrible savage voice cried out, "Wife, what do you have for my dinner? I bring some game—some elk." He was suddenly there in the kitchen. He caught his breath and paused. "Woman, what is this?"

"What?" she answered tentatively.

"Fee Fie Fo Fum, I smell the blood of human flesh. Where is the boy?"

"What are you talking about? There is no boy here! I swear! Perhaps it is the lingering sent of the last one or of the elk you carry with you; they are bleeding all over the place."

Jill boldly stepped from her hiding place. The giantess gasped, but the giant froze when he saw her. He had not seen a human girl in he didn't know how long. She bore the fairy queen's mark. He had killed plenty of fairies, but to incur the wrath of the fairy queen herself gave him pause.

"What do you want, girl?" he roared.

Jill hesitated, "My task is to restore peace to the upperworld," she answered.

"Then your task is suicide," he thundered. "Peace was destroyed long ago. All now is slaughter and destruction," and Jill heard the sorrow and regret in his voice as well as his resignation that this was the only way it could be.

Jill realized that she must make him see what he had lost and what he could have again. She pulled out one of the stones the fairy queen had given her and held it up on the palm of her hand. It transformed into a large crystal ball that Jill was just able to hold in her hand. "We could change that. This could again be a place of peace and love and harmony." Images swirled in the crystal ball—green fields and orchards, content villages and villagers. The giant and his wife looked at the images transfixed, and then the images changed and became more specific.

A younger giantess was lying in a bed holding an infant boy. They both gasped. "Benjie," the giantess breathed, and tears started sliding down her checks. The younger giantess moved in the crystal ball and handed the baby to a younger giant. The baby babbled at him, and he babbled back and covered his chubby face with kisses. And then the baby wasn't an infant anymore. He was walking away from them on unsteady feet, and then he was running, and they were chasing after him. He squealed in delight as they caught and tickled him and kissed him. The images froze in a picture of the three of them together, the boy seated on his mother's lap with his father hugging the both of them.

The giantess was sobbing softly, and the giant stared at the images—his heart aching but also somehow disbelieving. "My son … our son," he conceded but stopped himself. "Benjamin is dead," he added bitterly.

Jill squeezed the crystal ball, and the images changed. The giant and his wife appeared as they seemed now, but in the crystal ball, the giant was presenting his wife with different baby—a baby girl. The birth of this child was apparently so unexpected and a cause for such joy that both the giant and the giantess were crying and laughing at the same time, kissing the child and each other over and over again.

The giantess dared not say anything, but tears were streaming down her face. Another child, in a time of peace—there was nothing that she wanted more. The giant realized that he was holding his breath in shock. He remembered before—before the slaughter and betrayals—they had been happy and content with lives of farming, family, friendship, and peace. Could they really have it again?

"Girl," he began.

"Jill," she said interrupting him.

"Jill, why do you think that this is possible?" he asked, his voice significantly softer and slightly unsteady.

"Because, Gabriel, I know the story of another giant who was taken to heaven by the Christ child. In the same way that giant found joy in turning from anger to love and found redemption and a place in heaven, so you can find a better way and a way toward peace and happiness. Further, there is much in a name, and you are named after the angel who proclaimed the miracle of Christ and hence Christian forgiveness. Can't it be through you that peace is returned to the upperworld?" Jill asked.

The giant stared at Jill. It had been so long since a being had called him by his first name, and here this fairy-marked human girl was using it and offering him a destiny he thought had been obliterated by death and violence. He couldn't remember when he and his wife had used their true names. All the tenderness and intimacy between them had been stripped away when violence had taken over his life. He looked at his wife and saw her tearstained face, "Terry," he whispered, and he felt shame at what he had become and what he had taken away from both of them. She seemed to see it in his face and didn't want it to dwell there. She wanted a new start, a new chance for them. He could see it in the way that her eyes were lit with hope and possibility. "Gabby," she whispered back, "*please*," and his heart seemed to melt. They had known such horrible heart ache, but the violence didn't take that away; it just made him into an uglier and crueler being. Love, tenderness, kindness, compassion, empathy, forgiveness—these were the only ways to heal the heart, he realized with a sudden assuredness.

Could he convince the remaining giants? He didn't know. If Jill helped him, he might be able to. And what if he couldn't convince them? What if they took the opportunity and killed him trying to change things? And he realized that he didn't mind death—that the life they had been reduced to through violence wasn't even a life worth living. If he couldn't help make the upperworld a place worth truly living again, then it was better to be dead and end this senseless misery.

"What is the story of the angry giant?" he asked. Jill recounted the story of "The Selfish Giant." When she was done, they were all crying: Jill as always because of the beauty and sadness of the story, and the giants for its beauty and sadness as well but also because of its message of transformation and redemption.

"How … how … do we … change things?" the giant choked out.

"Do you think that if I showed them, the other giants, the images from the crystal ball and their own lives that they would be impressed enough to try?" Jill asked.

"Perhaps," he said carefully. "But it is not without risk too."

"I am not alone," Jill said softly.

"Who is with you?" the giant asked, his voice more menacing.

"The fairy queen, Tatiana, sent two of her knights with me," Jill confessed quietly.

The giant considered this. Might the fairy knights be able to marshal rogue magical creatures and beings hidden in the mountains and far places to stand with the five remaining giants and their wives as an added incentive to peace?

"Are the fairy knights marked as you are by the fairy queen?" he asked.

"Marked?" Jill asked, puzzlement clear in her voice.

"The jeweled star on your forehead is the mark of the fairy queen's blessing," he answered swiftly.

Jill felt her forehead. She did not understand. She felt nothing and had seen nothing on her forehead when she looked in the mirror the morning she left for the upperworld. The fairy queen had kissed her forehead the night before as she had Juniper's and Dusty Rose's. Perhaps it was a mark a human could not see. "Queen Tatiana kissed and blessed us three," she answered.

"Can you call them?" the giant asked.

"Yes," and Jill reached out with her mind the way that Dusty Rose had explained to her. "Dusty Rose, the giant is willing to try to convince the other giants to move toward peace. He wants to meet you and Juniper. Will you come? We need to make a plan."

A voice in her mind, Dusty Rose's, answered her. "Jill, how is it possible that you have subdued the giant so quickly?"

Jill thought back, "I have not subdued anyone. Remember that the queen said that this could only be accomplished through love. I have convinced him that he could have love again. Will you come?"

The voice rang in her head again, "My Lady was right. We are impressed. We will come."

"They are coming," Jill answered, and it seemed that only moments later, there was soft knock on the kitchen door.

The giantess opened the door and tried to stifle her shock at seeing the fairy knights. They were so little, so much smaller than even Jill and so beautiful. She had missed their beauty.

Jill spoke quickly. "This is Juniper," pointing him out, "and this is Dusty Rose." Both inclined their heads to the giants.

The giant said, "I am Gabriel, and my wife is Theresa. Jill has shown us a different version of the future. Is this possible?" he asked, and the hope and ache in his voice were nearly heartbreaking.

"Jill has used one of the fairy queen's gifts to show you that vision. It does not lie. It can be so if you do what is required to make it happen," Dusty Rose answered carefully.

"Can you reach out? Can you reach out to the hidden—so that they know what we are trying to do and show themselves to encourage this?" Gabriel asked.

"Yes, I can do that," she answered.

"And I can make them more inclined to accept your offer," said Juniper.

Though Theresa offered to make food for the fairies, they withdrew, and Dusty Rose communicated and met with the hidden beings. Juniper communicated with the magical beasts and told them of what was going on.

Theresa showed Jill a room after they had eaten, and she crawled into the bed gratefully and fell in to a deep and peaceful sleep.

She woke to brilliant sunshine streaming through the windows of her room, and she found Theresa and Gabriel shyly trying to rediscover themselves. She considered withdrawing when they sensed her presence and insisted that she stay. Jill had toasted bread, and by the end of breakfast, Dusty Rose's voice was calling to her. "Meet us at the south side of the castle in the woods there. We have collected forces and are gathering."

"But this is not a fight," Jill wailed in her thoughts.

"No, it is not a fight. It is a show of force. It is meant to make them consider Gabriel's proposition more carefully. If they ignore Gabriel's proposition, it may be a real threat—one supported by a host that five cannot hope to defeat," Dusty Rose answered.

So they came—Gabriel and Theresa and Jill—and in the forest they saw a great assembly of creatures and beings: unicorns, griffins, dragons, sphinxes, phoenixes, fairies, trolls, centaurs, dwarves, sprites, and pixies.

Jill was shocked to feel the eyes of them all on her. They expected her to lead, to have a plan. She swallowed hesitantly. "We go forward. I will show them what I can in the fairy queen's crystal ball. You stand by—a reminder of allies that were once enemies and that could be again if this goes badly. Gabriel and Theresa will be an example of commitment to this vision."

When they all nodded with positive assent, Jill felt that she might collapse with the pressure of their faith in her, but she dared not.

The host followed Jill, Gabriel, Theresa, and the fairy knights as they marched to the nearest castle. The host stopped in the field before the castle, and Jill, the giants, and the fairy knights went forward alone.

Gabriel knocked boldly on the castle door, "Gol, open up! It is Killroy. We must speak."

They waited anxiously until they heard footsteps. The door opened and the giant's wife stood before them. She gaped at them in shock, "What … do … you … want?" she stammered.

Theresa surprised them all by stepping forward and touching the giantess's arm, "Molly, we need to show you something, something incredible, show you and your husband. Will you take us to him?"

"Terry, are you mad? You have a human girl with you and fairies. Gol is likely to kill you all."

"There are more than just the five us," Gabriel said, motioning with his head to the field beyond them. Molly's eyes widened as she took in the host in the field. "Besides," Gabriel added, "for this cause, I am prepared to die."

"Truly, Molly, I think it is worth dying for," Theresa added, and she blushed scarlet as she felt her husband take her hand and squeeze it.

Molly stared at the pair of them, open-mouthed. "I … I …," but words seem to fail her. Finally, she shook her head furiously.

An angry voice rang out, "Wife, what the hell does Killroy want?"

Molly still shaking her head, muttered softly, "You're crazy. God have mercy on you." With those words, she opened the door to them. "To see you, Gol," she said more loudly. "He is in the kitchen," and she led them there.

Gol was standing when they entered the kitchen, a knife in each hand. Clearly, he meant to be threatening, but the sight of them together, the two giants, the human fairy-marked girl, and the fairy knights, surprised him so much that the shift in his glaring face to a blankly astounded one was almost comical.

"Goliath, we need to speak with you. I come as Gabriel, not as Killroy," Gabriel began.

Molly and Goliath both gasped and said at the same time, "Gabriel?" Goliath added with a sneer, "Gabriel is dead. That giant was destroyed long ago. We all were. Goliath along with him. There is only Killroy and Gol and the rest. Distorted fragments of what we were."

"What if we could be reborn or transformed? What if we could start again? I want to start again. We can start again together—but only together," Gabriel said quickly.

"Are you mad? Have you completely lost your mind? Is this some sort of fairy magic?" Gol asked, glaring at the fairies who ignored his insult stoically.

Jill step forward now, the crystal ball was in her hand—the images of the green fields and orchards and peaceful villages playing in it. All four of the giants stared at the images. Gol looked up and into the faces of his wife and Theresa and Gabriel. He saw the desperate longing in their faces, and his own heart swelled as he realized he wanted it too. Then the images changed. A baby was in the crystal ball. He gasped at the sight as did his wife. Nathaniel as a baby, and then images of him as a toddler. The images shifted, the twins, Maya and Maria. Molly was crying, and it was too painful. He couldn't bear this.

"Stop! It is too cruel. I cannot watch," Gol shouted at them, but he could not take his eyes away.

Jill squeezed the crystal ball, and a new image formed, a new unfamiliar baby filled it, and Gol and his wife gasped and stared at the image. Then, in the crystal ball, the baby cried, and Gol picked it up and brought it to Molly, and she adjusted her blouse so that she could nurse the infant.

"Goliath," Molly whispered to her husband.

He was shaking his head in disbelief. "This isn't real. It can't be. How could it be? Why torture us with what is impossible?" he said furiously.

"We must start again," Gabriel said softly. "We must fix what is broken."

"Tell them the story of 'The Selfish Giant,'" Theresa suggested timidly.

Molly had them sit around the table, and Jill told the story. Again, they were all crying by the end of the story—even the fairy knights who had not heard the story before. After much talking by Jill and reassurances from the fairies that the images from the crystal ball could come true, Molly and Goliath agreed to go with them to Ham's castle to try and convince him and his wife to try and fight for peace, and they won over Abraham (Ham) and

Sarah, and then Robert (Rob) and Rebecca, and Magnus (Mag) and Penelope, and Michael (Hael) and Lovana.

Having agreed on peace, a great cleansing ceremony had to be performed over the course of several days so that the land could be healed and blessed once more and so the emotional and psychological scars of years and years of war could be touched, shared, and forgiven by the souls that bore them. Queen Tatiana presided over this ceremony but representatives of all the beings and creatures were present to help their people as were Jill and her mother. On the first day, the land was healed and blessed. On the second day, the different beings and creatures worked separately to share, heal, and forgive. On the third day, together as one body the different beings and the different creatures worked again to share, heal, and forgive. The fourth day was simply a feast day where the beings and creatures of the upperworld rejoiced at a new beginning. Jill was acknowledged for her role in the peace of the upperworld, and she was given a fairy ring that would allow her to communicate with the upperworlders and to return to the upperworld if she was needed.

Jill had returned the queen's gifts (the knives which were not needed, the magical rope, and the stones) upon the completion of her quest. The last thing that Jill was given was a vial of liquid which she was to pour on the roots of the beanstalk after she and her mother had returned to the downworld. The upperworld and the downworld were separate after all, and beanstalk bridge between them had to come down. Though Jill poured the vial on the roots with reluctance, she did what was required of her. What did surprise Jill, was that the next morning, the fallow field, the one that had contained the beanstalk, was full of all manner of ripening bean vines (green beans, lima beans, butter beans, fava beans, even peas of all sorts). While it was a little hard to go back to downworld-village-life after the excitement of the upperworld, Jill settled into the routines of the farm and her work at the village school. The bean field which Jill and her mother started calling it after its third consecutive season of producing a significant bean crop (clearly a gift to them from the fairy queen) made them so much money that after giving significantly to the village school and the village shelter for orphans and widows that they sought to fund such institutions in neighboring villages. Every anniversary of the Great Peace in the upperworld, Jill and her mother came downstairs to a sumptuous feast that took them days to eat through, four days usually, and every once in a while, they were visited by Queen Tatiana herself where they exchanged happenings and stories of their worlds like old friends.

Beau and the Beast

Once upon a time, in a small and far away kingdom, there was a young, spoilt prince; his name was Nathaniel. His parents doted on him, and though they were sweet and kind and regal, he was not. He was short-tempered with the staff, the servants, and his peers. He was blessed with good looks: pale skin, big blue eyes framed by dark lashes, thick, curly, auburn hair, full lips, a square jaw, height, and a muscular frame. He was swoon material, and he knew it. Young women were always interested in him, but he wasn't particularly interested in them. No young woman he met caught his interest, and he often rebuffed them in the cruelest manner. No one dared to complain to the king and queen about their son's behavior, so they were naïvely unaware.

Nathaniel slowly came to realize that he was attracted to other young men. He lingered at training sessions and fighting practices. The muscular arms, shoulders, backs, and chests of boys and men excited and humiliated him. Homosexuality was unheard of; males liked females, and females liked males. There was not a male-likes-male or female-likes-female option. He did not feel any attraction to the numerous young women he had met. On the other hand, he felt seriously attracted to some young men. He would get hard-ons looking at and thinking about certain young men. He even dreamed about them. He masturbated thinking about young men—particularly about Luke—his regular sparring partner.

When Nathaniel was eighteen, he was particularly cruel to Isadora, the daughter of his parents' envoy to the neighboring kingdom to the south. She paid a lot of attention to him, and he made fun of her clothes, her looks, and her attempts to flirt with him. He had the audacity to call her a cow at a court party, and, mortified, she ran out of the party and sought the solace of the gardens. A sobbing young woman in the royal gardens caught the attention of Fairy Kate.

"Why do you cry, child?" Kate asked.

"Prince Nathaniel was beastly to me. He ridiculed me in front of everyone. He called me a cow," she sobbed.

Fairies, especially fairy queens, did not tolerate extreme vanity in humans, and Fairy Kate was a fairy queen. "Beastly?" Fairy Kate repeated, grinning with a sudden satisfaction. "I like it. Beastly he will become. I'll test him first, but I have heard about him before. A reckoning is in order." And with that, Fairy Kate left the young woman and waited.

On a stormy night, Fairy Kate sensed that activity in the castle was low. She sensed the young prince near the kitchens and knocked on the back door, transforming herself into the shape of a poor, old woman. A servant answered the door, and Kate asked to be let in from the storm and given a bite to eat. The servant led the old woman into the castle immediately and led her to the fire.

The prince, seeing the old woman, was aghast. "What are you doing?" he asked the servant.

"My prince, in this storm, we are obligated to give shelter and aid," she answered.

"To this troll?" he answered. "She is odious. Get her out of here. I will not stand her presence."

The servant stared at him. "My prince, it is not done. You could hurt yourself. She could hurt you."

"That hag? How on earth could she hurt me? She is nothing, a beggar," he scoffed.

"Please my prince, the fairy folk test us. If you fail the test, I hate to think of what could happen," stammered the servant.

"The fairy folk—do you believe in such wives' tales? Out! Get her out!" he screamed.

Mortified, the servant turned to Kate, "Oh, my lady, have mercy on me. I must obey my master."

"A blessing be upon you, my child. I am not dismayed by you. You tried to warn him," and she turned and looked at the prince and transformed into her most radiant fairy queen self.

Nathaniel was stunned, and he was suddenly afraid. He had revealed his most uncharitable nature to a fairy queen. He couldn't imagine the punishment. "My lady," he began.

"Silence, it is too late for apologies. You were beastly to Isadora and to me, and so a beast you will be and remain forever more unless you convince a mortal to love you," she smiled in sweet satisfaction as she spoke the words (because she couldn't imagine his arrogant personality ever swaying a mortal's heart beyond the monster she would make him appear to be).

She raised her hand toward him, and he felt it rip through him: pain and transformation. His body twisted and grew and sprouted. He grew huge: seven-foot, hair sprouted all over him, his jaw extended with his teeth turning to fangs, his hands and feet transformed into paws with claws. He howled in rage. Rage—

human reason in this form was difficult to attain and almost impossible to verbalize—he howled again. The fairy disappeared, and he raged against himself in the castle. He ripped through rooms, destroying everything in his reach. He refused to look at himself in a mirror. Finally, he took himself outside and simply ran on four legs through the forest.

He had done this to himself. He couldn't believe he had been so stupid. His mother had told him story after story about the dangers of vanity and false pride. Zeus and Hermes, the Ancient Greek gods, were notorious for disguising themselves as beggars and visiting humans to see if the unsuspecting humans showed the proper deference to a guest. One old couple, he remembered from the stories, had given the disguised Zeus and Hermes the best of everything they had and had been rewarded with a never-emptying stew pot and a never-emptying wine jug. Hubris, arrogance, human pride, had brought him to this, to being a beast.

As he calmed down slightly, analyzing his situation, he realized that he could sense the other animals in the forest. What surprised him was that the other predators were wary of him and scared of him. Was he so monstrous that he frightened even wolves, bears, and beasts of the forest? Yes, apparently so. When he was absolutely exhausted, he returned to the castle, found his bed, and passed out.

The light streaming through the windows woke him the next morning. Nathaniel lifted his head, and he saw himself in the mirror. He was like some kind of werewolf: huge, fury, fanged, clawed, hideous, an animal. He shattered the mirror. He wandered the castle and found that he was utterly alone. His life was horrid for a long time. He ran in the forest and through the grounds. He destroyed different parts of the castle, but he never touched his parents' apartments. Their spaces were the only places he found holy, touched with the unconditional love they had always shown him and, therefore, worthy of a reverence he had not shown other castle spaces in his rage and anger.

The castle provided for his wants and needs. A bath was provided for him at six in the evening, and the family dining room produced dinner for him at seven. Sometimes he ate there, but more often than not, his attempts at civilized eating infuriated him. He could not handle the cutlery with his paws and claws. Even handling the fine china plates and dishes reminded him of how different it had been when he was human. Thus, he often ate in the forest, taking down a deer, a beaver, or some other animal and eating it raw like the beast he was.

He longed for company, any company. He had never realized how devastating it was to be isolated and alone. Even the taunting fairy would be better than this abandonment. In fairness, he knew the fairy had not taunted him; she had corrected and punished him for his inappropriate behavior. But this knowledge did not end his loneliness. He started to seek out people—the odd wood gatherer or traveler—but whenever he revealed himself, they screamed and ran off in terror.

After several years of misery and isolation, he ran across an old woman who was preparing to camp in the woods for the night. Her grandson was out collecting firewood. She was sitting on log by the fire. She sensed him and called out to him.

"Hello, Stranger. Come and warm yourself by our fire. Can I offer you some tea?" she said kindly.

It had been so long that Nathaniel couldn't resist. "I don't want to frighten you or impose," he said hesitantly.

"Nonsense," she said laughing at the thought. "Where are you from?" she asked.

"Not far. There is a castle through the forest," he began. He wondered when she would start screaming as he drew close to the fire and to her, but she just sat there contentedly. When he sat down on the ground near her, she reached out with a tin mug of steaming tea for him. He was sure that she could see his face, though he kept up the hood of his cloak, and she could see also his clawed paws, and yet, she did not seem phased. By the light of the fire, he could see that she had light brown skin, dark hair streaked with gray which was braided in a single plait, and dark eyes. He took the mug from her awkwardly and thanked her for it.

"You're welcome," she answered. "A castle? There was the Brandenberg Castle, but there was a great tragedy there. I thought it was abandoned," she said slowly. "What is your name?"

"I am Nathaniel," he answered quietly. He couldn't look at her.

"Nathaniel Brandenberg?" she whispered.

He knew she knew then, by the way she whispered his name, and their chance encounter was about to be over. She would scream, and the grandson would come, and they would run away and never speak to him again. It was all too much. He started sobbing and choked out his response, "Yes … I am … he," and he forced himself to look at her. For the first time, he noticed that her brown eyes were rimmed with a whitish blue. Her face searching his, did not fill with terror but with a dawning sadness, and he realized that she was blind. "You can't see me, can you? What is your name?" he asked softly.

"No, I can't see you, Nathan." He gasped. His mother called him that. "I am Gwyneth, and I know you beyond your name. Do you know me?" she asked, a smile forming on her lips.

Gwyneth was the midwife who attended his mother through her miscarriages and then through his birth. There had been something she had said about his destiny after he was born. He had been told, but he couldn't remember. "Yes," he said hesitantly. "You were my mother's midwife. You birthed me," he said overwhelmed by the emotions that crashed over him—memories of his parents, his mother, their life as it had once been. He started sobbing again.

"I warned her," Gwyneth whispered. "The night you were born, the stars, the portents were … ominous. The deaths of the others … they would worship you too much, your parents. You could become the kingdom's undoing. And so you have, haven't you, my child," she added solemnly.

He choked out the words, "It … is … everything … you … say. I was spoilt. I insulted a fairy queen. I … am … a … beast," he said.

She got up then. She was a tiny, little woman at this point, but she sat down next to him and hugged him. He was so stunned at the gesture, at the contact, at the forwardness, that he didn't resist. He sobbed onto her shoulder, and he realized that she rocked him back and forth against her body. He sobbed harder; he was so lonely. This was the only contact with another human being he had had in so long.

"Grandmother?" a voice called, the voice tinged with surprise and alarm.

The old midwife released Nathaniel and turned her face to the voice, "Beau, do not be alarmed. We have a guest," she said firmly.

The firewood that had been in the young man's arms crashed to the ground. Nathaniel saw the young man's face change from alarmed surprise to full alarm and revulsion as he saw Nathaniel's face and paws clearly. "Gran, that is not a guest; it is a beast. Get away from it," and he drew a large knife from its sheath at his side.

"Beau, I know what you see, but the beast you see is not all he is. He is a young man underneath, and that is the part you can't see. Put the knife away and throw some new logs on the fire," she said commandingly. She waited, but the young man was frozen, gaping at her as if she had lost her mind. "Beau!"

Her shouting his name seemed to pull him back to himself. He hesitated, but then did as she asked, sheathing the knife and reaching for two of the logs he had dropped, throwing them on the fire. He kept his distance from Nathaniel and sat on the log near his grandmother. She patted his knee once he was seated. "Beau, this is Nathaniel Brandenberg. Nathan, this is my grandson, Beau."

The young man again was staring at his grandmother as if she had completely lost her mind. "That's not possible, Gran," he began, but she interrupted him.

"Nathan, tell Beau your story, all of it," she said demandingly.

That two people were still sitting with him, even though they knew what he was, was a miracle in and of itself. He dared not hope for anything further. He sensed that only complete honesty and humility with them would be tolerated. As a midwife, Gwyneth would have heard and seen it all (heard every lie and seen every deviant thing a human could do), and he had nothing more to lose. So he told them of his spoilt childhood and the vanity and arrogance and distain he felt for others, except his parents. He told them how he hid his behavior from his parents who had always tried to teach him to be kind, generous, and empathetic. He told them about his indifference toward young women. He told them about his attraction to certain young men. He told them about what he said to Isadora and then to the Fairy Kate. He told them about his transformation and his years isolated and lonely in the castle. Lastly, he told them about his attempts to see others and about his encounter with them.

He had watched their faces intently as he told his story. Both the grandmother and Beau had suppressed their reactions at two points of his story: his indifference to young women and his attraction to young men. Were they shocked and revolted? Surely, the old woman had known of same-sex relationships; she was a midwife. He couldn't be the only young man who got turned on by other young men, could he? The old woman had flashed a look at her grandson, and he had blushed and carefully avoided returning her look. Nathaniel knew that her eyes couldn't see, but her other senses must react in such a way as to give her an accurate enough impression of what was going on. It was as if she could see through her blind eyes. What did that mean? He gasped suddenly. What if Beau also was indifferent to young women and liked young men? He couldn't imagine the emotions flashing over his face, but he doubted that they could read them through the fur and beast's muzzle. He forced his face into the most neutral expression he could manage. The old lady was watching him intently with her blind eyes. A smile played at the edges of her mouth, and Nathaniel could have sworn that she made the tiniest nod of her head as if she had read his thoughts and was confirming their accuracy.

"How long?" Beau asked, a mix of emotions playing across his face, shock, sympathy, confusion, and curiosity.

Nathaniel looked at Beau before he answered. Beau had the same dark looks as his grandmother: he had light brown skin; dark, glossy, curly, short hair; sparkling, and strangely tender-looking, dark eyes; and though he was modestly dressed, his muscular frame was pronounced through his clothing. He was very different looking than the fair haired and blue-eyed Luke, but Beau was strikingly attractive, at least to Nathaniel. Nathaniel answered hesitantly, "I am not sure. It has been years, but when everything was misery, I stopped paying attention. I just don't know." Nathaniel's mind filled with the memories of the endless days of isolation and loneliness.

Gwyneth's voice interrupted his thoughts, "My prince, why don't you allow us to accompany you to the castle?"

That she could call him prince shocked him more than he could have possibly imagined. His animal rage flared. "Don't call me that," he said harshly. "I am a beast; there is nothing noble left."

Though he spoke harshly, she was unintimidated by his words. He guessed that women in the throes of childbirth had said unimaginable things to her (curses, threats, promises of vengeance). "But you are not a true beast. You are a human in a beastly form. Find your better nature and redeem yourself," she said quietly.

Nathaniel stared at her. Redemption, could it be possible for him? He shook his head softly.

"We have brown bread and cheese, Nathan," Beau said quietly. Nathaniel was surprised at being called by the endearment, but the young man's grandmother had used the name, so he understood. Beau rummaged in a bag by the fire and doled out the bread and cheese. Gwyneth got them all more tea. Nathaniel pushed back the hood of his cloak. He looked at Gwyneth as he did so, but the woman's expression only showed warmth, and perhaps, slight appreciation at being trusted with such a revelation. Nathaniel next sought Beau's face, which seemed to hold curiosity more than anything.

Once they had eaten their small meal, Gwyneth insisted on bed. Beau produced blankets from another bag, and they gathered themselves around the fire to sleep. Nathaniel, before sleep overtook him, felt profound relief. He was connected to people again. There was an irony to the fact that an old woman was that vehicle since an old woman (at least so he thought) had been the vehicle to his isolation. He felt hope for the first time in a long time. Even if neither of them came to love him, he would not be alone, and then sleep claimed him.

When the old woman stirred in the early morning, Nathaniel's beastly senses woke him, and he offered to get fresh water. By the time he returned, she had rekindled the coals from the fire and had the tea leaves in a pot waiting for the water. Beau still slept, so they spoke quietly to each other.

"You do not have to come to the castle with me," Nathaniel said, knowing that it was true and yet wanting it more desperately than he had ever wanted anything.

"No, we don't. But I am a midwife, and my primary task is to relieve suffering. You are suffering, and so is my grandson, though he will not speak of it to me," she said quietly.

Nathaniel knew only too well his own suffering and pushed it from his mind. He knew also that when the old woman spoke of her grandson's suffering, she was speaking of Beau's attraction to young men. "You are not repulsed?" he asked, genuinely curious.

"Child, insecure and hypocritical men are repulsed or fake repulsion. Love and desire are what separate human beings from the animals. Animals reproduce by instinct not love or desire. Sexual attraction and pleasure, not reproduction, drive human relationships. As a midwife, I know this. Just because reproduction happens between a male and a female doesn't mean that all males are sexually attracted to females or all females are sexually attracted to males. Neither does it mean that the sex between a male and a female is pleasurable. It should be, mind you. However, if pleasure is the defining characteristic of sexual relations, which I believe it should be, take pleasure where you will, female-male, male-female, male-male, female-female, and any other coupling you can think of among consenting human beings."

Nathaniel stared her open mouthed. "How can you say those things?" he asked.

She looked at him with all the compassion of her calling, "I bring life into the world, and I try to alleviate suffering. We are all God's creatures. I refuse to believe in a punitive model of God's relationship with human beings. A parent, a true parent, loves all his or her children, regardless of their idiosyncrasies and differences from their peers, their parents, or even their siblings. You are different for many reasons, Nathan. You are a prince, whether you acknowledge that or not. You are your parents' child—a position I hope you reclaim. And you like other young men—a situation you are not alone in—and you being open about that could change the world for all those young men (and others) who have, like yourself, hidden for too long. You all should come out and be who you want to be and love who you want to love."

He could only stare at her. He had hoped with wild desperation that she might understand but that she could articulate his barely self-acknowledged longings was incomprehensible to him. "Gwyneth, …I am … just a beast," he said.

"No, Nathan, no beast of the forest could talk to me of such things. Be the human being that you can be." She stood up, and for a tiny, old woman, her presence was powerful. Perhaps it was all the lives that she had brought into the world or saved from worms or whatever illness or broken bone. He quavered under her penetrating blind gaze.

"I am … unworthy," he choked out.

"So make yourself worthy," she spat back at him in a challenge.

Worthy? If he were worthy, he could be loved. "I will try," he answered.

"There are some who would answer that to try is not enough, but I will accept you trying," she answered.

Beau stirred, and Nathaniel and Gwyneth stopped talking and got a small breakfast together. With Beau up and about, they ate quietly and then packed up their things. The walk to the castle started well, but after a short time, the old woman was clearly struggling.

Just as Nathaniel felt a tinge of annoyance at having to slow his pace, he realized that the logical thing to do was to carry the old woman. Beau could do it, but Nathaniel was much bigger and stronger. He stopped and turned to face them.

"Nathan?" the old woman asked.

He smiled, or tried to; he wasn't sure he pulled it off too well. "Let me carry you," he said softly, and he took off his cloak and knelt down so that she could climb on his back.

"No, my prince, it would be unfitting," she said backing away from him, but he reached out and took her hand in his paw.

"There is no kingdom, so there is no prince. You honor me with your company. The journey is hard for you, but it is nothing to me. Allow me to ease your passage." He saw her face change from resistant to something softer and more accepting. He let go of her hand, and he turned to Beau who watched them both in surprise, "When she is in place, can you tie the cloak around us, to hold her better?"

Beau took the cloak and nodded. The old woman climbed on Nathaniel's back hesitantly. She was so tiny that her arms around his neck were almost uncomfortably tight, and her little legs barely reached around his waist. Beau wrapped the cloak around the two of them, his fingers fumbling awkwardly and his face flushing slightly as he tied the edges of the cloak across Nathaniel's chest. Once the cloak was secured, the old woman was able to loosen her hold, and Nathaniel laughed. It was strange sounding to him. A kind of bark with a laugh in it. He realized that he had never laughed in his beastly form. The thought was like a kind of grief—for all that he had lost.

"What is so funny?" she asked, a tinge of irritation in her voice.

Her question and her tone jolted him back to himself. He shook his head, clearing his thoughts. "You're just so light and tiny, like a child," he answered. More quietly, he added, "It has been so long," and he could hear the ache in his voice. He hadn't been touched since he had been transformed, except when she had hugged him the night before.

She seemed to read his thoughts. "Like a child, am I? Perhaps, then, it is fitting. It seems like yesterday when I held you, cleaned you up, and handed you back to your mother." He couldn't see her face, but her voice was gentle, and he felt her little hands patting his neck. He was touched more than he could say.

"Thank you," he whispered.

"Don't dwell on what you can't change," she said softly, and there was a sadness in her voice.

Nathaniel wondered what was the cause of that sadness. "Why did you leave the castle?" he asked.

"A blind midwife isn't very useful," she answered stiffly. "I chose to leave, to return to my family and life in the villages," her voice was warmer. "Beau is studying with me; it is unusual for a male to train as a healer, but then Beau is an unusual young man," her voice filled with pride.

Beau's head turned toward them at the mention of his name. "What are you two talking about?" he asked.

"I was just talking about your training," she answered raising her voice so that he could hear her clearly. "Tell us a story," she commanded.

Beau obeyed and launched into the story of "The Happy Prince."

Nathaniel listened, fascinated and charmed by the story. The prince and the male swallow clearly loved each other. It was a sad and sweet story. He wished it had a happy ending instead of the tragic one. The story had an author unlike traditional fairy tales, Oscar Wilde. Clearly, this man lived in a kingdom that did not condone male-male relationships—that had to be the cause of the tragic ending. They could love each other, but the people would reject them. Despite the intolerance of the people, God and the angel knew the love and sacrifices of the prince and the swallow were the most worthy things in the town. There was hope in that, Nathaniel thought.

They passed the rest of the journey amicably. The castle came into view, and he heard Beau and Gwyneth both gasp. He smiled. He hadn't felt pride at the sight of his home in a long time. Then he thought of the damage he had done, and he was filled with shame. His body stiffened with tension.

"What is it?" the old woman asked.

"After I was transformed, I was very, very angry," he said quietly. "Much of the castle ..." but he couldn't finish.

"You raged through the castle. I can imagine. It will give Beau and me something to do," she said softly, patting his neck again for reassurance, and they both felt the tension leave his body.

On the grounds, Nathaniel knelt down, and Beau untied the cloak and helped his grandmother down from Nathaniel's back. They entered the castle through the kitchens. Beau whistled at the destruction. "Is it like this everywhere?" he asked, more with curiosity than condescension.

Nathaniel shifted uncomfortably. "Not my parents' apartments. I will show you to those rooms. You must be tired."

"My prince, we could not," the old woman said firmly.

"You must stop calling me that," he said more loudly than he intended.

"Alright," she said, "but then you must call me Gwyn."

Nathaniel reigned in his emotions, "Okay, Gwyn," he said in a more measured tone. "My parents' apartments are the only rooms in which it would not humiliate me to put you."

"Nathan, Beau and I will find a room or rooms that we can tidy up and be happy with. We are servants," she began.

"No!" he said so loudly than she and Beau both jumped. "You are my guests, and I am a beast," he said lowering his voice in response to their reactions.

Recognizing the pain in his voice, she smiled, a warm, grandmotherly smile, full of understanding and compassion, "Show us the way."

She was humoring him, he knew. He led them through the halls and up the stairs. Beau took special care to lead his grandmother so that she wouldn't trip. They passed room after room; most bore witness to some kind of violence.

"Which ones are yours?" Beau asked, but he was amused.

"They are coming up, Beau," he said dryly.

Turning a corner, Nathaniel waved toward a door on the right, "These are my apartments," he said solemnly.

Beau ducked his head in and saw the overturned bookcase in the study and saw past that to the bedroom with the smashed mirror. He whistled again. "You must have been really angry."

"You have no idea," Nathaniel answered bitterly. "Being a beast didn't help either. I lost it for days. When I couldn't take it any longer, I would run through the grounds or through the forest. Anything to burn off the anger and rage."

"Well, you are not alone now," Gwyn said gently.

Nathaniel turned and looked at her, "No. Thank you for being here," he said sincerely.

"Whose rooms are these?" Beau asked. "They don't look disturbed."

Nathaniel followed Beau into the rooms across from his rooms, taking a turn at leading Gwyn. Once inside the rooms, he stared around him wildly. He remembered slashing through these rooms almost as viciously as his own rooms, but they were in perfect order now. The bookcase, the chairs, the tables, the bed. There was a note on the bed.

"What is it, Nathan?" Gwyn asked. She couldn't see the rooms, but she could read the distress and tension in his body.

"I destroyed these rooms," Nathaniel answered.

Beau had walked to the bed and picked up the note. "Um, these are apparently my rooms," he said, holding out the note, with a surprised look on his face.

"The castle is enchanted," Nathaniel said hesitantly. "Perhaps ..."

"Perhaps it knew we were coming?" Gwyn finished for him. She sounded excited. "Do I have rooms?" She tugged at his paw, and he laughed his strange barky laugh.

"Let's find out," he said, caught up with her excitement. "The castle has never fixed itself before," he mused.

"Perhaps it is not the only one changed," and she squeezed his paw.

He felt the tears prick in his eyes, "Perhaps," he said in a strangled voice, and he felt her squeeze his paw again. Gently, he squeezed back.

They crossed the hall again, and the rooms were again in order though he remembered abusing them. More interesting to him was that they were decorated in a more feminine manner than his or Beau's. Different than his mother's rooms but distinctly feminine. Additionally, there was a hand rail that ran at waist level around the walls of the rooms. Nathaniel led Gwyn to the rail and put her hand on it. The rail was at her precise waist-level. Holding the railing, Gwyn navigated the first room. She was approaching a set of chairs and a table that obstructed her way, and Nathaniel was about to cry out, but she stopped suddenly, and successfully felt her way around the obstructions.

"How did you do that?" he asked.

"The rail told me the chairs and table were there," she said in wonder. Then after a moment, she said, "Describe the rooms to me?"

"The walls are painted a marigold yellow," Nathaniel answered.

"I so love yellows," she said absently.

"There are solid, golden-colored, velvet curtains at the windows," he continued. "The bedding looks to be of the same golden velvet. There are flowers, roses, in vases, throughout the apartment. Your study has books and a desk." He fell silent as he watched her cross into the other room to the bed and feel the coverlet. Though she was an old woman, her excitement made her seem like a small girl.

"I feel like a princess," she said, giddy with enthusiasm, making her giggle and laugh at herself. "Our rooms here are bigger than our cottage, Beau." She flopped herself onto the bed. "It is so soft. It is like lying on feathers."

Nathaniel was both pleased and ashamed by Gwyn's pleasure in her apartments. She had been a trusted member of the royal household, but only as a servant. These rooms were grand compared to the servant quarters but nothing like the grandeur of his parents' apartments. What he took for granted was made splendid and special through Gwyn's vision of it.

"They will ever be your rooms, Gwyn, for as long as you live whether you visit often or only rarely," he said with conviction.

Gwyn sat up and looked at him, "Nathan, you can't do that."

Yes, he could. Whether she understood it or not, she and Beau were his family now, his only tie to his humanity. They had not run from him screaming in the forest, and they had agreed to stay with him. He would owe them more than they could possibly imagine. Before he could get emotional on that point, he shifted his thoughts. "Dinner is at seven, usually, in the family dining room.

The castle usually provides me with a bath at six, just in case it does it for you as well. We have a couple of hours until then, but you may like to rest and get to know your rooms, so I will take my leave and look forward to seeing you at dinner," Nathaniel bowed to them and left.

Nathaniel entered his own rooms a little bewildered. The castle had cleaned up Gwyn's and Beau's rooms but not his. Why? Perhaps it was not ready to accept that his rages were over. Could he really blame it? The first ones had lasted for days. A day of civilized behavior on his part was nothing compared to before. Instead of retiring to his room, he wandered the castle, following his paths of devastation and regretting them. Eventually, he retired to his rooms. He took the bath with more pleasure than he had ever remembered. Despite his fur and his claws and fangs, the water made him feel clean for the first time in a long time. After his bath, he found dress clothes in his closet and found that he dressed with anticipation.

Dinner was lovely. Though Nathaniel had smashed dishes and thrown cutlery, in the family dining room, it had escaped relatively unscathed, and whatever damage he had inflicted, the castle seemed to have mended, so that the room was as elegant and welcoming as it had been before Nathaniel's transformation. Beau looked unbelievable cleaned up, in a smart suit, smiling from ear to ear. Gwyn was bursting with happiness, her dress was golden silk and flattered her frame in all the right places. The table was set when they entered, the fire was comforting, and then the food just appeared on their plates, their favorite dishes. Beau helped his grandmother into her seat, and then he and Nathaniel seated themselves. Nathaniel was at the head of the table, with Gwyn at his right side and with Beau at his left. Nathaniel's meal was fingerling potatoes, cut glazed carrots, and beef steak which had been cut into strips. Though he was relieved that the steak had been cut, he flushed with embarrassment as he anticipated what a fool he would make of himself trying to use the silverware. Gwyn, perhaps sensing his tension, turned her face toward him. He clenched his jaw and concentrated on trying to pick up his fork. It fell from his clumsy paw, and he resisted the urge to slam his fisted paw onto the table. Fury coursed through him, but Gwyn's voice intruded on his dark thoughts.

"I have always thought that the excesses of table manners were ridiculous," she said softly, "and since the castle has gone to such trouble to give us all relatively bite sized portions and I can't see where the food on my plate is, I hope you won't mind if I use my fingers." She then moved her hand over her plate and found a piece of roasted potato and popped it into her mouth.

Nathaniel stared at her, and his fury melted away, and he felt only gratitude and compassion. Gwyn could hold the cutlery in her human hands, but she was right. Without her vision, she would not be able to spear the food on her plate with her fork without hacking at it. His paws were still clumsy, but he could spear his food with his claws and eat it effectively.

Beau, perhaps also sensing the tension in the room, breathed an audible sigh of relief, grabbed a piece of roasted duck with his fingers, and said, "Sounds great to me, Gran. I never know which damn fork you are supposed to use with what anyway." Then he put the duck in his mouth and ate it.

After that, they ate their meal contentedly and talked comfortably about what they might do the following day. It was decided that they would work at cleaning up the castle in the morning, and then in the afternoon, Nathaniel and Beau would go through the grounds and perhaps some of the forest collecting herbs and items that Gwyn always liked to have on hand as a mid-wife and that Beau should have experience preparing. Then if they had time, Nathaniel had promised to try to see whether in his beastly form, he might still be able to train Beau in fighting skills.

After dinner, Nathaniel led them across the hall to a small chamber he had not entered in years. Comfortable chairs and sofas were grouped together. There was a piano forte and several other kinds of musical instruments along the back wall. After Gwyn was seated in a comfortable chair, Beau went and picked up a fiddle and played folk songs for them, and so they spent a pleasant evening before retiring to their rooms for the night.

When the sun streamed through his windows, Nathaniel woke. He lay quietly for while feeling content and almost happy. He was not alone anymore, and he felt comfortable in front of Gwyn and Beau even though he was a beast. He looked forward to the day, and he couldn't remember the last time he had felt like that. Sitting up, he gasped in surprise. His mirror was intact, completely mended, as were the other things he had broken in his rage. Tears pricked in his eyes; perhaps Gwyn was right, and the castle noticed that he was changed. He dashed the thoughts from his mind. It was dangerous to hope for too much. He rose and washed and dressed himself. He knocked lightly on Gwyn's door, and she opened it almost immediately. They exchanged pleasantries, and he escorted her to the family dining room where a light breakfast was set out for them. Though the table was set for three, Beau was apparently sleeping in as could be expected from a young man (who wasn't a beast).

While waiting Beau's arrival, Gwyn suggested that Nathaniel read to her. He agreed, and he left her seated by the fire on a padded bench while he went to retrieve a book from the library. He braced himself at the door. The second day after his transformation, he had tried to read a book to distract himself, but he couldn't turn the pages and had wrecked the place. To his amazement, the library was perfectly in order when he opened the door. All the books were in place and nothing was broken. "Thank you," he whispered. "Thank you *so much*." A book lay on the nearest table, John Milton's *Paradise Lost*. It seemed fitting somehow, so he took the book and returned to Gwyn. He sat next to her on the bench and held out the book to her. She took it, opened it, and turned the pages until he told her she was at the start. They read together like that: he reading the words and telling her when he finished a page, and she turning the pages for him and listening to the story. They hadn't gotten very far when Beau joined them. He begged them not to stop and got himself a cup of tea and a slice of toast and joined them near the fire to listen to the story.

After Beau had eaten, they made their way to the kitchens to start cleaning at least one of them. To their surprise one of the kitchens was already completely in order, while the other two were not. Nathaniel quickly explained about his room and the library. Nathaniel led Gwyn to a table and chair, and he and Beau brought her jumbles of things that she could sort by shape and feel, like silverware and napkins and such. Nathaniel got out a broom and dustpan and set about sweeping up broken china and pottery. Beau picked up scattered pots and pans, washed them, dried them, and then put them away. After about an hour between the three of them, that kitchen was in order, so they moved on to the larger kitchen. This one took them two hours, but when it was done, Nathaniel felt so much pride and satisfaction that it surprised him. In his previous life, he had never really had to clean things. The servants had done all that, but completing the task from start to finish, seeing the transformation of the room from chaos to order, fixing a mess that he had made—all of these things gave him pleasure—and best of all, the work was much more pleasant in the company of others. Sometimes they talked, but other times they just worked in a companionable silence.

When they were done, they returned to the family dining room and found lunch waiting for them. After they had eaten, both Nathaniel and Beau expressed concern about leaving Gwyn all alone for the afternoon, but she scoffed at them. She had found a knitting basket in her apartments and had started on a shawl for herself. She knit so well that she didn't need to see what she did; she could feel what she did and needed to do. She had them escort her back to her rooms, showed them her newly started project, and sent them on their way. Beau brought with them his knife and a basket and a sack from the kitchens in which they could store their finds. The castle's kitchen gardens were not in as bad a shape apparently as Beau had assumed. They were full of weeds, of course, but a lot of the herbs were still alive, fighting for their spaces among the weeds. Beau cut swatches of lavender, rosemary, chamomile, tansy, peppermint, spearmint, and sage. He found rosehips in the formal gardens and collected those along with a range of different flowers (roses, foxgloves, dandelions, pansies, and others). Next they set out for the forest, and Beau was remarkably good at guessing where to find certain kinds of mushrooms, and he even found some truffles. Nathaniel watched Beau work with fascination. Some tasks Nathaniel could help with, but though he couldn't help with the majority, it was still interesting and educational to watch Beau foraging. Beau tried to explain what each item was and how it could be used in various remedies or poultices and other healing means. He was kind and patient and very much like his grandmother, Nathaniel realized.

When they returned after several hours, Nathaniel went to get Gwyn. Beau set out the different things on a big kitchen table in the smallest kitchen and got bowls for some things and string and scissors for tying up herbs to dry. Then the boys left Gwyn to work in the kitchen while they experimented in the training yard. By trial and error, they found that Nathaniel could wield a staff, while Beau tried to come at him with a sword. Nathaniel was over a foot taller than Beau and much stronger and faster as a beast, so that despite the seeming disadvantage of Nathaniel's staff to Beau's sword, they were in fact more evenly matched, especially with Nathaniel's extensive former training usually giving him the advantage, but he didn't take advantage. It was thrilling to do something more physical than just run. Thus, they spent several hours going after each other until they were both dripping with sweat and thoroughly sore and nursing various bruises and abrasions. A final competition ended in a draw, where neither one nor the other could get the advantage, and they finally collapsed to the ground laughing at each other. Nathaniel got to his feet first and held out his paw to Beau who took it and allowed himself to be pulled up.

They walked back to the castle together to see how Gwyn had made out. She was sitting waiting for them. Bunches of herbs had been tied together, and she had lengths of string ready for them. She set them to work hanging the herb bunches to the ceiling beams where they would dry. After the herbs, came the flowers. The rosehips would dry in a colander, and she had placed the mushrooms and truffles near the stove in case whatever sprites or fairies who created the enchantments of the castle wanted to use them for the food.

Then they retired to their rooms where Nathaniel and Beau were badly in need of their waiting baths. Dinner was again delightful. All three were served with sliced chicken in a mushroom truffle sauce with roasted vegetables and small squares of polenta. They ate contentedly and shared the events of their separate activities. After dinner, instead of music, Beau read to them from *Paradise Lost* until it was time for bed.

After retiring to his room, Nathaniel spent a lot of time thinking about his day, especially his time alone with Beau. He had not allowed himself to do so before because he did not want anything to be awkward between them, but now alone, it was all he could think about. He thought about Beau on the grounds and in the forest—his quiet gentleness and grace, his kindness and patience, his beauty. He was beautiful, a dark Adonis, and they had touched. They had clashed against each other, hard sometimes and other times only just slightly, and Nathaniel had held his hand, pulling him up from the ground. He tried to empty his mind, but he couldn't. He kept thinking about Beau and wanting to touch him more and wanting Beau to touch him too.

The days fell into a happy rhythm, cleaning in the morning with Gwyn and then Nathaniel and Beau foraging or training until it was time to think about dinner. On the odd rainy day, they played games or read in the afternoon. Nathaniel and Gwyn usually paired off against Beau in games. He became her eyes, and she became his hands. As the days turned into weeks and months, they grew incredibly close. Nathaniel wasn't sure exactly when it had first started, but Gwyn's good morning and good night kisses seemed so natural to him that it was hard to imagine life without them. The one pattern that did change was that one morning, there wasn't a room in the castle that needed cleaning. They had either cleaned those that were damaged or the castle had mended them. In the absence of that chore, they read or played games in the mornings until the young men went out on their own.

A couple of other things changed as well, Nathaniel's feelings for Beau only strengthened in intensity, and Beau began reciprocating those feelings. They held hands occasionally. In addition to training with the staff and the sword, they competed without weapons which almost always disintegrated into a wrestling match, which was a poorly disguised way for them to touch each other. During one such bout, Nathaniel had Beau pinned beneath him, his weight and height making this easy for him to do, and Beau had been struggling against him, but then suddenly Beau stopped struggling, and when Nathaniel looked down at Beau, Beau was staring at him, his lips parted, his breathing heavy, and a hunger in his eyes that made Nathaniel gasp. Nathaniel pulled away slightly.

"Nathan?" he heard Beau ask him.

"You can't want me. I am a beast," he said bitterly.

"You're not a beast. I do want you. Gran and I both love you; surely, you know that, don't you?" Beau asked.

"Love me?" the words were strangled. They were everything Nathaniel had ever hoped for, and yet he didn't feel worthy of them.

"Let me touch you," Beau pleaded, and he reached out his hand to touch Nathaniel's face.

Nathaniel felt Beau's hand on his face, through his fur, and then he felt as if he was melting, his fur, his size, his shape. It wasn't an agonizing burning, but it was definitely a melting, and the next thing he knew, he could feel Beau's hand on his bare skin, and he could feel the skin of his body against Beau's skin. He looked at Beau, and Beau looked just as surprised as he felt. They sat up staring at each other.

"Nathan, you're human again," Beau whispered.

Nathaniel couldn't believe it. He wept, and Beau wrapped his arms around him and let him cry. When the tears stopped, Nathaniel looked up, and Beau was waiting for him. He inclined his head, and they were kissing. Nathaniel had wanted to do this for so long that he nearly started weeping again, but he didn't. The kisses deepened, and they were touching each other. Then somehow they were naked, and in between touching and stroking, they made each other come, and they were so happy and so content that they laughed. Then they shrugged into their clothes, so they could go and find Gwyn. Nathaniel had to hold his overly large clothes to his body, but he didn't mind.

To their surprise, Gwyn was not alone in the kitchens when they entered. Fairy Kate was with her. Both women were seated and beaming at them.

"Prince Nathaniel, I have never been so happy to have been wrong," the fairy queen said with a radiant smile.

Somehow Nathaniel knew not only that the curse was broken but that he was forgiven, and he felt profoundly humbled, a state of mind he recognized as a gift. He inclined his head to the fairy queen, "I am not a prince, My Lady, but I am so truly grateful to be human again. It was a tough lesson, My Lady, but I am also grateful for it. I am happier at this moment than I ever could have been in my previous life," he said quietly.

"Though you are missing your kingdom, it will be returned to you in about an hour, and you will be worthy finally to be its prince. In a moment, you and Beau may want to get cleaned up, so that you can greet your parents in proper style," said the fairy.

"My parents … what … do I tell them?" Nathaniel looked awkwardly between Gwyn and the fairy, and they knew that he meant about loving Beau.

Gwyn spoke first. "They love you, Nathan, as I love you. They will want your happiness more than anything else. If you and Beau make each other happy, others will see that and want that for you, if they truly love you. Being different and/or bringing change is hard, but it is important."

"Plus, I have a gift for each of you," and Fairy Kate moved forward and gave each young man and Gwyn a kiss on the forehead. "You are all marked with my kiss, and the kiss of a fairy queen is not to be trifled with. It will protect you and bring you luck."

Gwyn gasped suddenly, jumped to her feet, and knelt at the feet of the fairy. "My Lady, how can I thank you?" she began.

Fairy Kate held out her hand and pulled Gwyn to her feet. "You are skilled, my dear Gwyneth, and you have much more life to live. To make the most of your skill and to aid your people, it is my pleasure to return to you your sight," she said softly. "It is time for me to leave. Live well all of you and enjoy each other," and she disappeared in a flash of sparkling dust.

Nathaniel and Beau and Gwyn all hugged each other. They were all so happy and grateful for so many things. They talked excitedly as they retreated to their rooms to get ready. After his bath, Nathaniel stared at his reflection in the mirror for a few minutes, turning and checking to see that on no part of him lingered a patch of fur or a claw or a fang. He checked to see that he was really, truly human again, and apparently he was. It amused him to open his closet and find a completely different wardrobe than the one that had presented itself to him that very morning. All these clothes fitted him as he was now, a human. He dressed in beautiful clothes that he picked out with his mother in mind.

Nathaniel, Beau, and Gwyn walked hand in hand through the castle to the grand ballroom and were not surprised to find the castle in a flurry of activity, with servants rushing about and guests milling around. Nathaniel led his friends into the ballroom and then froze when he saw his parents clearly on the dais looking the same as always, utterly unchanged and unharmed.

"It's okay, Nathan; you are the one who has changed, not they," Gwyn said to him quietly.

Nathaniel went forward purposefully then. He hugged his parents passionately, and they seemed bemused by his enthusiasm but did not remark on it. He presented Gwyn and Beau as his permanent guests at the castle and also presented Beau as his boyfriend. If either the king or queen found this information odd or uncomfortable, there was absolutely no sign of it on their faces. They welcomed Gwyn and Beau warmly, and with a light and happy heart, Nathaniel and Beau left Gwyn to catch up with the queen while they went to dance the night away.

Sleeping Beauty's Escape from Date Rape

Once upon a time, there was a land that was divided and ruled by variety of means. Some lands were kingdoms ruled by kings. Some lands were queendoms and ruled by queens. Still other lands were ruled by a counsel of representatives. Usually, the most peaceful lands were the queendoms or the counsel-ruled. The kingdoms tended toward violence and war either among themselves or with their neighbors.

In one queendom, Andelusia, Queen Natasha and her consort, Lord Kenneth, were blessed with a beautiful daughter, Maleficent. Maleficent grew to be a sweet and charming young woman. When she came to be of marriageable age, eighteen, Lord Kenneth's cousin, King John, from Conquest (the kingdom bordering Andelusia's northern side), begged the queen and her lord for a marriage between his son, Prince Edward, and Princess Maleficent. Both Queen Natasha and Lord Kenneth were alarmed by this proposal and felt great apprehension about it. They had hoped to make an alliance with another queendom with their daughter's marriage, but they had to consent to King John and his entourage's visit to Andelusia. What they did not know was that King John hoped to enlarge Conquest's holdings with Andelusia, and the marriage was a means to an end—a way to unite the lands and the families before showing his true intensions of killing off the queen, lord, and princess and taking Andelusia for himself and his son.

King John paid the dark sorcerer, Mortensen, to help him with his plans. Prince Edward understood his task was to woo Princess Maleficent by any means necessary. The prince was a cruel man who held women in contempt and would suffer this "game" to get the power that his father so desperately wanted.

Mortensen cast a powerful aurora around the king's party and around Prince Edward in particular. To any in their presence, King John's proposal was utterly sincere and trustworthy and Prince Edward was stunningly handsome and kind and generous. Spies had been sent previous to the arrival of King John's party, and Queen Natasha's sorceress, Cassandra, had been cleverly poisoned so that it appeared she suffered from a natural affliction so severe that she couldn't be at court and was in fact only vaguely conscious.

Queen Natasha, Lord Kenneth, Princess Maleficent, and their court were all taken by the enchantments Mortensen wrought on them. The queen and lord believed King John's proposal of peace and bonding, and they found Prince Edward an excellent suitor for their beloved daughter. Princess Maleficent was utterly charmed by Prince Edward and longed to be his wife.

Prince Edward played his part well and was aided by the sorcery of Mortensen, but he found that Princess Maleficent had an unexpected effect on him. She was beautiful in every way that he could imagine—her face, her body, the way she moved, even the way she smelled of rose water and rain. He realized that he wanted her in the most carnal way possible—to look at her naked body, to feel her naked body, and to have her completely—the way that a man can know a woman physically, sexually. He looked at her face, but the swell of her breasts and the fullness of her hips caught his attention too.

A date for the wedding was set, and when the day came, Prince Edward convinced his father to let him have his wedding night with his bride before the slaughter of the royal family and the nobles closest to them. Though the king agreed, Mortensen warned them against this plan. Alone with the princess, Prince Edward's enchantment would fail, and she would see him as he truly was. Prince Edward didn't care—he would have his princess—willingly or unwillingly.

And so it came to be; the marriage was performed, and the prince and the princess retired to private chambers for the consummation of their marriage. Maleficent and Edward started kissing. She was so happy and so in love, and he was lustful and eager. Edward's face had been soft against Maleficent's cheek one minute and then suddenly rough and scratchy the next. She pulled away to look at him, and her Prince Edward was suddenly different—not so utterly handsome, kind and gentle, but handsome and dangerous and cruel looking. The look in his eyes changed from loving to predatory. She gasped and pulled away further, scrambling to put some distance between them. Anger washed over his face; Mortensen had been right—she could really see him now—but he didn't care. He would have her whether she wanted him or not. He moved toward her, and when she tried to run to the door, he tackled her. She tried to scream, and he clamped his hand over her mouth and found a kerchief to gag her with. He tried to remove her clothes, but she fought him, so he ripped them from her—shredding the fabric of her bodice and ripping through her skirts. Tears poured from her eyes, and he hit her until she stopped struggling and crying and went numb with the torment she was being put through. He raped her and beat her and left her for dead.

When he left the bridal chambers, he found his father's men slaughtering. He joined them eagerly, and by morning the terrible coup was complete. Andelusia was part of Conquest. Prince Edward was king of Andelusia. What King John and King Edward hadn't reckoned on was that the princess's handmaiden had escaped the slaughter and had found the princess. The handmaiden found her brother, a stable hand, and together they secreted the princess away on two horses. They rode into the deep forest to the cottage of the ancient midwife, Hestia, in the hope that she could save the princess.

Hestia had been troubled for weeks—emissaries from Conquest, Cassandra's sudden illness, the marriage of the princess—all this was bad. Her anxiety lessened when Cassandra had been brought to her cottage, so that the midwife could look after the sorceress with her full range of potions and salves and poultices. Cassandra screamed in the middle of the night—sweat streamed off her body, and Hestia tended her, dread rising at what had happened that Cassandra could be so affected given her less than conscious condition. As Hestia wiped a cold compress against Cassandra's brow, Cassandra's hand flew to Hestia's wrist and her eyes shocked open, "The princess, Hestia. You must save her!" Before Hestia could ask a question, Cassandra was unconscious again, and the foreboding that Hestia felt became even worse. She made Cassandra comfortable and sat outside the cottage to wait for what she feared would come.

The sound of horses storming through the forest reached Hestia. There were only a few—perhaps two. She did not fear two horses and their riders speeding to her cottage. She stood and prayed to the Great Goddess and to the Moon for help, for strength, and for guidance. The riders appeared, a man holding a slight body, a woman's body, and a woman riding alone. They slowed at the sight of the cottage and Hestia. The woman dismounted and approached Hestia.

"Ancient One," the woman called, "the marriage is a sham. The royal family and those loyal to them are dead, slaughtered in their beds. The prince did unspeakable things to the princess. She is barely alive. I am her handmaiden, Maeve. This is my brother, Anthony. Please, will you attend the princess?"

Tears sprung to Hestia's eyes. This was worse than anything she could have imagined. All of Andelusia was in danger now. Only the princess could save them if she could be saved herself. "Yes, of course." Hestia moved toward Anthony as did Maeve. Together they held the princess while Anthony swung down and took their burden and carried her into the midwife's cottage. Hestia had Anthony place the princess on Hestia's own bed, and then she sent him to fetch fresh water from the stream. Together Maeve and Hestia unwrapped Maleficent from the blanket that Maeve had wrapped her in. The princess was bruised and swollen and bloody. Hestia gasped at the sight of the princess. Both the beating and rape had been savage. With the water still in the cottage, they cleaned the princess. Hestia applied poultices and salves to the cuts and bruises depending on their severity. For her internal wounds, it was too soon to examine. The poor woman was too swollen and raw for any such probing. Hestia fixed a tea with herbs that would help Maleficent fight infection and bring down the swelling and had Maeve slowly and carefully trickle drops down Maleficent's throat. Hestia dressed Maleficent in a loose gown and wrapped her in a clean sheet and blankets.

Anthony returned with two buckets of stream water. He was shy. He understood that he was male in a cottage of women who mostly weren't his kin. "Midwife, where should I be? What should I do? Where can I sleep?" he could barely look at her as he asked his questions.

Hestia smiled at him—that he could be so concerned and understand the awkwardness redeemed him. "Anthony, I am an old woman tending two unconscious women with your sister. You are an honorable man. We cannot afford to have you away from us—though what you or any of us could do against King John's men is not encouraging. I will sleep in my room on the floor with the princess. You and your sister are welcome to sleep on blankets by the fire. Cassandra is on a pallet by the wall. I will feel more comfortable with both unconscious women attended during the night. So you and your sister do me a favor in this."

Anthony felt all the emotions of the day crowd over him. His queen and lord were dead. His princess ravished and nearly dead. The danger to himself and his sister. Men, the men of the kingdoms, could they ever be trusted? Greedy, brutal, violent, why were they like that? "Ancient One, how do we recover from this?" his voice barely a whisper trying to contain all the emotion that he felt.

"Call me Hestia," she said firmly. "We will make these women well. Cassandra can teach Maleficent and possibly your sister too, and they will be a force that few will be able to reckon with. We will help them. We will help save Andelusia because that is what we must do or die trying. Death is not such horrible fate, especially if living in an earthly hell is the only option—and King John and King Edward would make Andelusia just that."

Anthony felt a surge of courage swell in his chest at Hestia's words. He wondered absently if it was just the words or some spell that she had cast to make him feel brave, but he didn't care. Andelusia, his Andelusia, their Andelusia, was what he would die for. Hestia then sent him out to stable the horses in her small barn.

That night he fell asleep and tried to block out the screams he had heard from the stable. He woke several times in the night to his sister's nightmares—her shaking and writhing and crying about the images she had seen. He stroked her arms and tried to sooth her.

In the morning, Anthony and Maeve found Hestia had lit a small cook fire to the right of the cottage and had a kettle of porridge cooking and another of sweetened and spiced apples for their breakfast. She had also been busy at other tasks. Several blankets had been spread on the grass. On one were many of her mid-wife supplies and remedies. On another were clothes and various kinds of bedding. On another were a variety of tools, weapons, and supplies.

Anthony was so surprised by these preparations that he forgot his hunger. "Are we going somewhere?" he asked haltingly.

"Yes, Anthony, as soon as your sister and you have eaten, your sister will stay here with Cassandra and the princess, and you and I will go to a cave near here where we can hide until they are stronger. We must take what we think we will need and then move Cassandra and the princess."

"You think they'll come looking for us?" Maeve stammered, fear clear in her voice.

"They won't find the body of the princess. When they enquire further, they will also realize that Andelusia's sorceress is missing too. I am an obvious person to question in these regards, and I have no wish to be questioned by King John's men," Hestia answered grimly.

They ate solemnly, sobered by the threats surrounding them. Once they were done, Hestia gave Maeve more tea to give to the princess and a series of tasks to do in preparation for their move. Hestia handed Anthony a variety of goods to add to the blankets. The smaller two she rolled up and secured to the horse she rode, and larger Anthony rolled up and secured to his horse. Hestia had them ride through a streambed for a considerable length of time, and then, on the other side, they doubled back to a cleverly obscured cave. People had obviously lived in the cave before. The floor was packed hard, along the back of the cave, sleeping ledges had been chiseled from the rock walls, brackets were driven into the walls to hold torches, some crude shelves had been mounted to the side walls, a large stone-lined cooking pit was in the center, and a range of rough furniture scattered the interior (stools mainly). Hestia and Anthony untied and carried their rolled blankets into the cave. Hestia emptied the bedding and clothing onto the sleeping ledges and had Anthony dump the tools and supplies in a pile on the ground to be sorted later. The medicines, she left rolled up, their storage needing more care and time than they had at the moment. They returned to the cottage as soon as they could.

Cassandra was murmuring in her sleep, calling the queen's name and the princess'. Maeve had given the princess the tea and had accumulated more piles of things for them to roll up and transport. Hestia helped Maeve and Anthony secure more things to the horses and waved them off. The princess woke and cried into the arms of the midwife who held her and tried to console her. Maleficent was terribly sore from the various ways she had been assaulted, but she had no fever for which Hestia was very grateful. Hestia explained that she wanted to flush the princess's body with warm water and a little vinegar to cleanse her after the rape. Though the princess feared the pain this contact might bring, she submitted to the midwife's care and was surprised to feel how gently the midwife touched her so that there was only the slightest discomfort. The princess ate some porridge and apples and more of the antiseptic tea. Moving gingerly, the princess went to sit with Cassandra, taking the unconscious woman's hand in her own and telling her and Hestia all that she remembered from the night before.

When Anthony and Maeve returned, the last of the supplies was tied to one of the horses, and the princess was placed with Maeve on the other horse. Hestia made the last of the preparations and readied Cassandra for travel. Anthony returned with both horses. Cassandra was secured to one horse, and Hestia rode with Anthony and the last of what they were taking with them. Once Cassandra was comfortably situated on a sleeping ledge and the last of the supplies taken into the cave, Hestia had Anthony take the horses through the forest to a secluded meadow where they might graze while she walked back to the cottage and set it on fire. She did her best to obscure their trail on horseback to the streambed and tried to leave a false trail into the forest. Retracing her steps carefully, she also tried to destroy the horse trail on the other side of the streambed to the cave. Exhausted, she returned to the cave to find Anthony and Maeve cooking a pair of rabbits they had snared in the forest, and just as they sat to eat, it started to rain, allowing all four of the conscious members of their party to relax and enjoy their food since the rain would even more securely make them hidden and untrackable.

They slept fitfully. The princess, Anthony, and Maeve had nightmares that, at best, made them sleep poorly and awaken disoriented and, at worst, made them wake up screaming and sweating, reliving the horrors they had seen or been through that horrible night. Hestia resolved to make a sleeping draught that they could take before retiring the following day.

The next morning the young people woke to find Hestia agitated and crouched by the cave entrance. The fire had burnt out and soon they understood why she had not lit another. The sound of dogs and horses and men could be heard some distance away. King John's men searched for them. They glanced at each other nervously, but as they looked, they also saw that at some point in the night the rain had really come down in pouring sheets of water—everything was muddy and saturated. Hestia handed them some dried fruit and meat with which to break their fasts and left them to tend to Cassandra. Soon after the sounds of the search had disappeared, Cassandra woke. Hestia fed her teas and asked the young people to cook some porridge and apples, which they did. After this for lunch, Anthony and Maeve went into the forest to forage and hunt. They set snares and explored. They found a large pond, and Anthony shot two ducks with one of Hestia's longbows. They found bushes of raspberries and blackberries, which they filled Maeve's apron with and then returned to the cave. Over dinner, all sated and conscious, they talked about what to do next.

"We need to leave Andelusia," Anthony said. "If we can get to Maidenport, we may be able to see Queen Charlotte and ask for her help. Lord Kenneth was her brother."

"But that is two lands away," Maeve said despondently. "And we only have two horses."

"Andelusia to the Commonwealth to Maidenport, it will be some journey, but what choice do we have?" asked Hestia. "We cannot stay here. Perhaps we could get help in the Commonwealth but our best hope lies with Queen Charlotte. We need to get well first, all of us. Then we can think of travel," Hestia said with authority.

And so they hid and healed for a week. Twice they heard some of King John's men searching the forest, but both times it was a much smaller group of men, and they never came close to the hidden cave. The second week, Hestia had them all train twice a day, building up their strength. They took long hikes. She made the young people climb trees and practice with her long bows and knives. Anthony, as a stable boy, had little combat training, but he had seen the pages and knights training, and he tried to explain anything useful that he had seen or learned.

One morning, Hestia assembled them and handed a fine pair of scissors to Anthony and instructed him to cut her hair to look like a man. The princess and Maeve looked at each other in alarm, but Cassandra only nodded. It would be safer for them to travel as three young men and two men than as a mixed party or four females and a young man. Cassandra had her hair cut next, and then the princess and Maeve. The young women were young enough that the butchering of their hair was painful to them, so though they submitted to the scissors, tears escaped their eyes as their carefully cultivated locks were cut off. Hestia gave them all male clothing to put on and get used to. The girls especially were surprised at the difference. The absence of corsets and long skirts and delicate shoes gave them an ease of movement that they had not experienced before.

Hestia combed through her possessions. She fashioned backpacks of a sort for each of them to carry. They each had two changes of clothes and a blanket. Hestia created two essential kits of her herbs and remedies. One she stored in her bag, and then other she gave to Anthony. She divided up the rest of the common gear among them (essential cooking implements and tools). Luckily, she had six skin sacks that had been treated specifically to hold fluids, so each of them carried one full of fresh water with one spare. Each carried a sheathed knife. Hestia gave the two longbows to Anthony and Cassandra. Anthony was sent to see if he could find the horses. By some miracle, they had not wandered off and had not been found and seized. Anthony located their hidden gear and bridled and saddled the horses and led them back to the cave. It was agreed that Hestia would ride one of the horses, and the other would carry their gear for the time being. What money they had, they divided among them. And then when Hestia seemed satisfied, they set off. They avoided villages and foraged and hunted in the forests and fields. They fished in streams and rivers. They traveled south.

As they traveled, Hestia and Cassandra taught the young people what they knew. Though Hestia normally would apprentice only young women, given the slaughter, she did not feel comfortable withholding the information from Anthony. She made sure the young people could identify the different trees and bushes that they passed. She explained which had edible fruits or nuts or berries and which had poison ones and which just had ones that were not particularly tasty. In the right circumstances, the knowledge of poison could be very valuable. She also pointed out herbs and fungi and explained which could be used for what purposes. She made the young people recite the different uses and applications of different herbs and things. She made them recite combinations of herbs and things to make teas or poultices or other remedies. She explained common ailments and parasites and how to treat them. She explained about broken bones and how to set them correctly and immobilize them so that they could heal. She talked to them about reproduction and sexuality.

At first, the young people were embarrassed by these topics, but both Hestia and Cassandra chided them about such feelings. They explained that men feared female sexuality because of its power to produce life and endless pleasure females could experience sexually. Men, therefore, constantly framed female sexuality in terms that made girls, women, boys, and men feel uncomfortable with it and yet accept male sexuality as normal and even inevitable. What was particularly terrifying to men was young female sexuality—hence all the emphasis on female virginity and the acceptance of male sexual urges as beyond a male's control. It was all nonsense, they scoffed. Girls and women were powerful sexual creatures with natural and different sexual responses than boys' and men's sexual responses. When the young people looked dubious, Hestia and Cassandra asked them how often they masturbated. Masturbated? The young people were speechless and then scandalized. The older women giggled like girls at their responses and encouraged them to try it sometime. Sex was supposed happen between consenting partners and to be about pleasure for both. What Prince Edward had done to Maleficent was deplorable, criminal behavior. Though the young people were still skeptical about their rights to sexual pleasure, they agreed that coercion, violence, and pain should not be part of sexual experience. Hestia moved on to pregnancy and childbirth, describing different changes in a woman's body during pregnancy, complications, and remedies and then the different stages of childbirth, complications, actions to help, remedies, other actions to try, how to handle the afterbirth, cutting the umbilical cord, caring for the infant, helping the mother nurse the baby. Sometimes it seemed overwhelming, but Hestia went over it again and again patiently.

In the evenings, when the children weren't working with Hestia, Cassandra began to school them in sorcery. Everything had a core essence, and with the proper knowledge and grasp of a thing's essence, one could, with the addition of special words and spells, manipulate that thing. They started with small things. Cassandra had them accelerate the blooms of flowers, making them bloom on demand. Enhancing a life force, doing a positive action, was much easier than doing something debilitating or negative. From making the flowers bloom, she had them work on transforming the blooms, making daisies bloom on rose bushes and making marigolds bloom on daisy stalks. Animals were different; they weren't things. They were sentient beings. If one could feel an animal's essence, one could call it and "request" a favor. In some ways it was a request, but with the addition of the magic words or spells, it was a request that few animals would refuse. They started with mice but moved on to larger animals and lastly to predators. Anthony asked if it could be done to human beings, and Cassandra explained that it was a great sin, the darkest magic, damnable magic, that even the darkest sorcerers would avoid. Free will separated humans from animals—it was sacred. No human being had the right to take another's free will away, to control him or her like that.

One evening, when Hestia had been entertaining them with stories out of Ancient Greek mythology, Maeve asked about magical creatures. Did they exist or not, sirens, sphinxes, griffins, dragons, harpies, phoenixes, and such? Cassandra was quiet for a long time. Finally, she told them that it was legend that such creatures existed, but not in living memory had any sorcerer ever been able to summon one. If the creatures had ever existed, they had not been seen in so long that no one could feel the essence of such a creature to call it and make a request. From that evening on, the young people only wanted to hear about magical creatures and beasts—demanding every story that Cassandra or Hestia had ever heard.

The young people grew powerful. They could request favors from deer and not just single deer but by requesting a favor from the herd leader, they could control the herd. Anthony was the best with predators. Cassandra and Hestia reminded the young people over and over that with great power, they had great responsibility. They told them stories about hubris and explained how people who flouted their place as mere mortals, people who abused power, could be tested by the supernatural and punished. They told them about how Zeus and Hermes tested the common people's response to helpless guests—punishing those who refused to offer hospitality and rewarding those who did offer it. They told the story of "Beau and the Beast" where Prince Nathaniel had been foolish not to offer shelter to the disguised fairy and was transformed into a beast until he earned the love of another human. They told them about Arachne and how Athena turned her into a spider and about Sisyphus who tried to outsmart the gods into a second life and was tormented in Hades with pushing a boulder up a hill and almost reaching the summit when it rolled down to the bottom and he had to start again forever. Humility and power had to go together. Women usually felt this as mothers. It was part of the reason why the queenships were more peaceful than the other lands. But women were not immune to the lure and corrupting influence of power. Power used with humility sought to elevate the human condition. Power exercised with humility sought service for the greater good, not power for its own sake.

More than anything, the princess wanted to be able to feel the essence of a magical creature, especially a dragon. If she could call a dragon and request something, it would be able to route King John's army and drive it from Andelusia. Part of her knew that she wanted revenge for what had been done to her, her family, and her household, but another part knew that she wanted to free her people and stop King John from hurting other people. So in her free time, Maleficent thought about dragons—about every part of them. She thought about their shapes, their powers, and the abilities: their heads, their snouts and mouths, their eyes (like a cross between an owl's and a cat's), the spikes (around their heads, down their spines, on the ends of their wings, and on their tails), their long necks, their wings (sort of like bat wings but grand and so much more powerful), their bodies, their legs, their claws (beautiful and deadly, sharper than any knives), their tails, their scales (luminescent), their hearts (with magical qualities), their hording tendencies, their special bonding to each other, their ability to communicate without sound (telepathy), their speed, their range, their fire (fierce and deadly), their magic (not just dragon hearts had magical qualities; dragons could do magic). Dragons! How she wanted to see a dragon!

One afternoon, the princess had separated from the others and was sitting in a small meadow thinking as pointedly as she could about dragons. Her thoughts were unfocused, and then suddenly they sharpened: dragon, the essence of a dragon, she felt it, and it felt different than any encounter with an animal she had ever had before. She called to it, not it but her, the dragon was female, and she was not just sentient, she was capable of higher level thought.

"Who calls me?" the she-dragon asked in the princess' mind.

"I call you, My Lady. I am Maleficent of Andelusia," she answered back.

"How is it that you can call me? No human has called me in millennia," the dragon asked.

"I am not sure," the princess answered truthfully. "I have tried to learn everything I could about dragons, and when I was thinking about dragons just now, it just suddenly came together—a sense of you, your essence," she struggled to explain.

"You have quite the imagination, then," the dragon said with what seemed like a chuckle. "What do you wish of me?" the dragon asked.

"My people have been slaughtered by an evil king and his men. I wish to vanquish them," the princess answered.

"They cannot be brought to the side of right?" the dragon asked indignantly.

The princess felt embarrassed. Of course, a nonviolent solution was the moral choice, the best choice. Dragons could read each other's thoughts. Maleficent thought to the night of her rape and the slaughter and brought the memories to the forefront of her mind and willed the dragon to be able to see them.

"STOP!" the dragon ordered. "They are beasts worthy of extermination. I will come to you."

The princess wondered how long it would take, but almost immediately, the sky shimmered, and a dark shape appeared in the sky and grew larger and larger. It descended more magnificent and overwhelming than she could have ever imagined. Her scales shimmered from purple to green and back again. The princess curtsied before the dragon. The dragon inclined her head. "I am Dragon Isis. You will not be able to 'request' things of me, little sorceress, like you do of other animals. We will need to work as a team. I will be your equal partner or not your partner at all. Is that understood? Do not try to do otherwise or I will never respond to your call again," Dragon Isis spoke in a clear voice that rang like thundering bells.

At that moment, Anthony, Maeve, Cassandra, and Hestia burst into the meadow, breathless and frantic. They gaped open-mouthed at the dragon and froze in their tracks. The princess faced her friends and chose her words carefully. "I have made contact with the Dragon Isis. She finds what King John and his men did despicable. We need to talk further," the princess explained. Her friends nodded mutely, overwhelmed by what they saw before them.

The dragon glanced at the new comers and dismissed them, turning back to the princess. "Do you have a plan?" the dragon demanded.

"I don't know," the princess began hesitantly. "In all the stories I have heard, there have been descriptions of dragons, what they look like, their abilities, but I have not heard stories about how humans and dragons work together or could fight together." She paused, summoning her courage. She didn't know if her suggestions would be sensible to the dragon or offensive. "I thought perhaps I could ride you, if you didn't find that too objectionable." She glanced up nervously, but the dragon did not look offended. "I had hoped that you had other friends who might be willing to help and that my friends and I and you and your friends could ride and fight together." The princess blushed with embarrassment. In truth, it wouldn't be much fighting, and it certainly wouldn't be much human fighting. It would be the dragons slaughtering King John and his men with perhaps guided suggestions from the humans.

The dragon's response surprised the princess. The great beast clutched her chest and seemed to chortle deeply. "Your second silent assessment is the better vision of what may come to pass, little sorceress. And it is to your credit to be honest in that assessment. Though I can rally dragons to your cause, it would be better if your friends," and she nodded at them, "could call to four dragons, then the five of us can rally other dragons more effectively than just I can. They now have the advantage of having seen me but have them come closer and really look at me. They can touch me too if they wish."

Dragon Isis held herself very still and waited. Hesitantly, Maeve, Anthony, Cassandra, and Hestia moved forward, circling the dragon slowly, feasting their eyes on the beast. Only Cassandra was brave enough to touch the dragon, running her hands over the dragon's scales, the excitement and awe and gratitude in her face were clear. The princess also went forward. Though she had called the dragon, the princess had not touched her, and she felt the same joy and awe at touching Dragon Isis as Cassandra seemed to feel.

In her mind, the princess heard the dragon, "I am pleased too. It has been too long since humans and dragons have worked together. I hope we accomplish good things. We did before when humans worshiped the Great Goddess in one form or another and we, dragons and serpents again in one form or another, were her helpers and sometimes her consorts in an age long ago. Perhaps we can bring peace and magic back to your world. That would be a heady accomplishment."

When they were done inspecting Dragon Isis, they stepped back slightly.

The dragon spoke out loud again. "You will need saddles, but since human knowledge of dragon saddles is doubtless lost, I suggest that you get elfin aid."

"Elfin aid?" the princess said, her face filled with both awe and confusion.

The dragon chuckled again. "I can send some elves to you. They abhor violence. I am sure they will be sympathetic. Take your friends, Maleficent, and tell them what you thought about dragons that allowed you to make contact with me, and then tomorrow in the afternoon, each of your friends should try to call a dragon. You and I are linked now, so you will be able call me easily. I will take my leave, now. Farewell." The dragon drew back from them and launched herself into the air. She rose gracefully and majestically, her powerful wings carrying her high in the sky.

They watched her climb through the sky with a silent reverence, which Cassandra broke.

"How on earth did you do that, princess?" Cassandra demanded.

So the princess tried to explain how she had visualized every aspect of a dragon that she could think of, the physical features, the abilities, the powers—and that it had all just clicked—and she suddenly felt the essence of the dragon and could talk to her in her mind. The princess explained the warning that the dragon had made about not trying to request things from dragons but to treat them like equals and partners.

"I don't think we need to leave Andelusia any anymore," said Hestia softly. "With the dragons' help, we can destroy King John and his men and restore Maleficent to the throne. We don't need to seek Queen Charlotte's help."

"Dragons," mumbled Anthony still stunned with this encounter with a living, breathing dragon.

"She was beautiful," added Maeve.

Cassandra, her voice choked with emotion, said, "The woman who apprenticed me predicted that I would see dragons one day. I had hoped when I was young, but I had lost faith in the prediction. Dragons in the world again; perhaps magic will come too."

"I hate to bring us down, but perhaps we should head back, find something to eat, and think about bed. It will be a big day tomorrow," Hestia said practically.

So they headed back to the camp. Hestia got the fire ready. Cassandra went to fetch water, and the young people went to forage and hunt in the forest. They ate and talked, trying to contain their excitement. When it was time for bed none of them felt like they would ever be able to sleep, but slowly they drifted off.

When the sun blazed through the sky in the morning, they woke eagerly. They had the princess go over everything she had thought of before making contact with Dragon Isis while they ate a hasty breakfast. Once they were done, they realized that they were not alone. Small figures stood silently at the edge of the forest. Realizing they had been observed, one figure moved forward. She was about the size of a ten-year-old girl and looked impossibly both very young and very old. Her hair was entirely white and long, and her eyes were a startling violet color, and they flashed with mirth, curiosity, and excitement. She was clothed in greens and browns so that she blended into the forest.

"Greetings, humans," she said with an almost hypnotic, sing-song voice. "Dragon Isis contacted us. You need dragon saddles, is that correct, for a just cause? I am Mia, an elfin rider and head saddle maker."

They bowed to the elfin woman, and the six elves with her moved forward. Maeve, Anthony, and the princess took turns explaining to the elves what had happened in the palace of the rulers of Andelusia and what they feared was happening across the country. As they spoke, the anxiety of the elves was palpable.

"Such acts of cruelty and barbarism are unconscionable. Long ago, when your peoples worshiped versions of the Great Goddess, such actions would have been unimaginable, and if perpetrated, resulted in the harshest possible punishment, death. Violence and cruelty destroy the magic of life, and we are a people of magic. We will make your saddles as a sign of good faith and hope that when you rid your land of these animalistic men that there can be greater contact between our peoples. Long ago we helped each other, it would be nice to restore that relationship," said Mia solemnly.

The princess did not know how to respond. Neither apparently did her companions. But they all realized the compliment or opportunity that was being offered them and bowed to the elves in acknowledgement. That seemed to be a satisfactory response because the elves moved forward and started measuring the five humans. The elves brought forth sheets of leather and set to work making the saddles and the straps that would secure them to the dragons. The princess wasn't sure what was skill and what was magic, but the saddles sprang into being with astonishing speed. The elves then had each human settle him or herself into his or her saddle mounted on an overturned log to check and adjust the fit. Once the elves were satisfied with their work, they placed the saddles in a circle, and then had the humans and elves form a circle around that circle. The elves reached out their hands and indicated that they should all clasp hands, forming an unbroken circle around the saddles.

Mia spoke, "Great Goddess, giver of life and death and magic, bless these saddles, the work of our hands, that they may do your work: punish the inhumane, unite the many peoples of the earth and those who have moved to other dimensions, encourage love and compassion and empathy, foster stewardship of the earth and her creatures, encourage the appropriate use of magic. My Lady, through these instruments, give us a better future." She inclined her head in a gesture of reverence, and everyone followed suit.

The elves walked with the humans to the meadow, magicking the saddles before them. The princess voiced the anxiety of her human companions. "It doesn't start today, does it?" she asked in a shaky voice.

Mia smiled reassuringly, "No and yes. You do not battle today, but you train and ride," she said, enjoying the effect that her words had on the princess and her companions. Once at the meadow, the elves withdrew to the fringes, and the humans separated and sank into their individual thoughts about dragons.

The princess immediately connected to Dragon Isis, "I come, child," the dragon said in her mind, and she said back, "Thank you."

She glanced at the others who all seemed to be having silent conversations with the dragons they had managed to contact. She was pleased that they all seemed to have connected. Cassandra had spent time with Hestia desperately trying to teach the mid-wife enough of what she needed to know of sorcery, so that the old woman might be able to call a dragon, and it looked like all that effort had paid off.

Dragon Isis landed in a flutter of wings, and the princess greeted the dragon, stroking her face and neck. The dragon's green/purple scales were surprisingly cool to the touch. The dragon made a low noise in her throat, and the princess again heard the dragon's voice in her head. "Though we can breathe fire, we are cold blooded, and you humans are not. The warmth of your touch is very pleasing to us," the dragon explained.

A thundering of wings then nearly deafened the humans, as four dragons landed in the meadow. A silence descended mostly, as humans and dragons spoke to each other telepathically. Sometimes the conversations became spoken out loud, but most communication was not.

At a certain point, the elves moved in and picked up the saddles. They showed the humans how to strap them on their dragons, having the humans do it over and over, until they could do it blindfolded, because their lives would depend on doing it correctly. When the elves were satisfied and the humans were satisfactorily mounted on their dragons, the elves withdrew.

Maeve's dragon was Dragon Gaia, small with yellowish/orange scales, Anthony's was Dragon Horus who was the size of Dragon Isis but with black and midnight blue scales, Cassandra's was Dragon Arinna, also small with flaming scales of red and burgundy, and Hestia's was Dragon Brigid, more medium sized with green and blue scales. One by one, the dragons launched themselves into the air. Dragon Isis and the princess going first. It was like nothing else that the princess had ever imagined. She felt securely bound to her dragon through the saddle, but it was terrifying to be hurling through the sky and watching helplessly as the ground receded. Reading her terror, she heard her dragon in her mind.

"Easy, little sorceress, this was your idea, you know," and there was amusement and sympathy in the tone of the voice in her head.

"Yes, but I have never been higher than in the upper branches of a very tall tree," the princess answered back defensively.

"Master, your fear. The saddle holds you securely, and even if you fell, I would catch you. We could try that if you like? Perhaps it would boost your confidence."

The princess knew that the dragon was making fun of her playfully. But the thought of falling through the air from such a height made all the blood drain from her face and made her physically shudder in panic. "I am sorry, Maleficent," the voice said full of contrition. "Of course, this is new to you, and it is as natural to me as breathing. What would you like me to do?" the voice asked gently.

"Could we fly lower to the ground for a while? Just until I get used to it?" the princess asked.

"Yes, but I shall fly faster, so you can see the difference," and the dragon altered her course and suddenly they were dropping down, flying just above the tree line, and just when the princess was beginning to feel more comfortable, the dragon accelerated. The princess had not realized it was possible to go so fast; she pressed herself against the dragon to lessen the resistance. With time, the princess' comfort level increased, and they flew high again, and the dragon twisted in mid-air. The dragon had warned the princess about this move, and holding on firmly, the princess found herself laughing in delight. After hours in the air, the dragons and their riders landed. They would practice the following day, and then the next they would set off to find King John and his men. Before the dragons took their leave for the evening, Dragon Isis asked a question that the princess had not considered before.

"Princess, what if at some point during the battle, King John and his men surrender or ask for mercy?"

The princess felt all eyes, human and dragon, on her. She had not thought of this possibility. Some part of her wanted to be merciful; another part of her wanted vengeance. And there was something else—that she could not quite articulate. The conflict must have been clear on her face because Dragon Isis followed up her question with a suggestion.

"We do not need an answer at this moment. Go with your companions and consider the matter, but we must have the answer before we set off," she said, her tone indicating that she appreciated the conflict her question posed.

They parted, and the young people and the older women chatted excitedly about their encounters with their dragons, what they had learned, and how terrified they had been at first. They had not forgotten the question they needed to discuss but were waiting for an appropriate time to raise the difficult matter. Cassandra and Anthony foraged and checked their snares, bringing back berries and two rabbits to cook for dinner. Maeve had gotten fresh water, and Hestia was busy making tea and getting the spits ready. After they had eaten, they discussed showing mercy to King John's men. It was the noble thing they agreed. But King John had not been noble or merciful. He had been a deceitful, murdering, land snatcher. It was not enough that he was horrid to his own people. He wanted to seize control of Andelusia, but he did not go about it the honorable way, if war for conquest could ever be considered honorable. He had feigned friendship and alliance to murder the rulers of Andelusia and take the land.

He set an example that others might follow. Perhaps not in Andelusia defended by dragons now, but what about in Maidenport or other lands whether queendoms or with counsels of representative like the Commonwealth. And what would King John and King Edward think of Princess Maleficent's mercy? They would find it a weakness not a kindness. The added benefit of not showing mercy would be that the people of Conquest, lacking a royalty after the executions of King John and King Edward and their nobles might create a counsel of representatives or a queendom, making things safer for the region. It was a difficult decision to come to, but no mercy would be shown even if King John and his men surrendered—their crimes were too great and the example had to be set.

After an exhausting day, physically and emotionally, the human companions drifted off to sleep easily. They were surprised to awake the next morning to find the elves waiting for them. Mia stepped forward to speak for her people.

"Princess, when you engage your enemy, you should be recognizably Princess Maleficent of Andelusia," she said kindly.

The princess ran her hand though her butchered hair. "I don't think that is possible, My Lady," she answered quietly.

"Ah, but you forget with whom you are speaking," and she gestured to her companions. One elfin woman came forward holding a magnificent suit of clothing in the Andelusian colors of red and bronze. The jacket was like a male riding jacket but cut for a more feminine frame. There was a plain white linen shirt underneath and fitted bronze colored pants and boots and matching gloves. The elfin magic was such that the pants, boots, and gloves gleamed like actual polished metal. On the back of the jacket was a silhouette of a dragon in the same gleaming bronze. Additionally, there were weapons. A fine bronze colored belt would circle the waist of the jacket holding on one side a dagger and on the other a short sword—both of which had hilts shaped as dragons. Then there was an elfin bow and quiver. The bow was smaller and more compact that Hestia's long bows, and the princess suspected much more powerful. Both the bow and the quiver also sported a dragon. They were magnificent gifts. The princess was quite overwhelmed.

"We have sets for your companions too," Mia said gently, and at another gesture, other elves moved forward to show the others the beautiful clothes and weapons.

"My Lady, you are so generous. We have nothing to give," the princess began, but the elfin woman held up her hand.

"Giving is its own reward," she said kindly. "Rid your land of these beastly men and restore friendship between our peoples and that will be a great gift for us all."

The princess ran her hand through her hair again, and Mia said, "There is one thing more," and at the snap of her fingers, four tubs full of scented water appeared in the camp. Mia laughed at the startled looks on the princess and her companions.

"Bath time?" the princess asked incredulously.

"Humor me," Mia said with a sly smile on her lips.

The elfin man holding Anthony's set of clothes and weapons motioned him into the woods.

The princess, Maeve, Cassandra, and Hestia stripped out of their clothing and got into the tubs. The bath felt to the princess like the most heavenly thing she had ever experienced. The smells and the feel of the water were almost intoxicating. All her worry and anxiety washed away from her. She felt confident that they would route King John and restore peace and order back to Andelusia. Nothing would bring back her parents or the slaughtered, but she and her people would heal and love again. So delightful was the water that it took the princess a long while to realize as she toweled herself off afterward that she was also toweling off her long flowing hair. She looked up stunned to see her dawning realization echoed in the faces of Maeve, Cassandra, and Hestia.

Mia's sing-song laughter filled the camp. "I did tell you both that you needed to be recognizably you and that you had forgotten with whom you were dealing," she said with satisfaction.

"The princess, yes," Hestia began, but again, Mia held up her hand.

"The sorceress and one of the best mid-wives of Andelusia should be recognizable as well," she added. "The king and his men should know that you survived and are exacting justice. Men of your world need to be reminded of the power of women." She waved her hands, and the tubs disappeared. Elfin women helped to dress the human women and braid their hair, and when the princess and her friends were properly dressed, the elves took their leave, disappearing into the forest. Anthony strode back into camp in his new clothes, visibly cleaner but otherwise unchanged.

They had a quick breakfast and went to meet the dragons. Once the dragons were called and assembled, the princess explained their decision about showing no mercy to King John and his men. The dragons all listened carefully and nodded in agreement when the princess had finished. Dragon Horus marked a series of trees with great Xs with his claws, and then the humans mounted the dragons, and they flew and trained. The dragons encouraged their mounts to try to hit the Xs with their arrows. They were all surprisingly good at it, and the princess suspected that elfin magic more than human skill accounted for this. When they stopped at mid-day to rest and for the humans to eat, the humans began to search for their spent arrows only to find that their quivers were just as full as when they received them from the elves. In the afternoon, they trained more, and the dragons encouraged them to try throwing the daggers.

"But I only have the one," the princess protested when Dragon Isis urged her to throw it.

"Have you learned nothing from your encounter with elves, Maleficent, the young woman with her hacked off hair now reattached?" the dragon chided her.

The princess then understood and threw the dagger as hard as she could. It hit the center of one of Dragon Horus' Xs perfectly, and then after coming to another target, the princess found the dagger was back in its sheath, waiting to be thrown again, and she smiled. Before the humans and the dragons parted for the evening, Dragon Isis explained that the dragons would come to collect them in the morning and as they flew north, they would be joined by about twenty other dragons. She anticipated that the battle would be swift. The human men would not be able to offer much defense against the dragons.

They ate a light supper—the gravity of what would happen the next day suppressing their appetites. They might have slept restlessly, but Hestia had put a sleeping aid in their evening tea, so they were all well rested in the morning. They dressed quickly and were again surprised to find the elves at the edge of the camp waiting for them.

Mia strode forward followed by a few of her people, who carried baskets of food to break their fast. Elfin bread, fresh berries, and some cheese. Mia gave them packets of bread and dried berries for later in the day, wished them all well, and blessed them in the name of the Great Goddess. Then the elves withdrew again, and the humans hurried to the meadow to call their dragons.

The dragons came quickly. They were impatient to be mounted and away. Excitement wasn't the word, the princess thought. None of them, human or dragon, particularly wanted the coming battle, yet it was necessary, and the anticipation of engagement filled them with the desire to be immersed in it immediately. The waiting for it, tortuous.

Suddenly the open sky felt crowded as dragons soared up to fly with them. The princess had grown used to the variety among her and her friends' dragons, but that was nothing to the variety that she saw before her now. There were ones far larger than Dragon Horus and Dragon Isis, and ones much smaller than Maeve's or Cassandra's. They came in so many colors—but always with a luminescence to the scales that made them shimmer in a range of color, not just one flat color. As with her friends' dragons, she could not read these other dragons' thoughts, but she could hear them when they spoke in Dragon Isis' mind. They knew the plan; they were jumpy with anticipation too.

Though it had taken the princess and her friends two weeks to travel as far as they had gone, by dragon, they could see the spires of the royal castle after only about two hours' journey. An army of men were camped outside the castle. Through Dragon Isis's acute vision, the princess saw the confused men. They did not understand what they were looking at, watching the in-coming dragons. They shouted out an alarm. A nobleman came forward, but he didn't understand either. They were joined by King John and King Edward who looked equally bewildered.

"Those two," the princess said in the dragon's mind, "they are the king and his son."

"Ready, little sorceress?" the dragon asked in her mind. "I think it is time to reveal ourselves and see what these brutal men are made of." The largest of the dragons took off with a burst of speed, keeping high in the sky to try to disguise themselves until the last possible moment. They were aiming toward the back of the encampment—where the tents and soldiers were closest to the castle. Dragon Isis wanted the men separated from the castle (a means of escape). The five charging dragons would drive the panicked men into the fields into the path of the rest of the on-coming dragons. The charging dragons dove down at the castle wall and discharged waves of flame, lighting tents on fire and sending panicked men and screaming horses stampeding to get out of the way. The dragons, pleased with their work, roared so fiercely that the ground shook, causing even more panic from men and beasts. It was mayhem. Countless men were trampled by their fellows and left for dead.

The princess and her friends, all with their dragons, now charged the mass of men coming toward them with five other dragons. The rest of the dragons hung back to see if they were needed. As the princess had predicted, it wasn't much of a battle. The bursts of flame from the dragons alone cut down the men. Because they were closer to the men, the princess could see them clearly, and they could see her and her friends. She recognized some of the nobles, and when they recognized her, their faces were almost comical in their utter disbelief at seeing her, Princess Maleficent, defeating them on the back of a dragon. They screamed in pain as they burned. The slaughter was grisly and sad really. Dragon Isis read the princess' thoughts.

"It is hard to kill, princess, but I have seen what you showed me, and Dragon Gaia and Dragon Horus have shown me what Maeve and Anthony saw. These men are butchers; they have lost their humanity. You are right. They must be made an example. We are nearly done," her dragon added gently.

The princess tried to take comfort in Dragon Isis's words.

A man on horseback tried to break away from the group. "It is King Edward, princess. Ready your bow, and I will take you to face him," her dragon told her.

She notched an arrow in her bow and moved it around into position to shoot. Dragon Isis circled around the fleeing figure, so that they now faced each other, and she slowed down, allowing the man and horse to come closer. At first King Edward's face only showed fear and grief, but then he saw the princess, really saw her. He recognized the colors of her clothes as Andelusian and his face furrowed in confusion, but then he recognized her, and a wave of fury swept his face.

"Shoot," commanded the dragon.

The princess let the arrow fly, and it flew true and struck the king in the chest, killing him instantly, but in the moments before the arrow struck, his ugly mouth struggled to spit out a word, "Who…" was all he was able to get out before he was dead. Dragon Isis followed the princess's arrow with a burst of flame that consumed the would-be king.

The princess was rigid with indignation—that he, a rapist and a murderer, could attempt to call her a whore was unbelievable to her.

"Easy, princess. I have more to say on this matter, but we need to see if we are done first."

There was no movement in the field. Heaps of corpses smoldered. A few horses had ridden to safety. Otherwise it was a field of burned death. The mounted dragons landed, but the unmounted dragons did not. They circled the skies and roared with victory, and then after about a half an hour without incident, Dragon Isis released them, and they flew away.

"Princess," Dragon Isis said softly in her head. "Men of your world devalue women in many different ways. Somehow the religions you chose legitimatize this for them."

"Our religions?" the princess interrupted.

"Yes, your angry male sky gods." Dragon Isis realized that the princess still didn't understand. "Your Jehovah is angry, punishing, and unloving, and he makes sex dirty or shameful, particularly for women. Your Zeus is violent, sexually and otherwise, and punishing with his thunderbolt. For both religions, the easiest way to utterly devalue a woman is to equate her with a prostitute. It is a male way to devalue women. Don't give it another thought, or perhaps do. You might think about the Great Goddess as an alternative where love, life, and pleasure are celebrated in all their forms and violence is condemned and pain is avoided where possible. Do not make yourself sick about what the king tried to call you. He was a beast and deserved much worse than he got. You gave him a clean and relatively painless death.

That was merciful. I wanted you to have that because killing is hard, even justifiable killing, such as this. It damages the soul. You will suffer for having had to do this, but perhaps knowing that you could have been crueler, you will suffer less. Dismount, child, and we will find the others," she added.

People poured out of the castle. Those who had escaped the slaughter cried with joy to see their princess and the sorceress well and they stared with nervous wonder at the dragons. Farmers came forward to see the field, the dragons, and the princess. Anthony had shot King John. Cassandra and Maeve told the story of their flight and meeting up with dragons to all who would listen, and everyone seemed to want to hear the tale. All gathered outside the castle were invited in to share a feast to celebrate Andelusia's freedom from the savage Conquesters. Before going inside the castle, the princess and her friends said good-bye to their dragons, and it was agreed that the humans would call the dragons in the afternoon the following day to figure out what to do next.

In the castle, mercifully, many of the servants had hidden in the dungeons or remote rooms or hidden passages that the servants used to traverse the castle and most others did not know about. When they could, they took guests of the castle with them. The castle artisans had escaped relatively unscathed—their services being of value to the murderous king trying to take the castle but needing to function in it after his slaughter. King John and his men had looted the kitchens, but the cooks had still managed to hide away a decent amount of food. It wasn't exactly a feast, but it was a meal. The people ate, and they laughed and cried in equal measure. The people were all mixed together. Farmers were sitting with servants and castle artisans and nobles. The princess found herself at a table with Hestia and some farmers, Maeve, and another servant who knew Maeve. The princess resolved to keep this mixing. It seemed healthy, and a way to make sure that she was in touch with her people, all of them.

The princess refused to sleep in the room where she had been raped or the room in which her parents had been murdered, so she was brought to a tower suite of rooms, and she found that she liked them immensely. There was a library/study, small sitting room, a bedroom, and large balcony that she thought could stand the weight of a dragon, perhaps even several dragons, and it was high up—taller than the tallest tree she had ever been in—so it reminded her of her beloved Dragon Isis and their adventures.

The servants had moved some of her clothes to the new rooms. She stripped out of her clothes, washed herself, put on a clean night gown, and crawled in a soft bed with clean sheets—and she felt like a princess. Of course, she was a princess, but it had been so long since she had had such comforts that they seemed unbelievable luxuries to her. Her mind wandered to the luxuries that her people experienced; all of them they should have access to some, and as she drifted into sleep, she wondered how she might make sure that all her people enjoyed some luxury in their lives—surely that would be the mark of a great queen.

She fell asleep to happy images of farmers with paintings or silver tankards or a fine waistcoat, and then her dreams shifted, and she smelled burning human flesh and she watched King Edward die by her hand. She cried out, and Maeve was there, her handmaiden once, but now her friend and her fellow warrior.

"I had nightmares too, so I came to see if you were alright," Maeve said by way of explanation.

"Would you … would you … sleep with me?" the princess asked.

"Of course, my princess. Whatever you desire," Maeve answered immediately, falling back into servant mode.

"Maeve, you are not my servant anymore. You are my friend and my battle compatriot. You can refuse my request," the princess tried to explain.

Maeve made an impatient clicking sound and climbed in bed with the princess, "I had nightmares too. If you didn't want me to sleep with you, I was going to look for my brother."

Knowing that the person who slept next to her understood her pain and trauma, the two young women fell asleep, and though images imposed themselves on them, the caress of a friend, allowed each to fall back asleep.

The next morning after breakfast, the princess tried to explain to her people that the people of Andelusia might unite with the magical world and have permanent contact with magical folk and beasts, citing the dragons and the elves. Some were incredulous. In a clean field near the castle, the princess had a great tent set up, one that might even accommodate five dragons as well as other guests. In the afternoon, the princess and her friends went and stood beyond the great tent and called their dragons. The dragons appeared as promised but with other riders. Dragon Isis carried the Elfin queen, Boann. Dragon Brigid carried Mia. Dragon Arinna carried Tatania, the tiny fairy queen, and Dragon Horus carried a fairy knight, Puck, and Dragon Gaia came alone, but she carried all the supplies from the camp that the princess and her friends had abandoned in their return to Andelusia.

Greetings were exchanged, and they moved to the tent that had been especially prepared for them. A low side board had been stocked with glasses, plates, pitchers full of water, fruit juice, a range of wines and ciders, baskets of bread, bowls of fruit, and plates of cheese. When each had what she or he desired, they ate amicably, and when they were done, they began discussing what they wanted. Earthly vegetables, herbs, and flowers were more desirable to elves and fairies than those in other dimensions, and they wanted to come back—if they were not hunted and spied on. The dragons wanted to access to the big game, the elks and the bison, the herd animals, the occasional elephant or rhino, and whales. So long as these animals were not hunted to extinction, the princess saw no objection. The elves wanted to be able to sell their wares, the magnificent weapons and jewelry that only their crafts people could make. None of the nobles who had been such valuable counselors to the queen and king had survived the slaughter, save Cassandra. In the vacuum, the princess had invited Hestia, Maeve, and Anthony to advise her. All of the terms were pleasing both to the princess and to her people, so the treaties were made and signed.

Then there was a more informal council. Dragon Isis began this. "You have taken care of your people's interests, young princess, but what do you wish more than anything?" she asked.

The princess thought quietly about this request before saying, "Dragon Isis has made it clear to me that my own culture encourages rape of girls and women and violence against them, and I wish that no girl or woman, or boy or man, for that matter, has a sexual encounter like I had."

Dragon Isis paused for a moment, "You understand that your culture creates predatory males and female vulnerability (through female desire to please others and the ideal of female sexual passivity) because of its adherence to violent sky gods?"

The princess hesitated a moment, "Yes ... but how do we change that?" She had explained her conversations on this topic with Dragon Isis to her friends when they had been alone.

Hestia spoke softly, "We could revive the ancient religion of the Great Goddess, but we would need help," she added, glancing nervously at Cassandra and looking at the tiny fairy queen and the elfin queen.

Both queens smiled and inclined their heads in assent, Queen Tatania's voice, sounding like the most delicate of ringing bells, answered Hestia's request. "It would be our pleasure. The fairy rites are slightly different than the elfin rites, but we can explain the different rites, ceremonies, festivals, traditions of each of our peoples, and you can choose those that best suit you and doubtless create some of your own."

"Yes, we can send you some of our priestesses, and the adoption of the Great Goddess will help, but it will take time, and there will be some resistance," Queen Boann added in her musical voice. "Will you make the Great Goddess Andelusia's official religion?" she asked carefully, her emerald eyes flashing with interest.

"No," the princess answered carefully, suddenly aware that her answer was very important. "Force is not the way of the Goddess, is it? It may be my religion and the religion I encourage, but the people will be able to choose. Forcing a religion on my people would only create more resistance."

Both queens inclined their heads in approval, and the princess felt a wave of relief. In her head, Dragon Isis said, "Well done, little princess." Out loud, she said, "It still does not take care of the immediate problem of eliminating rape or sexual violence, and for that, I think that between dragon hatchlings and fairy knights, we may have something to offer," and the princess saw that the fairy queen and her knight grinned at Dragon Isis's words.

"But it is more than rape and sexual violence," Cassandra said suddenly. "There is the problem of sexual coercion. When a girl or woman says no by gesture or word, she is too often ignored. People have to accept that no means no the first time and limit their behaviors to what is acceptable to both partners."

"Point well made, Sorceress," Dragon Isis said solemnly.

Between Dragon Isis and the fairy knight, they explained that older dragon hatchlings and the some of the fairy knights could be trained to sense sexual predators and could intervene. Their magic would allow them to sense a sexual predator. The princess could only imagine the surprise with which a young man might find himself interrupted from his sexual conquest by a small, talking, fire-breathing dragon with deadly claws or the sword and words of a fairy knight. The princess consented to the plan, and after helping themselves to more food and drink, the different parties took their leave of each other, agreeing to meet in a week's time. The princess and her friends watched the dragons fly off with their small riders until they could see them no longer.

Shortly thereafter, the lustful, young farmer, Tom, had successfully lured his neighbor, Katarina, into a hay loft and was kissing her aggressively. He kept putting his hand on her waist beneath her shirt and kept trying to move his hand up to her breasts. She kept pushing his hands away. After the third time, she broke the kiss and said, "Please, Tom, stop." He was about to ignore her yet again when he felt a blade at his throat. Startled, he pulled away from Katarina, and they both stared at the female fairy, fury radiating off her, who held a sword at Tom's throat.

"The lady said 'no,' you wretched beast. She said it in gesture three times and once in words. How stupid are you?" the fairy demanded.

"But ... it is always like this. Young women resist, and young men push them," Tom sputtered. "I have needs."

The fairy pushed her sword against Tom's throat harder, and he felt the blade pierce his skin, and a few drops of blood drip down his neck.

"Not anymore," she answered, his lame excuses only making her angrier. "From now on, when she or any girl or woman says no (by gesture or word), you will respect that or I will find you, and I assure you that if I am compelled to visit you again, Tom, you will not find my blade at your throat but at another part of your anatomy. Perhaps with its loss or alteration, your needs will not make you act like such an animal." Tom whimpered at the thought. "You should also know, both of you, that though she may say no and mean it, she may also say yes and mean it. Be a good boy, Tom, and wait for the yes." The fairy looked at Katarina. "Are you all right?" she asked, her voice gentler.

Katarina hesitated. She wasn't sure what to say. She had a fairy godmother, it seemed. "Yes, thank you, My Lady," she replied softly, respectfully.

"Call me Crystal. Think of me if you have need of me again, now that we have met, I will be able to sense you. Do you wish to remain with this thug?" the fairy asked her.

"So long as he does not behave thuggishly," she answered slyly.

Crystal smiled at the young woman's response. "What say you, Tom?" she said easing up on her blade. "Are you done with your thuggishness?"

Tom nodded carefully, and the fairy withdrew her sword. "Tell your friends, both of you, no means no and yes means yes." She threw something in the air, and she disappeared in a shimmer.

In a fine manor house, Lord Phillip had given the beautiful Lady Aurora a drink laced with sleeping potion and planned to have his wicked way with her after she passed out. He was watching her carefully, and as she began to feel the effects of the drug, he steered her to a bedroom and locked them both inside. He helped her stagger to the bed, and then he straddled her and started to take off her clothing. She tried to push his hands away from her clothes. She tried to tell him to get off, but she was falling unconscious. He reached for her bodice again, and he felt claws at his throat and on his back. Something had landed on his back.

Hot breath warmed his ear uncomfortably, and an angry voice spoke to him, "You foul, evil, little man. If you ever do this to a girl or woman again, I will hunt you down and eat the precious part of your anatomy that you think entitles you to such behavior." Phillip winced. "Further," the voice continued, "you must respect the sentient refusal or consent of a girl or a woman to any and all sexual activity. Failure to do so will reward you with another visit from me, and my claws may not be as sharp as my teeth, but they are plenty sharp," and Phillip felt the claws at his throat and on his back tighten and break the skin.

"Please," Phillip begged. He felt himself jerked from Aurora's body, and he was suddenly standing on the floor, the claws still digging into his throat and back uncomfortably.

"Are you quite reformed now, little rapist?" the voiced asked, dripping with indignation and contempt.

"Yes, I swear." Phillip felt the claws release him, and he turned, staring in disbelief. A small dragon, the size of a large dog, was hanging in the air before him, its large wings flapping, holding it aloft. The sun streaming from the open window made its scales dance in bright yellows and oranges.

"Go, reformed rapist, and tell your friends," the dragon ordered, and to compound his threat, the dragon released a small burst of flame, which had Phillip scrambling with the lock and out the door.

The dragon chortled at Phillip's retreating figure and settled himself on the bed to wait for Aurora, a sleeping beauty, to wake so he could tell her what happened and advise her to always get her own drinks in the future.

In a small school, Teacher Sam had kept young Harry after school with the excuse of tutoring the boy in math, and Teacher Sam had tutored Harry for a while. Then he began pressuring Harry. He put his hand on the boy's thigh. He saw Harry's discomfort and alarm, but the school was abandoned. Even if Harry screamed, no one would hear, but they rarely screamed. They plead to be left alone. Occasionally, they cried. That was very off putting. He hated when they cried.

"Please, don't," Harry whispered, trying to push Sam's hand away.

"You owe me," Sam said leaning over and kissing Harry's cheek. Just has he was about to move his hand to grope the boy's genitals, he felt a blade at his throat. He jerked back, but the blade remained at his throat. He saw with astonishment that a fairy held his sword to Sam's throat. The tiny fairy radiated righteous outrage that made Sam flush with shame.

"You monstrous, disgusting, horrid, predator," spat the fairy. "I am not sure a warning is all I should give you. You do realize how criminal your behavior is, don't you? First, you are an adult attempting to have sexual relations with a child, which is rape whether the child consents to it or not. But the child is not consenting to it; the child is resisting, and you add physical rape to statutory rape. Next, you are a teacher, an authority figure over the child, which constitutes another form of statutory rape. Lastly, as a teacher, you are a trusted figure who has emotional sway over the child, your abuse of that trust, your manipulation of that trust, is another form of statutory rape. So you are attempting to rape this child on four different levels. If it were up to me, I would castrate you on the spot," and the fairy pressed the blade into Sam's throat further.

Sam shuddered at the thought and whimpered a lame, "Mercy?"

The fairy turned to the child, his expression gentling immediately. "Harry, are you all right?" he asked.

Harry started to nod, but then he really wasn't sure. The fairy was watching him intently. Harry wasn't sure he could speak. He was upset, very upset, he realized. The fairy held out his other hand to him.

"Touch my hand, Harry," the fairy ordered. Harry touched the fairy's outstretched hand, and a calming sensation flowed through the boy.

"Thank you," Harry whispered. He didn't want to talk. He just wanted to be home.

As if reading his thoughts, the fairy said, "Go home, Harry, straight home, and tell your parents. Tell them everything. I will tell your princess, and they will figure out what to do with this disgusting filth," and the fairy again pressed his sword into Sam's throat, this time breaking the skin.

The fairy waited until the boy was out of sight and then he withdrew his blade. Sam clutched at his throat and started to speak, to try to make some excuse. But this only angered the fairy, who was suddenly brandishing his sword in Sam's direction again.

"Don't even think about trying to make some excuse. There is none. Nothing justifies your behavior. You will pack your things up. You will never teach children again. Go home and wait to see what your princess will have done to you. Try to run, and I will find you."

Sam quavered at the threat. The fairy sheathed his sword, and throwing something up in the air, he disappeared in a shimmer of light.

And all over Andelusia, individuals seeking to coerce or force sexual relations from unconscious or unwilling victims were interrupted by hatchling dragons or fairy knights, and girls and women and boys and men were talking and thinking very seriously about what was consensual sexual contact and what was not.

Over the next few weeks, the princess was crowned queen, the fairy and elfin priestesses shared their knowledge about Goddess worship, and Maeve worked at becoming a human priestess of the Goddess. Female Andelusians were quick converts to the new religion and some male Andelusians found welcome freedom in a religion that allowed them a far more diverse set of roles than the masculinity of the other religions. It would be interesting how many more men and boys converted as it became more established. Fairy men and elfin men could imagine no other religion for themselves, so there was hope for Andelusian males. Dragons were seen flying the skies of Andelusia, fairies gathered herbs and flowers and fruits from the wild places or traded magic services for such things from farmers. Elfin crafts people sold their wares in Andelusian markets, and the Conquesters adopted a counsel of representatives. The queendom flourished, and emissaries from different lands came to observe the new Andelusian way and the peace and equality it fostered.

In a rare moment, when Queen Maleficent and Dragon Isis were able to fly through the skies together, the queen was thinking about how her life had been transformed by the power of a dragon. She was so profoundly grateful. The Andelusian symbol was now a dragon. The queen had even considered having her skin marked with a dragon image.

"You don't need an image, my little queen. You have me, but perhaps, someday in the future, a girl marked with a dragon tattoo may be a champion for girls and women who have been victimized by evil men," and she chortled at the thought.

The Twelfth Princess

Once upon a time, in a kingdom far, far away, there lived a king, King Richard, his queen, Queen Elizabeth, and his twelve daughters, the princesses, Catherine, Jessica, Rose, Constance, Beth, Lauren, Leila, Maeve, Alexis, Mary Ann, Joan, and Sophie.

Sophie was the youngest, the twelfth princess. She was petite compared to most of her sisters. She had auburn hair that curled at the ends, and she had pale blue eyes like her father's. All of the girls were beautiful, seeming to have inherited the best qualities of their mother and father, but Sophie was startlingly beautiful. She was also willful, the most stubborn of the twelve girls, to her mother's embarrassment and her father's chagrin. Fortunately, she was so sweet and kind that her stubbornness was often overlooked.

When the girls were little, they had a nurse-maid who took care of them, Medea. Medea told them all the traditional stories, "Cinderella," "Sleeping Beauty," "Little Red Riding Hood," and "Snow White." But Sophie begged for a different story, a story where the girl was more active and took her life into her own hands, a story where she saved her own life and maybe that of her love's too.

Medea was uncomfortable with this, but when all the girls pleaded her for such a story, she admitted to hearing a story or two when she was a little girl, a story of the old world. In the old world, she told them, men and women were equal partners; they worked together inside and outside the home, they cared for children together, they had sex together for mutual pleasure; one did not have power over the other. The story ignited Sophie's imagination, and it saddened her to watch her sisters dismiss the story as fantasy, but they did. When Sophie was alone with Medea, she got the old woman to tell her other stories about the old world.

As the years passed, Sophie watched her sisters marry. King Richard negotiated the terms with the kings of different kingdoms, and Sophie watched her mother and the other queens look on stoically at the matches of her sisters to princes like they were the least worst-case scenarios possible.

Though the kingdoms celebrated these great unions, there was something about them that was disturbing to Sophie. The queens seemed both happy and sad and so did her sisters. At Alexis' wedding, Sophie found Medea who had been in her cups too much, and Sophie asked her why her sister was sad.

"Because, women are slaves in our culture, Sophie. Pretty, dressed-up slaves, but slaves nonetheless," Medea answered bluntly.

"What do you mean?" the girl asked, alarmed by the description.

"As wife, you will be your husband's servant. Your property becomes his. Your labor is his to command as is your body. You will clean, cook, and care for him. You will warm his bed, have sex with him, and bear his children. You will then need to take care of his children and clean, cook, and tend for them, too. He will give you no credit for the work that you do, as wife and mother; he will feel he is owed your services. If you are lucky, he will not mistreat you. If you are not so lucky, there is nothing that you can do. Slave. A well-dressed slave, but slave nevertheless."

"What about in the stories?" Sophie demanded.

"Stories?" Medea asked right back at her.

"Like Cinderella? She finds the prince and lives happily ever after, right?"

Medea scoffed at the idea. "She just traded one kind of servitude for another, evil step-mother for tyrant husband. Notice the story ends before you find out what Cinderella's life was like under her new master," Medea added bitterly.

Sophie's mind reeled; was it all so awful? Was marriage for a woman in her culture a legal slavery? Was there anything else? Once upon a forgotten time, yes, there was or seemed to be something else. "And in the older world?" Sophie asked.

"Hush," hissed Medea, her voiced hushed and trembling. Medea looked nervously around them, but there was no one near them. Sophie had been careful to catch the old woman alone. Medea took a deep breath and steadied herself. She looked at the princess and said in a barely audible voice, "Princess Sophie. I ... I shouldn't have told you about that time... your parents ... they wouldn't want you ... to think about an alternative." Recovering herself, she continued more firmly, "Women marry. Your father will find someone nice for you." She smiled reassuringly and waved vaguely in the direction of the thrones.

But Sophie would not be put off, "Walk with me in the garden," she commanded, surprising both herself and her nurse-maid with the authority in her voice. She walked to the back of the hall with Medea following behind her. Quickly they navigated the passages, and Sophie brought them out into her mother's rose garden. Even in the gathering dusk, they were surrounded with the intoxicating scent of the flowers. Sophie took Medea's arm, linked their elbows together, and started them walking down one of the paths. "Tell me, Medea, please," Sophie begged.

"I don't know anything beyond the bits of story I have already told you." She paused, "You cannot mention what I have told you to anyone, Princess. Promise me. I fear for you, child. You are too willful. You are unlike your sisters. You remember and believe the old tales—and it is dangerous for you to do so," Medea whispered urgently.

The tales implied such a different system of order between men and women and between parents and children that Sophie imagined these people had a different relationship even with the divine. Medea had never said anything about their religion, but she knew that Medea's grandmother had told her other things. "How did they worship in the old world? Where? What was sacred to them?" The questions exploded in a rush.

Medea stopped dead in the path and gaped at her. "Why do you want to know? Why would you think I know anything about that?" she said wide-eyed, the surprise of the questions still showing on her face.

"I am just curious, Medea; please tell me if you can," Sophie said sweetly, patting Medea's arm gently.

"Curiosity killed the cat," Medea answered dryly. "You will not just get yourself in trouble; you'll get me in trouble too," she said accusingly.

"No one is going to get in trouble. I don't intend to ever tell anyone, but you don't want the knowledge to die with you. I know you. I have seen the pleasure you took in telling the stories and your disappointment that my sisters were not interested. It scares and pleases you that I know and believe. I won't be stupid, but please tell me what you know," and Sophie gathered the old nurse-maid's hands in her own and kissed them.

"Lord, help me," Medea said and crossed herself. "I don't understand it all. I am not sure how it is possible, but it would have been interesting to see," she said softly. Sophie had been right; Medea wanted to share this information. "They also had a trinity but the opposite way—not the triangle with the pinnacle at the top—but with the point at the bottom; the points of the trinity stand for the maid, the crone, and the mother. Human beings were the much beloved children of this holy trinity of women and their consorts instead of the errant and punishable children of the angry Father of Heaven. They followed the phases of the moon (the new moon, the quarter-moon, the half-moon, the three-quarter moon, and the full moon). The ever-renewing cycle of life was sacred to them—so animals or insects associated with renewal and rebirth were holy (butterflies, frogs, snakes, bears—creatures that transform, hibernate, or are born a new). Caves were important for some ceremonies and rituals. Being enclosed in the earth and then re-emerging could be a symbolic rebirth. Sex was sacred as part of the holy cycle of life instead of something shameful or dirty. Love and pleasure were the bonds between human beings, not status and power. Women and men chose each other for as long as attraction or lust lasted, so relationships could be casual and fleeting or intense and exclusive. Some relationships lasted a long time, but others did not."

Sophie struggled to process the onslaught of information. The mention of sex so bluntly made her flushed with embarrassment. "They didn't marry?" she managed to blurt out.

Medea thought for a moment. "I guess they could, but many of them didn't."

Sophie thought about this, if women could choose to have multiple partners, then, "The women didn't need to be virgins?" she asked softly.

"No, they didn't. Sex was supposed to be fun, pleasurable for both the woman and the man. Can you imagine?" she said, the old woman giggling a little at the scandalous thought.

Sophie shook her head a little. If sex was part of the cycle of life and for pleasure and fun—it was as natural as eating. If desire for sex was natural, then all the shame she was made to feel about her body was absent for these people. Her bleeding once a month wasn't dirty, it was natural. Her vagina wasn't a curse but a sacrament; V—the trinity inverted—sex was sacred. It all fit. If love and pleasure were the highest goals for these people, no wonder women and men were equal; they were partners in everything. Sophie had a sudden and powerful longing for that lost time and a young man who would want to be partnered with her. A new thought occurred to her, "But what about families—about children? Men want to marry virgins to be sure their children are their children. How would it work if children were only known to be the child of the mother?" Sophie asked.

"Children were sacred to them—gifts from the goddesses—they were everyone's children. The children were everyone's responsibility. I am not sure how that worked. All I have ever known is this—clans and families who only protect their own and compete against each other for power and status. Somehow these other people loved each other and shared everything. They were inclusive instead of exclusive. The common good was most important to them—all children were equal—instead of some privileged and some paupers," Medea said wistfully.

Sophie was suddenly acutely aware that she was royalty and Medea, a servant; she was privileged, and Medea a pauper. She flushed with shame. It was too much. She shook her head again. Lost in her thoughts, she realized that Medea was telling her other things and was drifting off into one of the stories. Sophie guided them back to the palace.

Back in the great hall, she looked around her, and she let her gaze drift from couple to couple—watching them, assessing their body language, trying to imagine from how they sat together what they were like intimately. Her parents were companionable, familiar. They sat together closely, his hand on her arm. Possessive almost. Long years together and twelve children, but there didn't seem to be passion and fire. Perhaps once. Sophie sighed. She didn't even know what she wanted. True love might be nice, but it could be dangerous too—to feel so much for someone—to love beyond reason. Maybe being friends was the best thing. Avoiding a brute was essential.

Her eyes scanned over her sisters. Jessica and her husband, Scott, did not touch, and there was a cold, formal feel for the way they regarded each other. Sophie's heart ached for her sister. Catherine and her husband, Jeffrey, sat together closely, and Sophie realized they held hands in the folds of Cathy's skirts. She smiled. She found various states of companionship or tolerance from the postures of her sisters, and then her eyes found Leila who shrank away from her husband, Thomas. Sophie remembered that she had never liked him when he visited. He had always seemed to be acting too hard—that wasn't right—it had seemed to cost him enormous effort to act kindly toward not just Leila, but to all of them. It struck her now as she watched him engaged in animated conversation with another man, that Thomas didn't like women because he thought them beneath him—his wife, his mother, his female children—they were means to an end, bothersome possessions that occasioned his being, and the means for his line to continue. The only people he regarded has his equals were other men. Sophie shuddered and felt a horrible sadness for her sister.

She looked at other couples, Alexis and her husband, Mark, seemed genuinely enchanted with each other. They sat together closely; they held hands, and he whispered to her at moments, slyly brushing his lips against her ear in gentle kisses that caused the color to flush in her sister's checks and neck. They seemed promising, Sophie thought, and yet, men could be tender one moment and horrid the next—because they could. In the old world, clearly they couldn't—because they would be alone—no woman would choose to be with such a man if she had a choice, and there in that world women could choose.

A thought struck her that made her suck in her breath. What if the old world had not disappeared? Medea had mentioned the caves. What if old worlders had found another place when the ancestors of her people came and claimed the land? What if there was a passage between this world and the old world through the caves? Her skin rippled with goose-bumps. Somehow she knew this was true. There was a way through, and she realized that she wanted nothing more than to go through to the old world. She wanted … what did she want … she wanted to be wanted, to be desired, and to be respected and loved with the same intensity that she would want and love another human being. She withdrew into her own thoughts, and when it was reasonable, she retired to her room. Sleep came slowly—and her dreams slipped from weird visions of horrid relationships and wonderful ones. The images blurred, but one lingered—a young man with piercing gray eyes, black curly hair, bronze skin, and a muscular frame—and he touched her with such reverence and tenderness that she wanted to weep with joy. A dream, she knew, and yet she clung to it. In the days and weeks that passed, the dream reoccurred, and its power and pull stayed with her.

She was allowed to ride accompanied by her groom. She searched the countryside for caves. Systematically she sought them out, and she found cave after cave. None seemed very interesting. She felt that she would know—that there would be a sign. Her groom bore her searches as best he could. He plainly thought she was ridiculous—a mindless woman poking her head into caves looking for God knew what.

One day, when she had nearly given up hope, she walked the grounds of the palace instead of riding. There was a small wood to the south, and she followed a deer trail into its depths. She was startled when the path shifted and climbed. She heard a stream before she reached it. She stopped and drank from her cupped hands and splashed water lightly on her face and neck. She scanned the other side of the stream and saw the hills covered with foliage from the trees, bushes, and ground cover, lush with greens and browns. The darkish brown/gray spot caught her attention by its contrast, and she walked toward it. Sophie felt the hairs on the back of her neck prickle as soon as she walked into the cave. There was something about this one. She fashioned a crude torch, lit it, and moved it so it illuminated the walls of the cave. Nothing, nothing, nothing. And then inverted triangles and butterflies and snakes, V and Vs in patterns, a trinity of Vs on the wall by a small pool of water at the back of the cave. This had to be the place. Full of excitement, she went back to the palace and waited for the full moon.

When it came, she waited for everyone to fall asleep, and then she stole out of the palace and made her way to the special cave. She had taken care to mark the way with specific stones that would shine in muted light. Her lantern shone only through the front pane—she hoped attracting the least amount of attention, especially with her body blocking the faint light moving away from the palace.

It seemed to take forever, the trail, the stream, the uneven way to the cave. Her heart pounded so hard when she entered the cave that it seemed to echo off the walls. Once inside the cave, she opened the darkened panes of the lantern and moved to the markings on the wall. Nothing happened, so she traced her fingers over the marks. She could feel a tingling as her fingers touched the marks in the stone. It was strongest on the trinity of Vs on the wall by the pool. There was a sudden whoosh—an unexpected gust of wind—and everything went dark. The open lantern was extinguished, and Sophie felt panic. She was alone in the dark in an unfamiliar cave. But it wasn't absolutely dark, she realized. A streak of moonlight shown through a slit in the cave wall—the source of the wind. The moonlight shone on a trinity of Vs on the floor of the cave by the pool that she hadn't noticed before. Sophie moved into the center of the trinity, and she felt the pull. She couldn't describe it, but she knew there was a place to cross to, she knew she could cross, and somehow she knew what to do. She took off her shoes and striped down to her shift. Ideally, she should go naked into the pool, but she wasn't that bold, so she wore it as she waded into the pool. The water was surprisingly warm and comforting; she swam toward the center, and at some point she felt completely disoriented.

The pool in the cave had been small, but the body of water she was swimming in now was large. She couldn't feel the bottom. She felt a surge of fear, but she realized that she had crossed somehow. She was somewhere else. That knowledge calmed her, and she continued swimming. She could smell the grasses and flowers before she felt the bank beneath her feet. She climbed out of the water and found herself on the shore of a large lake. She turned around and was surprised to find a young woman apparently waiting for her. The young woman held out a cloak for her, which Sophie gratefully accepted and wrapped about her.

"Welcome," the young woman said softly, smiling as she said it. "I am Tara. I was hoping you would come tonight." Tara was about her own age, eighteen or so, but she was different than any girl Sophie had ever seen. She was dark, dark haired, dark skinned, and dark eyed. Her black hair, she wore in many thin braids that hung loose and unbound around her shoulders and back. Her skin was a warm brown color like walnut wood, and her eyes appeared black in the moonlight. She was robed in a white gown tied around her body with red cord.

Sophie stared at Tara, trying to take her in, "You were … waiting for … me? Why?" She felt a shudder run through her. How could they know? She pulled the cloak around her more closely.

"The Greatmother read the signs," Tara said quietly, glancing absently at the moon and the lake. "Come, you should eat. There are few people to meet tonight and then you should rest. Tomorrow will be a busy day," she added. Tara led the way. Sophie was startled to see they were on a path. It led to a large sprawling stone building. Lights sparkled through the windows.

Voices could be heard toward their right. The path split, and Tara purposefully led Sophie away from the voices.

They entered a building, and Sophie was surprised to see a beautiful balcony overlooking sprawling gardens. The lush gardens so distracted her that she didn't see the small group of people waiting until a woman's voice called out to her. "Greetings, Changeling," the soft musical voice said. Sophie realized that she hadn't told Tara her name; she flushed with embarrassment.

"I … am … Sophie," she said haltingly.

"I am Gaia, the Greatmother here. This is my consort, Pan, the Greatfather" and she motioned to the man standing beside her. Gaia was a petite, older woman. Her hair was red, its vibrancy toned down by streaks of gray and white. Her eyes were a mossy green. Pan, beside her, was about her age, his black hair grayed similarly with silver and gray, his eyes a cat-like golden color, his skin a rich golden color, darker than Gaia's and her own but not so dark as Tara's; he bowed his head in acknowledgement.

"Welcome," he said, his voice, rich and gentle. "May I present Winter, our Grandmother, and Hunter, our Grandfather, and you have met Tara, our Goodmother, but this is Max, our Goodfather," he said, inclining his head toward the others in turn. They nodded to her in acknowledgement, their eyes sparkling with warmth and curiosity. Their faces lit up with smiles of welcome, and Sophie felt a deep joy of acceptance and welcome. They led her into a small room with several tables. One was set with glasses and plates and food and wine. They dished out portions and talked quietly. Sophie realized that, with effort, her hosts were restraining themselves from the questions they had; she was grateful and suddenly so tired that her eyes fluttered.

Gaia saw and got up, "Come, child. You are exhausted. I will show you to your chamber, and we can talk in the morning."

Gaia held out her hand, and Sophie took it and let herself be led away, murmuring good-nights and receiving them back as she went. Gaia stopped at a door and opened it; inside was a small but inviting chamber. The bed looked comfortable; a candle was burning on a small table by the bed. There was a small washstand with a pitcher and basin next to a wardrobe opposite the bed. Gaia gestured toward the wardrobe, "There are clothes in there that might fit, Sophie," she said gently. Sophie looked up to see Gaia staring at her closely, and she flushed in response. Gaia continued softly, "You will meet the others tomorrow. You will stay with us awhile, and you are welcome here, but you must decide your own path. You can choose to stay with us, or if you should wish to go back, we can help you." The green eyes looked with a scrutiny that made Sophie uncomfortable. She looked away and nodded mutely and felt firm but gentle hands grasp hers. Sophie looked up, and the green eyes had softened, Gaia's hands squeezed gently and then released hers. "Sleep well, child," Gaia said quietly and withdrew from the room.

Sophie murmured a thank you but was relieved to be alone. She took off the cloak and hung it on the peg on the door. She looked through the wardrobe and found a clean shift to wear. She used a small cloth to sponge herself down with the water she poured into the basin, and she washed her feet off from the lingering dust and mud from the lakeshore and the path. She put on the shift and climbed into the bed. She was asleep before she could even think about it.

She was dreaming of green fields and flowers. Butterflies flitted from bloom to bloom. She felt a deep contentment. She turned, and a red-haired woman embraced her and presented her to a hall full of people. Images blurred after that until a young man with curly ebony-colored hair and startling gray eyes held out his hand to her, and she took his hand and smiled at him, and they walked away together into the open fields, into the light which brightened slowly at first but then blazed so intensely that she couldn't see. She felt panic and didn't know why until she realized that she couldn't see him. He was gone, and she felt bereft. She gasped, and she heard herself. She opened her eyes and found herself in pool of bright sunlight. She shook her head, trying to clear it, but gray eyes persisted in her mind's eye. There was a knock at the door, distracting her. "Come in," she called, hastily getting herself out of bed. Tara strode into the room holding a white gown, blue cords, and a pair of blue slippers.

Tara asked how she had slept and set about helping Sophie groom and dress. She brushed Sophie's hair and arranged it gracefully around her shoulders. Sophie put on the gown, and Tara set about tying the cords around her body, so that the seemingly shapeless gown clung to her body, blue cord wrapped under her breasts, pressing them up where they were slightly exposed by the low bustlines of her shift and the gown, and then crisscrossing between them, accentuating them further. More cord wrapped around her waist and hips. Tara stopped and looked at her handy work, clicking her tongue approvingly. Sophie realized that the gown corded around her was much like what she would have worn at home, except that it was more comfortable for the lack of corset, and it was shorter, exposing her calves. It also occurred to her that she had never been in public with her hair down before; it wasn't allowed. Women's hair down and loose was sexual—but not here, because here women could be just as sexual as men. It was fascinating—the smallest things had such surprising repercussions. Tara pulled Sophie out of her thoughts and took her arm and led her through the corridors. As they walked, Sophie began to appreciate the freedom of movement that her new clothes afforded her. She could really breathe, and the shorter skirt and comfortable slippers gave her legs a freedom of movement that her longer skirts did not. She laughed to herself, as she realized that she could probably run in this gown. Tara looked at her questioningly, and she answered that the gown was comfortable, very comfortable.

She also liked the luxurious feel of her hair brushing her shoulders and her back as she walked.

They turned a last corner, and Sophie found herself at the back of a large hall full of people seated at tables, eating, drinking, and talking. As they stepped into the hall, the conversations died, and a painful silence was broken by a buzz of whispers. Sophie felt like every eye in the place was trained on her, and she froze in sudden self-consciousness. Tara tugged on her arm, and whispered to her, "Relax, Sophie. They are just curious. You will be presented to them later. Eat something, and then we need to meet with the Greats and the Grands and Max." Sophie's appetite had died, but she let herself be led by Tara. She accepted a steaming mug of sweet smelling tea and an apple tart bathed in honey. Tara led her to a table where Max greeted her warmly, and then turned and engaged Tara in conversation. Sophie felt the eyes upon her, but the mundane conversation between Tara and Max made her feel at ease, and her appetite returned enough for her to sip the tea and feel it warm inside her. Half way through the tea, she was hungry enough to taste the tart. It was delicious, and she had eaten the whole thing before she realized it.

When they had all eaten, Tara and Max took her to the Greats and the Grands. They all questioned her at great length about the world she had left and about what she wanted. They seemed to know a surprising amount about her world. They were deeply interested in what she knew of their world and why she sought refuge with them. After their questions, they told her about their world, their gods, the Maiden, the Crone, and the Mother and their consorts, their ways and customs. The Greats, the Grands, and the Goods were the leaders of their people, but they did not rule them like her father and mother had done at home. She felt the difference. The leaders shared with their people. No one was poor. They thought of each other as equals; everyone had a voice, even the children. And the children, the future generation, were everyone's children, communally reared—attached to a specific mother and often a specific father but of importance to everyone. Later Tara and Max walked her around. The large building was the palace in which most of the kingdom's inhabitants resided. It was so unlike her own home where the palace excluded more than included. Some of the farmers choose to live near their fields, but they were always welcome in the palace for ceremonies, rituals, and festivals.

After dinner, she was presented to the people of Little Knonos. Faces and names were introduced to her in a blur; Tara whispered reassurances that Sophie would get to know them all in time. There were about two hundred people. Tara and Max took care to point out and reintroduce some of the young men and young women Sophie's own age, and Sophie flushed as she realized they were trying to pair her up with a partner, for the night or for longer, she wondered. In her mind, she understood that these people were freer about sex than where she was from. But the idea that she could select anyone and do whatever she wanted or didn't want to do with that person was staggering.

Tara laughed, seeing the emotions flash over Sophie's face. "You don't have to do anything with anyone, if you don't want to," she said softly. "We just wanted you to know that you could if you wanted," she added.

"I … I … I knew … you …were different … about … that … but … I," Sophie struggled to find the words.

"You aren't ready," Max said gently. "It is okay, Sophie. It will take some getting used to, I imagine." He smiled, his blue eyes sparkling with amusement. Music continued to be played at the back of the hall, and some couples danced together before retiring for the night. Once aware of what was going on, Sophie saw that people were clearly coupling for the night. Gaia and Pan held hands, but Winter was dancing with a tall blond-haired woman, and Hunter was un-mistakenly flirting with a small brown-haired woman. Sophie found herself looking at Tara and Max, trying to figure out what was between them. He winked at her, and took Tara's hand. Tara squeezed his hand in acknowledgement. "We are happily coupled," he said. "For now," Tara added, but the way she said it teased more than threatened or rebuked. Sophie flushed and looked toward some of the young people she had been introduced to. A young man with dark curly hair was looking at her with interest. He smiled when he saw her looking at him. She felt a shock of recognition—he was like the young man in her dreams. She blushed and smiled back. He rose from his seat, and she panicked and took a hasty leave from Tara and Max who looked after her with curiosity.

Alone in her room, she brushed her hair to soothe herself. She slipped out of the slippers and the gown and got ready for bed. Clearly, she didn't need to be sleeping alone tonight, but she had never done anything sexual to anyone—not even herself. She had never been kissed romantically. To suddenly be contemplating being fully sexually aware was alarming. She knew that male animals put their penises into female animals' vaginas, but trying to visualize a young man putting his penis into her vagina was hard; it seemed like it would hurt—the flesh was so tender there. What did one do to make it easier? Her hand traced the soft skin of her neck and then skimmed over her breasts through the shift and then down over her belly and between her legs to the mound of flesh there. She stopped and slipped out of the shift, her hands reaching for her breasts and fingering them, squeezing them gently, enjoying the feeling of her nipples getting firm and hard under her touch. The sensations activated other throbbings, and one hand reached between her legs. Touching her breasts had caused her vagina to secrete fluid that allowed her fingers to slide into herself easily. The greatest pleasure came from rubbing her clitoris, which got firm and hard under her touch. As she concentrated, she could feel a building pressure. She felt like she was reaching some edge, some critical point, and then a shocking pleasure hit her like a wave and radiated out sensation. Wow. Was it always like that? Sex felt good, and she could see how it could be seen as sacred, too, like the way the Greats and Grands and Goods had described it. It was transcendent for that brief moment of ecstasy.

The next day, Sophie rose and got dressed. She braided her hair loosely. She found the dining hall and got some sweet smelling tea and some fruit. She found Tara and Max waiting for her. They ate, exchanged pleasantries and plans for the day, and then they rose to leave. Sophie was outside and headed to the orchards with a basket when she heard someone call her name. She turned to find the dark-haired young man from the night before coming up behind her. She stopped and waited. He was looking at her so intently that she flushed and looked down at her feet.

"Sophie," he said again. "I am Tobin. May I come with you?" he asked, his question puckering his brow. His eyes, a warm clear gray like crystal, searched her face. He was unnervingly familiar and very handsome. His skin was slightly tanned from outside work, his hair was a mass of jet curls, his eyes were beautiful and framed in long dark lashes, his nose and jaw were angular. He was taller than she was but not by much. He was simply dressed in a blue homespun shirt and a pair of brown leggings. He held out his arm for her, and before she could think about it, she linked her arm around his, and they set off. He asked her about her world, and she found it easy to talk to him.

They came to the peach orchard, and they picked the ripe fruits together and continued talking. When they had filled the basket, they sat down together, and he pulled out a small knife from his belt and cut up a peach, feeding her pieces with his fingers. She blushed when she first realized that he meant to feed her; it seemed an intimate thing to do and they had only just met.

And then she remembered that everything was different here. They could be intimate in more ways than just feeding each other, today, right now for that matter, and it could mean nothing or everything. She looked at him and blushed an even deeper shade of red. Something told her that she didn't want it to mean nothing. She was flustered; it must have shown on her face, because she felt his fingers trace the side her face as he spoke softly to her, "Sophie, you are very beautiful, and you are easy to talk to, but I want to get to know you, and I want you to know me." He paused a moment, "What I mean is that we are in no hurry."

His fingers were soft on her cheek; she felt her stomach go queasy. This must be what they meant by butterflies in your stomach, she thought. Why? She wasn't nervous and yet she was. He seemed to like her. Did she like him? Yes, she thought she did. He was attractive; he was easy to talk to; he was gentle and attentive. She wondered what his fingers would feel like on other parts of her body. She flushed again, and brought her hand to his, linking their fingers and bringing them to her lap. "Thank you," she whispered, looking up at him from their linked hands.

"I have dreamed of you, Sophie," he said softly.

"Have you?" She was surprised, but then she confessed, "I have dreamed of you, too." Her memories of the dreams of him were so clear in her mind; she was curious about what he could have possibly dreamed about her. "What did you dream of me?" she asked.

He looked at her, and his eyes went the softest gray, burning with intensity, "I dreamed that you were my heart's true love and that you crossed a world for me, and you did."

"I didn't do it just for you," she whispered, but her heart was pounding. She left to escape the kind of male-dominated marriage and society she knew—but she also did it for the beautiful young man that she saw in her dreams—Tobin, Tobi.

"I know, but the act for me is no less beautiful for that," he said, and she flushed with color. He broke her embarrassment by saying, "Shall we go?" a radiant smile lighting up his whole face. He stood and helped her to her feet. He carried the laden basket and kept his free hand linked in hers. In the kitchens, a cook set them to peeling and pitting the fruits, which they did contentedly. Tobin was called to help with the sheep, and he left her reluctantly, squeezing her hand and touching her face in parting. When she came into the dining hall for dinner, she was relieved to find him waiting for her. Tara and Max didn't seem surprised to find Tobin accompanying Sophie. Max winked at her as they sat down. After dinner, Tobin took Sophie for a walk and then saw her to her room.

In the days that followed, she found that she enjoyed gathering things for the kitchen. Sometimes she was sent to get fruit, and sometimes to gather vegetables. She also worked in the kitchen garden pulling weeds and gathering herbs for the cooks to use for cooking or the healers to use in healing. She also enjoyed talking to the children and schooling them in letters and numbers. Almost everyone was involved with the children in one way or another. Sophie began to understand how they were everyone's children, the communal responsibility and legacy. But most of all Sophie enjoyed being near Tobin. They often did their chores together. There was a growing intensity between them. When they were together, they could barely keep their hands off each other. They stole kisses as often as they could.

Being with Tobin confused and excited Sophie. All the unspoken rules about relations between a man and a woman in her world were at war with what was allowed here. She could have sex with him at any time. She could have sex with him and with anyone else she wanted. But she didn't want that. She wanted him, and he seemed to want her. Men needed sex, she had been taught. It occurred to her that though Tobin wanted her, his need might drive him to be with another, and the thought disturbed her powerfully.

One afternoon, they were kissing in the gardens. The kissing and groping had escalated, so that they were half-naked and pressed against each other, greedily exploring their naked flesh. Sophie could feel his penis erect and hard through his leggings and her gown's skirt. She knew he wanted her and reached for the lacings of his leggings, but he stilled her hand.

"Not yet, Sophie," he whispered, trailing kisses beneath her ear and down her neck.

"But … don't you need to?" she asked breathlessly, flushing.

"Need?" Sophie felt his body stiffen as he asked the question. "What do you mean, Sophie?" There was an edge to his voice that Sophie didn't understand.

"Don't you want to?" Sophie asked, flushing further, and daring to glance up at him.

Tobin was looking at her with a strange mix of emotions on his face, tenderness and the flush of passion interrupted, but there was something else. She had insulted him somehow she realized. He was affronted. "Yes, I want to," he said carefully, "but desire does not justify action. I am not an animal, Sophie. Tara and Max, the Grands and the Greats, they talked to me about your world—about how it is between men and women there. Rape is a heinous crime here, Sophie. I want us to go slowly. I want you to really want to before we make love," his voice softened at his last words, and he bent and kissed her cheek, his body relaxing again and molding around hers.

She was embarrassed at having insulted him but confused too. If he wanted to, but wasn't doing it with her, was he doing it with someone else? She didn't think it was possible to blush any further, but she must have, and her thoughts must have shown on her face—because she felt his body stiffen again and pull away from her slightly.

"Do you really have such a low opinion of men, Sophie?" he asked incredulously. His gray eyes were searching her face imploringly. She was insulting him again. She was terribly confused.

"I … I … don't … I … just thought … I don't know. It is different here," she said desperately. She looked away from him, trying to hide her embarrassment.

She felt his hand on her cheek—coaxing her gaze back to his. His eyes softened at her discomfort, and he pulled himself closer to her. "I could be with another, but I don't think you would like that, would you?" he asked, but his eyes sparkled with a slight amusement. He knew that she wouldn't like that. They had never talked about it in words, but still he knew—just as she knew that he didn't want her to be with anyone else but him.

"No," she whispered.

He looked at her with a mixture of exasperation, sympathy, and tenderness. "I am not an animal, Sophie, that ruts senselessly by instinct or driven by a period of heat. I can control myself even when I desire to do otherwise. If I am not with you, it doesn't mean that I have to seek out another. I am perfectly capable of satisfying my own desires," he said matter-of-factly—as if this was obvious to even the smallest child, and Sophie realized that, here, it was obvious to the smallest child. Individuals here only had sexual relations with others with mutual consent and for mutual pleasure. To do otherwise was unthinkable, criminal and monstrous. One always had oneself if no willing partner could be found.

Her embarrassment melted away. He would wait for her. He wouldn't push her. He wouldn't seek out other partners. Their relationship would evolve naturally. She relaxed against him, and they pulled each other closer and resumed kissing, touching, and exploring.

They started sleeping together just so they wouldn't be parted, their bodies wrapped innocently around each other. He kept them from having sex, refusing to do it, until he thought she was ready. Finally, they fought over it, and they were ready. They loved each other; they wanted to love each other every way possible.

They undressed each other and lay naked on her bed, running hands down each other's body, admiring each other. She ran her hands over his muscled chest, shoulders, and arms, and he traced the shape of her breasts and lower around her navel and the round the curve of her hips. They kissed gently at first but then with more fire. His hands caressed her breasts, his mouth moving up and down her neck and back to her mouth. She kissed him back and touched his nipples, making him gasp. He moved one of his hands between her legs, gently inserting his fingers and working her up to orgasm. She moaned and cried out softly in pleasure, and he thought he would explode from desire. Her pleasure was wildly erotic to him, and when he eased his penis into her and felt the wetness of her arousal, it only took him moments to come as well. They lay in each other's arms, completely content, whispering "I love you" and each other's name. When his penis contracted enough to disengage their bodies, he reached for the small cloth on the washstand to mop up the aftersex, and they snuggled into each other's arms for sleep.

She didn't know when the dream had started. One moment she was warm and loved, and the next she was dreaming. She was back in her parents' palace. The palace was ablaze with activity. She wandered through the familiar halls trying to figure out what was going on. There was to be a wedding, and with horror, she realized it was her wedding. Her father and mother had arranged for her to marry Prince Henry. He wasn't a bad young man but he wasn't nice either, and she felt no attraction to him whatsoever. She was begging her mother to find some excuse to delay or stop the wedding, but she knew it was useless. She had to marry Henry, but she couldn't marry Henry. She had Tobin. Desperately, she called out his name, "Tobin, Tobi!"

"Here, love," came a sleepy answer. "Are you okay, darling?" and she felt him kiss the back of her neck, and she felt his body spooned behind hers, solid and firm and warm. His arms hugged her closer. She flipped around to face him, kissing his chest and neck, smelling the scent of him, breathing him in in reassurance.

"Yes, I am here; you are here. I am home," she answered softly. She felt herself calm. She nuzzled against him, comforted, and waited for sleep to take her again.

The next day Sophie went to see Gaia. She told the Greatmother about her dream and about her desire to stay with them at Little Knonos and to stay with Tobin. Her life felt meaningful to her here, and it fell into an easy rhythm with chores to do and Tobin to love, and she had no desire to go back. She had found a paradise where there was meaningful work to do, plenty of food to eat, pleasures to be had, people to care for, and people to care for her. It was a simpler life, and sometimes she missed her family, but she was happy. She wasn't a princess anymore and she was no one's wife; she was her own person; she could couple and uncouple as she liked, and with a smile, she realized that so would her children, and they would be loved and cherished and have good and meaningful lives too. There was nothing more to wish for.

Snow White and the Huntsgirl

Once upon a time, there was a king and a queen who loved each other very much and wanted a child more than anything. Queen Theresa and King Michael were good and just rulers, and because of that, when the queen asked the fairy queen for her help in granting them a child, a girl with hair as dark as ebony, skin as white as snow, and lips as red as blood, the child was conceived and then born. They named her Snow White, and she was a sweet, kind, and loving child. She was also very beautiful.

When Snow White was eleven, her mother grew ill, and despite the doctor's efforts and the constant tending of King Michael and Snow White, the queen's condition worsened, and she died. The king and Snow White were bereft, and they withdrew from society. The royal court allowed them their grief for a while, but then they demanded their re-entry. It was easier for Snow White; she was a child after all. She made appearances and then disappeared to the kitchens and was coddled by the cooks. From the kitchens it was easy enough to escape to the kitchen yard with the other children. Shirking off her royal status was often a blessing, so she often felt like a regular child and not a princess.

Her father drifted. Sometimes incredibly attentive, and sometimes incredibly absent—lost completely in his grief. A half-brother drew him abroad. Months dragged by. Snow White was so lonely, and then suddenly they were back, and her father, her half-uncle, and their entourage; a woman accompanied them. Lady Lauren was stunning, one of the most beautiful women Snow White had ever seen. Where her mother had been fair, Lady Lauren was dark with golden brown skin, thick, tightly-curled, dark brown hair, and cat-like golden brown eyes.

Her father and Lady Lauren were married shortly after the royal party returned, and they were happy. Queen Lauren loved King Michael, and she was kind and loving to Snow White. And then a sickness fell upon the land, and King Michael was struck with it. Queen Lauren and Snow White cared for him in shifts, but to their horror, they watched him deteriorate. He was dying, slipping away from them, and there was nothing they could do, so they loved him as much as they could for the time they had left. When he died, they knew that each of them had done everything that she could have done and that they had loved him with their complete souls and hearts.

Snow White withdrew into herself, and the queen let her as much as she could. Queen Lauren dealt with matters of state as best she could, and she was amazingly good at it considering that she was a foreigner. Snow White heard the compliments that were made about her step-mother and was pleased. The queen oversaw Snow White's education, placing her in the capable hands of Lady Jessica, a distinguished tutor. The queen made time each day to lunch alone with Snow White so that they could talk intimately. Snow White grew to love the queen, not as a replacement of her mother but as a kind of second mother, and the queen loved Snow White and never tired of noting what looks the princess had inherited from her father or what mannerism of his that she used quite unconsciously. It made Snow White feel closer to him somehow. So the months passed in a contented rhythm, and soon it was years, and Snow White found herself facing her fourteenth birthday.

Though Snow White had not found the idea of turning fourteen any different than turning thirteen, she realized that she was mistaken. When she had finished her morning lessons with Lady Jessica, Lady Jessica led Snow White to the queen's private council chambers. There Snow White found herself being formally introduced to the queen's advisors. She had known them for years of course. What excited and frightened her now was that she was being introduced to them not as a child but as a peer and equal. The queen now expected Snow White to learn to rule and to do so she would need to work with these ladies and lords. She glanced nervously at Lady Jessica, but she had withdrawn. She next glanced at the queen, who smiled at her reassuringly and nodded to confirm that Snow White had guessed quite correctly. After the introductions had been made, the queen led Snow White to barracks of the Queen's Guard where she was likewise introduced. Captain Davidson winked at her and introduced his men with authority and respect. The queen then took Snow White to meet the chief cooks and housekeepers and healing women and doctors. It struck Snow White that the queen knew all these people by name and details about their lives and their families. Finally, they ended up in queen's private dining room where a small lunch was laid out for them. As they took their seats, the queen handed Snow White a round flat package. It contained a delicate diadem which the queen took from Snow White's hands and placed carefully on the girl's head.

"You have been a young woman for some time, Snow White," she said tenderly, "but now you are a queen in the making. It is time for you to wear a symbol of what you are," she said sweetly, and bent to kiss Snow White on the forehead.

"Thank you, my queen," Snow White said shyly.

"Don't be silly, my child. Nothing significant has changed between us. You must use my given name when we are alone," she said with a smile. "Eat," she commanded, and so they ate, and the queen explained that Snow White's days would change now. She would have morning lessons with Lady Jessica as usual, but on days when there was court business to attend, Snow White would attend the queen and watch and learn. On days when there was not court business, there were other things the queen wanted to show Snow White.

Learning the business of becoming a queen was often incredibly dull, but other times it was full of unexpected surprises. In formal court session, about a month after Snow White's birthday, she was shocked to hear King Arthur of the neighboring kingdom ask for Snow White's hand in marriage for his son, Prince Kenneth. Snow White thought that she might burst into flames at her embarrassment until she caught the mocking gaze of Captain Davidson watching her with such suppressed mirth that she felt a rush of anger. He saw her change of expression and amended his face to a more deferential attitude of apology that was somewhat convincing. She later learned that princes had been asking for her hand for years with both the king and the queen putting them off on account of her youth.

Another surprise was the deference with which the queen held the household staff (the cooks, the housekeepers, the healers/doctors, the teachers and tutors of the children). "Never dismiss the servants, Snow White. They run the castle; they know things. You need them as your allies, and they need to know that you respect them and value them. Have the servants as your enemies, and you fail because you fight on all fronts. But it isn't just politics, Snow White. They are good people; you have selected them as such—acknowledging them as such, it is just what is due. Life has granted us privilege, Snow White, but never forget that you could be one of them and lucky at your good fortune." Snow White bowed her head in acknowledgment. She knew this was true from her time in the kitchens with the cooks and their children.

One afternoon, the queen led Snow White to her private apartments. Snow White had been their many times when it had been her parents' apartments, when her father had shared it with the queen, and in the time since her father's death when it had been the queen's alone. The queen led her into the large changing room. Snow White followed, increasingly puzzled. The queen opened a large armoire at the far end of the room. Snow White came to stand by the queen's side, peering curiously at the inside of the armoire.

"Come, Snow White, this is my greatest secret," the queen said very softly, and Snow White felt the queen take her elbow and help her inside the armoire, shutting the doors behind them and casting them into darkness. Snow White felt a rush of fear, but then the queen waved her arm, pushing aside a dark curtain that Snow White had mistaken for the back of the armoire, and there was a little hidden room before them. It was small and sparsely furnished. Two small couches sat by a large low table. In the center of the room, a brazier burned un-natural blue, steady flames gently lighting the little room. Opposite the couches stood a great, magnificent mirror, gilded with both silver and gold. Runes made a winding, twisting silver band around the edges of the great mirror while pictures of animals real and imaginary made another in gold.

Snow White stared at the great mirror and then at the queen. "What is this place?" she asked in a whisper.

The queen steered them to the closest couch and sat down. Snow White sat next to her. "Your father let me store the Magic Mirror here. We used it together while he lived, and I have used it since to rule the kingdom," she said simply.

"Magic Mirror?" Snow White repeated numbly. "What does it do?"

"It grants wishes, Snow White," the queen answered.

"Wishes?" she found herself repeating again. "Any wishes?" and Snow White found herself both excited and alarmed at the prospect.

The queen straightened herself and looked at Snow White carefully. She felt the scrutiny of the queen's gaze, probing her, trying to decide if she had been mistaken in trusting this secret to the girl. "The Magic Mirror is a powerful object, Snow White. It can be used for great good or great evil. I am only human, but I have tried to use the mirror for good—to enhance the lives of our people. In my own land, my cousin learned of the mirror and wanted it. He was a cruel man, and I knew he would use the mirror poorly, so when I met your father and he seemed like such a good man, I asked the mirror about him, and it showed me that he was good and that we could have a good life together. So I confided to him the secret of the mirror, and he helped me hide it and then get it here safely. Not even your half-uncle knows about the mirror. Now you are the only other person who knows about the mirror."

Snow White shook her head, trying to process this information and trying to order the questions that were screaming in her mind. "How does it work?" she asked speculatively, looking from the queen to the mirror, glistening in the odd blue flames.

"Snow White," the queen said sharply. "It is not a toy. It is a great responsibility to have access to such an object. You must be very respectful with how you use it."

"How do you use it?" Snow White asked sincerely.

The queen relaxed a little. "I use it to see things in the kingdom that I would not otherwise see. I try to alleviate suffering where I can, but I also try not to pry too far into the lives of our people," she answered.

Snow White still clearly did not understand. The queen sighed and turned toward the mirror, "Mirror, Mirror, on the wall, show us those who suffer in our land so that we might lend a hand."

The queen reached quickly for a large notebook that had lain on the table and a quill which she adroitly dipped in an inkpot. Snow White had failed to notice these objects on her first scan of the little room. She could not imagine what the queen wanted with them, until suddenly the mirror flashed to life. A baker's store front came into view, and inside in the living quarters an angry man was lashing his son savagely. Angry red marks cut into the boy's bare buttocks, and both Snow White and the queen flinched as they watched the beating. The queen scribbled notes in the notebook, and the image changed. A woodcutter's cottage deep in the forest, and a woman's face gaunt with hunger divvying out a meager stew to her four skinny young children. Another entry in the notes. The image changed again—a tavern, two men sat conspiring, one was being paid to set fire to the other man's neighbor's barn. More notes. The image changed again, a girl was being coerced into a marriage that she didn't want and was too young for. The images flickered, and the queen wrote about it all in the notebook. When the mirror went clear again, the queen picked up a different, smaller notebook and made a copy the notes in the larger book. Snow White sat quietly watching, and as the queen finished this second set of notes, she asked, "What will you do?"

"Captain Davidson will see the baker and send his men to see about the farm dispute and some of the other situations. There are things where it is better for a male intervention than a female one, but there are others that are suited to me and, now, me and you. The woodcutter died a little while ago; I should have realized, but I had forgotten. With children so young, she should be moved out of the forest. We will pay her a visit and help her get relocated. Some nanny goats and chickens would help her support her family," the queen answered.

So Snow White began to be schooled in the power of the Magic Mirror. Beauty, the queen counselled, was as much in the soul and heart as in the face and the body, and the beauty of one's heart and soul could be seen in the actions one performed for others. The danger of the mirror was that one could see too much. Seeing too much could strip people of their powers of free choice and their agency over their own lives. Help where needed was the goal, not control over others. The prayer was for the sight to help, and Snow White felt a profound satisfaction traveling with the queen and giving aid to her people. Most were unabashedly gratefully. The queen's gifts were answers to their most secret prayers. The woodcutter's wife had fallen to their feet crying and sobbing strangled thank yous. A few prideful to the point of idiocy tried to refuse the queen's gifts, but she skillfully turned the gifts into loans which they were to repay with interest.

That spring it seemed like the countryside bloomed in invitations, dances, balls, festivals, and/or ceremonies. Snow White could not remember a season with so much activity. The queen had a dressmaker come specifically to update Snow White's gowns and to make quite a few new ones. Her new gowns were different; they were more fitted and sophisticated. They were not the gowns of a child, but the gowns of a young woman, and Snow White realized that the flurry of invitations was in acknowledgment of her being of marriageable age, and she felt a sense of dread at the thought.

At lunch with the queen, Snow White asked about it, "Do I have to marry?"

The queen looked at her, the startled expression on her face softened as she read the anxiety on Snow White's face. "No, my child. You don't have to marry, but you might like to, some day," she added gently.

"Some day?" Snow White toyed with the words. Relief that imminent betrothal was not her fate washed the tension from her body.

"You are very young, Snow White, but it is time for you to be presented to the neighboring royalty. Perhaps in a few years, you may get to know someone you like. Our lands are relatively peaceful; we have allies already, and I do not see the need for marriage alliance, but if one should present itself that wouldn't be undesirable either." The queen paused. She saw that her words did not comfort Snow White. "Your desires are also important, Snow White. I would not see you married against your will."

The queen and Snow White went to ever after event. Snow White was introduced to scores of young men. She danced and talked with them, but Snow White had always been a solitary child. She liked being with mother and father, with Lady Jessica and some of the other tutors, with the cooks, with her father and

Queen Lauren, and then with the queen. She had acquaintances among the ladies-in-waiting, but no close friends. Her closest friend was Tanya, the Huntsman's daughter, who often accompanied Snow White when she rode. Tanya had taught Snow White how to hunt with a bow and arrows, and they had an easy friendship. The spring had been so busy with Snow White's turning fourteen, assuming more adult responsibilities, and being presented to royal households that Snow White had scarcely seen her friend.

One evening, Snow White was dancing with a young man with straight black hair and dark russet skin; he smelled vaguely of the outdoors and horse, and Snow White wished she were dancing with Tanya. They would be laughing easily at all the fuss over dresses and costumes and all the intrigue over who might marry who. Some of the young men she met were handsome; some appeared to be very nice; some even appeared to be handsome and nice, but none of them grabbed her attention, and none of them were as fun to be around as Tanya.

The next evening, they were at her half-uncle's castle. Lord John and Lady Rebecca had introduced Queen Lauren and Princess Snow White to the ladies and lords present, and Snow White was dancing with her half-cousin, Lord Peter, when a party of guests arrived late and was introduced. Lord Thomas and his sons were presented, and suddenly, the queen was at Snow White's side.

"Lord Peter," she interrupted, "please get Snow White out of here as discretely as possible and then go and fetch your father," she whispered. Both Snow White and Lord Peter were alarmed at the strain on Queen Lauren's face and the deathly pale of her skin. Before they could say anything, the queen disappeared into the crowd. Her half-cousin followed the queen's example and disappeared Snow White into the crowd and out of the back of the hall.

Lord Peter took Snow White to his father's private counsel chamber and left her there with the queen while he went to get his father. Lord Peter returned with Lord John and the head of the Lord's Guard, Captain Richards. Queen Lauren explained that Lord Thomas was her cousin, the man she had fled when agreed to come away with King Michael. Lord John understood enough to know that the queen and Snow White were in danger, and he ordered his son and Captain Richards to take half his guards and return the queen and the princess to their castle and remain with them. Lord John would see what could be done to get rid of the unwanted company and feign ignorance about the queen and princess.

They travelled as swiftly as they could in the darkness; it was dawn before they reached the castle. Grooms saw to the horses, and cooks and housekeepers saw to feeding and housing of Lord Peter and his father's men. The queen sent Davidson to fetch Tanya and her father, and she had clothes brought to her private rooms. The clothes, Snow White realized, were boys' clothes. The queen laid out several changes of clothes and had Snow White change into one of them. She packed three other changes of clothes. Davidson ushered a bewildered Huntsman and his daughter into the queen's rooms and stood waiting. He was rigid with tension.

"My cousin has found me," she explained. "He showed up at Lord John's. I don't think he saw me, but even with Lord John's denials, he will find out that I was there and about Snow White. He will try to force a marriage alliance one way or another with me or with one of his sons and Snow White. He wants something from me, but I will destroy it to keep it out of his hands if I have to," her eyes looking meaningfully at Snow White. She nodded in acknowledgment. If the queen should fail to destroy the mirror to keep it from Lord Thomas, Snow White was to do it herself.

"Snow White must go into hiding. Tanya, will you take her? Disappear into the forest. Go far away. Keep her hidden," the queen implored.

"I will go with them, my queen," said the Huntsman.

"No, my friend; I can't let you go. It would be too obvious if you disappeared. Tanya we can make excuses for, and knowing my cousin's contempt for women, he will not think much of Tanya's skill and resourcefulness."

"What about me, my queen?" Davidson asked.

"You must remain with me also, my captain, but is there one among your guard that you would trust with such important task?" the queen asked.

"Yes, my queen, Nathan Daniels is a good soldier and a good man. I will go and make the arrangements," and he bowed and took his leave, pausing to wink at Snow White and wish her well.

The Huntsman embraced his daughter and wished both her and the princess well. Davidson returned with Daniels, and he led the three through the castle to the stables where he saw them mounted, armed, provisioned, and off. They were to ride for a few hours so that they were well clear of the castle and then find a secluded place to rest.

The three of them were so stunned by the recent events that they didn't talk much. The distractions of the spring countryside keeping them entertained. They rode through any stream or creek bed they could find; they forded one river and then another. By about noon, they were well up in the mountains, and when they found a shaded clearing, they made camp. Snow White fell asleep at once after her sleepless night, and Tanya and Nathan took it in turns to watch the sleeping princess and hunt. They woke the princess at about five. They ate a happy little meal of roasted rabbit and wild yams, bread from the castle, and fresh raspberries. Snow White tried to explain what she knew about Lord Thomas to Tanya and Nathan (excluding the information about the Magic Mirror). Nathan had tried to use formal address with the princess and Tanya, but Snow White demanded that they use their given names under their distressed circumstances. They told each other stories after that and then bunked down for the night.

They rose at dawn and continued traveling. They stayed away from villages and settlements. They hunted and fished and gathered for food as their meager castle provisions were consumed. The days fell into a quiet rhythm. They were all anxious: Snow White about the queen, Tanya about her father, and Nathan about his brothers-in-arms and the queen. By unspoken compact, they didn't discuss their worries. After about a week of hard travel, they slowed their pace. It had rained twice since they had left—between not knowing the direction they had traveled, the rain, the measures they had taken to disguise their paths, and the significant delay Lord Thomas and his sons would have faced in beginning looking for them, they were pretty sure that they were beyond his grasp. Tanya and Snow White spent significant portions of their days together. They bathed together, and then they hunted and gathered together. Sometimes Nathan joined them to hunt and gather, but he seemed to enjoy his time alone too.

Weeks passed, and Snow White worried that if everything was resolved peacefully that no one from the castle would know how or where to find them to bring them back, but Nathan assured them both the Queen's Guard and the Huntsman would know. Spring turned into summer, and Snow White and Tanya bathed daily, and something began to change between them. They had always been friends, but Snow White realized one day sitting on the river bank watching Tanya combing her fingers through her hair that Tanya was the most beautiful person she had ever seen. With her dark hair and skin and her golden-yellow eyes, Snow White was reminded of a dark jungle cat from the stories she had heard. Desire flared in the bottom of Snow White's stomach, and she blushed at the direction of her thoughts. She remembered that night at a dance when she had pictured herself dancing not with the young man who held her but with Tanya. As if divining Snow White's thoughts, Tanya looked up suddenly and saw Snow White looking at her and blushing. Tanya smiled ruefully at her friend and came to join her on the river bank. Snow White didn't know what to say. Apparently, she had been attracted to Tanya for some time but had not articulated the idea to herself. How was she supposed to explain it to Tanya? What was more, how did or would Tanya feel about the matter?

Tanya didn't speak but simply took Snow White's hand in her own and squeezed it. Snow White turned to look at Tanya who was looking at her with the same desire that Snow White felt, and all the awkwardness of situation seemed to fall away, and they kissed. It was gentle at first and exploratory, and then the intensity of it increased, and they were kissing passionately and running their hands across each other's body.

At first, they hid their relationship from Nathan, but he surprised them by telling them he not only knew but didn't care. Same sex relationships were not apparently as uncommon as Snow White thought. Nathan's paramour was the head stable groom, Harry Fraser. Nathan gave them his blessing—noting that now he wouldn't be responsible for the princess "technically" losing her virtue or getting pregnant—concerns that had apparently troubled the guardsman with their living rough in the wilderness.

Since Nathan knew, Snow White and Tanya curled up together at night, held hands when they wanted, and exchanged fairly innocent kisses. They continued their intimate moments when they were bathing or in the woods, and Nathan gave them a wide-birth for their exploits.

As summer drifted into fall, tensions ran high. All three of them were anxious for news from the castle, and though Snow White and Tanya could distract themselves with each other, Nathan missed Harry and could be snappish and irritable.

One morning, they woke to frost and the sound of hoof-beats. They took strategic positions in the trees, arrows notched, and waited. The Huntsman, Captain Davidson, and Harry Fraser came in range and were hailed. It was a joyous reunion. Lord Thomas had tracked Queen Lauren back to the castle. His sons went after Snow White but couldn't find a trail. The queen claimed that she had left the mirror in her homeland and that it must have been destroyed if Lord Thomas had not found it. She allowed Lord Thomas' men to search the castle, and they tore apart every room they searched, but they failed to find the secret room behind the armoire, so they eventually left with Lord John's and Captain Davidson's threats that they should never enter the kingdom or threaten the kingdom, Queen Lauren, or Snow White again.

They rode hard to return, but opportunity was given for Nathan and Harry to spend time together. The Huntsman and Davidson got themselves used to the idea of Snow White and Tanya and were even happy for their obvious joy. Though they were not sure how the queen would take the news, they could and would attest to the happiness of the couples.

Queen Lauren was only happy and grateful. They were free from her cousin, the mirror was safe and could continue to be used to help their people, Snow White had come home, Tanya was returned to her father, Snow White had found a caring and attentive partner, Nathan was returned to the Queen's Guard and reunited with his lover, and Queen Lauren was re-bonded with Lord John's family. Snow White found it both bizarre and comforting to think of her life as queen with Tanya at her side, but she had many years to get used to the idea, learning and growing into the role under Queen Lauren's patient tutelage.

The Frog and the Transgender Prince

Once upon a time in a small kingdom, there lived a princess. She was the apple of her parents' eyes. They showered her with affection and love, but she was not a happy child. Stephanie never felt quite right in a way that she couldn't explain to herself. Her father was dark skinned, a deep dark brown that was nearly black. His hair was kinky and wiry. He wore it in tight thin braids and usually tied it back in a pony tail of sorts. His eyes were dark, nearly black. Her mother was fair skinned with wavy light brown hair and crystal blue eyes. Stephanie was somewhere in between. Not quite the image of her father and not quite the image of her mother. Her skin was a lighter brown than her father's but much darker than her mother's. Her hair was raven black but had the texture of her mother's fine hair except that it was crazy curly—in tight corkscrew curls that were impossible to tame. Her eyes were a light brown flecked with green, but it wasn't just her skin, hair, and eyes. She never felt graceful like the other girls at court or in the castle. They seemed to glide through their actions, and Stephanie always felt like she plodded along. Once she hit puberty, she felt even more miserable. Other girls were naturally shapely in a feminine way, and she just wasn't. She didn't have hips; her waist was thick rather than slender, and she had broad shoulders. There were other things. She loved history and philosophy; she hated needle work and was not a good musician or singer. Her dancing drew the frown of the dancemaster who often made the compromise of having her dance the less complicated male leads of the dances.

Feeling so out of sorts, she had few close friends. When she could, she went riding to be alone. She enjoyed hunting, and though women rarely accompanied hunts, her father allowed her to come with them because so few things seemed to give her pleasure. She watched the boys and men of the palace train with interest. The physicality of what they did looked like fun and engaging, but watching was all she was permitted to do.

For her eighteenth birthday, the princess had been given a golden ball. A travelling sorceress had given the ball to the king and queen, assuring them that the ball would transform the princess' life and lead her to true happiness. Stephanie had thought the whole thing was ridiculous, but knowing how her parents grieved over her discomfort, she had accepted the ball.

Shortly after her birthday, she had ridden deep into the forest. She had dismounted and was leading her horse through a stand of trees when the trees thinned suddenly to reveal a beautiful small pond. Her horse drank eagerly from the water. Stephanie sated her own thirst and then walked absently around the charming pond, admiring the wild flowers that grew around it. After her initial exploration, she sat down at the edge of the pond and ate her small packed snack of bread and cheese and dried fruit. She fed an apple to her horse and found herself drowsy, so she spread out her cloak and fell asleep to the peaceful sounds of the pond and the forest.

She woke with a start and had the uncomfortable feeling that she was being watched. She got up and gathered her things warily, but her horse was completely peaceful and contented, so she convinced herself that it had only been her imagination. To distract herself, she took out the golden ball and started playing with it. She threw it up in the air and caught it. Such a small and insignificant thing, she thought; how was a ball supposed to change one's life? Still it was made of gold, a precious metal. Perhaps that was the price of change—something precious. Frustrated by the seemingly futile train of her thoughts she threw the ball up higher than she had intended, and she realized that she couldn't catch it on its way down. She watched helplessly as the golden ball dropped into the pond and disappeared.

She was shocked by the depth of emotion that accompanied the disappearance of the ball. She had not truly believed that the ball could do anything for her, and yet with its loss, the potential for her true happiness was lost too. She sat down on the edge of the pond and wept. She had been so consumed with grief that she did not notice that something was trying to talk to her. Finally, she realized that a voice was speaking to her, and she looked up in shock.

"Miss, please, miss, why do you cry?" the voice said. It was coming from a frog who seemed to have come out of the pond or had otherwise appeared out of thin air. The princess stared at the frog. I have finally lost my mind, she thought, and looked around frantically to see what her horse was doing. If a frog could talk, perhaps Star Blaze had grown wings and could fly as a Pegasus. But, no, Star Blaze stood grazing happily, four legs and a tail and no wings. Stephanie looked back at the frog who seemed to be eyeing her with amusement. There didn't seem to be any choice, so as foolish has the princess felt, she spoke to the frog.

"Are … are … you speaking to me?" she asked, the incredulity clear in her voice.

"Well, yes," the frog said softly. "You seem so upset. What is wrong?" it asked again.

Stephanie felt ridiculous, but she tried to explain. "My parents gave me a golden ball for my birthday, and I have lost it in the pond," she answered.

The frog looked from Stephanie to the pond and back again. "I could get it for you," the frog said slowly, "but you would need to do me a favor in return."

Without considering the consequences of such a promise, Stephanie answered immediately. "Of course, anything you want, so long as you fetch my ball for me."

"Anything I want," the frog repeated, looking at Stephanie carefully.

Stephanie felt a tinge of panic—what was she promising this creature obviously touched by magic? It is just a frog, some voice in Stephanie's head answered, dismissing the fears that suddenly presented themselves to her.

As if reading Stephanie's mind, the frog looked into Stephanie's eyes and asked, "Who are you and where do you live?"

With the vanity of nobility, Stephanie announced herself, "I am Princess Stephanie, the heir of King Marcus and Queen Rose." Realizing too late that she was giving the frog more information than she intended if she didn't intend to honor her promise, which she didn't, she lied about where she lived, waving vaguely in the opposite direction from her father's palace.

The frog nodded. "I will hold you to your promise, princess," and then it turned and hopped into the pond and disappeared.

Stephanie stood and found herself worrying her hands together in anticipation. Just when she was concluding that she had imagined the whole thing, the frog hopped out of the pond and hopped to her feet, spitting out the golden ball from its mouth.

Stephanie stooped down and snatched up the ball. "Thank you," she said, and she meant that part. "Now it is time for me to return home," and she snatched up her cloak and started for Star Blaze.

"But, your promise, princess," the frog protested.

Stephanie ignored the frog, mounted her horse, and was gone without giving her broken promise a second thought.

The following day, Stephanie had convinced herself that her encounter with the frog had been a dream. So that evening at dinner, when the page announced the frog as "a guest of Princess Stephanie, heir to King Marcus and Queen Rose," Stephanie was just as surprised as her parents. The frog slowly hopped its way through the royal family dining room and stood before the king and queen.

"What is the meaning of this, Stephanie?" the queen asked.

So Stephanie told the king and queen the story of her encounter with the frog at the pond. Both her parents looked stricken when she explained that she had promised the frog anything it wished—and she began to realize that promising anything was a very dangerous thing to do.

"What is it that you wish of our daughter?" the king asked cautiously.

"For now," the frog said politely, "I only wish to be the princess' primary companion. To eat with her and to be with her through the days and nights."

The king and queen relaxed slightly hearing these words. The king turned to his daughter, "You have heard the request, my child. Make the frog feel welcome in our home." Stephanie looked at her father, trying to recover from her shock. He was dead serious. He wasn't even faintly dismissive of a frog requesting to be her new best friend. She started to say something in protest, but her father shook his head slightly. There was no argument to this request; it was an order. Whether she wanted to or not she had to befriend the frog. The frog hopped up on the table and helped itself to small scraps of her stewed meat. When they were all finished dinner, the princess retired to her room to save herself the humiliation of entertaining the frog in front of the court. Alone in her apartments, the princess ignored the frog. The frog didn't seem to mind and contented itself with looking through her books and possessions.

Stephanie was miserable. Previously unhappy and out of place, she now felt herself the butt of every joke, the subject of all the gossip in the palace, the object of every stare. She tried to ignore the frog as best she could, but her parents grilled her every day about how well she was being companionable to her guest. Worse, the frog talked to her. It told her all its favorite stories. It talked to her about its favorite periods of history and favorite philosophers. Stephanie found herself listening to the frog despite herself. They spent long hours alone in Stephanie's apartments. The frog would page through the princess' books. Sometimes the frog would read to Stephanie. The frog began to be fascinated by poetry and would read out its favorite poems. Once the frog had gone through all the volumes of poetry in the princess' apartments, Stephanie took it to the formal library and let the frog choose volumes of poetry to take back to their rooms.

Slowly, Stephanie began to talk to the frog. She talked to it about all the ways she didn't feel comfortable with herself and her life in the palace. She told the frog things that she had never told anyone. She wondered why she could tell it such things. Perhaps, she mused, because no one would believe a talking frog or perhaps because, as a frog in the palace, it was as out of place as she felt.

One day, they had been reading a story about seal-man whose pelt had been stolen by a human woman, so that he had no choice but to marry her and live with her in his man form, but she had grown to love him in that selfless way that is the way of true love, and she had given him back his pelt so that he could return to his home and his people. She had truly expected him to leave her then, but he had grown to love her as well so he stayed with her until she died and only then returned to his home. The transformation part of the story fascinated and excited Stephanie. If she could only transform, perhaps then she would feel like she belonged. But transform into what?

"If I could transform into anything, what do you think I would be best be suited to turn into?" Stephanie found herself asking the frog.

The frog stared at her for a long time. Stephanie thought there was a desperate longing in the eyes of the frog, but it shook its head and turned away from her.

"What is it?" Stephanie asked. "Tell me," she demanded.

"Nay, princess," it said softly, "I cannot tell you. It is a selfish desire of my own, and I love you too well to speak it." The last few words were spoken so softly that the princess could barely hear them.

Stephanie stared at the frog. The whole crazy situation seemed to make perfect sense now. How could she not have seen it? How could she not have guessed? How could a frog talk? How could a frog read or know history or philosophy? How could a frog know the obligations of court and royalty? Only if the frog had in fact been a human and been transformed him or herself. "Who are you?" Stephanie demanded.

"No one of consequence, princess," the frog answered, but Stephanie did not believe it.

"Yes, you are! You are of consequence to me. Who are you and why were you transformed?" Stephanie demanded again.

The frog looked at her again with the sad longing present in its eyes. "Once I was a child every bit as spoilt as you, but I had the misfortune to be rude to a fairy queen who transformed me into a frog."

Excitement coursed through Stephanie's veins, "But then I can free you, can't I? If I love you and tell you so and kiss you, I can free you?" she said in a rush. And she felt like she had never wanted anything more. This was it; it was all true. The golden ball was transforming her life. It had brought her the frog, and the frog was a prince, her prince, and she would be happy. "I love you," Stephanie said breathlessly, and she bent and kissed the frog on the head. She stepped back to see the transformation clearly, but nothing happened.

"Nay, princess, I am a princess myself, and though I love you dearly as a friend, I need the love of a prince to save me," the frog explained slowly.

Stephanie stared at the frog. She felt as though the world had shifted under her feet. Of course, that was it. She sat down and looked out the window. She had never been comfortable as a girl, but it had never occurred to her to be a boy. The rightness of it took her breath away. Would her parents care? No, she thought firmly—they had only wanted her happiness. The frog could ask for anything—even her life. The frog could have demanded that Stephanie become her prince, but the frog loved her well enough to remain a frog forever, and she loved the frog well enough to make the change into a prince as much for her own sake as for the frog's.

Her name was even suited for it; she would change from Princess Stephanie to Prince Stephen. She laughed at the thought. "What is your name?" the princess asked.

"Julia," the frog answered softly.

"Julia, my sweet, Julia, I will be your prince, and you will be my princess, and we will be happy forever," Stephen answered.

"I cannot ask it of you, princess," the frog said carefully.

"But I give it freely. Nothing would make me happier—and you know this better than anyone could," Stephen answered firmly. "I love you, Julia; take me as I will take you," and Stephen kissed the head of the frog. There was a blinding light. Stephen felt a deep glowing flowing throughout zir body. Ze could not see. Ze could only feel the glowing coursing through zir body. Slowly the glowing stopped and the bright light faded, and he sat on edge of his bed naked, now Prince Stephen. Next to him sat a beautiful young woman with russet skin and long straight black hair with dark brown/black eyes.

"Julia?" he asked softly.

"Stephen?" she asked at the same time.

They nodded at each other and laughed. Shyly they reached out their hands and explored each other. Touching progressed to kissing, nibbling, sucking, and licking. Julia seemed to discover her own body as Stephen explored it, and perhaps she did, having been a frog for he didn't know how long. Stephen certainly found that he discovered his own body through Julia's exploration of it. His proportions all seemed much more natural in male form, and he felt a deep genuine contentment and self-satisfaction that he had never experienced with himself as a female. He made her climax using his fingers—his former self-pleasuring in female form—aiding this particular sexual skill. The sexual intercourse part was harder. They both knew that his penis needed to go into her vagina but beyond that both were novices. He was gentle. He entered her carefully and slowly. As they both got used to that, he proceeded slowly. Gradually, he could move in her easily, and when he climaxed, it was wonderful—filled with the same transcending sensational experience as it had been before—but different—the semen exploding out of him in pulsing spurts. They lay in each other's arms, kissing and talking softly. Mostly, they were so grateful to each other and so happy and fully together after having been alone for so long.

Finally, Stephen wrapped himself in a blanket, went to the outer room, and called for a maid. The young woman nearly fainted at the sight of him. He was recognizably Stephanie only a young man now, not the young woman she had been an hour before. Stephen demanded the maid go to the dressmaker for a suit of men's clothes that would fit him. Next, he looked through his former clothes and helped Julia dress in the most beautiful clothes he had. Once the maid returned, Stephen dressed himself as best as could, the novelty of male clothing being new to him. Assured by Julia that he was thoroughly presentable, Stephen led Julia through the palace to find his parents and present themselves.

The king and queen were in their royal apartments. The queen was doing needle work, and the king was writing a letter. They looked up as Stephen entered. Their eyes went wide with both shock and recognition. Stephen smiled hugely at them and motioned Julia to his side—grasping at her hand and linking his fingers through hers.

"Mother, father, I have the most wonderful news. Julia is my frog, and I am her prince, and we are happy, really truly happy," he said in a rush.

The king and queen made the two tell the story again from the beginning. Having either Julia or Stephen go over bits they found particularly confusing again and again, until at last they understood. They also understood the joy and love that flowed through and around the young couple, and they gave them their blessing. They were married in the following weeks, and the kingdom rejoiced that the princess had found her true self as a young man and that their new prince had found joy with a princess who loved him.

Hansel and Gregory

Once upon a time at the edge of a great forest, there lived a lonely woodcutter and his son, Hansel. The woodcutter's wife had died in childbirth some years before; the child, a baby girl, had also died. The woodcutter had so loved his wife that he withdrew from all society except his son. There was a village nearby, but the woodcutter always sent Hansel to sell their wood to the villagers. Their life had a pleasant rhythm. They woke at dawn and fixed a modest breakfast—usually of porridge and goat's milk. Hansel would then feed the chickens and gather eggs while his father fed and milked the goats—separating the milk for drinking and cooking with the milk to set for cheeses. Then they worked in their small garden, weeding and picking ripe vegetables, fruits, and herbs. Done these husbandry tasks, they packed lunches of cheese, bread, and fruits and made their way into the forest with their axes, knives, bows, bundles, and Donny, the mule. Two dogs, Ben and Bertha, they left behind to guard the chickens and goats, but Sampson, the great boarhound, accompanied them. They set snares for rabbits and other small game as they made their way into the forest, knowing the sounds of their labors would send terrorized animals fleeing toward the waiting traps. Once set to cutting felled limbs, the work was hard but rewarding. After four hours or so, they had usually filled their bundles and secured a sizable load of wood in packs on Donny. Sometimes they managed to collect and cut an excess, which they would stack neatly to be retrieved the next day in a double run. Other times they would hunt or fish before returning with their loads and the contents of their snares to their homestead, the cottage, the garden, the smoke shed, the well, and the barn with the great lean-to that sheltered their wood and their wagon.

The evening before market day, they would eat a hasty supper and load the wagon with bundled wood. On market day, Hansel would hitch up the wagon to Donny and make his way to the village, leaving his father alone. Occasionally, Hansel would spend the night in the village with a friend. It was lonely, after all, for the young man with just his father and the animals, but he returned home in the morning with a few coins and the goods they needed like salt and oats, fabric, and the odd tool or book. It was a quiet but contented existence, and then everything changed.

One afternoon a storm came with particular intensity. It drove the woodcutter and his son home. They baked bread and read by the hearth. They mended clothing and made arrows. As evening drew close, the dogs started barking, and Hansel went outside to find the dogs ringed around a horse and two frightened figures on the horse. Hansel quickly called the dogs off; they retreated but sat watching the newcomers warily. With the dogs calmed, a young man about Hansel's age swung down from the horse and introduced himself.

"Good evening. Pardon our intrusion. We lost our way. I am Gregory Griffin, and this is my mother, Elena Griffin," he said politely, gesturing to his mother.

Hansel looked from the young man to his mother; they were strangers. He had never seen them before. They weren't from the village; villagers knew to keep their distance. Hansel flushed. He knew his father would be uncomfortable with guests, but there clearly was little alternative. Gregory and his mother would need shelter, and there was no one else around for miles. They would just have to make the best of it.

Hansel grinned at Gregory. "I am Hansel Hansen," he said. "Please, you must come into the cottage and warm yourselves."

Gregory was already helping his mother off the horse. Hansel took the woman's arm and turned to lead them to the cottage. He paused a moment when he saw the cottage door open and his father's strained face eyeing the guests and making a grim appraisal of the situation.

"Father, we have company," Hansel called, watching his father carefully. He sighed with relief as he saw his father carefully set his features and nod stoically. Reassured that his father would manage the situation, Hansel waved the Griffins toward the cottage and then led their horse to the barn where she could keep Donny company. As quickly as he could, Hansel took the mare's saddle and bridle off and got her a portion of oats. Bubbling with excitement, he ran from the barn to the cottage.

He found the Griffins divested of their sodden traveling outwear and holding mugs of steaming tea on a bench by the blazing hearth. His father looked embarrassed but was busying himself at the far end of the hearth over the smaller flames with basting the roasted goose that was to be their supper. Hansel got himself a mug of tea and joined the Griffins on the bench by the main fire.

Up close and out of the rain, Hansel looked over their guests. Elena was a pretty woman with thick chestnut colored hair, tamed in a plait, but the humidity had changed the small wispy hairs around her face into a mass of corkscrew curls that was most becoming. Her eyes were a strange golden color like a cat's. Gregory's hair was a mass of short, wavy sandy brown with a few of his mother's corkscrew curls at his temples and the same golden colored eyes. They had been trying to get to the village, but the storm had spooked the horse, and they had lost their way. She was a seamstress and knew her trade well, Hansel thought. Her bodice and gown were fitted and flattered her frame quite well. The soft browns and mahogany piping matched her eyes and found an echo in the color of her hair. It turned out that Elena's husband had died in a fire five years ago. Her trade had kept them fed. Gregory worked when and where he could and made decent contributions to their maintenance especially in the last few years. Elena's brother was the local smith, Tom Bradley. They sought his protection. In their home village, on the other side of the ridge, the local brewer and pub owner, Jack Stephens, had been increasingly threatening in his desire for Elena's hand in marriage. So they had left, leaving before dawn and having the ill luck to be traveling on the day of such a storm.

Fortunately, given the current circumstances, Hansel and his father had expanded the cottage. Originally, it had consisted of his parents' bedroom, his bedroom, and the main room with the great hearth. But they had added on two rooms on the far side of the main room. Hansel had taken the larger of the two for his bedroom. After drinking his tea, he retired to his room to retrieve some of his essential belongings, so that Elena could have his room for the night.

After depositing his things in the small bedroom next to his parents', he helped with the dinner preparations, getting bread and cheese and placing them on the table. Though a stranger, Elena knew her way around a kitchen and set out the dishes, cutlery, napkins, cups, and a pitcher of hard cider. Hansel's father took the goose off the spit and placed it on a platter on the table. Hansel found it easy to talk to Gregory and his mother. The three of them chatted companionably. Elena seemed intuitively aware that his father was unaccustomed to company and was content leave him to his silence. Gregory followed his mother's lead and did not try to engage Hansel's father in conversation.

When the table was set and ready, Hansel's father surprised him by stepping forward and holding out a chair for Elena. "Madame, permit me," he said in a soft voice. Hansel's mouth dropped open, and he caught the look of surprise on Gregory's face as the young man looked to him for guidance.

Elena blushed but took the proffered seat gracefully. "Thank you," she said in an equally soft voice. "Please, call me Elena," and she smiled at him.

Hansel's father nodded awkwardly, "I am Hansel also." He paused thoughtfully. "Big Hansel long ago, but I suppose Old Hansel now," and he smiled at his son. He drew out his own chair and sat down motioning the young men to sit as well. Once they were seated, Hansel's father said grace and wished the Griffins safety and success. They ate, and Hansel continued talking with the Griffins. The earlier tension surrounding Hansel's father's awkwardness was lessened somehow with the exchange of first names and the breaking of bread and the sharing of drink. Hansel watched his father surreptitiously and realized that his father was watching Elena just as covertly as Hansel was watching him. His mother had been dead for ten years. He had been six when she and the baby died. His father had withdrawn from others in his grief, but Hansel wondered now, looking between his father and Elena, whether his continued isolation was more habit now than unrelenting loss. He gazed at his father—surprised to see him as a middle-aged man, solidly and muscularly built with russet skin, short black hair, brown-nearly-black eyes, and broad handsome face. He was stunned to realize that his father was attractive. The fact had not occurred to him before. He glanced at Elena who blushed slightly as she caught him looking from his father to her. He glanced at Gregory who seemed to be making the same assessment that Hansel was; he too looked slightly embarrassed and amused at the same time.

Elena seemed suddenly flustered and self-conscious. "Hans, thank you … for your … for your … h-hospitality," she said awkwardly, flushing.

"It is nothing, Elena," his father answered quietly, and he reached out his hand to pat hers, which rested lightly on the table next to him. She blushed even further, and suddenly, the atmosphere at the table seemed charged. Hansel felt like he was intruding on something private and powerful. Gregory went pale next to Hansel. Elena pushed back from the table, rose, collected her plate and cup, and took them to the washstand. Hansel and Gregory rose also with their things. Elena insisted on doing the washing. She seemed desperate to have something legitimate to do, so Hansel let her and collected his father's things and one pot from the hearth that needed cleaning.

Hansel's father sat himself in an armchair near the hearth. With the distraction of routine food storage and washing, the awkwardness receded. Hansel, Gregory, and Elena resumed lighthearted conversation seated around the fire. Hansel's father didn't speak, but he looked at each of them, his eyes lingering on Elena when he thought no one was looking. When it was time, Hansel made sure that Elena and Gregory had fresh water in a pitcher and a basin in each of their rooms and a chamber pot. Wishes for pleasant dreams were exchanged, and each retired to a bedroom.

Hansel was too confused to try to talk to his father that evening. He retired to the little bedroom feeling relieved to be alone. He stripped out of his clothes. He tried to process the evening. He has heard of sudden attraction, the thunder bolt, some people called it. He had seen goofy infatuations between the village teenagers, but they usually ended, sometimes as fast as they had started. This was different—the charge was like a heat pulsing between them, his father, Hans she had called him, and Elena. She seemed affected by it too. It embarrassed her. If they acted on it, they would have sexual relations. It was strange to think of his father as sexual. Of course, he must be. Humans were sexual from birth to death despite the best efforts of the church fathers to pretend otherwise. Thinking about sex aroused him. He touched himself with increasing vigor until he climaxed on a soiled towel and allowed himself to relax into sleep.

Hansel woke at dawn and was surprised to smell bacon being cooked—an extravagance usually reserved for holidays and special occasions. He hurried with his morning ministrations, relieving himself, washing, and dressing. He found his father looking simultaneously embarrassed and unrepentant. He wore one of the finer shirts he owned and was sitting on a stool frying bacon over a small fire, the pan suspended by chains above the flames.

"Pappa, what on earth is going on?" Hansel demanded.

His father blushed but looked into his son's face. "I don't know," he said honestly, "but I hope to find out." His father smiled sheepishly and continued minding the bacon. "Get some eggs and fresh milk and then see about the bread. Elena wrapped it in a damp towel, so it should be fine this morning."

As if divining the mention of her name, Elena emerged from her bedroom. She nodded at them. "Good morning, Hans and Hansel," she said quietly. She moved into the main room. Hansel's father watched her move across the room transfixed. By the time she reached the table, the two of them were blushing furiously. Hansel shook his head, grabbed a pitcher and a basket, and left the cottage. Any trace of the storm was gone, and the sun coming up shone brilliantly. He fed the chickens first and collected six eggs. Then he got feed for the goats and milked them. He used the pitcher that he'd brought and a bucket in the barn. He would see about setting the extra milk for cheeses later.

As he was getting food for the Griffins' mare and for Donny, Gregory came into the barn looking exasperated.

"Good morning," Gregory said politely, but the effort it took him to say the words casually gave him away.

"I have never seen anything like it in my life," Hansel said sympathetically.

Gregory's handsome features spread into a mischievous grin, and he laughed ruefully, "At this rate, we could be brothers in a week." He shook his head, "I have never seen my mother act this way."

Hansel laughed as well, "Nor I my father. Quite frankly, my father has avoided people since my mother died. I can't remember the last time he talked to someone besides me," he said gravely.

Gregory looked at him thoughtfully for few minutes. "Perhaps, we should be happy for them," he said a little tentatively.

"Perhaps," Hansel admitted, "but I wish they could tone it down a bit. It makes me uncomfortable to be in the same room with them."

Gregory laughed again, "Why do you think I am here? Thank God it is a nice day. I can't imagine being stuck in the cottage with them all day." He was smiling, and Hansel found himself smiling back. The prospect of spending the day with a person his own age was exciting. He did interact with the kids in the village on market day, but his primary activities were selling the bundles of wood and getting the supplies they needed. And it might not be just a day if this crazy thing between his father and Elena was as serious and powerful as it seemed. Could he have a brother and a mother? Could they be a family? Gregory went over and patted the mare; her name was Patsy. Hansel picked up the pitcher of milk, and Gregory grabbed the basket of eggs. They walked to the cottage and found themselves hesitating awkwardly by the door. Gregory coughed loudly, and Hansel fumbled with the door handle for a solid minute before opening the door.

Hansel's father was scooping two fried eggs onto a plate that Elena held. The table was set with three other plates of eggs. Bread, cups, napkins, and cutlery were on the table. Hansel put the pitcher of milk on the table, and Gregory put the basket on the counter near the larder. Hansel's father stood up and followed Elena to the table, holding out her chair for her and seating himself next to her. Hansel and Gregory took their chairs. The time alone seemed to have benefitted Hansel's father and Elena. Hansel could still feel the charge between them, but there also seemed to be an understanding between them about just what to do about it and that helped. Hansel glanced at Gregory, who winked at him; he felt it too. They talked and ate amicably. As they finished the meal, Hansel's father suggested that the young men gather wood in the forest and do some hunting. He didn't suggest what he and Elena would be going in their absence. Hansel and Gregory flushed slightly, but they were only too glad to go into the forest. Hansel's father got them lunches while Elena started cleaning up at the washstand.

Hansel led Gregory to the barn, and they equipped themselves with axes, knives, bows, bundles, Donny, and Sampson. Hansel showed Gregory how to set snares as they walked through the forest. They talked. Gregory told Hansel about life in their village, Littletown. His father had been a carpenter. Life had been good in the village when both his parents had been alive. They had plenty to eat and nice clothes and possessions. It was harder after his father died. At first, he was slightly too young to get steady work, but it had been easier since he turned fifteen and looked more like a young man than a child. Hansel, in turn, told him about life in the woods and about the village. Hansel knew Tom Bradley. He admired the smith and told Gregory about him. Having met Elena and Gregory, Hansel could see the family resemblance. Tom had green eyes, but his sister's curly auburn hair. As a smith, he was well built and muscular like his father—something that Hansel had always admired about the smith. Looking at Gregory, Hansel could imagine him filling-out like the smith and found himself blushing at the thought. Hansel tried to do most of the axe work to spare Gregory's hands, but Gregory wasn't put off, working up quite a set of blisters by the time they stopped and tried a little hunting. Though unsuccessful at hunting, they had more luck with the snares and brought home three rabbits along with the wood. Hansel had Gregory drop his bundle and take the rabbits in to the cottage while he started unloading the bundles. Gregory returned quickly, shaking his head and snorting.

"I don't know whether it is better or worse," he said trying to make light of the situation. "But they are definitely *together*."

Hansel looked Gregory over carefully. "What do you mean?" Hansel asked.

Gregory smiled a little bitterly and said, "That charge thing is back. They are being careful, but you can feel it is an effort not to be touching each other. I have heard about love like that—love at first sight. But it is quite something to actually watch it happen—and to *my mother*. I don't know whether to be scandalized or glad to know that love is something one can enjoy past one's youth." He shook his head in a gesture that so completely expressed his bafflement that Hansel found himself snickering in agreement.

Finished with the wood, the young men returned to the cottage. The leftover goose had been made into a hearty stew with carrots, potatoes, onions, herbs and goat's milk. Hansel's father set the stew pot on a metal trivet on the table, and Elena dished out bowls of stew on to cubes of stale bread. Each poured cider for him or herself. After grace, they talked about their days, eating in between descriptions. Hansel's father and Elena admitted to walking around the property, working in the garden, and taking a walk in the woods where they gathered mushrooms and wild strawberries. Gregory showed his mother his blisters, and Hansel's father glowered at Hansel for not doing most of the axe work, but Gregory silenced both of them by saying that given the circumstances it looked like he needed to build up the calluses. After a brief silence where both of the adults turned a satisfying shade of pink, Hansel had them address the immediate future.

"So what happens now?" he asked. "You're crazy about each other; we get that," darting a glance at Gregory who nodded in approval and support. "Don't you think that you are rushing just a bit recklessly. I mean flash fires, flame suddenly, but they burn out. Have you thought this out or is it all impulse?" Hansel struggled through the last couple questions blushing furiously, but they all felt his genuine concern.

When Hansel couldn't continue, Gregory asked, "What are we doing, mother, are we going to the village or are we staying here? Is there any plan?" Gregory glanced at Hansel who smiled at him gratefully for intervening.

Hansel's father reached out and took Elena's hand, twining his fingers through hers. Looking at Gregory, he said, "I would like you and your mother to stay … for a bit." Then he turned and looked at his son pointedly.

"Yes, of course, we would like you to stay," Hansel answered his father's demand automatically, but he felt another wave of pure excitement washing over him. Gregory would stay; Elena would stay. He was happy and then another batch of questions struck him. Where would they stay he thought with horror—and all the implications of that thought. The last place he wanted to be was in the room by his father's bed—if she came to him in the night or if he brought her to his room—his room—not his parents' room. As these last few thoughts flashed through his mind, he caught a glimpse of Gregory's face draining of color—as if the same thoughts in reverse were occurring to him.

Hansel looked at his father who was blushing furiously but who also seemed to understand the discomfort of the two young men. He nodded curtly. Hansel understood that to mean that Elena and he would change rooms. All of them blushed at that point, and Elena started nervously reaching for bowls to excuse herself from the table. Gregory grabbed cups, and Hansel cleared off the cutlery and the empty stew pot.

Hansel darted into the small bedroom and again removed his essential belongings. Gregory, in full sympathy with his distress, opened the door of his room, so Hansel could stow his things there until Elena had moved her things. After the delicate dance of musical rooms, they sat by the fire and Gregory and Hansel took turns reading. Elena sat in an arm chair next to which was a basket of assorted yarns and needles. One project, apparently started in the absence of the young people, was a scarf, Hansel judged from the short width of it. His mother's things, he thought, but pleased to see them put to use.

The next few days fell into an easy rhythm. They ate breakfast together and avoided discussing sleeping arrangements. The young men packed lunches and left the happy couple to the domestic and husbandry tasks of the homestead and to getting to know each other in every way possible (their histories and their dreams as well as their bodies and bodily pleasures). The young men grew close too, talking about everything from their pasts to their parents to their lack of success in relationships of their own.

Market day approached, and Hansel's father made the remarkable announcement at supper that they would all go. Hansel just stared at his father dumbstruck. Elena took his father's hand and squeezed it. "We need to see my brother," she said softly, "and arrange a wedding." They all went slightly pink at the statement, but the dinner of roast rabbits in mushroom sauce with fresh bread distracted them.

On market day, they loaded the wagon. Elena rode on the wagon with Hansel's father, and the young men rode together on Patsy. Hansel rode behind Gregory and was startled to find that about an hour into the ride that he was aroused. Gregory's tight, firm buttocks rubbing against him couldn't be ignored. He flushed with embarrassment and thought again of Gregory's uncle and how Gregory might fill out so muscularly. Gregory's back stiffened in response. Hansel felt a surge of shame. Was he repulsing Gregory? Were his feelings un-natural? Surely, his father and Gregory's mother would think so. Attraction for them was between a man and a woman. His attraction to Tom Bradley's muscular form and his lack of interest in the village young women suddenly seemed to make sense. He liked males, not females. But Gregory was close to being his brother. How would that complicate things for his father and Elena and Gregory and himself? Startling him, was Gregory relaxing against him, feeling his erection but not moving away from it. Gregory, it seemed, liked males too, like him. Hansel flushed with pleasure and excitement.

As they neared the village, the people that they passed stared at them. Old Hansel Hansen's return to society was taken due notice of. By the time they reached the smithy, Tom Bradley was waiting outside. He stood erect—tense trying to read the face of his sister and the faces of her three companions.

"Elena, are you well?" he asked, anxiety clear in his voice.

"I am well, brother," she said clearly and firmly. "We got lost in the storm, and the Hansens have been very kind to us." She smiled at him, and he smiled back, but eyed Old Hansel and Young Hansel.

Tom helped his sister dismount the wagon and led them all into the smithy. The accumulated crowd was left to stare after them as they disappeared indoors. Inside, Hansel's father asked consent to marry the smith's sister. Tom stared at them both, shocked at the proposition, but then Hansel and Gregory chimed in—explaining the circumstances and the attraction, and Tom looked at the bond that was so clearly between Hans and Elena. The marriage was arranged. Elena and Gregory would spend a few days with Tom and his family, and on Saturday they would be married, and then could permanently retire to the Hansen homestead.

They shared a spectacular lunch, and then it was time for the Hansens to leave and go back to the homestead. Tom looked curiously at the pained expressions of both his sister and his nephew as they saw Hans and Hansel off. Happy to be re-united with family as they obviously were, there was a melancholy about them too. Tom thought he understood, if Elena could meet and be committed to marriage in a matter of days, the separation would be hard. His nephew's grief, however, puzzled him. Did he miss his future father so much? That seemed unlikely. Did he miss his future brother? And if so, how? He shook his head. The impossible was happening. Hans Hansen had left his solitude—had left his solitude for his sister. Jack Stephens had been moving to compel his sister to marriage, and this thwarted his efforts and protected her in a way Tom would have been willing to do himself, but this was better—Hans, Hansel, and Gregory—but they were so isolated where they were. Could he get them to move closer to the village or even to the village? That would be best, he thought. He let it drift from his mind as he integrated his sister and nephew into the fabric of his family, his wife and two daughters and two sons.

Tom watched as he saw his sister and nephew interact with genuine pleasure with his family and yet feel a grief at their separation from the Hansens. It made him wonder exactly just what had passed at the Hansen homestead. He felt a vague sense of jealousy and confusion as the two primary warring emotions. What exactly had happened there? Jack Stephens and his men had arrived three days ago demanding Elena. Tom had been shocked, scared for his sister, and glad that she was not there. Now, now what? Elena loved Hans, and Hans loved Elena—that was plain. But what was it with his nephew? Why was he pining as much as she was at the separation? Was he in love too? That would be disastrous.

The days passed in a bustle of activity; it would be a small wedding in the Bradley home. Elena was to be dressed in a new gown of pale browns with copper colored lace highlights. Gregory was provided with new clothes that similarly brought out his eyes and hair color. Tom had had the dressmaker size up Hans and Hansel before they left town, and she had made matching garments for both of them. As soon as the Hansens entered town, they were ushered to the Bradleys to change for the quiet ceremony.

Tom watched with a mingled satisfaction and confusion at the joy of this re-united family—his sister, Hans, his nephew, and Hansel. Some of the dynamics he understood, between his sister and Hans, but between Gregory, Hansel, and Elena, he did not understand. But it was loving, he knew that much. And wasn't that all that really mattered? Yes, the voice in his head answered.

Formally married, Hans and Elena retired to the Hansen homestead, taking Hansel and Gregory with them. As the honeymoon wore off, Hans started to join the young men in the afternoons to harvest wood and haul it. That still left Hansel and Gregory the mornings (and presumably their parents) to be alone and intimate. And they were; Hansel touched Gregory, and Gregory touched Hansel.

The young men had gone fishing and had stripped completely to avoid soaking their clothes. They had caught a dozen trout between spearing them and using a net. Hansel was placing the last of the fish on the bank of the small lake when he turned to find Gregory staring at him with blatant desire and longing. They had embraced before and kissed, but something held them back—some sense that others wouldn't understand—even their parents. The church fathers were very clear on the matter of who were the appropriate partners of romantic love—and two males weren't an option. Plus with their parents married, it was like incest even though they weren't real blood brothers. But there alone, naked in the shallow water, it didn't seem to matter. They were in each other's arms suddenly and all the suppressed passion and emotion of the last couple of weeks flamed. Kiss followed kiss. Hands roamed touching face, neck, breast, nipple, shoulder, back, buttock, balls, and penis. They made each other come and lay on the bank in each other's arms. When the languidness of post-orgasm faded and brought them back to more rational thought, they were engulfed in a sense of panic.

Gregory touched Hansel's face, "What do we do now?" he asked, his voice tense with anxiety.

Hansel looked into the golden eyes and shook his head. "I don't know. I … I … don't think we can go … go … back," he choked out. The thought of abandoning his father was devastating. But it was equally devastating to think of abandoning Gregory or attempting to live with him and not be with him as they were now, lovers. The bleakest thing was thinking of the disapproval his father would express at the subject of Hansel's love. He couldn't face that. He looked back at Gregory whose face was flooded by similar dark thoughts.

"I think you're right," Gregory said slowly, the regret and sadness clear in his voice.

They dressed slowly. They didn't need all the fish for just to the two of them, so they took four and went in search of a sheltered spot in which to spend the night. They found a cave, made a fire, ate, and snuggled into the comfort and the pleasures of each other's arms for the night. The next day they wandered in the forest. They brought down two ducks and found shelter beneath an overhang of rocky ledge. The following day they continued deeper into the great forest. They had not found shelter, and it was nearing twilight when they smelled wood smoke.

Following their noses, they came across the most curious cottage they had ever seen. At first glance it seemed to be made of food—of every delicacy imaginable—of candies and pastries, of tender slices of meat, of carefully cooked and seasoned vegetables, of wonderfully ripe fruits, of generously buttered breads, of flavorful cheeses. Gregory stretched out his hand to touch the wall closest to them, and the images changed. Suddenly, the two of them were staring at naked bodies, male and female all in the act of self-pleasuring. The two young men gasped and blushed furiously. They stared at the images before them, too shocked to speak. Hansel looked at Gregory. Yes, Gregory was seeing what he was. The pictures showed people of all ages and colors and sizes in blissful sexual ecstasy. It was both horrifying and exciting. If sex was natural, why not?

Hansel reached for Gregory's hand, and the two of them silently walked around the cottage to the next wall. They gasped again. The images were just as explicit except that they were of males and females in a wide variety of acts of sexual pleasuring, fellatio, cunnilingus, and intercourse. Again the people came in all colors and shapes, but the ages of the actors did not include prepubescent children. They stood staring for some time working up the courage to see what was on the next wall of the cottage.

The next wall was full of images of female couples engaged in sexual play—cunnilingus but also pleasuring with hands and fingers and dildos. The females came in all colors and shapes again and again excluded prepubescent children.

With anticipation they rounded the final corner and gasped again. The wall was full of images of male couples engaged in sexual play—fellatio but also hand-jobs and anal sex. The male participants were youthful and old, black and white and yellow and russet. Some were lean and muscular, but others were flaccid and plump. All were post puberty judging from their pubic hair. Gregory and Hansel glanced from the images to each other. Perhaps, if the cottage could display all this variety in human sexuality, they weren't so abnormal after all—their faces said more clearly than either one of them felt capable of articulating. Gregory grinned and touched Hansel's face, which was breaking into an answering grin.

"Good evening," said a voice, jolting Gregory and Hansel back to their surroundings. Hansel let go of Gregory's hand, and they turned to see the person standing in a doorway they had not noticed. There was something odd about the person. Hansel couldn't tell if it was a man or a woman; he glanced at Gregory who looked similarly confused.

"Good evening," the young men answered cautiously. They moved toward the person—whoever this person was—he or she had answers for the questions they had about themselves and others. Closer, they froze and gasped—trying to process the aberration before them. He/she/it was half male and half female—a hermaphrodite—ze seemed the better pronoun under the circumstances—a combination, not a single gendered identity. That accounted for the oddness. Ze's hair was shoulder-length and a sandy blond color, but one side of the face and body had softer female features and parts (a big blue colored eye and long lashes, full lips, soft, hairless cheek, a feminine shoulder, a developed female breast, a slender waist, a full hip, the mounded pubic area of a female, a long shapely leg, a delicate ankle, and a small foot) the other side of the face and body had harder male features and parts (a heavier brow, a smaller blue colored eye, narrower lips, check and chin sprouting day old stubble, a broad, muscular neck, shoulder, chest, and arm, all sprinkled with coarser masculine hair, a tapering waist, a narrow hip, pubic hair that nested a ball and a penis, a hard muscular leg also coated with coarser masculine hair, and a larger foot). Ze wore a sheer robe, so the young men saw everything.

"Children, I am Herim. How can I help you?" Herim bowed theatrically to them.

"What is this place?" Hansel asked.

"It is my palace," Herim answered. "In the time before history, all knew my palace and found pleasure there, but patriarchal culture drove me into the depths of the forest or secret places. It made any sexual activity beyond sexual intercourse between the active male and the passive female forbidden or wrong. As if anyone should be passive or dominant in sexual activity; it's just the wrong metaphor. Mutually empowered, mutually pleasuring, and by mutual consent—that is the better dynamic. You pleasure each other, do you not? You love each other. You would not cause each other pain or force the other to do something that he did not wish to do, correct? I rant a little, excuse me. Being persecuted tends to distort your perspective—or at least, it distorts mine. Sexual pleasure is as natural as the need for food and drink, sleep, love (parental, platonic, and romantic)—it is a part of both platonic love and romantic love."

Hansel and Gregory both exchanged glances of incredulity at these last words; Herim noticed and continued.

"Sex is just sex. Jettison it from the morality that you were taught. Restructure your world around pleasure for all and security for all. Love is the answer. Love is always the answer. Love is the better way—be the better angels of your natures. How could it be anything but better? Acceptance not exclusion. Enough. Enter my palace children and see the ways of love." Herim ushered them inside.

Herim wasn't kidding. Stepping across the threshold, the modest cottage changed into a vast, sprawling palace filled with guests. People milled around in happy conversations; the atmosphere was festive. Herim encouraged the young men to explore the palace, but before Herim excused zirself to attend other guests, ze warned them.

"There is one absolute law for finding pleasure here; there is no coercion, no force. There are sheets of paper and pens in every room or alcove. In any sexual encounter, each participant must write down what he or she or ze wishes to do and wishes to have done to he/she/ze, even if that only consists of watching. Each contract is subject to verbal amendment. A request to stop must be honored by any and/or all participants. Violation of the contract (written or verbally amended) will result in public humiliation and punishment, including if necessary, banishment. Do you understand?" Herim asked severely.

Hansel and Gregory flushed at the explicitness of Herim's statements and their implications but nodded in agreement. The young men found all sorts of people flirting and dancing in the grand ballroom. In small private rooms, every kind of coupling seemed to be taking place including group sex—threes and even more.

Hansel and Gregory passed an empty room, and Gregory took Hansel's hand, and they walked into it together.

"What do we do now?" Hansel asked breathlessly.

"Anything we want," Gregory answered, moving toward the waist-high table in front of them with a blank contract laid out. They entered their names and the date. They blushed writing down what they wanted to do to each other and laughed together. It seemed strange and yet liberating to be so explicit about what they wanted. Both noted the "subject to verbal amendment" clause at the bottom of the page. They embraced and started kissing. They found themselves on the bed. They stripped each other of their clothing. The touching escalated, and they brought each other to climax—kissing, licking, gently nibbling/biting, sucking, blowing, stroking, and touching. After their lovemaking, they wandered around the palace. A man dressed as a woman offered them bits of roasted meat on small bits of toasted bread. A young woman about their age offered them glasses of cider. They continued to wander. In one corridor, they heard a smacking sound that they both recognized as flesh striking flesh. They looked at each other in alarm, not knowing what to do. A pair of women were nuzzling each other against one wall, but one of them noticed the young men's distress.

"It's is okay," she assured them. "They do it all the time. It's part of their contract. He likes to be spanked. The slight pain excites him and helps him climax. Different strokes for different folks, right?" she smiled suggestively, and then laughed at their embarrassment. "There is lots to learn here," she continued. "Find couples who don't mind being watched, and you'll see that there is much more variety than you might have thought." She laughed again at their deepening blushes, but then stopped as her partner tugged on her hand and suggested that they find a room of their own. The women disappeared down the corridor.

Hansel and Gregory found their way back to the grand ball room and contented themselves with dancing and watching the other dancers. As it got late, Herim found them and probed them about their future plans. They tried to explain why they had left. How they were sure that their relationship would not be approved of and might even be punished.

"Are you sure?" Herim had asked them. "Do you really think that Hans Hansen and Elena Griffin could stop loving his/her child because of who the child is attracted to when attraction refuses to obey laws of reason?"

Gregory and Hansel stared at each other and then back at Herim, "You know our parents?" they both exclaimed wide-eyed.

Herim laughed. "Yes, I know your parents. You'd be surprised at the people I know, though much fewer admit to knowing me," he said with a sly smile that held a mingled mirth and regret. "Let's see what tomorrow brings, shall we?" ze said and showed them to a bedroom that they could call their own for the duration of their stay.

Alone in their room, the young men felt overwhelmed by the revelations of Herim's palace. By un-spoken consent, they did not entertain the implications that their parents knew Herim, had been to the palace, and knew its secrets. Both silently wondered in what capacity their parents had come there, but they forced such thoughts from their minds. They took off their clothes, climbed into the inviting bed, and found comfort and sleep in each other's arms.

The sun was up when they woke the next morning. They used the chamber pot, but they didn't dress. Hansel grabbed a contract and wrote out his desires while Gregory read them over his lover's shoulder, smiling and waiting to write out his own. Once the contract was written, they commenced to fulfill its particulars with great enthusiasm. Sometime later, they cleaned themselves off and got dressed. They found a small dining room and had just finished a light breakfast, when a boy appeared and said that Herim wanted to see them. The boy led them to an elegant library. Herim was seated at a grand desk. Two travel-worn, cloaked figures stood in front of zir.

Herim cleared zir throat at the sight of the young men, and the figures turned revealing themselves as Elena Griffin and Hans Hansen—both of whom wore twin expressions of anxiety and worry. Those expressions faded at the sight of the young men to be replaced with expressions of relief and hurt.

Hansel felt a wave of guilt, and glanced nervously at Gregory who was also looking mortified.

"Hansel!" "Gregory!" Elena and Hans exclaimed at the same time.

Herim stood up. "I told you they were fine," ze said to them softly. Then Herim turned to the young men, "Let's all take a couple of deep breaths and sit down," waving to the four chairs clustered around the desk.

Herim had Hansel and Gregory sit directly in front of zir with their parents on either side of his and her son. With everyone seated, Herim spoke, "Elena and Hans, the young men ran away because they are gay and thought you would disapprove."

Hansel and Gregory flushed and looked at each other sheepishly, and then shot tentative looks at their parents. Hansel saw his father's face change from a forced calm to a one of contrition and self-remonstration. Hansel's father glanced past his son and nodded at his wife. His father took a deep breath, and then addressed himself to both young men.

"Hansel and Gregory, do you really think that we didn't know?" he asked softly.

Hansel stiffened. Know, how could his father know? Hansel hadn't even known himself. He felt Gregory go rigid next to him, apparently having a similar reaction. Hansel didn't remember talking to his father about his interactions with the kids of the village on market days—or at least not much. He certainly hadn't talked about romantic attractions because there hadn't been any. He gave up trying to tease it out when his father started speaking again.

"Do you think we care more for whom you are attracted to than for you?" his father continued.

Before Hansel or Gregory could respond, Elena cut in, "Do you disapprove of your father and me?" she asked.

Disapprove—Hansel thought with shock—they were adults, and they were heterosexual. It was sudden, yes. It was embarrassing to think of his father as sexual, yes, but he didn't feel he was entitled to disapprove. "What is there to disapprove of?" he asked in exasperation. "And even if we did, it wouldn't be our place to say anything; it is between the two of you."

"Exactly," both Elena and Hans said together. "What happens between romantic partners is their business. The church fathers have poisoned people's ideas about sex and sexuality," Hansel's father said quietly.

“Surely, even your short time here helps you see past the narrow teachings of the church fathers?” Elena added.

Gregory glanced at Hansel, and the two of them smiled with relief. Herim smiled broadly and cleared zir throat, rising to zir feet. “Ah, my dears,” ze said to the young men, “I told you.” Then sweeping his look to the whole group, Herim said, “You are all welcome here as you see fit,” and then narrowed his gaze on Hansel and Gregory, “You can return and stay with your parents’ permission.” Herim bowed then and left them to attend to other matters.

It was decided that the young men would return with their parents to the Griffin-Hansen homestead where the young men would share the larger bedroom in the new addition of the cottage, but they would be free to return to Herim’s palace in the future.

They took their leave of Herim and thanked zir for zir hospitality. The young men rode together on Patsy, and Elena rode Donny with Hans leading the mule. And with occasional visits to Herim’s palace, they settled into a happy routine of work and pleasure and lived happily ever after.

HP

Lenora's Prince

Lenora stood at the window. It had all the makings of a spectacular day. It was cool, and mist clung to the hills, but the sun was blazing through in patches, lighting up the moisture on the trees and grasses like diamonds and silver beads. Despite the magnificence of the day, she felt an odd sense of foreboding, which was only increased as her gaze was drawn to the small stable roof where a large raven sat cleaning its feathers. A loud "caw" interrupted its grooming, and the bird was suddenly joined by another raven, and then, her heart sinking, a third. They seemed nearly as startled as she felt; they looked at each other and then at her, and then in an explosion of wings, they flew off to the west.

Three ravens. An ill omen. And flying west—to the land of the dead.

Lenora shook herself. She would not allow herself to think such thoughts. It would be an important few days. There would be court business this morning. She was already dressed for it. Her maid, Katie, had put up her hair elaborately, and she was dressed in a beautiful gown of soft golden browns that set off the colors of her hair and her light honey-colored eyes. There would be feasting that afternoon and evening. There was a hunt the following day, competitions between the fighting men, and more feasting. The next day there was to be a spectacular ball. She looked up at the hills and was comforted to see a faint rainbow stretched between a patch of mist and the blazing sun.

She made her way down to the Great Hall. Her father was seated on his throne. Her step-mother, Queen Margaret was absent, but she was hugely pregnant and had been feeling unwell of late. Lenora was worried for her; she hoped that her step-mother's unwellness was not indication of the labor that the poor woman would need to soon endure. Her father motioned her to the queen's throne. After she seated herself, the other counselors, ministers, and members of the court seated themselves. Lord John, the queen's brother, sat closest to them as was usual. The herald shouted out the order of business, and the petitions began. It was the regular stuff—disputes, quarrels, thefts, assaults. King Arthur dealt with most of it with his quiet authority and dignity, but some of the thornier conflicts he set to her, grooming her for her turn at rulership. The session was easing up, when the herald interrupted and announced the arrival of Lord Everett. Lenora was surprised. Glancing at her father, she saw that he was just as surprised and slightly uncomfortable. Lord John stiffened beside them. Lord Everett had wanted to marry Lady Margaret, but she had chosen her father, and the two men had not spoken since. It had been at least five years. Lord Everett had in fact left the kingdom for a time, travelling to distant lands it was said; he had in fact only recently returned.

Lord Everett was a powerfully built man of about forty. His dark hair framed his face. He was followed by a few of his men. His face had shown a brief glimpse of disappointment when he saw Lenora in Margaret's place, but that was replaced by another look that made the hairs on the back of Lenora's neck pickle. She looked hastily away. She felt her father stiffen in his chair and saw his hands clench the arms of his throne, the knuckles going white with fury.

"My King," Lord Everett's voice boomed into the sudden silence, "I bring you a rare gift." He knelt where he stood, and his men parted, kneeling also and revealing a young man. The hall buzzed with surprised and shocked whispers. The young man was nearly naked with his arms bound behind him. The man behind him pushed the captive roughly to his knees and then knelt himself. Lenora was just as shocked as the rest. The young man was unlike anyone she had ever seen. He had beautiful dark skin, green-yellow hazel eyes, like a cat, and curly black hair that was cropped close to his head. She had rarely ever seen a young man in such a state of undress. He was tall and well built, with powerful arms, shoulders, and chest muscles. His skin shone, and she imagined it would feel like oiled walnut to the touch. She flushed with embarrassment.

"His name is Achilles; he is learned, I am told. He is my gift to you, my King, that the rift between us may be healed," Lord Everett added, his voice carefully controlled. It was said sincerely enough. The whispers in the hall approved—that was clear enough. But Lenora felt threatened. Lord Everett's look before belied this act of reconciliation. She glanced at her father; King Arthur was similarly troubled, and Lord John was frowning ever so slightly.

"Thank you, Lord Everett; please join us later for the feast, you and your men," her father said politely, and he inclined his head to the man and then raised his hand, releasing them. Lenora watched as Achilles was pulled to his feet. Despite his bonds and his state of undress, he held himself like a prince—his head held high, his back straight and erect. He kept his face carefully impassive, but she saw his eyes travel across the room. She watched as he looked at her father and then at herself. He was scrutinizing them, she knew. She would have given anything to know what his assessment was in that flash of first impression. The king then motioned to Lord John who stepped forward to take custody of the slave. Lord Everett and his men stood, and a page led them from the hall to find them accommodations. Lenora saw Achilles' back then, as Lord John walked him out of room, and was horrified to see the web of scars that crossed it. What on earth had been done to him? She didn't want to think about it—but she knew. He had been whipped, and the thought nearly made her sick.

The court returned to the business at hand, and the last few petitioners were heard and dealt with in less than an hour. The king and Lenora retired to the royal library where they found Lord John waiting.

"A slave! What on earth is the man giving me a slave for?" the king demanded.

"To get between you and my sister," Lord John answered matter-of-factly, his face troubled.

"What do you mean?" the king asked, startled.

Lord John was fair-haired, blue-eyed and attractive like his sister, but his face darkened as he thought about how to respond. Steeling himself, he cleared his face, "It is a great secret in our family," he said slowly. "Our great-aunt was abducted and sold into slavery. They were unable to get her back, though they tried. No one in our family would ever have anything to do with slavery as a result. How Lord Everett has come to know this information I do not know. Margaret never would have told him; clearly she hasn't ever told you—though you are her husband." Lenora watched her father's features react to this information and saw alarm and irritation. Lord John did too, and added hastily, "Don't be angry with her. It is a closely guarded family secret. I would not be telling you now, but I feel you have to know, so that you can counter whatever Lord Everett is planning appropriately."

King Arthur nodded reluctantly. "Where is the boy now, the slave?" he asked.

"Temporarily, I had him placed in a cell in the dungeon," Lord John answered.

"Arthur," Lord John added softly, "did you see the boy's back?"

"I did, John," the king answered grimly.

An interview with the slave was decided upon. Lenora wanted to stay, but she wasn't sure she would be allowed. Her father wanted a female point of view, and once it was established that Achilles had been provided with proper clothing, guards were sent to bring him up. The king seated himself at the great desk. Lenora sat next to him and Lord John stood behind them.

Achilles' hands had been rebound. He wore brown breeches and a white shirt. He had been given boots. It made Lenora uncomfortable to see him bound and flanked by two guards. Apparently it made the king and Lord John uncomfortable, too. The king had the guards stand back and he, himself, stood, walked around the desk, and cut the ropes from the boy's wrists.

Achilles looked at them warily as the king retook his seat. "My King, I am your servant," he said in clear but slightly accented English, and prostrated himself on the floor.

"Please, rise, Achilles," the king said hastily. He motioned to one of the chairs in front of the desk when the young man was on his feet again. "Tell us about yourself, Achilles. How do you find yourself a slave and how you have come to be with Lord Everett?"

Achilles nervously sat down. His discomfort made Lenora wonder how he expected to be treated. It turned out that Achilles had been from a royal family in Alexandria, Egypt. He was nineteen, but he had been taken the year before by his uncle who thereby cleared the way for his own son to head the family. He was educated; he spoke Arabic, French, and Latin in addition to English. He was not Muslim, but he was evasive about his religious background—not Christian either, perhaps. He knew horses; he had been trained in arms and was a fair hunter by his own estimation. Lord Everett had bought him in the slave market in Zanzibar, far from his home. His lordship had not been particularly interested in him. He had not questioned Achilles. He had seen him fed and monitored but had largely ignored him. The journey "home" had been long. Several of Lord Everett's men had contracted a fever on the ship. Achilles had gotten a mild version of it, but one of his lordship's men had died of the fever. The trip overland was easier; they had been back for two weeks before today.

King Arthur listened carefully as did Lenora and Lord John. They were in a fine pickle, Lenora thought. Achilles had been presented to the court as a slave gift to the king. To free him would be an insult to Lord Everett—a rejection of his gift—and a personal condemnation of Lord Everett's character as a man who would hold a slave. Yet to keep him would be a deep affront to Queen Margaret and Lord John (though no one but the four of them would know and understand that). Additionally, Lenora was sure that her father did not view slavery as legitimate. The poverty of some of his people pained him personally, and he did all in his power to alleviate it, but his people were free people. Even apprentices, maidens, and married women had rights under the law. It was not so in other kingdoms, she knew.

King Arthur shook his head and sighed. "Achilles, Lord Everett has set me a fine trap with you at its center," he said reluctantly.

Achilles' shoulders tensed noticeably, and he made his face go carefully blank.

"Nay, lad, do not fear from us," the king said, reading the young man's distress. Her father glanced at both Lenora and Lord John. Their faces mirrored his own. "I cannot have a slave nor can I let you go. You must appear a slave, I am afraid." He hesitated. "John, what do you think?"

Lord John stepped forward, "I agree, Arthur. He could be useful in the stables with all the extra horses here," he said carefully. "Do you understand, Achilles? Would it suit you to work with the horses and the other grooms?"

Achilles looked between them warily; whatever he expected, this clearly wasn't it. Instead of decreasing his fears, this apparent civility increased it. Lenora felt his panic; she ached to comfort him. "Achilles," she began softly, "it really is okay." More firmly, she added, "We mean you no harm." His eyes shot to hers. She felt the intensity of his gaze might burn her, but then they softened. He believed her.

"A groom?" he repeated cautiously, looking between the three of them.

"Yes, for now," the king said. After a moment, he added, "You might also teach the children Arabic and work with them on their Latin and French, but we will consider that after the current festivities have finished." Seeing the puzzled expression on Achilles' face, he glanced at Lenora and explained, "There is Lenora, obviously, but she has step-brother who is four, and we are about to have another baby. Then there are children of my counselors and ministers." He looked back at Achilles. "Will you do it?" he asked. "Play the servant?"

"Play the servant?" Achilles repeated, uncertainly. "You mean that I will not be a true slave? I will have full authority over my own person and body?"

"Full authority over your own person and body?" the king asked, finding the phrasing odd.

"No one can beat me or abuse me bodily without due cause?" Achilles said, his eyes blazing with a kind of defiance.

The king was appalled. Emotions flashed across his face in an instant showing clearly the extent of his revulsion at the notion. "No," he said firmly. "No one can beat you or abuse you. You will have full authority over your own person." He hesitated, "Due cause?" he asked.

"For punishment of a transgression of rule or law," Achilles explained.

"You will be treated like any of the other servants in my employ. Generally, we are a happy family, and there is little transgression or punishment, but it does happen on occasion. I prefer peaceful means of settling conflict whenever possible. I find it much more effective than corporal methods of punishment," the king explained.

Achilles listened carefully, his shoulders relaxing slightly. "Employ?" he asked in a surprised whisper.

Lord John chuckled, "Aye, lad, wages. Though first you'll be exercising your wages in clothing, room and board, and supplies or goods such as you need. I am in charge of the king's purse."

Their business concluded; Lenora was put in charge of showing Achilles around a little before bringing him to Old Joe, the Master of Horse. Lord John and the king went to find the queen and appraise her Lord Everett's presence, his gift, and the arrangements for Achilles.

Lenora felt a little awkward, but Achilles was so happy and excited about the changes in his fortune that she got caught up in his mood. He had two brothers and two sisters at home; his parents sounded nice; they had loved him. He missed his family very much, but he assumed that he would never see them again. The thought made Lenora sad. She introduced him to Mistress Isabella who presided over all housekeeping workings in the castle. If Old Joe didn't have a place for Achilles in the stables, he was to report back to her for a room. She sat them down at a small table and got them both a few hot rolls liberally spread with butter and raspberry preserves and two cups of cider. Achilles consumed the first roll in two bites and drained the cup. Mistress Isabella clicked her tongue in disapproval and had a girl bring more rolls and cider.

"When is the last time you ate?" Lenora asked quietly.

Achilles flushed with embarrassment. "They gave me something this morning; it was barely edible. I am not even exactly sure what it was supposed to be," he answered. Mistress Isabella clicked more disapproval but then left them to oversee the preparations of the coming feasting.

Sated, they made their way to the stables. Old Joe was happy for another groom, and Lenora left them talking horse and made her way back to her apartments. She felt oddly connected to Achilles. Her thoughts kept drifting back to selected moments when he had smiled unguardedly or his eyes had flashed with emotion. He had such beautiful eyes.

The feast was a success. Mistress Isabella had out done herself as usual. There was plenty of food and drink for all. A small band of musicians played at the back of the Great Hall as entertainment. It was a pleasant affair except that there was slight tension in the air that she thought most of the guests must be oblivious to, but she felt it. Her father and Lord John felt it too. All three of them were just slightly tense. The casual observer wouldn't notice it if he or she didn't know them very well. It was Lord Everett and his men—there was a quiet menace about them. They didn't mingle with the others but kept to themselves. Their eyes roved over the crowd with cold calculation.

Lenora found herself searching through the crowded hall. When her eyes finally lighted on Achilles, she felt a warm glow of relief. Lord John had found the young man some dressier clothes for the evening, and he wore a dark brown coat and waistcoat. He looked handsome. He was sitting with some of the other grooms, but he too was rigid with tension. As though divining her eyes upon him, he looked up. He smiled and nodded to her and then resumed his conversation. Her eyes came back to him regularly. She saw him glance at Lord Everett every once in a while and knew that he felt what she felt; there was danger here. She glanced at her father and then at Lord John seated with them.

Lord John nodded, "The boy is caught up in it too. Did you notice, Arthur?"

"Yes, I noticed," he replied, frowning.

The tension was draining, and Lenora took the first opportunity to excuse herself from the feast. When she stood, she felt Lord Everett's eyes upon her. His expression showed irritation and disappointment in her leaving. Lord John stood abruptly, "I will see you to your rooms, Princess," and he held out his arm, and she went with him gratefully, her father murmuring a thank you to his brother-in-law and a benediction to her while he watched Lord Everett with hot fury.

Four guards stood rigidly outside the rooms. The royal family was all billeted in her parents' apartments, so guests could take other rooms. Lord John and her step-brother, Prince Anthony, were bunked in the study. Princess Lenora was bunked in the sitting room. The queen was awake and pacing when they entered the apartment. The prince was asleep, so they closed themselves in the sitting room, and Lord John and Lenora told her the events of the evening. Queen Margaret was by turns furious and anxious.

"He means her harm, John," the queen said quietly.

"So it appears," Lord John answered grimly.

"Tell me more about this Achilles," she demanded. Lord John recounted the boy's account of his enslavement and associations with Lord Everett, and Lenora told them the things he had told her about his family and his life before.

"Trained in arms?" the queen repeated. She glanced at the clock; it was only nine o'clock. "John, would you find the boy and take him Master Flynn? Test him. If he is adequately trained, arm him."

Lord John bristled at that. "Do you think that wise?" he asked. "He was a slave until a few hours ago."

"What is your sense here, John, Lenora?" She looked between them. "He is a slave who has been freed by our family. He is beholding to us for that alone. Arm him, and he will know that we understand the risk we take but that we trust him. For a young man of royal birth with a sense of honor, what would that mean? I would think it would mean a great deal, and if he is anything like his name-sake, honor and fierceness in battle he will have. And most importantly, Lord Everett has no idea of the boy's skills and history. Arrogant as ever, he is blinded by his limited notions of people and his hunger for power."

"What do you mean?" Lenora asked, surprised by the bitterness in the queen's last words.

"Achilles is black and his back is scarred. That is all that Lord Everett will have registered about him. Is that all that you have noticed about him?" the queen asked her.

Lenora blushed scarlet and looked at the floor, "No, Achilles carries himself like a prince. I noticed that before I knew," she admitted.

"You and I, Lenora, are female," the queen continued. "Perhaps you can imagine how little regard he holds the 'fairer sex' if he is willing to dismiss a prince as a mere ignorant heathen because of the color of his skin?" She paused, "This is to our advantage, brother," she said, turning to look at Lord John.

Lord John looked at his sister appraisingly. "Okay, I'll test him with Master Flynn, but you must tell Arthur before he is armed." He bowed and left them.

The queen and Lenora talked some more, but Lenora was truly tired, and the queen sent her off to her sleep. Lenora slept badly. In her dreams, she saw the three crows looking at her and then exploding into flight. She struggled to replace the image with the rainbow. Then the menace of Lord Everett rose to be countered by the smile that Achilles had given her in the Great Hall and happiness that had radiated from him as she showed him around to be undone again by the scars on his back and the whipping that must have been the cause. Startling her most of all was the scene of a young woman being abducted and sold into slavery. In a flash, the faceless woman, who she somehow knew to be Queen Margaret's and Lord John's great-aunt, changed, and it was her own face—she was being abducted by Lord Everett, his dark features looming over her, his menace not so much about wanting her as about punishing her father and her step-mother. She screamed in protest. It was in the dream—the screaming she thought—but suddenly her father was grabbing her thrashing wrists and holding her still.

"Lenora, child, it's okay. You're safe. Lenora! Lenora! Do you hear me? Lenora!"

The screaming hadn't been in the dream, she realized. She had awoken screaming. Had she scared them all? She looked up to see Lord John and the queen standing by the door way, anxiety clear on their faces. Prince Anthony was huddled behind his mother, tears on his cheeks.

She struggled to control herself. "I am … so … sorry," she said. "I had a nightmare. Lord Everett," she began, but her father stopped her, stroking her face.

"We know or we suspect too," he said. "We won't let Margaret out of the royal apartments until he's gone. First, she is not feeling up to it, and second, she would be a target for him. You, by default, will have to fulfill royal functions of hostess over the next few days. That means attending the hunt, the feasts, and the ball. The hunt is the most worrisome. You will be attended by guards and Achilles."

"Achilles?" she said in surprise.

"Yes," Lord John said from the doorway. "The boy is quite accomplished in arms. Master Flynn and I are quite satisfied with his skills. He will be armed in the morning, and so will you," he said pointedly.

"Me?" she said weakly.

"Daggers and a short sword, I am afraid," her father said softly. "We want your weapons hidden or to look decorative. Your best defense is to appear helpless, though you are not. There will be guards, but should those be thwarted or diverted for the few moments it would take for Lord Everett's men to take advantage, you and Achilles will be enough," her father explained.

She found a funny sense of ease in knowing that Achilles would be with her. He was so beautiful in his way, and he looked so strong. She could imagine him easily using a sword or knife or bow and arrow—his muscles flexing and contracting in the wielding of weapons. She saw his beautiful chest and then remembered his ruined back. Suddenly, she saw herself pressed against his chest, warm and soft but firm. She blushed slightly.

Her father cocked an eye-brow at her. "Are you all right, child?" he asked.

"Yes, Father," she answered evasively.

They left her then, and she settled into a restless sleep where she tried not to think about Achilles but found her thoughts drifting back to him—to the hunt and him being with her—to a fight and him defending her—to a fight and her defending him—to them being together—kissing, embracing, touching, more touching, and the ultimate joining. There was something else, too, but she couldn't explain it. He seemed to call at something essential about her, but she had just met the young man. Could it really be like that—that intense? It had been that way between her father and Lady Margaret. Lenora had felt ashamed to be in the same room with them. She had felt strangely comforted, then, to find that Lord John felt the same way around the smitten couple.

Her maid helped her dress in the morning in a different dress that brought out all the browns and chestnut colors of her hair and the gold of her eyes. She blushed as she realized that the same colors that brought out her coloring also brought out Achilles'.

The royal family took their breakfast in the royal dining room. Master Flynn brought in Achilles and joined them. Achilles was nearly bursting with pride. He wore a sword and dagger. Lenora was sure he wore more daggers concealed. He looked so pleased with himself that she wanted to touch him. He shot a glance at her, and they both looked awkward. The adults around them exchanged curious glances.

The queen with Prince Anthony withdrew while the others went to take their places for the hunt. Two guards were assigned to the princess. They hunted boar. For a while, nothing happened. Then, there was a loud squeal. Someone had hurt it. Suddenly, four men rushed at them. The guards were surprised. They killed their attackers, but that left the two. Achilles flew into action, cutting down the two remaining attackers with his sword and dagger. Lenora stared at him in a shocked daze. She had known there was danger, but actually being attacked, surprised her.

Before he thought about what he was doing, Achilles had sheathed his weapons and strode to Lenora. He hugged her, clutching her to him and moving his hands over her body, checking her for signs of injury, she assumed. He said her name over and over again, but as a question, asking if she was okay. She was startled at how natural it felt to be in his arms—like she belonged there.

"I … am … okay," she whispered, shaking in his arms. He seemed to realize suddenly that he held her in an embrace and let go of her, stepping back. The guards stared at them stupidly. There was a series of soft thrumming sounds, and Achilles pushed Lenora behind him roughly. He grunted suddenly, and his body convulsed slightly. She looked up to see the two guards collapsing with arrows in their chests. Achilles snapped an arrow shaft that protruded from his left shoulder. He drew his sword again and stood in front of her.

Lord Everett stepped from the trees followed by two men, swords drawn. Lenora's heart sunk at the sight. They were going to die. Achilles was hurt, and they were outnumbered. With determination, she drew the short sword and dagger. She would not be sold into slavery, and she would not be taken prisoner by Lord Everett.

He sneered at them. "Achilles, step away, you little monkey, before you get yourself really hurt."

Achilles was rigid with barely reined in tension. He didn't speak but shook his head and didn't move from his place in front of her. Lenora could feel his rage.

Lord Everett motioned to the two men. They rushed at them, and Lenora had the satisfaction of seeing the surprised looks on their faces when they realized too late that Achilles was a deadly opponent. Lord Everett stared in disbelief for a moment and then charged them. Achilles' sword clashed against Lord Everett's. It was a more even contest. They danced back and forth, striking and parrying. Lenora could see no opening through which she might help Achilles, so she stood back, though she kept her blades ready. Achilles managed to wound Lord Everett's right arm, but he brought his dagger down piercing Achilles' thigh. He cried out, and Lenora moved suddenly bringing her short sword across Lord Everett's throat, spraying both of them with his blood. Lord Everett fell then, a look of surprised anger on his face.

Achilles was on his knees. He jerked the dagger out of his thigh with a grunt of pain. Lenora cut a length of cloth from one of the dead men's jackets and tied it tightly around Achilles' leg above the wound while he sat pressing a wad of cloth on the wound itself. With his leg addressed, they turned to each other. He reached for her, and she rested her head against his uninjured shoulder. She was shaking and crying a little. His hands stroked her head. She felt safe in his arms—more than that—she felt home. Something about him completed her. He would do anything for her she realized, and she felt like she would do anything for him. It was insane. It didn't make any sense. It was dangerous. But when she lifted her face toward him in invitation, he bent his towards her in answer. He pressed his lips against hers, and she kissed him back, her arms wrapping around him while his good arm wrapped around her.

Moments later Lord John crashed through the bushes followed by her father and several guards. They gasped at the apparition of before them. The two figures broke apart suddenly. Lenora saw that Lord John was smirking at them; the king was having more trouble with the image and was trying to control in his emotions. "Children!" he said in a strangled voice.

"Father," Lenora said, in a voice she found growing more determined as she spoke. "He protected me; he saved me."

"She was in danger … I … wanted to … help." Achilles said, blushing furiously, "I … care … for her."

"You barely know each other," the king argued.

"I have dreamed of you," Achilles said looking at Lenora.

"I have dreamed of you also," Lenora answered breathlessly.

"This can't be possible," the king said desperately looking from one to the other kneeling on the ground before him.

"Well, it sounds a hell of lot like what happened when you and Margaret declared yourselves foresworn," Lord John said, his voice full of amusement.

The king shot his brother-in-law a venomous look; he was about to say something, but Lenora interrupted him.

"Father, he's hurt," she said.

"Yes, I see," the king answered curtly. He motioned to the guards. Two of them stepped forward and helped Achilles to his feet. "What about you, Lenora; you're covered in blood. Are you hurt?" he asked anxiously.

"I am okay; it is Lord Everett's blood," and she gestured to the corpse and rose to her feet.

"Nice work, Niece," Lord John said, examining the body and moving to look at the others. "You too, Achilles," he added.

They walked back to the main group of men. The boar had been killed and was being strapped to a crudely constructed travois. Lord Everett's men were dead, two archers and nine other men in addition to his lordship. Six men and Lord Everett had gone after Lenora; the five others distracted the king and his men. Besides the two guards killed by the arrows, the archers had killed four other guardsmen before they were killed by the king's guards. There were some sword wounds among the men, but nothing too bad. A wagon had been sent for to transport the dead. Lord John had Lenora ride with Achilles, unsure whether the young man could make it back to the castle without fainting. King Arthur wasn't exactly thrilled with that prospect, but Achilles looked faint.

The injured were brought to the infirmary which was run by Mistress Abigail, a mid-wife and capable healer. The king left them to attend to other matters. Lord John stayed with Lenora. Achilles was the most severely wounded, so Mistress Abigail tended to him first. Lord John had Achilles squeeze his hand first for the removal of the arrow and the cauterization of the wound and then Mistress Abigail went to work on his leg. Lenora wiped the sweat from his brow. At a certain point, Achilles passed out. The smell of Achilles' burning flesh made Lenora think that she might pass out too, but the strong smell of crushed garlic cleared her head. She watched Mistress Abigail spread the poultice on the wound and dress it. She had cleaned the wound as well as she could, she told Lord John, but the deep nature of the puncture wound worried her. He had nodded solemnly and then left to find the king. Mistress Abigail roused Achilles and had Lenora fetch him some fresh water. Satisfied that Lenora would mind her patient, Mistress Abigail moved on to other patients. Lenora and Achilles talked quietly. Lenora held his right hand. She told him little things about her childhood. After he nodded off, Lenora sat for a time watching him. What was it about him, she wondered, that so bound her to him. She noticed that there were triangular tattoos that circled his wrists, and she wondered what they meant. Reluctantly, she left and went to change for the latest feast.

The atmosphere at the feast was charged. Most people were outraged that assaults had been made on the princess and king. That Lord Everett was dead along with his men was more than they deserved was the general feeling. Queen Margaret was at the feast and Prince Anthony with her. Lenora listened to the talk, but she was worried about Achilles. The wounds he received were on her behalf. What Mistress Abigail had said weighed on her mind. Infection and fever were the new dangers. Suddenly, all the events of the day caught up with her, and she felt herself sag in her seat. The queen sent her off to bed with the prince. She was asleep before she even thought about it.

In her dream, she was pressed against him again. He was trembling and feeling her with his hands, terrified that she was injured. But she was fine. She could smell him, feel him against her body. He was touching her face lightly. She reached up to put her hand over his. She woke touching her cheek with no hand beneath hers. He had been touching her, holding her in the dream. She sighed and got out of bed. Katie was waiting. She helped Lenora dress in a fairly simple dress; there would a much more elaborate dressing session for the ball. For the first time ever, she wasn't excited about a ball. There was only one person she wanted to dance with, and he was too injured to attend.

She went to the royal dining room to get breakfast. She had the server bring her a bowl of strawberries to take to Achilles.

She found Lord John in the infirmary checking on the few men still in Mistress Abigail's care and talking to the lady herself. He smiled at her. Lenora went to Achilles. He was propped up to a sitting position. His face burst into a huge smile at the sight of her, and she blushed but walked to him purposefully. She presented him with the strawberries, and he laughed. It was the best sound she had heard in days. Filled with happiness, she took a strawberry and offered it to him. His green-gold eyes widened in surprise, and she blushed, belatedly realizing the intimacy of hand-feeding him. He took a bite of the strawberry, and a thin stream of juice ran down his chin. His face flushed with color, and he hastily moved to brush it away. Boldly, he grasped her hand and ate the rest of the strawberry, his lips touching her fingers. She blushed furiously, and her fingers burned where his lips had touched her or perhaps she imagined that. She wanted his lips to touch her other places. She didn't think it was possible to blush further, but she felt she must have. He smiled reading her distress and seized a strawberry from the bowl, holding it out for her. She started to reach out for it as he had, but the intimacy of it surprised her. He smiled and it brought to her lips. She took the whole thing in her mouth, not wanting to deal with the possibility of juice running out of her mouth. Her lips brushed his fingers this time, and she watched with some satisfaction as his face flushed with sudden color.

Lenora looked up suddenly and saw Lord John watching them. He had the funniest look on his face. He was both bemused and somehow relieved. He approved, she realized with a rush of excitement. Achilles followed her gaze. She looked back at him, and his answering smile made her heart ache. Lord John left. They sat talking together. He told her more about his life before. His family was a very old family, one that worshiped the Great Goddess in her glory before she was transformed to the asexual mother of God or a sexualized consort of the Devil. The V shapes on his wrists stood for the human manifestations of the Goddess, the Maiden, the Crone, and the Mother, he explained. Lenora marveled at the religion he described. Women were at the center of everything—the sources of life and pleasure. Part of her mind wondered what that would translate to in terms of being intimate with him—if female pleasure was so highly valued, how would he touch her? She blushed. Life seemed so much in harmony in the universe he described. Her own religion espoused love and tolerance—but it had been so often distorted to justify the grossest atrocities. It cast female sexuality as bad, dangerous, and/or dirty. The treatment of women and children, she realized, were a measure of a society's capacity for peace. Her father's family had always valued women and children—they had rights in their kingdom. But it was different in other kingdoms, and Lord Everett was a representation of that line of thinking. Achilles told her his uncle was another—embracing the Muslim faith manipulatively to gain power and subjugate the women of the family. Lost in conversation, the morning flew by, and they ate lunch together. As afternoon came on, she knew that she had to ready herself for the ball; she left reluctantly. He kissed her hand before she left, and she hesitated. He pulled her back to him with this good arm, and she went willingly—his mouth meeting hers—softly at first and then more urgently.

"Achilles," she breathed.

"Nora," he whispered, and she buried her face in his chest; it was the endearment that her mother had used with her; it brought tears to her eyes, and he wiped them away and kissed her hair. "Lenora … Nora … my love …"

She jerked away from him, and he pulled her back, his eyes searching her face, her eyes answering his. Her arms wound around him, and they kissed.

"Do … you …" she hesitated, "do you think … it's because you saved me?" she asked anxiously.

He pulled back enough to look into her eyes. His eyes burned with intensity. "No," he said softly. "I have dreamed of you." He was silent for a moment. "I am not sure I can explain. I felt your soul or spirit—my match. When I first saw you, I wondered." He shook his head before continuing; looking back into her eyes, he said softly, "Then when I touched you… when I thought you were hurt and I thought I would rather die … I just knew … besides … you saved me too." He smiled at her, and her eyes filled with tears.

"Yes," she whispered. It was exactly like that she thought, and they were kissing again. She felt the most amazing sense of contentment—but more than that—of completion. Together they were whole. She was his match, and he was hers. She didn't really know what would happen now, but they would be together, and that was somehow all that really mattered.

Jane's Knight

Sir Christopher was out hunting with his page, young Jimmy. They had been lucky and had brought down a deer which Midnight tolerated, but Jimmy had to keep coaxing the horse. When the two men burst through the shrubbery in front of them, Midnight lost it completely; whining her protest, she reared and dumped her burden. Jimmy somehow managed to stay seated, clinging to the beast, his hands woven through the horse's mane, until she calmed. Christopher only had time to take in the shabby dress of the two men astride the handsomely draped and saddled mare. Obviously, they had stolen the horse. Their shocked and worried faces at encountering Christopher and Jimmy only confirmed his suspicions. He would have gone after them, but Jimmy needed help. Christopher was off Perseus in flash, tethering the stallion, and grabbing Midnight's reins.

Once Midnight and Jimmy were both calmed, Christopher loaded the deer and Jimmy onto Perseus, and he, himself, rode the skittish Midnight. They set off in the direction from which the bandits had come. They heard the woman weeping before they actually came upon the scene of a woman weeping over her dead groom. She heard them and looked up.

Christopher knew her, Lady Jane. She was high born and stunningly beautiful. Even with the tracks of tears on her face, she was breath-taking with her large hazel eyes; long, dark eyelashes; fair skin dusted with a trace of freckles; full, deep, pink lips—all in that perfect heart-shaped face, crowned with the mass of wavy brown hair that sparkled even then with gold and chestnut highlights.

"My lady," he said, "can we be of service?" He reined up Perseus and handed the reins to Jimmy. He dismounted and was at her side in a moment, kneeling next to her. She looked at him, the desperation and grief in her face made his heart ache. Impulsively, he reached out to her, his arms circling her slender frame, and unbelievably she embraced him back, sobbing and pressing her face against his chest. He held her, emotions rippling through him. He felt her grief and outrage and sympathized with those, and yet he felt more. He wanted to protect her, to avenge her, to have her want him the way he suddenly realized he wanted her, to make her his as he would be hers. "Stop!" he thought desperately; "nothing good can come of such thinking. She is beyond your station."

Seeming to realize his thoughts, she pulled away from him. "I am sorry. They … they … killed … my men … they robbed us … they killed my men." Tears streamed down her face.

He stroked her cheek, wiping some of the tears away, "I am sorry, my lady, we are here now, and we will not leave you," he said firmly. He heard movement. He glanced up. Jimmy had heard it, too. He had dismounted and tethered the horses. He nodded at Christopher and moved toward the noise.

She pressed herself against him again, "I ... am ...scared," she whispered.

He pulled her more tightly against him, her head against his chest, and his heart was hammering, the scent of her flooding his nostrils, the desire for her making him tremble slightly. "I won't let anything happened to you. You are safe now, my lady," and he kissed her head, her hair tickling him.

They both pulled away, recognizing their sudden intimacy.

"Thank you," she said quietly, mastering herself. She disengaged herself from him completely, and he felt a jolt of pain. He helped her up. Her advisor, Lord Thomas, had been killed too, and his horse stolen by another pair of men. They had been hidden in the tree branches and had jumped down upon them suddenly, taking them by surprise. They had stolen Thomas's purse, but the horses and flight seemed to be their main objectives.

Christopher moved Thomas's body next to Kevin's (the groom's). Jimmy returned leading a beautiful grey mare. The horse was wary of the two bodies but nosed Jane in recognition and assurance that seemed to hearten both the beast and her mistress. Christopher and Jimmy strapped the deer to Genevieve, Jane's horse, and Perseus bore the two bodies. Jimmy mounted Genevieve. Jane and Christopher rode Midnight with Perseus tethered to them. Jane had not objected to these arrangements; they were practical after all. Jimmy rode ahead of them.

Jane kept her back straight as was becoming of a lady of her status, but Christopher wondered if her effort at such posture in their particular circumstances was a way to keep a degree of separation from their forced intimacy. Her buttocks and hips rested between his thighs, and his right arm draped across her body to hold the reins of the horse. They didn't speak much as they rode. Perhaps because of her rigid posture, he had a fine view of her hair, disheveled from her misadventures, escaping its pins and combs in places and revealing wispy curls that sparkled in soft golden and copper colors. He could see the back of her neck from her hairline to the back of her bodice. She smelled of lavender. Her skin was so pale and soft looking. The same light that brought out the highlights in her hair revealed the soft, pale, downy hairs that dusted her neck and shoulders which were otherwise invisible. He longed to touch her there. As if divining his thoughts, her skin erupted in goosebumps.

"Are you cold, my lady?" he asked. He wished he could see her face straight on. Sudden color was flushing what he could see of her cheek, neck, and ear.

"No … well … yes … perhaps," she said awkwardly. He brought his left arm up over her and switched the reins to that hand, while he fumbled with his free right hand in his saddle bag for his cloak. He pulled it out and draped it over her shoulders. She secured the clasp around her throat and murmured thank you.

Not long after, they arrived at the castle. Lord Edward, Jane's father, was furious. Men would be dispatched in the morning in search of the murderers and thieves. Lord Edward had thanked Christopher and Jimmy for their aid to his daughter and then had shepherded his daughter to their apartments in the castle. Jane had thanked Christopher formally and given him back his cloak. He had knelt before her and kissed her hand in parting. When her hand rippled suddenly with goosebumps, he had glanced up at her face to find her flushed with color, her pale skin glowing pink, her eyes widening in surprise and embarrassment. She was so beautiful like that, and he was so proud to be the cause of her disquiet that he smiled in response. Lord Edward glanced between them, and then he was hurrying her away. "That was stupid," he thought belatedly. He'd probably never be alone with her again, and the thought pained him. He rose to his feet slowly. Jimmy was staring at him. Christopher ignored his page and went to see what had become of the horses and the deer.

King James had sent men to aid his brother's men. Lord Edward over saw the funerals. Christopher and Jimmy attended. Lady Jane was there, but she was up front with her father and the other nobles. Christopher watched the ceremony, but he found himself watching her. Tears glistened on her cheeks, and he ached for her pain. He remembered brushing the tears off her face two days before, but that seemed like weeks ago. He had caught only fleeting glimpses of her in the days that followed. A feast followed the funerals. People offered testimonials of the characters of the deceased. Lady Jane spoke briefly about the generosity and wisdom of Lord Thomas and the attentiveness and diligence of her groom, Kevin, her voice trembling in places due to the depth of her emotion. Christopher talked and joked with the other knights and men-in-arms, but his attention returned over and over to Jane. His reward was a moment when her eyes found his; she smiled at him and was then distracted by a young woman next to her.

Lord Edward's and the king's men returned that evening; they had found both of the horses and killed the two murderers, bringing the corpses back with them. The other two had fled into the mountains. Life returned to normal at the castle. Christopher saw Jane regularly at dinner but always from afar. And yet, she looked for him. Their eyes would meet across the great hall; they would exchange sly smiles. Though his days contained only cursory contact with Jane, his dreams were filled with thoughts of her. He relived holding her on the ground by Kevin's body, the feel of her in his arms, her face stained with tears; then the ride, the feel of her bottom and legs between his own, the smell of her, her hair, the back of her neck and shoulders, the pale skin; and the kiss on her hand, when his lips were just pulling away, the burst of goosebumps, the blush on her face. He imagined all sorts of things. He imagined kissing her, and she kissing back. He imagined more; he wanted more. He woke frequently from his dreams ejaculating onto himself or his sheets or so desperate with desire that he brought himself to climax. It was so bad that he had stolen an extra sheet so that he could wash the one himself, so the chambermaid didn't need to know. And it was all so hopeless. She was King James' niece; Lord Edward clearly had other designs for his eldest daughter. Assumption was coming, and it was widely known that the king and queen from the neighboring kingdom would visit with their children. Everyone was speculating about whom would be betrothed to whom by the end of the festivities.

King Richard, Queen Catherine, their children, Prince William, Princess Tara, Princess Margaret, Prince Phillip, and Prince David, arrived two days before Assumption with a guard and some select members of their court and their children. The castle buzzed with activity. Many people were bunked together to provide the guests adequate lodging. Christopher was bunked with his friend and fellow knight, Mark.

There would be feasting and dancing for the three days—the most magnificent ball on the evening of Assumption. Christopher watched in agony while Prince William flirted with Jane and danced with her. Other boys from among King Richard's nobles danced with Jane. She was graceful, polite, and attentive. But she didn't look doe-eyed or smitten by any of them—though quite a few of them couldn't take their eyes off of her. Toward the end of the evening, Christopher moved boldly toward her and asked her to dance. To a host of raised eyebrows and surprised faces, she accepted and moved into his embrace. As her arms wrapped around him, he felt his flesh erupt in goosebumps and his face flush with color.

She blushed as well and smiled, "Nice to return the favor," she whispered, smirking a little, her hazel eyes flashing.

He pressed her closer to his body; she gasped. "I think of you all the time," he said softly.

"I think of you too," she whispered, glancing up at him.

He smiled tentatively, "Jane," and nuzzled his face against her hair and neck, taking in her scent, feeling her body against his.

"Christopher," she answered back, breathlessly.

They moved well together. He led, but he was attuned to the movements of her body. When she shifted, he followed through. "Yes," he thought, "lead me anywhere." She nuzzled against him, startling him from his thoughts. He felt her tremble against him, and he realized that he was trembling too, their breathing coming short in each other arms.

"Jane?" he asked.

"Find me tomorrow. My father knows that I care for you. He doesn't like it, but he loves me. I don't think he will force me to marry, and he will be watching us now."

"And what does he see?" he asked, eager to hear what he hoped came next.

"Me, pressed more tightly to you than any young man I have danced with all evening," she whispered in his ear and kissed him. He wasn't sure it was possible to press her closer, but he did and kissed her opposite ear.

She left him reluctantly, and he hated being parted from her, but they had agreed to meet the following day in the apple orchard. He watched her. Lord Edward was clearly annoyed; Lady Isabella, Jane's mother, less so. Christopher had not paid her much attention before, but her gaze was locked on him now. Mark and the others teased him, but he refused to engage them. "Let them think what they want," he thought furiously. Jane accompanied her younger sister, Sarah, when she withdrew from the festivities, meeting his gaze with a faint smile. He smiled back and went pink feeling Lady Isabella's eyes upon him. He left after that himself, hoping to be safely asleep and immersed in his dreams by the time Mark retired.

The next morning he was surprised to be summoned by Lady Isabella. The maid led him to a small library. Lady Isabella was seated at a large desk, leafing through a book.

Christopher knelt before her, his heart pounding in his chest.

"Rise, Sir Christopher, and be seated," she said softly. He rose warily; her face gave nothing away. She was a beautiful woman; Jane looked like her, except for the green eyes and hair touched with grey. He sat in the chair opposite the desk. He felt he should say something, but he felt completely inadequate. Jane could choose anyone; he was just a knight, and yet he was not a servant.

What on earth was he to say? "Start at the beginning," he thought desperately. He stared down at his hands in his lap. "I …" he forced himself to say, "I … found … your daughter, Lady Jane, … in the woods … after the attack…. She was upset," and he blushed, remembering. He looked up. Lady Isabella was watching him closely.

"And you comforted her?" she said coldly.

He flushed an even darker shade of red. He wanted to look away, but he knew he couldn't. Lady Isabella had to be convinced of his sincerity. This was a test. More important than her father's approval, Christopher had to win the favor of Jane's mother. He looked at her with determination, "Yes, I did," he answered, meeting the glare in the piercing green eyes. "And she let me," he added.

Something changed in Lady Isabella's eyes. "I saw you dance with my daughter last night."

He didn't see the connection. "She dances well; it was a pleasure to be partnered with her," he said, floundering for something appropriate to say.

"Did you see her dance with the others?" she asked.

"Vaguely," he hesitated. He hadn't wanted to watch her in the arms of other young men. He knew she danced with a range of partners, Prince William at least twice, but more than that he hadn't noticed. "I … didn't …" he couldn't finish; it sounded petty. He looked away and was puzzled by the look she was giving him when he looked back.

The hint of a smile played on her lips, and her eyes were softer, though still wary. "You didn't want to watch her in the arms of others?"

"No," he said quietly.

"Then you didn't notice the difference?"

"The difference?" he echoed stupidly. He flushed again remembering holding her as closely as he could.

A real smile bloomed on Lady Isabella's face, "Not just your proximity; she returned your embrace after all." He thought he might burst into flames. He remembered pulling her closer and her pressing against him, their bodies fully engaged with each other, nothing but the fabric of their clothes between them, the way their breathing had changed while touching that way, the hint of what they could do if they were completely alone. He looked at Lady Isabella helplessly; he didn't understand.

"You followed her lead," she said. Obviously, Lady Isabella thought this explained everything.

"We were partnered," he answered automatically.

She chuckled and shook her head. "Is that what you want from my daughter—to be partnered with her?"

"Yes, of course," he said, meeting her questioning gaze with conviction.

She pointed at the book in front of her. "Do you know any poetry, Sir Christopher?"

He had in fact been reading Conon de Bethune, the one poem seeming to capture his desperate desire for Jane and the impossibility of being worthy of her. He looked at his hands and recited the second stanza quietly:

> I know now, no being can be worth
> as much as this lady I have so often sung about,
> for now I have seen her and her beauty
> and know she is so great
> I must be outrageous and crazy
> to love so high—higher than I need to.

And yet many a poor knight
is born to great honor by a noble heart.

He looked up to see the startled expression on Lady Isabella's face. It changed to warm and welcoming smile. She stood up, and he scrambled to his feet, "My lady?" he stammered, bowing before her.

"Rise, Sir Christopher. Go cautiously with my daughter, but you have made a favorable impression on me. Pray don't make me regret that assessment," she said dismissing him.

He felt like his heart might explode with happiness. He left the library barely conscious of what he was doing. With Lady Isabella's approval, now he only needed to make sure he still had Jane's.

P Pan and Beyondland

Krystal and Kyle Barry were very close; they were twins after all. They played with each other always. They fought some, of course. A girl and a boy; she played princess and so did he. He played knight and so did she.

They could tell that their parents found them odd. It bothered their mother and father that the children could switch from female to male and male to female. They never said it explicitly, but Krystal and Kyle could tell. Their parents tried and tried to separate the children, but they snuck into each other's beds at night—to give each other comfort and support.

At school, the expectations were clear—there were boys and girls but nothing in between. They acted their parts. Krystal was a girl, and Kyle was a boy. It was so confining. Girls were supposed to be feminine—"Sugar and spice and everything nice": affectionate, cheerful, compassionate, gentle, loyal, shy, soft-spoken, sympathetic, understanding, warm, tender, yielding. In contrast, boys were supposed to be masculine—"Snips and snails and puppy dog tails": aggressive, ambitious, analytical, assertive, competitive, dominant, independent, individualistic, self-reliant, self-sufficient, stoic. Krystal and Kyle were so much more when they could move in between—when they could be both and more and anything in between. Wasn't that the point of being a full human being (being sympathetic and assertive, tender and self-reliant)—and didn't that mean being a blend of masculine and feminine? All they knew is that they didn't fit in.

One night they threw open a bedroom window and cried to the stars the heartbreak they felt. To their surprise, in the middle of the night, a figure loomed above their bed.

"What do you want and who are you?" Krystal asked timidly.

"I am P Pan from Beyondland, but please call me P. With what you said to the stars, I think you might like to come to Beyondland."

Krystal and Kyle listened to the words and then looked at each other. They looked back at this P and decided that they couldn't tell what he/she/ze was—ze was the better term they realized without being told. P was someone like they wanted to be, something in between or multiple instead of binary (male/female). Ze was about fifteen maybe with light stubble on zir face but eyeliner and lipstick, shoulder length hair, the front pieces braided off to keep out of ze's face, tight-fitted clothes that only favored ze's ambiguous form.

"What are you?" Krystal and Kyle blurted out the same time.

"I am a human being," P answered, "the same as either of you; it's just that, in Beyondland, I can express any aspect of myself that I desire. That's why some choose to leave their homes and come and live with us."

"But are you a boy or a girl?" blurted out Kyle.

P cocked zir head, "I am neither or both. I am non-binary. In Beyondland, gender is a spectrum—like a spectrum of colors from whites to yellows to greens to reds to blues and to blacks or like a big multifaceted rainbow. There isn't just white and black or male and female—there is a whole range of ways to see one's self." P paused, studying them. "From the things you said, I thought you were looking for somewhere where being more than 'girl' or 'boy' was appealing, but perhaps I am mistaken."

Krystal had taken Kyle's hand under the sheets and squeezed it. "Yes, P, we are, but we didn't even know a place like Beyondland existed. All we know is how it is here," Krystal struggled to explain.

The children weren't sure what to do. They loved their parents, but they also knew they didn't belong. They played at being a boy and a girl, but the roles were wrong—they weren't true to the core people Krystal and Kyle knew themselves to be. All these thoughts flitted over the children's faces.

P looked between them and smiled a sad smile, "It's a lot to take in and a lot to give up. You know how to reach me. Call me again if you're ready for Beyondland." With that, ze bowed and walked to the window—which the children suddenly realized had been open the whole time.

"P!" shouted the children as they watched ze leap out the window. The children, in horror, leaped from their bed and ran to the window to find P floating just outside the window and chuckling with mirth.

"Didn't I tell you or didn't you guess? There's magic in Beyondland. How else could I hear you to answer your pleas? Good night, sweet children, and call if you need." P then raised zir arms and flew away.

The children, too astonished to speak, stared after zir until they couldn't see zir anymore. They got into bed and whispered to each other their imaginings of what Beyondland might be like—what the children did there, what they could do there, and how they lived. The next morning they half convinced themselves that P's visit had been a dream—but they had never before dreamed the exact same dream. Then as they were washing up in the bathroom, getting ready for school, the bathroom mirror steamed up, and the two children froze as the words, "Beyondland is real," formed on the glass. Krystal wiped the words away, and afterwards, Kyle squeezed her hand—it was a secret between them—that was the pact.

School was tedious—the burden of the roles they played at school and for mum and dad—made Krystal and Kyle feel as if their true selves were being lost—consumed by the gendered performances that put others at ease. Then something frightening happened. Harry and Jamie, two young, sweet, kind boys, were found in the choir loft kissing. The two boys were dragged outside by a gang of older boys, yelling insults like "fagots," "Nancy boys," and "fairies." Krystal and Kyle were horrified. The boys circled Harry and Jamie, jeering at them and punching them. Some girls stood by looking uncomfortable while other girls took up the chants of "fagots," "Nancy boys," and "fairies." A few female teachers appeared and moved to break things up, but male teachers appeared out of nowhere and blocked their way. Harry and Jamie were beaten bloody before it was through. Krystal and Kyle couldn't bear to watch, so they slunk away. The guilt they felt at not being able to help the two defenseless boys from the savage attack overwhelmed them. They had feared being exposed as different as well, and they had feared being beaten too. So they hadn't intervened and had left. They found themselves vomiting alone in their separate gender-assigned bathrooms—rinsing the sick out of their mouths and the tears off their faces, and trying to compose themselves, so they wouldn't become targets themselves. Mercifully, the school day ended shortly after the disgusting spectacle without any explanation from the teachers or headmaster—making it clear that same-sex attractions were punished by the cruelest of means and that boys better act like boys and girls better act like girls—nothing in between would be tolerated.

Krystal and Kyle fled home. Nanna made them snacks and talked to them. Nanna was always so kind and supportive. They let their guard down in front of Nanna. That particular day, Nanna seemed to know there was something very wrong with the children. She probed them, and finally Krystal blurted it out.

"Two boys were caught kissing at school, and the teachers let some of the older boys beat them up and call them names," she choked out, tears running down her checks. Kyle was crying too.

Nanna opened up her arms, and the children went to her and let Nanna comfort them. "There, there now, my sweets. There are always people who are different—that doesn't mean they're bad. Other people, unfortunately, feel threatened by people who are different, so they dehumanize them and persecute them, bully them, punish them. The good Lord gave us the golden rule: 'Love your neighbor as yourself.' He didn't qualify neighbors as people just like you. Neighbors are people from different households, from different families—people who are different—so the golden rule really is to love people who are different than you. But people in power are threatened by the idea of too much love and togetherness especially among common people. No, they find it more effective to seed conflict, to pit groups of people against other groups of people. People who like people of their same sex are generally gentle and peaceful, people who just want the freedom to live in peace and as they choose. What was done to your friends is horrible, and you should be upset. That more people aren't upset says a lot about the intolerance and division that our culture spreads. I am sorry, for you and for them."

Krystal and Kyle felt comforted by Nanna's words. They knew what was done to Harry and Jamie was wrong, but they couldn't articulate why it was wrong, and Nanna had explained that. She had also explained why people encouraged conflict and hate. They knew it was probably a lot more complicated than that, but Nanna had explained it to them in a way that they could understand. But more than anything, Nanna understood about people who were different, whether attracted to people of the same sex or people like them, and they knew that Nanna knew about them, and she still loved them. "Oh, Nanna," they murmured.

"Hush, my darlings. The world can be a cruel place, but you are loved at home. You know that, don't you?"

"Yes, and no," Krystal whispered.

"What do you mean, my sweet?" Nanna asked.

Kyle squeezed Krystal's hand, "We don't think Mum and Dad ...well... we don't think they understand about us ... about people who are different," he struggled to say.

"Oh, my darlings, your parents are good people, and they love you. I am sure they'll stand by you," Nanna answered a little too hastily. "Now off with you; you have studying to do." And with that, she sent them away.

They went over their lessons in Kyle's room, and when they were called down to dinner, they ate with their mother and father and talked superficially about pleasant things. After dinner, they all sat in the parlour where the children took turns at playing the piano. While Krystal was playing, Nanna announced there was a call for Mr. Barry. Their father stepped into the hall to take the call. It didn't take long—perhaps five minutes. And then, their father was back.

"Is there something you children want to share about your day today?" he demanded, something strange and tense in his voice.

Krystal and Kyle looked at each other alarmed. "Why?" they stammered together.

"That was Master Laurence on the phone. Two fagot boys were caught kissing at your school today. The Master called to say that they had been punished and expelled from the school."

"What?" Krystal and Kyle cried together.

Their father looked at them in alarm. He bristled and shook his head. "Quite right, children. We can't have this sort of thing. Boys should be boys, and girls should be girls. Boys should like girls, and girls should like boys. That is the natural way."

"It's true, children; it is just what is done," Mother Barry added after a pause.

Krystal and Kyle nodded mutely as the colour drained from their faces. They excused themselves as soon as they could and kissed their parents good night and good bye. They retreated to their separate bedrooms and got ready for bed. Once the house was quiet, Kyle slipped into Krystal's bedroom where they threw open the great window and called out to P.

"P, P Pan, we are ready; we want to go to Beyondland. Please hear us and come to take us away!" they called to the stars. Then, they gathered a few of their favorite books, fairy tales mostly and a few books of poetry, a couple of changes of clothes, their brushes, combs, and toothbrushes, and things like that, and stuffed them into Krystal's pillowcase. They wrote out a note which they left on the bare pillow:

Dear Mother and Father,

We love you so much, but we are different. You've always known this, and it has always made you uncomfortable. Those boys you condemned from our school are more like us than we are like you or how you want us to be. Because you seem to hate them so, you must also hate us the way we truly are. So we have gone somewhere where they don't care. We wish we didn't have to go, but we don't want to be beaten and expelled.

With love,

Krystal and Kyle

Then they laid down together in Krystal's bed and waited. Not much later, a familiar figure flew through their window.

"P!" the children cried.

"I told you I'd come," and then P stopped, and ze looked over the children more carefully. "What has happened? You're traumatized. Tell me," ze demanded.

And Krystal and Kyle poured out the whole horrific story—the brutalization of Harry and Jamie, their guilt and shame at not helping, and then, worst of all, the words of their parents. "P, could you help Harry and Jamie too," they ended.

"We leave here to get Jamie, but Harry isn't ready to go," P said gravely.

"Why?" the children asked.

"He loves his parents and sisters, and his parents know and sympathize. They are going to move and try again. Maybe it will work. I hope so. It gets a bit easier when one is a young man or a young woman. If one is discrete, there are communities of people who are different and who give each other the love and support they need. There are risks, of course. But some people never choose to leave. I don't judge or try not to. I offer shelter in Beyondland for those who seek it; that's the duty of a Pan—to offer aid to other human beings," P explained.

"A Pan? What is a Pan?" Krystal asked.

P smiled and shook zir head. "I forget that you probably don't know our stories. I really should be better at this by now," P said to zirself. "I am a Polly Pandora—one of the many descendants of Pandora who was sent by Gaia, the Great Mother Goddess, to counter the harshness of the world of the Titians' and then the Olympians' making."

The children looked at each other in puzzlement. This was not the version of Greek mythology that they were familiar with. "But Pandora was a trick that Zeus and the gods sent to mankind in punishment for Prometheus giving men fire and then showing them how to keep the better cuts of meat rather than offering them in sacrifice to the gods," Kyle said in a rush. The children had always enjoyed Greek mythology and were quite proud of their knowledge of it.

P chuckled and shook zir head again. "Not a bad answer, but you have, in your answer, the source of your misinformation."

"Misinformation?" Krystal repeated slowly, pondering what P had said. Krystal looked from P to her brother and then back again at P. She laughed. "Mankind," she said softly, "a world of men—that part always bothered me. It seemed ridiculous."

"What do you mean? Ridiculous?" Kyle asked, just a tad defensively.

"I mean the idea of a world of just men is ridiculous. They can't reproduce. In the story, all the other animals are there—male and female (I mean the animals for the sacrifice aren't all male or they'd go extinct)—and humans are just supposed to be a single sex race of specie. Common on, Kyle, it is ridiculous. The Greeks hated women or saw them as subhuman—so of course they are trivialized in all kinds of ways. A race of all men with a woman as a punishment and the source of all evil and sadness in the world.

God, it's just another version of Adam and Eve. Men are the story tellers, so women get the bum-rap. That's right, P, isn't it? So what is the real story?" Krystal said in a rush.

P was chortling with mirth, but ze mastered zir features and answered, "Very good, Krystal. Pandora was a daughter of Gaia and one of the old gods. It was her task to offer aid and shelter where there was violence and conflict and hurt; she was hope and sanctuary. By following the Titians and the Olympians, human kind followed paths of violence and cruelty, hence rape and slavery and all the other misery that accompanies the pursuit of power over the pursuit of love. When Prometheus was punished for his aid to humans, Pandora healed him and set him free. Zeus was furious and took away her immortality. But as an old god, Pandora had power that Zeus didn't realize, and so Pandora's magic passes down her line from one Pandora to the next and the next—the Polly Pandoras or the many Pandoras, and I am one of the many, P Pandora," P said, bowing with a flourish.

"But why P?" asked Kyle.

P cocked zir head, looking at Kyle. "Not really sure; it just seems true to who I am at my core. I don't really see myself as either a complete boy (whatever that is supposed to be) or a complete girl (again whatever that is supposed to be). Other Pans have; there have been Peter Pans and Polly Pans, Paul Pans, and Pamela Pans, but there have also been Paul Pans who have switched to Paulette Pans and Phoebe Pans who have switched to Patrick Pans. And Pat Pans have been somewhere in the middle. P Pan just seemed to suit me when I was called to serve as a Pan."

"Called to serve? What does that mean?" Krystal asked.

"Well, we age, but not like regular humans do. Beyondland is special; it's magical and beyond the scope of earthly time, but still we age. Pans intervene for children, so a serving Pan should be a child, someone from 10-17 or at least look like a child of about that age range."

"Why that age range?" the children asked together.

"Because in many places, children are most vulnerable at puberty and while trying to figure out their gender identities and sexual orientations. In rigid cultures where only the binary of male/female is accepted, that is in most cultures, children need a Beyondland option, like you two and Jamie."

"Jamie," Krystal repeated. "We didn't help Jamie …we …" but she couldn't finish her thought.

"It's okay. Make it up to him. You will all meet lots of new and supportive people in Beyondland, but it will also be nice for the three of you to have each other. Shall we go? Do you have a few things to bring with you?" P asked.

Kyle took Krystal's hand with one hand and grabbed the stuffed pillowcase with his other. "Yes, I think we are ready," he said, his voice full of nerves.

"It's okay. I won't let you fall. Each of you need to take my hand."

Krystal let go of her brother's hand reluctantly and moved to P's other side. Hand-in-hand they moved to the great window. "Don't look down," P commanded. "It might be better too to shut your eyes—at least for the initial leap."

Krystal whimpered softly, but pushed her chin up and shut her eyes tightly. Kyle didn't make a sound, but he shut his eyes too.

P pulled the children close to his sides and said, "Now when I say, 'Jump,' we all go together, okay?"

"Okay," the children repeated softly.

"Jump!" P shouted.

The shout so surprised the children that they jumped without thinking. Suddenly, they could feel the night air on their faces and blowing against them. Krystal opened her eyes and stared in wonder. She was flying, holding P's hand and flying. London seemed so different from the air, she thought. She looked around P to see her brother grinning back at her, flying on P's other side. Krystal had almost forgotten Jamie when she realized that P had stopped flying and had them floating down in front of a smart Brownstone house. One of the windows was thrown open, and P gently pushed the children, one by one, through the window before flying in zirself.

A surprised voice called out, "Krystal? Kyle? Is that you?"

Jamie stood before them, with a pillowcase in hand and the most surprised look on his battered face.

Krystal burst in to tears at the sight of him. "Jamie, my God, your face. I am so sorry. We're so sorry. We should have done something," she stammered as she gave him a hug.

Kyle was there too, laying a hand on Jamie's shoulder, "I am sorry as well."

Jamie pulled back from Krystal's embrace, his eyes watering with tears; he shook his head and looked at P. "P, I don't understand?"

"They're like you, Jamie, in a way. They don't belong here and want to come live in Beyondland," P said simply.

Jamie looked from P to Krystal and Kyle. The brother and sister smiled a little awkwardly and shrugged. Jamie laughed, part in relief and part from nerves, and the others joined in.

P, then, got their attention. "Right, that bit sorted, let's be on our way. Jamie, you have what you need?"

"Yes, P, I am ready," Jamie answered.

P opened a small pouch at zir waist. "We fly a much greater distance this time," ze said addressing the twins. "You'll each need to fly on your own, though feel free to hold hands as you will. And for that, you'll need fairy powder." And before any of the children could ask, each found her or himself covered in a light dusting of glittering, simmering powder. It tickled and prickled the skin. Krystal was about to object, when she felt P pick her up by the waist and launch her out the window. She was about to scream, but then she realized she wasn't falling but flying, and the tickling and prickling feeling had disappeared. She was quickly joined by Kyle and Jamie whose faces flashed what must have been the confusion of her sensations just moments before. Each of the boys held a stuffed pillowcase, but that didn't impede their flying ability one bit. P joined them then—more gracefully, Krystal noted, P's magic creating a more natural flight. P led the way, and Krystal watched as London fell away beneath her, the mass of twinkling lights receding. She felt sad in a way, but excited too for her new life.

P let the children enjoy the novelty of flying before ze started explaining things in Beyondland. There were chores to be done each day, some domestic chores and some gardening and husbandry chores. There were various gardens, the herb and medicinal garden, a three-sisters garden (maize, beans, and squash), a green beans and potato garden, a carrot and garlic garden, a broccoli and cucumber garden, an eggplant and spinach garden, and all sorts of other companion vegetable gardens, lined with marigolds and nasturtiums to keep the pests away. There were beds of strawberries, blackberries, raspberries, elderberries, and blueberries. There were small orchards with apples, pears, peaches, almonds, walnuts, chestnuts, figs, cherries, and apricots. The children raised chickens and goats and sheep, so there were egg collecting, milking, and cheese making tasks. The children made things from clothing from woven flax and sheep's wool to pottery and crockery, baskets, tools, cider (both regular and hard), and cabin making and maintenance. Children were assigned bunks at first and then moved in with a group of friends usually. Cabins usually housed four to six children. There were lessons on basics subjects for all. Quarterly, there was a week-long arts festival with competitions on anything one could think of from paintings to knitted or crocheted items of clothing to song writing and singing to play scripts and performances to the best apple treat. The absolute rules about Beyondland were that one, all were welcome and supported. Two, that no one could coerce another person to do any activity, and sexual coercion was especially forbidden. Third, that no sexually mature person could have a relationship with a prepubescent child. Beyondland was an inclusive rainbowland of people from different races, religions, ethnicities, gender identifications, and sexual orientations. They were to become each other's family members now, and they needed to act like it. That didn't mean there weren't tensions and fights, but children were encouraged to work out those disagreements or tensions constructively through contests or writing about them or expressing them creatively in some other way. Someone who abandoned the principles of tolerance, acceptance, respect, and peaceful conflict resolution was subject to banishment. That had never happened, but that didn't mean that it couldn't. P had explained all this before, but ze did it again to reinforce the importance of the commitments they had made in coming to Beyondland.

Krystal had been contentedly holding Jamie's hand, so the two could share stories about all that they had hidden from their parents and their schoolmates before, when she realized that they were descending. The beautiful night sky, so lit up with more stars than she had ever imagined, was beginning to fade. Jamie squeezed her hand, and she followed his gaze to see a cluster of islands beneath them, and at the horizon, the threat of the sunrise was just beginning to light up the sky.

"Beyondland," P announced loudly. "The Main Camp is on the Big Island. That's where we're going."

"What's on the other islands, P?" Kyle asked.

"Crescent Island, that first one, has Crocodile Cove in the pocket of the crescent, and the Merpeople generally school around the outer crescent."

"Crocodiles?" said Krystal in alarm.

"Merpeople?" said Jamie.

"We're a pretty peaceful lot," P began, "but we've been attacked before by pirates. Our bask of crocodiles is led by Ali Oop; he's a sly old devil. He caught the pirate captain unawares—ate the whole bastard himself—hat, watch, boots, and all. Not really sure what kind of magic watch that captain had, but it is still ticking. Ali still has his stealth but that tick-ticking often gives him away now. The Merpeople are fierce fighters. After defeating the pirates, we all agreed to move Crescent Island to the front of the Beyondland island formation for defensive purposes."

"Move an island? But that's ... impossible?" exclaimed Kyle.

"I told you there is magic here," P said solemnly. "The Pans have magic, the crocs and the Merpeople have magic. The fairies have magic, and the children begin to absorb it too. It's kind of hard to explain, but the way we live here creates a magic—between the land and creatures and us—the more we have, the more we give, the more it seems to grow."

"Fairies?" repeated Jamie.

"Not an insult, Jamie, real fairies, little people with wings and magic. You don't want to mess with fairies; there a long-lived people who can make a lot of trouble if you get on their bad sides," P responded.

Fifty or so cabins ringed a great series of common areas. They landed near what appeared to be a communal dining and eating area with tables and benches. It was still largely dark, but the glow of the impending sunrise was stronger than ever. The children were startled when two figures moved out of the shadows. One was an old woman, and the other a middle-aged man.

"P, we are glad you are back," said the woman, smiling warmly at P and the children.

"Who have you got with you?" asked the man, also smiling a greeting.

"Wendy and Peter, this is Krystal and Kyle and Jamie," P answered.

"Children, this is Mother Wendy, our chief mid-wife and healer, and Peter is a former Pan."

The children said their hellos, and then Wendy showed them to an empty cabin, showed them the outhouses, and bade them to get a little sleep or rest before being introduced to the whole crowd. Krystal wasn't sure she could sleep, but snuggled against her brother in a soft bed with clean sheets, she was asleep before she realized it.

Krystal woke with a jolt when she realized a bell was ringing in their cabin. "Children, have you had a good rest? It is about noon, and we are breaking for lunch, so I thought this might be a good time to introduce you to our band of Beyondlanders," Mother Wendy called. Krystal heard Jamie open his door and stumble out.

"Mother Wendy, I'll try," Jamie mumbled, clearly still groggy.

"My, my, what did they do to your beautiful face, my lad," she said softly. "Come see me after you're groomed and feed, and I'll see if I can put something on that to ease the swelling and bruising."

Kyle and Krystal came out of their room a little unsure of their reception, but Mother Wendy didn't bat an eye. She smiled, instead, and chuckled, "You two look as groggy as Jamie. Groom yourselves as quick as you can; there's food to eat and people to meet." Then she left them.

The three of them stood there a little awkwardly. Finally, Jamie broke the silence.

"Are you together, then? I thought P said you were more like me? I don't understand," Jamie said.

Krystal and Kyle blushed a deep red; he squeezed her hand, and she answered, "It's not like that between us. It's completely platonic. I am not sure I can explain it exactly. We are twins. We've been together since the womb—we're just attached. I don't know what that means when we become attached to others, but I guess we'll deal with that when it happens," Krystal paused. "Do you have siblings? Do you know that special love and devotion that many siblings feel for each other—or that they should feel for each other?"

Jamie was struggling to keep up, but he understood the part about loving one's siblings. "Yes, I love my brothers and sisters. They know about me, even though my parents don't understand."

Krystal laughed, "Children always know—that's why Pan must be a child," she said both to herself and to her brother and Jamie. "I think we are more like P than like you. I am thinking of changing my name to Kay—I feel gender fluid—not one or the other. I think Kyle feels much the same way, but he'll have to make that decision himself. I told you about how uncomfortable we felt growing up. We didn't need a beating to know they'd hurt us for being different. After what happened to you, and then what our parents said, well we knew we needed to leave."

"Children," called Mother Wendy from outside the door.

They walked out the door to join her, where they found P and Peter too. Each took someone's hand, Mother Wendy took

Jamie's, P took Kyle's, and Peter took Krystal's. Peter introduced them all, and then let the children wander. Krystal and Kyle came to know that children were there for all kinds of reasons from physical abuse like beating and lashings and genital cutting to sexual abuse from uncles or step-fathers or teachers (in extremes forced marriages, rape, and sexual slavery).

Jamie, Kyle, and Krystal discovered that some children were straight and identified as boys and girls, but others were different and identified as everything from gay and lesbian (homosexual) to bisexual, transgender, queer, questioning, and asexual. People dressed in whatever they wanted. Some girls wore dresses and so did some boys. Most wore form fitting clothes. Many adorned their outfits with an accessory or two of a bright colour. Nearly everyone wore make-up of some kind, and many sported elaborate braids. Clearly, grooming for the day was a communal event.

After they'd had something to eat, the children were surrounded by other children. They were together but in the center of a swirling group of children who asked them questions and studied them.

Krystal heard Kyle and Jamie being asked questions, but she got lost in her own grilling.

"What kinds of things do you like to do?" a girl of about sixteen, with dark straight brown hair braided in a crown around her head and golden brown skin, asked her. "I am Athena, by the way."

"I don't know. I like to read," Krystal replied.

"No, no. We want to figure out how to dress you. Do you climb trees? Do you run? Do you like dresses or not?" Athena asked.

Krystal stared at Athena a little unnerved. Girls didn't climb trees and weren't encouraged to run. She couldn't remember ever not wearing a dress or a shirt and a skirt. Then, she remembered where she was. She could be anything she wanted here. Within reason, she could do anything she wanted here. Krystal, no, Kay, she thought. She focused her attention back on Athena, who seemed to be grinning at her. "I don't know," she said slowly. "I want to be Kay. I've never climbed a tree or been encouraged to run, but I think I would like to try."

"Good, that's a start," Athena said quickly. "Listen up, everyone, this is Kay, do you hear?"

"Kay," a chorus of children repeated.

"Ze's a small; find Kay some leggings and a shirt," Athena commanded. "Is there a bright colour that you like, Kay, and how do you want your hair?"

"Oh, Athena, let me do ze's hair. You know how I love long hair," said a dark-skinned boy in a form fitting pants and shirt set, accented with a bright yellow fabric flower at his throat. "I'm Pansy, and the pronoun I favor is he. May I?" he asked, his hand poised near zir head.

"Sure," Kay answered hesitantly. And then ze felt his fingers undo zir braids and run his fingers through zir hair gently. He started brushing zir hair and yet there was something different about the way he brushed. Kay realized he was taking the measure of zir hair, the feel of it, the weight of it. He walked around zir, playing with the ways zir hair could frame zir face.

"Colour?" demanded Athena, pulling Kay out of zir thoughts.

"Purple," ze answered absently as a small olive-skinned girl stepped forward with a tray of what had to be make-up.

"I'm Camille, and I am a she. I love to do make-up. Would you let me do yours?" she asked softly.

"Okay, I guess," Kay answered timidly. Ze had never really worn make-up before and was a little daunted by the quantity of colour on Camille's face. Her eyes were a yellowy-green, and her lids were painted a bright green that brought out their colour with kohl eyeliner accenting her eyes. Her lips were painted a pale sharp pink, and a dusty rose coloured her cheeks. "Over the top like me?" Camille asked preening. "Or just a test?"

Kay laughed at the pose, and answered, "Just a test, I think, today."

Camille gave a fake pout, but then set to her task, "Close your eyes." Kay felt Camille apply a line of paint across zir lids. "Good, now open and look up at the sky," and Kay felt a line of paint applied just under zir eyes. All the while Pansy was positioning zir hair. "What about zir lips, Pansy? I mean look at the colouring, such fair skin, with the dark hair and the blue eyes."

"Too dark, Camille. Ze just wants a test; there will lots of other days—when ze's ready," the boy answered. Kay felt a sense of relief at the words. "What do you think of Kay's hair?" And Kay felt the end of a braid being tied off with string, and Pansy was done.

"Lovely," answered Camille. "Hold still, Kay; just a minute longer. Part your lips just a bit." Kay complied and felt a thin layer of creamy paint applied to zir lips.

Pansy and Camille stepped back to look at Kay, and then what seemed to be a boy in a form fitting dress stepped forward, "I am Suzette, and I am a she." She held up a shirt and a pair of leggings in a dusty blue, "What do you think?"

"Wait, wait," called a young girl with curly, short, blond hair and a shock of painted butterflies adorning her face, "I am Melissa Blue; I am a she, and I just love butterflies, don't you?" and she held a tray of brightly coloured fabric butterflies on one side and brightly coloured fabric flowers on the other. "See anything you like?"

Kay felt drawn to a beautiful purple bearded-iris, so ze chose that. "Think about where you would like to wear it while you change. We could put it in your hair, or around your neck in a choker, or at your waist in a belt."

"Or at your wrist in a corsage," Pansy added. "Go to that cabin there and change. Think about whether you want to keep your old clothes. If you don't, they'll be added to the communal store."

Kay did as ze was told, but it felt odd. Ze didn't know whose cabin it was, but it was neat and quiet. Ze stripped off zir dress and petticoats and things. Putting on the simple clingy shirt and leggings felt strange. Ze was fully clothed and yet ze felt so exposed. Never had zir true body shape been on such display. It had always been covered by the layers and layers of clothes. Kay felt zir hair; it was braided around zir head, ze guessed somewhat like Athena's. Then Kay realized that ze had been so busy with zir own transformation that ze didn't know what had happened to

Kyle or to Jamie. Ze grabbed zir old things and rushed out the door.

The crowd of children was back. It made way and gently urged zir into the center where Kay found zirself looking at two children she knew and yet didn't. Before ze could speak, Athena's voice rang out. "Attention, everyone. I would like to present our guests. They are trying some identities out, and they are new at this, so those identities might change as they try to find out what represents their true selves. First, this is Jamie, and he's trying out being a gay boy."

Pansy stepped forward and took the clothes Jamie handed him and passed them off to someone else. Then Pansy took the pale pink fabric rose that Jamie held in his hand, "Where would you like it?"

"Around my neck," Jamie answered softly. A young girl handed Pansy a length of ribbon, and Pansy fastened the flower to the ribbon and then fastened the choker around Jamie's neck.

Jamie laughed nervously, but pirouetted around. He was wearing heavy make-up like Camille and form fitting clothing much like Kay had on.

"Welcome, Jamie," the children responded, and there was clapping and whistling to emphasize the welcoming words.

"Next," Athena continued, "is Kyla who is trying out being a girl," and Kay found zirself staring at zir brother, zir sister, ze corrected in zir head. Kyla looked like a girl, her hair had been styled differently, her make-up was much softer than Jamie's, but she wore more than Kay, and she wore a form fitting dress much like Suzette. She was pretty, this Kyla, in her own way, Kay realized with a smile (different than the prettiness Kyle had had) but pretty all the same.

Again, Pansy stepped forward to take the clothes Kyla handed him. Next, he took the bright yellow butterfly that Kyla held in her hand. "Where would you like it?" he asked.

"In my hair," Kyla answered quietly. The same young girl handed a small bobby pin to Pansy who attached it to the butterfly and pinned it neatly in Kyla's hair behind her ear.

Kyla looked nervously at Kay. Ze felt a mixed set of emotions at the weight zir approval or disapproval held over zir twin. Ze returned Kyla's nervous look with a blazing smile, and Kay felt zir eyes well with tears just as Kyla's did as she smiled to the crowd and spun around to the words, "Welcome, Kyla," and the clapping and whistling.

"Last, but not least, this is Kay who is trying on being non-binary."

One last time, Pansy stepped forward and took Kay's clothes. Then, he took the purple flower from zir hand and asked where ze wanted it.

"In my hair, like my sister," Kay answered. Pansy accepted another bobby pin and placed the flower in the center of the mass of Kay's encircling braids.

Thus adorned, Kay stepped forward and spun around to, "Welcome, Kay," and more clapping and whistling.

"Alright, alright, introductions are through. There's still daylight yet and some chores to do. Off with you now, until it's supper time," and with that, Athena dismissed the crowd.

Kay, Kyla, and Jamie weren't sure what to do, but Peter appeared. "Let me show you around, and then tomorrow at breakfast you can pick something you'd like to do or be assigned to a task." So Peter walked them around to the various gardens, through the orchards, to the chicken pens and yards, to the meadows with the goats and the sheep, to the various food makers and craftspeople, to Mother Wendy's infirmary, to the small lake and to the nearest beach. It took them several hours, and the children were beginning to feel very weary indeed when Peter left them to themselves in a small orchard not far from dining area.

"How do you feel?" Jamie asked the twins bluntly.

"Good," Kay said slowly, "different ... even a little outrageous. I didn't know I could present myself to others this way. I am not even sure that I am not presenting myself to myself in a whole new way. I don't know whether that makes sense. Does it?"

"Yes," answered Kyla, taking ze's hand and squeezing it gently. "I feel like I am acting out a part of myself that I have never been able to make public before. And the presentation is as much for myself as it is for others. It does feel almost out of control because I never felt I was allowed to do this before."

"I know," said Jamie excitedly, "and we can keep trying other identities out. I like this one, but I know I also want to try being a girl and then a non-binary. Is that weird?" Jamie asked suddenly self-conscious.

"No, it's not weird, not here anyway, and here's where we are. Three cheers for Beyondland and P who brought us here," exclaimed Kay.

“Hip, hip, hooray! Hip, hip, hooray! Hip, hip hooray!” they cried.

And just like that, Kay and Kyla, and Jamie settled into life in Beyondland and rarely ever gave their old lives second thoughts.

The Mirror

"This is the only way to have power," the sorcerer said angrily. "You control others or they control you."

Some small part of her fought against his words. The mirror stood off to the side, as imposing as ever, a steady reminder of how much of herself she had sacrificed in the name of power under the sorcerer's tutelage.

The poisoned knife lay on the table. She needed only to slay her new husband and imprison his daughter, and she would be queen. The knife glinted in the afternoon light, and something about it brought on a rush of memories.

"Snow White, there is an ancient curse that sends women preying on each other," the voice of the mid-wife, echoed in her head. "You will be the innocent victim of the corrupted queen, but then you will become the queen herself and repeat the cycle. Only a Snow White and a Queen can break the cycle. Snow White, do you hear me? Do you understand? The curse can be broken."

"But how? I'm just a girl," she heard her young voice cry, full of fear and doubt.

"Love, my child," Cassandra answered. "Men dismiss love all too easily, but love is one of the greatest powers on earth. Yes, it is vulnerable, and yes, it can be betrayed and even warped, but love is one of the few building forces. Today, too many men try to use power, violence, and fear—but they don't understand that the use of power without love only sows fear, resentment, and anger, and violence and fear only sow those negative feelings faster.

Snow White suddenly remembered her own mother. The joy, love, and absolute security Snow White had felt nestled in her mother's arms or having her mother brush and braid her hair or during their outings gathering flowers and herbs. Her mother had wanted her so badly, "Hair as dark as ebony, skin as white as snow, and lips as red as blood." She missed her mother so badly. Yes, love was vulnerable, but that didn't make it less powerful. The light flickered again, and she refocused on the knife laying on the table and sorcerer standing in front of her.

"When I was young, the midwife told me that power wasn't everything," she said in protest.

"And your midwife today, how fares she?" he asked with a sneer.

"She is dead," she answered resignedly.

"Of course, she is. See what love got her. Take up the knife; fulfill your destiny, and the kingdom is yours!"

Obediently, Snow White turned Queen picked up the knife. It felt wrong in her hand. She wanted to drop it, but she had committed herself too much to her destiny to truly resist.

When the time came, she plunged the knife into her husband's heart. The blood surprised her. It was everywhere. There was so much more than she expected. It sprayed all over her and her clothes—it coated her hands and arms. It was so much more than red; it was purplish and thick and slimy. She couldn't seem to get it off. She washed and washed. But it was more than the blood; murder was foul and unnatural. It marked her soul—even more than the compromise that she had made to the sorcerer for the power of the mirror. She was tainted and corrupted in a fundamental way; she felt it in her heart. When she finally felt like she had gotten most of the blood off, she forced herself to stand in front of the mirror. Standing in front of it, she still felt the taint of the blood, and she saw herself reflected in its image covered again in her husband's blood. She closed her eyes in shame, and when she opened them, she saw the strangest thing—she saw her image refracted and more images than she could count beyond her own. Queens, like her and not, the same dark hair, the same pale skin, the same red lips, yet each different in her own way, but with the same horrified expressions on their faces, blood spattered on their faces and covering their hands.

Staring appalled at the images, the full impact of the scope of the curse shocked her, "women preying" on other women in an endless cycle. "Only a Snow White and a Queen can break the curse." But how, she wondered.

The mirror changed. Gone was the image with the endless refractions of horrified, murdering queens, replaced by an image of her own mother holding her in her arms and singing to her. The song echoed softly in her head: "Sleep, baby, sleep! Thy father watches the sheep, and tendeth the lambs upon yonder hill, but mother watches one dearer still, sleep, baby, sleep!" It didn't matter that her father had never tended sheep or lambs in his life. Her mother had wanted her so badly that she had tended to her even as infant instead of employing a wet-nurse or some other surrogate. Secure in her mother's arms, with her mother's love raining down on her just like the simple words of the common lullaby, bathing her in comfort and sending her off to sleep—that was the truest image of love she knew. Love, of course, was the answer. Tears formed in her eyes, and she knew what she needed to do. The king's body had been removed and the chamber cleaned, even so, the place was the site of murder and unclean despite surface appearances. She had the mirror moved to a new suite of rooms, and she sent for Snow White, the king's daughter. She had the sorcerer seized and executed. The action was harsh, perhaps, but the "mischief" of such men was on the hands of all those sister queens in the mirror, and now that she had reached this moment of clarity, she wouldn't let more blood be split or more souls damaged if she could help it.

Snow White regarded the Queen warily, and the Queen regarded the young woman before her—a younger version of herself—like all who had gone before and all who come after if the curse remained. She was a blossoming young woman, ripe for sexual awakening. The striking coloring of the ebony hair, the white skin, and the blood red lips could be unsettling, and yet on a Snow White it always worked somehow—the un-naturalness of it, all the more alluring and appealing, usually set off with sapphire eyes, not light or crystal blue, but the dark blue of the stones—with just enough contrast to be different from the raven black hair. The Queen remembered herself at the age. Everything seemed possible. Her father's love protected her, the sting of the loss of her mother, eased just enough, the future waiting—a prince perhaps, marriage, a family—and then it was all taken away. It didn't seem that way at first. Her father, yes. The mad escape from her step-mother, but then the marriage to the prince. But he had died, and his younger brother claimed the throne and drove her from the kingdom. A Princess/Queen in name only, and then the sorcerer arrived with the mirror, and it had all gone wrong. She couldn't even remember how she had been convinced that power was worth the sacrifice, but she had made the vow. But she could stop it now. She hadn't been able to save the king, but she could save the version of herself who stood before her.

With the help of the mirror, the Queen explained about the curse, the sorcerer, the mirror, and death of Snow White's father. Snow White was by turns horrified, frightened, and angry.

"Why do you tell me all this?" Snow White demanded. "Is it some final way to gloat before you kill me?"

"No, Snow White. Don't you see? It has to end with us. Through an act of love, we can start a new story," the Queen tried to explain.

"An act of love?" Snow White screeched.

"Yes, through an act of love. For you, Snow White, the girl I once was, I sacrifice myself for you, in the trust that you will be a mother to your people and love them as your children. Promise me?"

"Promise? Sacrifice? What are you talking about?" Snow White stammered bewildered and panicked at the same time.

The Queen grabbed Snow White's hand and clasped it in her own. She looked deeply into Snow White's eyes, imploring, "Promise me?"

Snow White looked into the Queen's imploring gaze and was surprised by what she found there. There was a desperate need to be understood and forgiven. Part of Snow White recoiled at the thought, and then all the images of the blood-stained queens passed unwillingly across her memory. She looked again at the Queen and watched as the older woman's features softened and Snow White could see the Queen as a version of herself, the same stark coloring, another beautiful young woman. They could be sisters, and now somehow through this moment of silent communication and connection, they were sisters—absolving each other and giving each other the strength to write a new story that freed both of them, their sisters in the mirror, and the young women who would live out other stories rather than the one where women preyed on other women—or that least this particular manifestation of that story (the Snow White/Queen cycle). Snow White found herself calmed and resolute in her choice, "Yes, my Queen," she answered.

"No!" the Queen interrupted. "Promise me as your sister."

"Yes, my sister, I promise," and Snow White realized that she meant this as a sacred vow.

Upon hearing the words, the Queen released Snow White's hand and straightened up. She calmed herself and smiled a bitter sweet smile. Then, she kissed Snow White on the forehead and went and stood in front of the mirror. Too late, Snow White seemed to realize what would come next.

"No!" she shouted, moving forward. But the Queen stepped into the mirror and vanished. The mirror seemed to tremble. Snow White found herself trembling in front of the trembling mirror. She didn't know what to do. Somehow she seemed to realize how the storyline was supposed to go. She was supposed to be the innocent victim, and the corrupted Queen was supposed to try to kill her or to try to have her killed. But that hadn't happened. The Queen had sacrificed herself to the mirror. What did that mean? And all those women, Queens, former Snow Whites turned into corrupted Queens. The cycle of women preying on women—who has started that? Well, at least that answer was easy, men, men like the sorcerer. But what now? She was all alone. She found herself sobbing in front of the mirror—the surface now still and calm.

"What do I do now? I am all alone," she sobbed.

Voices called out from the mirror, "No, sister. You are never alone. We are always here." And a woman, a Queen, not the queen Snow White had known, but another, appeared. "Do you remember what your Queen told you? Do you remember your promise?" she asked.

Snow White forced herself to focus. The Queen had asked her to be a mother to her people, to love her people as her children. Love not power, she thought. Her father had always said that power corrupted, and she thought sadly of the all the corrupted Queens in the mirror. But weren't they all something else now? They had called her sister. The Queen had asked to be called sister. Was this the making of the new story, she wondered. "I promised to be a mother to my people—to love my people as my children," she said softly.

"Good, Snow White," the Queen answered.

"I am not sure how to do that," Snow White added. "The voices in the mirror said that they would help me, but I don't understand."

"Your Queen," the Queen began.

"My sister," Snow White was shocked to hear herself interrupt, but the distinction had been so important to her queen, their relationship had been altered from one holding power over another to one of loved equals, sisters, and the voices in the mirror had called her that too.

The Queen in the mirror bristled for a moment, and then her features suddenly softened and she laughed awkwardly for a moment. "That will take some getting used to," she said almost to herself, and voices in the mirror giggled or chuckled and laughed in response. "Our sister," she began again, "has changed the story and asked you to keep changing it. We will help you. We are all your sisters now. Do you understand, Snow White?"

"I understand that I need to rule with love, and I welcome your help, but how can you help?" Snow White asked.

The sister in the mirror, smiled yet another bittersweet smile, and her image faded. Then in the silver pool of the mirror, one of the village schools appeared, and Snow White saw the haughty Master Beckett and watched him terrorize and humiliate the children instead of teaching them, and worse, she saw him using the ruler and the switch on the children leaving raised welts that made Snow White's eyes run with tears and fury burn in her belly. She summoned the king's guards and had them seize Master Beckett. A date was set for an inquiry where the students and their parents gave testimony about Master Beckett. He was found abusive and unfit to teach. He was driven from the kingdom, and a Head Mistress was appointed in his place.

And so the mirror revealed injustices to Snow White, and Snow White sent the queen's guards to seize wrong doers or accompanied them herself. Wrong doers always had to have evidence presented against them and the chance to defend themselves, but when they couldn't defend themselves, they were driven from Snow White's queendom.

Snow White loved her people and looked after them with the help of her sisters in the mirror, and the people loved Snow White, the Queen Mother, they called her, and they all lived happily ever after.

Anton, the Steadfast Soldier, and Tatiana, the Steadfast Dancer

The clock struck twelve, and the Nursery was bathed in a strange silvery-blue light. The Steadfast Soldier was surprised to realize that he alone among all the toys seemed aware. Well, that wasn't completely true. The lovely dancer stood in her beautiful castle and held his gaze as she so often did, but her gaze stayed locked on him and did not wander the light-filled Nursery. Looking around him, the Steadfast Soldier found all his fellow toys frozen in the normal pre-midnight enchantment poses—even all his twenty-four brothers. But glowing in the center of the Nursery stood what could only be a fairy. Shimmering in the silvery-blue light, she stood with her wings spread, a wand in her right hand, and a broad smile on her beautiful face.

"Steadfast Soldier, do you know why I am here?" she asked.

"No," he answered hesitantly.

"You have been very brave," she said. "The Nursery troll cast you out into the big wide world. You were put at the mercy of street children, tormented by a rat, and swallowed by a fish. And after all that, you landed in the kitchen to be returned to this same Nursery. 'Fare Forth! Fare Forth, Warrior! Thou shalt suffer Death!' Well, you have, in a way, more so than any of your brothers who have only engaged in play battles and skirmishes here in the Nursery."

"I didn't do much," he said in protest.

"Steadfast Soldier, don't you know that ordinary heroes never start out to do much?" She smiled looking at him. "It's the fact that they go; they don't turn back, and they do the best they can. They go forward to be the best human beings they can be." She smiled more broadly as she watched him accept the truth of her words.

"Ordinary heroes," he said in wonder.

"An ordinary hero," she confirmed. "And your bravery has won you a reward. I, as a Nursery Fairy, can grant you life."

"Life?" he stammered. "Me? Again in the wide world? Alone?" He glanced down at himself in dismay—his one leg and the paint of his uniform all but gone except in a few very stubborn places.

The fairy watched him with interest. "Would you wish for something else?"

The Steadfast Soldier looked at the beautiful dancer in her lovely paper castle. "What about her? Could you give her life?" he asked, his voice tinged with both longing and regret.

"Why?" asked the fairy.

"She has been my companion here in the Nursery," he said simply.

The fairy just raised her tiny eyebrows and waited.

"I thought she was like me," he said slowly, blushing slightly at the vulnerability he betrayed by wanting someone else to be like him, disabled, misshapen and broken. "I mean, I know she's not now," he said in a rush. "She's a dancer. She's standing on one leg with her other one raised high behind her. But she's steadfast too, and she looks at me. She's kind."

"How do you know?" the fairy asked.

"I don't, I guess," he answered, "but she's so beautiful."

"Looks can be deceiving, but in this case, you might be pleasantly surprised," she said, winking at him. The fairy raised her wand in a flourish, and two strands of sparks shot from her wand—one bathing the dancer in light and the other bathing the Steadfast Soldier.

He felt himself warm and glow and throb in the strangest way. One moment, he was himself, a tiny tin soldier, and then the next he was a breathing, heart-pulsing young soldier, standing on the floor of the Nursery, utterly bewildered. Only the sight of the dancer, transformed like him into a breathing, pulsing young woman, looking similarly disoriented and bewildered, pulled him out of his own distress. She was even more beautiful alive than she had been as a paper dancer. She stood before on him on her two legs and two feet, looking at him with the oddest expression on her face.

"Thank you," she said. "You didn't need to do that," she whispered, both startled and pleased that she could speak. She curtsied before him in the most graceful, dancerly way. Her beautiful dancer costume replaced by a more practical every day dress—but even that had been cut so it hinted at her dancer past. Looking at her clothes, he glanced at his own. His uniform was crisp and perfect and neat—but he realized with horror that he was still one-legged, his left leg missing. The shock of the realization nearly threw him off balance. He swayed on the spot and was surprised to feel the dancer's arms clutch his right arm, steading him. He glanced from her to the fairy, his face flushing with embarrassment and a bit of anger.

"I'm alive but broken?" he asked. He felt the dancer stiffen beside him, and he saw the look of suppressed outrage on the fairy's face.

"Broken? Steadfast Soldier. You are in life what you were as a toy. As a one-legged toy, you became the companion of the dancer. As a one-legged toy, you went out into the wide world and faced adventures such as no toy in this Nursery has encountered. As a one-legged toy, you earned a reward. You have been given what you asked for, your companion's life and your own. Are you ungrateful?" she challenged.

Her words left him speechless for a moment. "I just thought," he struggled to say.

"We are grateful," the dancer said, quickly filling in for him. She squeezed his right arm gently.

The fairy turned her withering gaze from the Steadfast Soldier to the dancer, and her expression softened.

"We are just surprised, my Lady. Why we haven't even been properly introduced," she said startled at the realization.

"Names! Of course, you can't go into the wide world as the Steadfast Soldier and the dancer." Her expression clouded as she lost herself in thought. "Tatiana!" she exclaimed, after a moment. "That's a good dancer's name." She paused, "What do you think?" she asked, looking at the dancer and then at the Steadfast Soldier.

"Tatiana," the dancer said slowly, trying the name out. "Yes, I like it," she answered smiling.

"Tatiana and … Anton … How's that?" her gaze now firmly on the Steadfast Soldier. "Sergeant Anton Annelowitz."

"Sergeant Anton Annelowitz," the Steadfast Soldier repeated. His chest puffing slightly. He felt the dancer squeeze his arm again.

"You don't have to …" he struggled to say to her.

He watched Tatiana roll her eyes and attempt a stern expression, but the kindness in her eyes undercut that. She reached for a pair of crutches he hadn't seen and handed them to him. "I am your companion, Anton. Remember, you said so to the fairy, so I am Mrs. Anton Annelowitz. Where ever we go, we go together," she said firmly.

"But I am not whole," he started to protest. Both the fairy and Tatiana shot him disdainful looks.

"Whole isn't all it's cracked up to be," said the fairy.

"You're whole to me," Tatiana said. "I have never known you any other way, and I wouldn't want you any other way."

"Are you sure?" he asked, taking the crutches and placing them under both underarms.

"Yes, I'm sure, Anton," she answered emphatically, loosening her arms while he got the right crutch in place.

"Settled, are we?" the fairy asked, a little impatiently. "Sergeant, for your service, you have a pension." She twirled her wand again, and Anton found that both he and Tatiana were outfitted in warm cloaks, his matching his uniform and hat, and hers having a matching bonnet and purse. "You both have money, but more importantly, you have each other." She stopped then and flew up and kissed them both on their foreheads. "Be good, and remember to treat others kindly, and all will go well with you." She smiled and directed her wand at the Nursery door which opened, its opening echoing the noise of the front door opening below. Then, she turned the wand on herself, glowed brightly for a brief instant, and was gone.

After a few moments of stunned surprise, Tatiana smiled at Anton, "Shall we?" she asked.

He smiled, finally feeling a great peace in himself (validated in a way he had never expected and most importantly loved). The future lay before them, and he looked forward it in a way he had never felt before. "Yes, Tatiana, my love, I am ready. 'Fare Forth!' as they say."

"Fare Forth!" she repeated, and they left the Nursery and made their way down the stairs and out the front door, to a new day that was breaking and a new future, the Steadfast Soldier and the Steadfast Dancer, no longer toys—not entirely perfect—but ordinary heroes set on being the best human beings they could be.

THE END.

23418493R00186

Made in the USA
Columbia, SC
12 August 2018